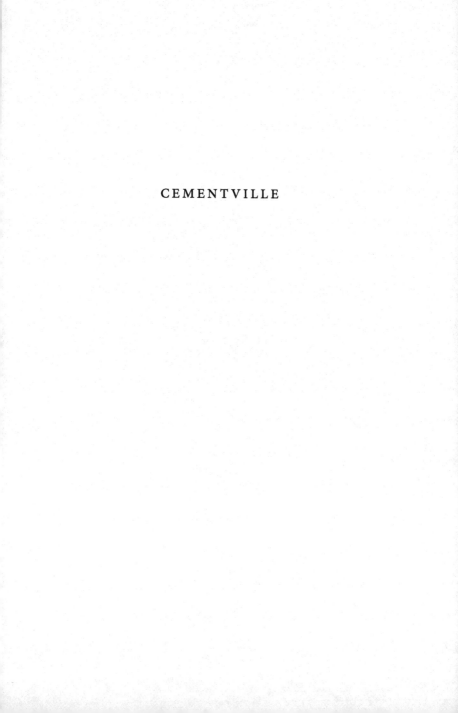

CEMENTVILLE

# Cementville

*a novel* | Paulette Livers

COUNTERPOINT PRESS

Vietnamese poetry of Ho Xuan Hu'o'ng, who wrote around 1800, is used here
in translation with permission of translator John Balaban. © John Balaban, *Ca
Dao Vietnam: Vietnamese Folk Poetry* (Copper Canyon Press, 2003), and © John
Balaban, *Spring Essence: The Poetry of Ho Xuan Huong* (Copper Canyon Press,
2000), reprinted by permission of the translator.

Earlier versions of portions of this text have appeared in *The Southwest Review*
and the audio journal *Bound Off.*

Library of Congress Cataloging-in-Publication Data is available.

ISBN 978-1-61902-476-2

Cover design by Michael Kellner
Interior design by Domini Dragoone

Counterpoint Press
2560 Ninth Street, Suite 318
Berkeley, CA 94710
www.counterpointpress.com

Printed in the United States of America

*for David*

# PART I

*Hear: Tell your children of it, and let your children tell their children, and their children another generation. What the swarming locust has left, the grasshopper has eaten. What the grasshopper has left, the caterpillar has eaten. A menace has come with the teeth of a lion to lay waste your land, Eden before them, a desolate wilderness behind, your trees and vines dead-white.*

—PROPHETS: JOEL REDUX

WE FEEL THEM COMING, THE LOW VIBRATION OF THEIR wheels, a dark convoy descending upon us, pitching north like a swarm lobbed from the fist of a spiteful deity. The military cortege moves toward us up the new toll road from Fort Campbell. Each black hearse with a small flag fluttering from its antenna, each containing a flag-draped coffin. See him, in front, the driver of the lead hearse? He no doubt finds the wide, flat road boring and wonders momentarily whether he needs to keep his eyes open at all, the thing is so damn straight.

We have wondered the same thing—some of us have tried it out, closing our eyes and keeping the wheel steady, the gas pedal to the floor, our tires singing as we plunge headlong down that smooth, perfect surface. The lead hearse driver, let's call him Corporal So-and-So, stares ahead at this unswerving trail of asphalt and hears the smoky voice of his great aunt, quoter of Scripture: *Wide is the gate, and broad is the way, that leads to destruction, and many there be who go there.* He glances in the rearview at the long shiny box behind him. He did not know the kid in the box, not being from around here. One of the other drivers told him about the bad luck of the boys from Cementville.

Corporal So-and-So's car is the only one to also include a passenger with a pulse, and he wishes this fact did not make the road all the more lonesome. He glances sidelong at the newly saved POW hero in his dress blues, with his big square jaw clamped in pain, the single leg restless, shifting around like it's looking for the gone one. Only thing spoken so far is moans. Finally So-and-So says, "You alright, sir?"

But the hero's eyes trace the passing cliffs, sheer limestone walls weeping rust-colored water from deep in the earth.

"Were you with the dead boys?" So-and-So asks. He knows better. The POW is a commissioned officer, West Point all the way, not from the National Guard like the boys who bought it. The driver is just trying to make conversation, only wishes to make the ride less tiresome. "Bet you're looking forward to the parade. All that home-cooked food," he tries.

We don't have to be in that hearse to know there will be no response. The cells of us are familiars of the cells of Lieutenant Harlan O'Brien, and the cells of the dead boys degrading even now in their seven individual boxes. We know their lives and their deaths as we know our own. We know our own. Our own.

Some distance behind the line of hearses rolls a Greyhound, wherein GIs stretch in various states of repose and disengagement. Some sleep, a few pass a pint of Heaven Hill. There is an air of half-hearted celebration. Two GIs warily eye another soldier who sits off by himself, faking sleep.

One says, "He don't look old enough to even be in the army, much less getting out."

The second GI says, "They say he kilt a man."

First one says, "It's war. Ain't that the idea?"

Other says, "Kilt one of us. And it *wasn't* friendly fire."

What feeds Corporal So-and-So's relentless yammering all the way to the end of this road is the dread of contagion. Our television screens flicker nightly with images of death in a steamy jungle. Walter Cronkite delivers Cementville its first shot in the national spotlight.

Soon the convoy will pass under the tattered banner at the town's northern mouth welcoming the rare visitor. *CEMENTVILLE,* the banner reads, *Solid through the Hard Times.* Someone long ago thought the pun clever and strung it between two stone bluffs on galvanized aircraft cable, all that remained from the soured dream of an airport. Our valley stretches between knotted parallels of knobs, making a fecund lap in which rest tracts suitable for pasturing or rose gardens, for webbing with snug lanes bordered by dry stone walls cobbled nearly two centuries ago from cleared bottomland. We are little more than a handful of stores and a clutch of sound old houses, protection from the storms that howl across the floodplain as if fighting the grip of the river.

Our town's reputation had been built upon the production of two things: passable cement and remarkable whiskey. And now it will be remembered by this new catastrophe. Along with a profusion of wreaths and baskets of lilies, out-of-town relatives have been sending clippings from the national papers, articles that wonder at war's appetite for plucking up farm boys and returning them home in wooden boxes.

Tiny Cementville, people all over the country are saying, population a thousand and three, suffering a loss out of all proportion to its size. Seven local boys, gone all at once in one horrific night. Boys whose parents thought they were safe, having signed on with the National Guard to protect the homeland. Not to be shipped out to some faraway place we never heard of.

# ONE

Nearly the end of May and the air is cool and damp with the threat of a storm trapped at the narrow end of the valley since sun up. The strange dry spring has hung on longer than usual this year, or so it seems to Wanda Ferguson Slidell, perched on the enormous limestone overhang that her grandfather christened Weeping Rock years before she was born. When Wanda was small, he held onto her ankles while she dangled over the edge of the cliff and cupped in her hands the spring water that oozed from the rocky wall. She lapped the water like a pup, splashing it over her face. Not until she was twelve or so did Wanda stop believing it to be the ice-cold tears of the earth.

She scans the undulating horizon of Juell Ridge across the valley, the gentle shape her grandfather said was a sleeping woman who, every spring, was draped in a velvet mantle of soft new leaf. Dogwood. Hardrock maple. Redbud. In winter though, it became a slumbering giant, the black trees against snow making the giant's grizzled beard; jutting rocks were his shoulders and elbows, his knees drawn up like an overgrown child.

Wanda would die living in town. The bustle of those thousand souls scurrying around in the fifteen or twenty-odd blocks that comprise Cementville, it would do her in. She is glad to be up here on this place her grandparents left to her and Loretta. This is hers, this knob of craggy land. It's where she belongs, clinging like some endangered raptor to this weeping carapace of limestone clad in a thin layer of poor soil. From her aerie, Wanda has the view of the entire Slidell Valley. She can trace the Louisville Road winding toward Cementville from several miles out, all the way to where it becomes Council Street and meanders southeasterly through town, crossing the river three times as it slaloms the valley floor. She peers toward the south to see if she can spy the hearses coming. Maybe they've already pulled in behind the Duvall Funeral Home. Once the mansion of some vanished founding family, it was converted decades ago to fit the needs of the grieving. The mortuary sits among the better houses in town, fine examples of eighteenth-century architecture as prized by their inhabitants as they are by historians at the state capitol who are hell-bent on designating the area a historic district.

Halfway up Juell Ridge across the valley, Wanda can see the little frame house Jimmy Smith built for his war bride. Everybody in town had assumed when the mysterious Giang arrived here three years ago that she spoke no English, and they talked openly about her within earshot of both Jimmy and Giang, the strange-sounding name nobody pronounced right. "*Zsjang*," Wanda practices out loud, as if to test her own worldliness. Charlene Cahill told Wanda about how the young Vietnamese woman interrupted the gossip of the Garden Club meeting at Happy's Soups, how with three elegantly crafted sentences she threw a dead silence over the entire gathering. Wanda has yet to meet Giang Smith but has rehearsed in her head what she might say to her on such an occasion.

At the south end of the valley, behind the distillery's big gray warehouses, Wanda can make out the rusted tin roofs of Taylortown, the neighborhood that until recently the whites called Coloredtown. After Civil Rights came, the old name wore off and the whites started calling it what the blacks themselves had named it long ago, after a family of abolitionists who settled there. The Taylors shocked everyone by moving in amongst the shacks of the freedmen, paying no mind to the invisible line demarcating one part of town from the other. There is a story, never corroborated by any real evidence Wanda knows of, that a freedom tunnel runs under it.

She holds her hands in the air to make a cropping frame so the rectangle of palm and thumb block out the cement plant. The town would be picturesque without it. But she gives up finally, unable to ignore the slumbering dragon lying in the belly of the valley. Its old body, scaled in iron, yields the occasional smoky belch. She remembers creeping out here to Weeping Rock with her grandfather before dawn, back when the plant was operating twenty-four hours a day. How she and Poose loved to watch the lights, the fires blinking from under a score of brazen eyelids. It was nearly beautiful then, in a vaguely terrifying way, cloaked in the dying night. Wanda and Poose would wait for the sun to rise across the way behind Juell Ridge, lighting the tip of the smokestack so that it looked like a colossal match leaning over the town.

The plant is dark today, the town shut down in honor of the war dead. In seeming collusion with the mourning pall, the clouds had not allowed for much of a sunrise. No match lit, colossal or otherwise, except in the sanctuary of Holy Ghost Church. Father Oliver and the Altar Society would be already making the preparations for the multiple funeral Masses to come. Seven in all, spread out over the next week, all the families having insisted on individual funerals for their boys. Or is it eight? No, seven is right; seven Catholic dead from the National Guard unit that was never supposed to have gone overseas in the first place.

There is an eighth, a cousin she barely knew, a boy ordered to his slaughter by the draft's roll of a die. But there'll be no Mass for him, the Fergusons being of Scot Presbyterian persuasion, or were so persuaded at one time. It's doubtful most of them can be said to be any religion at all anymore, Wanda included.

Wanda's branch of the Ferguson tree had severed ties with the rest of the family before she was born. Her grandfather's determination to make something of himself had set them off as the uppity side of the family, long before Wanda's mother married a Slidell. And her late granny, Mem, never missed the opportunity to remind people. Johnny was the only legitimate landowner among the Fergusons, the rest plain sharecroppers, and bad ones at that.

The couple of sentences buried in the obituaries said Daniel Ferguson was in another part of that embattled little country, far from where the National Guard unit was attacked. "Killed in separate fighting," the *Picayune* said of Daniel, out on some kind of night patrol. His body isn't due to arrive for a few more days. Nineteen years old, the paper said, drafted right out of high school.

Surely Loretta won't insist they attend the funeral service. Wanda flushes with embarrassment at her self-centeredness. But all those poor, sobbing creatures! Her heart thumps around her ribcage like a wounded rabbit. She grows light-headed at the thought of entering the suffocating rooms of the Duvall Funeral Home, walking down its dark central hallway, the horrid red wallpaper flocked with velvet swirls.

Wanda has to lie back against the mossy rock to get her breathing to ease.

She is glad this place is hers. She has earned this safe place on her windblown ridge: She has worked it, eaten from its soil, slept and dreamed in the small gabled room at the top of the house Johnny Ferguson built for his cantankerous Caroline. For Wanda, this soil, her hill, this house, her room, they are the locus of the beautiful plague of dreams that have shaped her life.

HER POOSE (MEM HAD ALWAYS called the old man Papoose, and Wanda's toddler lisp shortened it to 'Poose) gave names to everything as if the naming lent extra legitimacy to his claim of ownership. Around the farm were signs painted on bits of board and affixed to outbuildings and trees, even stretches of fence and gate. For instance, the big tree that stands sentinel down by the road, planted in 1911 after Mem's sister sent her a copy of *Howards End*. Poose was illiterate in those days, and when Mem read the book aloud to him, he heard the name of Mrs. Wilcox's magical tree with protective powers, a *wych-elm*, and figured his newly purchased farm needed all the help it could get. He procured an elm sapling and stuck it in the ground at the mouth of his road and had a sign maker letter up a placard naming it "Witch Elm." Mem enjoyed telling this story on him more than Poose enjoyed hearing it. "He'll soon be sticking it with hogs' teeth and chewing its bark like old Mrs. Wilcox," Mem said. Her teasing was the goad he needed to finally tackle his illiteracy. When the tree not only survived the Dutch elm disease that ravaged elms around the county, but grew into an imposing sentry at the entrance to his farm, Poose felt vindicated.

Once he could write, there was no stopping him. He continued his labeling campaign. Their farm was Hanging Valley, after the way April rains washed numerous gullies across the rocky surface, creating small but dramatic waterfalls that noisily joined the river below. The house itself he called Maiden's Rest, commemorating the birth of their only child, Loretta, in 1923, and he nailed a board above the kitchen door declaring it so. Mem swore it put a curse on them, as baby Loretta never slept through the night again after the sign went up.

Poose claimed the right to a nomenclature with the tone of those great hunters who roamed the land before the whites: Cherokee, Shawnee, and the others, natives who supposedly called the area "Dark and Bloody Ground" because its wooded hills were rich with game. Poose's own people were Melungeon, he said, and so could claim all the races if they wished to, white, red, black, although perhaps not the Oriental.

"Melungeon my foot," Mem would grumble when Poose went tearing off into his version of history and genealogy, and she would point to the bright hair growing sparsely on Poose's head, in thick ringlets on Wanda's, and hanging in a gorgeous braided rope down Loretta's back, hair that ranged from the color of a blood orange on Wanda to ripe muskmelon on Poose to strawberry blond on Loretta. "Fergusons are Scots-Irish or I'm the Queen," Mem said.

"Why, Uncle Bertram passed for colored in juke joints up and down the Mississippi!" Poose cried, and Wanda had to look away. She did not like to see her grandfather's eyes go watery, even when she was little.

"Humph. Bootblack, no doubt." Mem, keeping her broad back to them, the clopping circles she dragged through the oatmeal on the stove never ceasing.

Poose nailed a board above the outhouse a few days later: Queen's Roost.

Wanda could take herself back to this scene and others from those days if she closed her eyes and concentrated. Mem busy over pots on the stove, steam from boiling mutton swirling above her. Wanda's mother, Loretta, might be spinning the batts of fleece from her parents' sheep, the prized wool for which their farm had gained a reputation, or she might be reading or otherwise occupied in her mostly silent pursuits. Poose would push on the arms of his recliner (new and shiny back then) and he was always startled when his legs went flying into the air. It had fallen to Wanda to pull his muddy shoes off when he came in from the fields; she rubbed his toes to get the blood circulating.

"It was the mouth harp he played. Everybody loved Uncle Bertie," Poose would protest softly some minutes later, his gaze lost in the mug of thick coffee he held in both hands, all skin and bone and knuckle. And he would begin to hum some old tune. Poose, born John Knox Ferguson and called Johnny by everyone in town, had been the finest tenor in the county, highly sought after for singing at weddings and funerals.

"Tell how you got started singing," Wanda entreated. "Tell about the Sacred Harp, and how Uncle Bertram taught you the old songs from the Spanish Wars." That was how she coaxed him away from his tears, and back to her.

SHE LEANS ON HER ELBOWS now, sinking into the green cushion of Weeping Rock's mossy surface, and lets her head fall between her shoulder blades so she has an upside-down view of the locust grove ringing the side yard. A breeze rushes up from the valley floor and the trees rain their creamy blossoms. A few catch in her hair as if kowtowing to her earlier musings and, releasing the spring of its debts, let summer in at last. By tomorrow the fragrant petals will belong to the soil, doing their part to feed the blades of new grass carpeting the grove. Old Jimbo gives a whinny from his pen next to the chicken house.

"I know, I know, you're ready for the dang-gom plough," Wanda calls out to him. The garden should be in by now, but she has dreaded breaking into the hard ground, wrestling the clay into another year of submission. A heavy sky threatens to rupture over the valley. The sun has not managed to part the purple veil of clouds. She really should turn the soil today. With her luck, if she waits and it finally rains, the soil will go from hard and dry to too soggy to plough. Winter was mild enough that the cole crops from the fall garden didn't die off, and Wanda and her mother have enjoyed fresh greens every day to the point of being sick of them. A few root vegetables too, from seed she scattered in late February. But there are only so many knobby carrots one can crunch before a person will kill for the stinging citrus burst of a tomato in her mouth. The weather will turn hot soon enough.

Today is the last Saturday of the month, and normally she would have already driven to the A&P and back. It's up to her now to get groceries in since, for all practical purposes, the lupus has turned her mother into a cripple. They've worked out a system with the store manager whereby their grocery order is assembled and waiting for Wanda so she can pull into the parking lot a few minutes before the doors are unlocked, rush in and pay, and rush out before any other customers have shown up. But even that feels like an impossibility today, given the arrival of the bodies.

Wanda shivers. Please, God, she thinks, don't let my mother take a notion that we ought to call on cousin Arlene, offer our condolences for the loss of her Danny.

Besides her cousin and the seven soldiers blown to bits at Blacksnake, there's another that will return today. A maimed POW is to be feted at a parade—though the coming storm may have something to say about that. The article in the *Picayune* said the soldier had lost a limb, had to be airlifted to a hospital in the Philippines after the Green Berets got him out. The war has made her nearly glad that she and Loretta have forgone the luxury of a TV set. Although, sitting in Charlene Cahill's living room, Wanda had watched, breathless, the coverage of the POW's daring rescue. She remembers Harlan O'Brien before he was a prisoner of war, a handsome, smart boy behind her by a grade or two. She was always too shy to speak to boys like him. As they say, he comes from good people.

Wanda has allowed Charlene Cahill, reigning monarch at the Saint Brigid College Library since everybody can remember, to talk her into volunteering a few hours a week. Cementville is not big enough to have its own real public library, but there has never been a time that Saint Brigid College did not open its doors to anybody who wanted a book. Charlene is pestering Wanda to come work for her. "Just part time," she tells Wanda. "You love books. And it would bring in a little money."

It's no secret in town that Poose left them land and a house and little else. Loretta tried to hang onto the sheep but finally sold them off a year after he died. Buck Farber has driven up the hill three times already this spring to see if they're ready to put the farm on the market. "What with your mother so ill," he says to Wanda, smacking his lips as though he could eat the place right there for supper. The real estate man always stands with one white-shod foot in the doorway. She never invites him in, with his country-club white oxfords and matching white belt and the pants so bright green they hurt your eyes.

Wanda has not ruled out going to work at the library. Maybe only for a day or two a week. Enough to keep the county taxes paid, and Buck Farber away from the door.

In idle hours she invents stories for the busy people in town below, imagining lives in which things actually happen—or hold that potential, anyway. Some stories she doesn't have to invent. Gossip has a way of traveling, even up to Hanging Valley Farm, even to the infamous hermit Wanda Ferguson Slidell. Her best invention is the one she has made of herself: Thirty is already long in the tooth in these parts, and she was never all that attractive anyway. The only man to ever look her way was crazy Carl Juell, and everybody knows what became of Carl—last fifteen years in the nuthouse. The newest rumor around town has it he's coming home soon. Wanda breathes in and wraps both arms tight across her ribs to quell the thumping.

She is not ashamed of her hermit status. In fact, she has considered nailing a second sign to the Witch Elm at the bottom of the hill: The Hermitage. The issue of marriage, or any other life than the one she has, has never come up. In her experience it all ends in hard work and heartache anyway, something she would as soon do alone.

Look at her grandparents. Poose had to convince Mem to marry him, to leave her own father's comfortable house in town and help him make a life on top of this hardscrabble knob rising above Cementville. He was set on recovering the Ferguson family name, which was associated in these parts with horse thieving and sloth and cattle rustling and drunkenness. He worked himself to the bone to scrape together the down payment for this land and carried his reluctant sweetheart Caroline here on the back of a mule one April morning in 1909.

And Loretta too had to be snagged into marriage by Stanley Slidell, although anyone who knew the circumstances would not have imagined it such a difficult job. She was poor, if beautiful, and a Ferguson to boot. He was handsome and rich, the only son of the founding family, the last Slidell, and sure to inherit what was left of the original fortune. The Slidells owned the town when you got right down to it, said it was them who built it, ignoring the bent backs of the other five hundred some odd who had dug the sewers and hammered the nails and worked the stills and the vats and guarded the barrels at the distillery. They who had quarried the lime and ground the cement and got it into trucks to be hauled to wherever.

But Stanley. He wooed and he crooned. To see pictures of him, your first thought would be *lothario*, or at least *trouble*. But he was devoted to Loretta, when he wasn't gambling and drinking. Then, then he was just gone. Over and over, Wanda had to make her mother tell how it happened, how before daylight that morning the sheriff knocked on the door of the carriage house behind the Slidell mansion. It was where Evelyn Slidell allowed them to stay, her son and his unworthy bride and their new baby (Wanda herself). Stanley had already been gone three or four days.

"Didn't you wonder where he was? Hadn't you reported him missing?" Wanda wanted to know. But Loretta said she was accustomed to it, him disappearing for even a week at a time, when he was in his cups.

"And what did the sheriff say when he knocked on the door? How did he tell you?"

That Stanley was sleeping (Loretta did not call it *passed out*) in the backseat of Buck Farber's Buick, while Buck went in to visit the bootlegger Shine Calhoun, leaving the car running out at the curb (it was late November, and quite cold); and a poker game took hold of Buck and he lost track of time. He didn't know the carbon monoxide had gotten Stanley until he tried to rouse him in front of the Slidell mansion.

"And what did you do?" Wanda would hold her breath and wait.

"When you started crying, I fed you," her mother told her for the umpteenth time.

Thinking on it now, Wanda found it the perfect ending to a devastating story, although at the time she was never satisfied. Her incessant requests to hear about her father's death must have held the childish hope for a different end, in which he staggered up the iron steps of the carriage house and kissed his wife and baby good night before tumbling into bed to sleep it off. He might swear off liquor and cards, and the three of them would go for lunch together to Happy's Soups and More, or walk around town on moonlit nights.

And Wanda would not be afraid of anything.

It was the kind of thing that made Poose shake his head and say, "Wishing don't make it so."

LORETTA WILL BE UP BY now. Wanda stands and stretches her long backbone in an arc and heads for the henhouse to gather eggs. Clutches of new chicks follow close behind their speckled mothers, scratching beneath the horse chestnut. They run toward Wanda for the corn they've come to expect at the sight of her approaching. There is Jimbo, sleeping on his feet. She would not have thought mules could grieve, but he has been off his feed since his sister Julie passed on this winter.

People always say a mule lives to kick you, that if they live to forty, on their last day on earth they'll use their final breath to shoot out a leg that can kick in any direction and give you one solid. You'd never prove that by Julie and Jimbo, gentle as any house cat the entire of their lives. Wanda pulls a couple of carrots from her pocket and Jimbo puckers his mouth into a hoarse whinny that ends in a heehaw.

She does not let herself wonder how much longer he can hang on. This is the thought she is letting go when she sees them enter the valley, the caravan of long black cars carrying the boys home.

# TWO

Maureen Juell at thirteen is on the cusp of knowing memory's vagary. Even for an imagination as wild and dramatic as hers, the accretion of events on a Saturday in May will make her wonder later if it wasn't too much, if a single day could hold all that, or if it would turn out to be another crazy concoction that would someday come tumbling down around her head. Pieces of the story she will not stop claiming with some confidence: That this was the day seven young men, once alive, came home not; that a storm blew into their lives, changing more than they reckoned. It may or may not have been the day her mother confiscated the Ouija board, or the day their downhill neighbor, the wife of the town no-account, left him, this time she swore, for good. These events on their own might have been enough to cause the Juell family to miss the parade in town commemorating the fallen and welcoming a one-legged hero back from the war.

Of this much she is certain. It was on this day that her brother walked up the gravel road from the Greyhound station in town and knocked on their family's front door like a stranger.

ALL MORNING THE SWOLLEN SKY leaned and loured over the valley. The view from the kitchen window was exactly what Maureen imagined it would be right before Judgment Day, not a soul moving, not a bird twitching or a leaf falling.

Her father said, "I don't like it, Katherine. Looks like trouble." Her mother rolled her eyes and shook her head at what she called Willis's prognostications of gloom, his penchant for signs and omens. Katherine Hume Juell was a reluctant convert to the staunch Catholicism that cast a wide net over the region. She had moved to Cementville as a teenager to live with her uncle, Judge Freeman Hume, when her parents vanished on a trans-oceanic flight. Katherine maintained that nothing in Scripture should be taken literally. She certainly did not believe in the End Times, as Maureen and her father liked to. Her people were Unitarians from Connecticut. Whereas the Juells reached generations back to when the town was founded, and Cementville was a place where such things mattered. Their brand of the faith was a peppery blend of the mysticism of Aquinas and Matthew's Baptism of Fire.

Willis was swigging his coffee to its dregs when their downhill neighbor's high-pitched wail preceded her up the driveway. Her stick arms pumping, Ginny Ferguson powered up the hill at a forty-five-degree angle to the earth. She could be heard from out by the mailbox. Katherine walked out to meet her. She took Ginny's hand and led her into the kitchen and sat her in Willis's chair. Willis slinked off to the front room to read the paper.

"Levon Ferguson has done it this time, Mizriz Juell. Goddamn bastard staggers home this morning, smelling like that shit-heel June Cahill's cheap Evening in Paris shit perfume," here the woman spat through clenched teeth, "and he hung my Clancy on the clothesline till that poor little dog thrashed his self to death."

Katherine Juell was not a woman who cursed, but she did not hold it against Virginia Ferguson for doing so. She believed there were women who had every reason to curse. Maureen had asked her mother once why swearing and taking the Lord's name was okay for some and not for others. "Hands have been dealt to some women that look more like a foot," Katherine had explained. She supported a woman's right to leave a mean man, papal dispensation or no. "You can work with mad, but there's not a whole lot you can do with mean," was how she put it.

So she kept her neighbor's coffee cup filled and repeated the words "I know, Virginia," the only two things the woman seemed to need. Virginia Ferguson was called Ginny by all but Katherine Juell. The way her mother clung to such formalities was a source of embarrassment to Maureen when people her own age were around, and of pride when they were not.

Perched in her spying spot in the corner between the refrigerator and the window, Maureen opened the new red diary she had received for her birthday. It had a golden lock and key, and a little gold pen attached by a ribbon. *May 24, 1969*, she wrote. She watched the grownups go about their business. She wanted to be ready when adulthood struck. The annual pixie haircut Katherine administered at the beginning of each summer had given the girl the look of a trouble-seeking imp, dishwater blond bangs jutting from her forehead a good two inches above a single eyebrow. Maureen had complained bitterly that she was too old for such a baby-fied haircut, but Katherine shushed her, saying short hair made it easier to spot ticks, that if she weren't such a tomboy, there would be options beyond the pixie.

Little sore nubs chafed raw under the crop top of her new shorts set, even though her mother insisted she was not ready for a bra. Maureen worked not to stare at Ginny's ponderous breasts and wondered whether she really did want such things plastered on the front of her. True, Ginny was expecting. Katherine had explained that a woman's breasts swell as they get ready to feed a new baby. Ginny's pillowing belly heaved under great sobs while her cheekbone took on an extraordinary shade of blue. Katherine gave Maureen the nod, and she hopped down from the stool and fetched ice and wrapped it in a tea towel for Ginny's face. The woman's hard-luck life never failed to fascinate Maureen, no matter how often its woe was wrung out in their kitchen, and how much the story remained unchanged. For her part, Maureen thought her parents never should have rented the old tenant house at the edge of their farm to Levon and Ginny Ferguson in the first place. But Katherine had taken one look at poor Ginny when they showed up on Juell Ridge that day and said yes before Willis even had the chance to think it over. Maureen had been sitting in the swing when Levon's truck flew up the hill, and she saw him get out with something wadded in his fist. After they left she fetched it out of the ditch where Levon had thrown it—the For Rent sign Willis had taped to the window of the tenant house.

Willis popped his head into the kitchen now as if checking for the all clear. "I ought to finish that order for Rafe Goins. I expect he'll be here directly to pick it up," he said, stepping into his coveralls.

Maureen stuck her diary into the waistband of her shorts and followed her father across the yard to his shop. She ducked through its low-slung door and sucked in the lush air, the smells that belonged specifically to her father: pinewood and machine oil and red cedar and varnish. This was where her father made his living, machining mysterious parts of this and that from hunks of metal. But it was also where they worked on projects for the house, Maureen and Willis and Billy too, before he went off to the war. Whatnot shelves, magazine racks, ashtrays. She climbed into the driver's seat of the old Hupmobile that had stood in the center of the shop for as long as she could remember. Willis's uncle had left it to him, and over the years he had restored every inch of it, inside and out.

"Can we take the Hupmobile out today?" Maureen said.

"They're calling for rain. No sense in chancing it." Her father always cleaned and polished the old Victoria's body after they drove around the countryside so that it gleamed like new.

"Will we go to the parade for Harlan O'Brien and the dead boys?"

"I'm not sure that is on your mother's to-do list for today. It wouldn't surprise me if they postpone it anyway. Storm's coming."

Maureen sat down at the small workbench her father had built for Billy (she had laid claim to it after her brother left for the army), a scaled-down version of Willis's own. She sanded the spurdle she was making for Katherine, a late Mother's Day present that she hoped would be an even better surprise for being late, plus it might cheer her after the recent bad news. Her mother was against war. Well, maybe not war in general, but *this* war. When Katherine and Willis's friends with sons in the Kentucky National Guard were notified that their boys' unit was shipping out to Texas for training and then on to Vietnam, some of them were baffled and outraged. They had understood the Guard to be meant for emergencies close to home. Katherine had gone to Frankfort to protest with some of the parents, despite Willis's efforts to talk his wife out of it. Maureen kept expecting Katherine to say to Willis, *I told you so*, but so far she hadn't.

She stopped sanding her Mother's Day project and hovered at her father's elbow, watching him drill tiny holes of progressively larger diameter into odd shapes of metal. She hopped from one foot to the other and waited for him to turn off the drill and take off his mufflers and safety goggles and look at her.

"What do you think's going to happen when Uncle Carl comes?" she said.

"I expect we'll welcome him home and see to it he's got someplace to sleep." Willis drew his goggles over his eyes again.

In front of Maureen her parents pretended not to be concerned about the fact that a certifiable nut was about to move into their house with them. But she had heard them talking when they thought she was absorbed in *Johnny Tremain,* sitting in the glider on the porch. Katherine had made clear to Willis that she did not intend to move Willis's crazy brother Carl into Billy's room. "Well, what is it you plan to do with him then?" Willis had asked her last week, which Maureen thought was a good question. Her mother did not appear inclined to answer. Maureen had watched out of the corner of her eye as Katherine took a stack of sheets and blankets out of the closet and put them on the daybed out on the screen porch that wrapped around the house. Other than that, no particular plan had been put in place.

"You're not scared?" Maureen asked her father now.

"What, of Carl? No!" Willis rarely got as exasperated with Maureen as her mother did, or if he did, he was better at not letting it show. He blew metal shavings away and went back to his work.

She tapped her father's elbow once, twice. Repeatedly. Willis turned off the drill.

"Mother said that once Billy gets home we'll have to wait and see." It's not that Maureen was trying to stir up trouble; she needed to get the lay of the land. It was still almost a whole year before her brother was to return from Vietnam, but still. All Maureen wanted to know was what would happen once Billy—the person who was *really* supposed to be coming home at some point—got home. "Will Uncle Carl have to go back to the insane asylum?"

"People do not call them that anymore, Mo." Her father breathed in long and let it out slow. "Why don't you let Curly into the garden. She can root out the old corn stobs. Your mother's on me to get the soil turned over before the rain comes."

This new summer was not even started and was already so deadly dull that even small tasks were welcome. Maureen sighed with exhaustion and obeyed. She knew it was wrong of her, but she was almost glad for the bodies coming home—at least it was something. There would be a whole week of funerals. She could barely remember the last time she was at a funeral. Would her mother even let her go? She picked up a stick on the way to Curly's pen and jabbed at her foot with it as punishment for thinking so selfishly. She stabbed a little more, hard enough to make a tiny spot of blood pop out on her white skin. Of course she wasn't glad those boys had died. It was awful and sad and the worst thing her town ever had to face. Her eyes watered and she clamped her mouth tight.

The enormous pig lay on her side in the dust, her broad belly rising and falling with the gentle effort of breathing. Through the fence Maureen poked the pig's bristled back.

"Curly, you fat thing, get up." The sow groaned with pleasure, thinking Maureen meant to give her a good scratching. "I said, get up." Curly rolled upright and waited with somber grace for Maureen to lift the wire strap from the gatepost. She followed Maureen to the garden. The garden sat on a rise near the bluff and was edged by a loose amalgam of wire and post meant to keep Levon Ferguson's hounds from running roughshod over the vegetables. Maureen noticed without alarm that the clouds had come to occupy a third of the valley's ceiling. At least a good storm would be something to write about.

Yesterday, she had begun writing her memoirs in the new diary. She had written about her mother's refusal to buy her a bra, and about the mean thing a girl had done to her at the last-day-of-school party. But she had run into a dead end at the bottom of page two after crossing out *I wonder what Eddie Miller is doing today.* Maureen and Eddie were in the same grade at Holy Ghost, eighth come fall.

She went to the swing under the big white oak, where she and Eddie used to take turns being pushed by their pretty young mothers. She stood on the swing's plank seat and pumped herself high enough that her head brushed the new leaves. She could not let herself think about Eddie now, because thinking about Eddie made her think about his brother Brandon, who was one of the seven dead boys coming home today. Maureen's mother had been visiting Eddie's mother, Raedine, often since the Millers got word. "That woman is prostrate with grief," Katherine said each day when she came home from taking soup and muffins and little presents and puzzles to distract the Miller kids from the fact of their family being torn to pieces.

All of which made Maureen think morbid thoughts about her own brother, upon whom they had not laid eyes in a year. She had not forgotten the day Billy left, saying the hell if he was going to throw his life away grinding Portland cement same as every other poor bastard in this shit-hole town—this he'd said to Maureen, of course, not to Katherine and Willis. Billy was not yet at the point of cursing in front of their parents. He was only seventeen at the time. It occurred to Maureen, thinking on it now, that he'd had a birthday in a foreign country, lucky duck. But was somebody really lucky, being in a place where things were exploding every other minute? Her brother had wanted to go, he wasn't drafted by the government or tricked like the guys who were in the National Guard. He'd signed up for it. She remembered sitting on her brother's bed, watching him throw T-shirts and underwear and a toothbrush into a sack. "I'm the kind of man that demands adventure, Mo, here tomorrow, gone today," he said. She took the underwear out and folded them neatly—the way their mother would have done if she was still speaking to him—and she put them back in the sack and reminded him that seventeen was not, strictly speaking, what you could call a man. To which he had squinted at her all James Dean. He peered into the mirror on his dresser. "*Asia*," he whispered to his reflection, like he was conjuring a steamy land where flying howler monkeys and screeching birds made your spine tingle in the night. A blind person could see Billy Juell had plans.

Maureen had not blamed her brother one second for itching to get over there.

She wrote to him early on, but he did not write back, not once, not ever. Their mother was faithful, and now and then Maureen stuck things in her envelopes to Billy. A drawing of the horse they did not own, a stupid poem she'd gotten an A on, or lame drawings of Billy's dog Paco whose skull had been squashed flat by the wheel of Jink Riley's Corvette on Halloween. She remembered all the blood, and running home in her costume, wailing all the way.

She clambered down the stone steps now to the springhouse half-submerged in the side of the hill and took a ladleful of water that came from the ground, so sweet and cold it made her teeth hurt. This was where her father's father and his father before him had drawn water as a boy. In the olden days, water had to be toted up to the house a single wooden bucket at a time, Willis told her, until they got to where they could pump it through a pipe up the hill. Now the city has dammed the river ten miles downstream, making the big lake everybody calls The Reservoy. Gradually all but the remotest areas are going on city water. The big blue water tank can be spotted from almost any direction.

Maureen caught a skink and carried it to the swing and sat petting it with one finger. When she turned it over to tickle its soft scaly belly, the skink slipped between her fingers and ran down her leg and into the tall grass by the fence. She sat, barely moving like the air around her, waiting, waiting. But for what? For her crazy uncle to come and turn their lives upside down? For her brother to get home—another whole year from now? For the funerals of the dead National Guardsmen? Yes that, all that. And this other thing: She was ready for her life to begin.

She pumped her legs half-heartedly a few times but quickly gave up and hung there from the tree limb, still as a windless bell. She sighed deeply. Katherine's fat sow grunted soft agreement from the vegetable garden.

Maureen pulled the diary out of her pocket. The anvil-shaped cloud that had been assembling itself into a purple caul at the end of the valley moved almost imperceptibly closer. Maureen dragged a winter toe, pink and tender as a baby's, through the worn spot under the swing, pausing now and then to jot down a note. *For my life to begin.* She fell to imagining someone watching her, rested her chin in her hand, and set her gaze across the valley, picturing in her head how she might look to her voyeur. Her wrist fell asleep. She pitched the diary to the ground and twisted the swing's ropes tight, then let herself spin out, dragging her foot in a narrowing spiral in the dirt. She was sick to death of this edginess, of the way the second hand of a clock seemed to sweep in slow motion around the inside of her skull, reminding her that time was passing and the world was passing and she was just here, here, here. Instead of winding down like a normal clock, she could feel springs inside her being coiled tighter. She was amazed that pieces of her didn't suddenly go shooting off this bluff, blasting across the valley in bloody rain. She shoved her feet into her new flip-flops—it was the first day her mother had let her wear them—and flapped her arms awake to get the pins out.

A cool breeze brushed her neck, and in minutes the purple curtain wrapped the whole sky. She heard the grating screech of the screen door and waited for what she knew was coming.

"Maureen, get inside right now," Katherine called.

Maureen gave a last good twist to the ropes of the swing, leaned back, and whirled around, her body a stiff plank spinning in air like an acrobat. She stood and staggered a bit, relishing the dizzy buzz, then headed for the house. She was still giddy and grinning when, halfway across the yard, the hair on her forearms lifted and the air split and crashed together again and everything went white.

Suddenly her mother was lifting her off the ground and her father was running to them, still wearing his safety goggles. *It's not even raining*, Maureen meant to say out loud but wasn't sure whether she had or not, it was all so dreamlike. A vibrating burning shock ran from her heel to her pelvis and feathered out into her belly. In the dream the three of them turned together in slow motion toward the garden where Curly lay on her back as if playing a serious game of possum, four legs stiff in the air. Maureen did feel rain then, spare gentle drops glinting through wan sunlight. *Look, the sun!* she tried to say. A second snapping strike hit so close her mother screamed, its clap a gunshot in their ears, and they were running toward the house, Maureen's legs dangling and flopping from Willis's arms. She was looking over her father's shoulder and was the first to see it: The giant oak hanging over the machine shop shuddered and swayed as if to some music only it could hear, and in that long moment Maureen wondered if it would refuse to fall. The only sound was of her father's heavy breathing in her ear. And then the sky unfastened with a sudden driving rain, the kind that makes dry ground roll up into little dirt balls for a split second before everything gets soaked brand new.

"Sweet Jesus in heaven!" Virginia Ferguson said, waiting for them at the door, her voice trembling. She was staring beyond them. Then Willis, following the line of her gaze, saw it. His machine shop was buried under the oak tree, its massive trunk bisecting the roofline. The grownups all stood as if they had sprouted roots right through the kitchen floor.

"You can set me down, Daddy," Maureen said. But he carried her upstairs and her mother put her in bed against her protests.

*Are you all right, she'll be all right, I'm all right.* Ginny Ferguson had followed them upstairs, and all three adults were exchanging opinions on the extent of damage, real, potential, and imagined. Then there was the litany of blessings, the discussion of luck that always seemed to mean a lot to grownups at such times. Maureen herself could not decide whether she had been lucky or cheated out of finally having something truly exciting happen to her. She did not feel the way she imagined you were supposed to feel after being knocked down by a bolt of lightning. Katherine pulled the sheet over her and rubbed her arm.

"Mr. Juell, I believe your girl saved your life," Ginny said. "Her and Jesus."

Katherine and Willis stared at her blankly.

"You ran out to get to her only seconds before that tree came crashing down and cut that shop smack in two," Ginny said.

This was an angle Maureen had not thought of. She looked back and forth between the three adults to gauge how magnificent this thing might be. She felt a poem coming on, but as quickly as a phrase came to mind it vanished, just as the lightning bolt had done. She sunk into the pillow and looked at the ceiling where a spider the color of putty picked its careful way toward the corner.

"The main thing is nobody is seriously hurt," Katherine said. She did not place much stock in coincidence, much less divine intervention. "You don't hurt anywhere, do you, honey?" She rubbed at Maureen's heel, which did not look a lot different from the way it looked before.

"Ow," Maureen said without conviction. The truth was the sting had disappeared minutes after it had all been over. "Curly got hurt," she said. "Curly's dead, isn't she?"

"We'll worry about that later. You rest," Katherine told Maureen, "and stay away from the windows."

Maureen listened to the grownups trundling down the stairs, their voices falling into that odd sorting of what to do next, as adults will after a hubbub. Ginny sounding fractious and entirely ready to be off this hill, Katherine trying to persuade her to wait out the storm, Willis insisting that he would drive her home.

On her bedside table sat the stack of summer reading Maureen had brought home from the library. The room had grown dim enough with the storm that she switched on the lamp and settled into her pillow with *Bleak House*. She skimmed the first page, determined not to be put off by the fact that she did not know what a chancery was. Dickens was a first-class noticer of gloom and smoke and rain and fog. All the books she had chosen had scary titles that sounded as if they might shed light on possession by spirits. *The House of the Seven Gables. We Have Always Lived in the Castle.* Maureen believed she lived in a house haunted by ghosts—four, as best she could count—and she had resolved that this would be the year she finally communicated with at least one of them. The lightning strike might actually have been a stroke of luck in this regard. Granny Ricketts, the closest thing Cementville had to a witch, had told her that people who survive a lightning strike often end up with special powers.

Maureen closed the book and pulled a cardboard box from under the bed. She opened the hinged game board flat. The four corners each held an answer: Yes, No, Hello, Goodbye. Maureen took out the heart-shaped wooden pointer thing (Augrey Ferguson called it the *planchette*, which sounded very authentic) and placed it in the center of the board. She rested her fingertips on it lightly the way Augrey had shown her.

"What. Is. Your. Name?" Maureen whispered, and waited for the pointer to move among the letters of the alphabet arched across the board. Nothing. She did not want to believe she'd been gypped. She kept an ear cocked toward the staircase lest her mother decide to check on her. Regarding matters of the occult, Katherine was at least in partial agreement with the nuns at school—such things were gateways, if not for the devil, certainly for morbid thoughts that ought not occupy an adolescent mind.

Not to mention Maureen had traded her brother's Led Zeppelin album for it, her first real foray into dicey behavior. The thrill of stealing (*borrowing*, really, since she absolutely would replace the album before Billy got home) was enhanced by association with the notorious Augrey Ferguson. Some people called Augrey a slut, but she had offered to throw in a deck of tarot cards for a forty-five of anything by the Temptations, which Maureen thought was nice. "My brother doesn't have any soul," Maureen had told the girl, "only hard rock. Won't your mom get suspicious if too many of her things go missing?"

She could not translate Augrey's snort.

Maureen suspected it was the misfortune of being born a Ferguson that gave weight to the rumors about Augrey. Augrey's mother, Arlene, had six or seven kids whose several unknown fathers she had never bothered with marrying, and she lived in a house trailer (a "mobile home," Augrey was always correcting people) in Taylortown with the blacks and the other poor people. Augrey's big brother Levon, who blacked the eyes of poor Ginny, was hated or feared or both by everybody in Cementville.

It occurred to Maureen that this was the sort of stuff she ought to be writing in her diary. She jumped out of bed and ran to the window, because it also occurred to her that she had left her diary in the grass by the swing, and now it was buried under a three-hundred-year-old oak tree, its clean white pages surely soaked to a pulp.

There were her mother's footsteps on the stairs. Maureen folded the Ouija board into the unmarked box and tried to shove it under her bed. Too late. Katherine set down a tray of toasted cheese sandwiches.

"What—?" she started to ask.

Maureen burst into tears. "My diary . . . it's under the tree!" she managed to get out between sobs.

"We'll get another. It only came from Newberry's," Katherine said. She took Maureen in her arms and rocked her as she had not done in a good while. "What were you putting away when I came in?"

Maureen dried her face with her arm. "Nothing."

Katherine bent over and pulled the box out. She glanced at Maureen once, giving her a last opportunity to come clean, before opening the board wide enough for a good look.

"Where did this come from?"

Maureen stared out the window. The rain seemed to be slowing. "My diary . . . " she tried weakly again, almost forcing her voice to tears.

"Maureen, I'm going to put this away until you're ready to tell me where you got it."

"I traded something for it. With a girl I know." She looked at her mother again. "Please. I need it."

"Need it? Sweetheart, there is nothing this meaningless scrap of cardboard can do for you."

"Then why won't you let me keep it?" Maureen was crying in earnest now.

But Katherine thrust the box under her arm and turned for the door.

Maureen said, "Granny Ricketts said people who survive a lightning strike can take on special powers—"

"Have you and Edward been pestering Adelaide Ricketts again? You know that poor woman isn't right in the head."

"She gave Bran Miller a snakestone after he got struck by lightning, and let him keep it for a whole year to protect him from becoming a human lightning rod. Because snakestones give you dreams that make you prophesy!" Maureen could see she was getting nowhere fast. "Eddie told me all about it, see, you can prophesy and know when the next storm is coming. Granny said being struck once is almost guaranteed magic, but twice could be curtains." The words gushed out, and a sudden pounding in her head made her fall back on the pillows again. "Miss Raedine made Bran give it back and now look what's happened to Bran!"

Her mother sat on the bed and pushed the short bangs from Maureen's forehead and felt for fever. "I don't care what Willis says, I'm calling Doctor Carruthers." She examined Maureen's heel again.

"Mom, just think," Maureen said, whispering now, "Between the new special powers and the Ouija board, and maybe a snake-stone, I might be able to talk to them."

"Talk to who, honey?"

"You know." Maureen gave her a knowing look.

Katherine's face shifted from concern to impatience. Maureen wondered if her mother believed in anything at all that was truly mysterious. She longed for Katherine just once to come out and say that Maureen was right, there certainly was a whiff of the Forsaken Bride's perfume in the northwest bedroom closet, or to admit that, during the night, she had heard the shuffling gait of the Bloody Groom in the downstairs hall. Maureen had given names to all the ghosts in the Juell house, at least the ones she could identify so far. Another thing to be annotated in her diary—which now would have to be replaced.

"For the last time, there are no ghosts in this or any other house. Anyway, we're not even sure you were actually struck by lightning," Katherine said. "The charge had probably dissipated by the time it reached you."

"What difference does that make? You never want anything extraordinary to happen in my life!"

It was obvious her mother was trying her best not to smirk. "Something tells me your life is going to be extraordinary, regardless of what I want."

Maureen tried not to be pleased.

Katherine brought the tray of toasted cheese sandwiches to the bed, and the two of them ate together. It was a rare treat, getting to eat in bed. Her mother wasn't even minding the crumbs.

"Will we go to the funerals?"

"I don't know if that's a good idea. I mean, I'm sure either your father or I will try to attend most of them. But sweetheart, it doesn't sound like an experience you need to go through."

"Not even Bran's? Eddie is practically my best friend." Maureen had not admitted to her mother that Eddie Miller was in fact her only friend. But thinking about the funeral Masses that would be spread through the week, the smoky incense trailing out of Father Oliver's brass censor, the candles and the choir, it all made her suddenly very tired. "Do you think the Hupmobile is all right?" Maureen asked.

"I hadn't even thought of that." Katherine held her sandwich in midair. "Don't mention it to your father," she whispered, as if Willis might hear. "Oh, he's going to be grieving if anything happens to that—"

Maureen knew she was about to call it a hunk of junk. Katherine would never say such a thing to Willis's face, but Maureen had heard her talking to Raedine Miller about the Hupmobile. Old cars were on the list of things Katherine Juell could not see the purpose of; she would be the first to acknowledge that she wasn't much of a sentimentalist.

"Don't worry, Mother. I know how Daddy is. Remember when Blue died? How he wouldn't look straight at anybody for two days? You always know he's eaten up with something when he gets that way." Willis had been forced to shoot his old bluetick hound after he was bitten by a rattler.

Katherine ruffled Maureen's bangs again. "Such an old soul! Are you hurting anywhere, honey? Tell the truth now."

Maureen shook her head. Before she could make another plea for the release of the Ouija board, she was asleep.

WHEN SHE WOKE, THE SUN was full out, as if it really had all been a dream. Outside, voices strained to be heard above the rumble of her father's tractor. Katherine was directing him toward a suitable burial spot in a corner of the garden. Maureen watched from the upstairs window as Willis looped a chain around Curly's hindquarters. Unbidden, a vague memory floated up to her, of the day Curly had come to them, an anniversary gift from Willis's elderly Aunt Janine. "What on earth—" her mother had said before bursting into tears. That she detested the smell of pigs was a known fact. That Willis's jealous maiden aunt still saw Katherine as a city-bred outsider, years after her nephew had brought her home for a bride, was equally known. But the pig, a blotchy pink thing just off its mother's milk, followed Katherine around like a dog, ensuring that the sausage mill would not be her fate. She soon grew into a handsome Chester White with black spots. Katherine said, "Oh, Will!" when he teased her about being a city girl with a pet pig, but it was clear that Curly was destined for a life of ease and table scraps. Until this day anyway.

Maureen ran to the garden and followed along behind the tractor as it dragged the pig's carcass to the hole her father had dug. Curly rolled with a dull thump into her grave. Low thunder grumbled in the distance.

"The storm's moving off," Willis said.

Katherine, wary of the angry clouds still glowering over the south end of the valley, was not satisfied. "It's foolish for us to be out here. Maureen, come inside, and Willis, you get this contraption put away and—" A deafening boom made Katherine jump.

"That'll be the transformer down in town," Willis said, swinging down from the seat of the tractor. He shoveled dirt over Curly. It started to rain again, and Maureen and her mother ran to the house. The radio Katherine kept on top of the refrigerator had already fallen silent and the house lights were dark. Maureen brought out the kerosene lamp and Katherine let her light it. From the sideboard in the dining room Maureen fetched a deck of cards. Playing cards by the kerosene lamp was what they did when the electricity was out. It was always Maureen's secret hope that the power would stay off so long that people forgot about it and life went back to the way it was in the olden days. Her family would keep a stable full of horses and ride into town on Saturdays for provisions. Lumber, fabric for sewing clothes, cornmeal. Not sugar, because her family would keep bees and tap trees for maple syrup.

Willis came in from the barn and slung his wet jacket over the hall tree. Her mother poured the last of the coffee. "I suppose the shop will have to be rebuilt?"

"That's what insurance is for," Willis said. No mention of the Hupmobile. He looked at the clock. "You want to try to make it down to town for the parade?"

"It's been postponed. Lila O'Brien called—they decided to move it to Memorial Day. Evidently the storm and some semblance of sanity or sensitivity or *something* has prevailed among the Daughters of the Confederacy or whatever that group is that has put itself in charge of all things *patriotic.* . . . " Katherine bit off her words and threw a dish rag into the sink.

Willis reached out to put a hand on her shoulder but stopped. "How's Ginny doing?" he said.

"She's mad enough to be good for her. Pray to God this time it sticks. She'll stay at her cousin's for a few days until she figures out what to do." Katherine pressed her temples with her fingertips, pulling herself together. Neither Willis nor Maureen went to touch her, knowing she hated that when she was collecting herself. Ever since Levon and Ginny rented the little house from them at the bottom of her driveway, Katherine seemed to have taken on saving Virginia Ferguson as a personal mission. Sometimes, after Ginny left, Maureen found her mother poring over *The Feminine Mystique*, which Katherine said was about the conventions that had kept so many women under the hard boot of men. When Maureen asked her mother if Willis had *her* under his boot, she had laughed and said, "Hardly!"

Katherine wasn't laughing now. "She's got to get out of here, Will. Otherwise I believe that man's going to kill her one of these days, I really do."

Maureen and Willis were staring at the linoleum when they heard footsteps on the front porch and a knock on the door.

Maureen ran into the dim hallway. Through the glass and the gauze curtain she could see the shape of a tall man in brown holding a satchel. She opened the door. His hair was buzzed close to the scalp on the sides and combed up flat on top. His eyes made her think of windows in a house with nobody home. Blood whooshed through her ears and she felt herself blink in slow motion.

Maureen flung herself like a torpedo into her brother's arms. He caught her, just. Their parents heard the commotion and came running. Willis had to prop Katherine up when she nearly fell into the potted fern. They pulled Billy into the hallway as if they were rescuing him from the jaws of some invisible monster set to grab him off the front porch. Katherine used the bottom of her skirt to wipe him off and said, "You need to get out of those sopping wet things." Then Katherine, Willis, and Maureen stood as still as if a ghost had floated into the house, and they watched Billy pick up the satchel and climb the stairs to his old room. He hadn't spoken yet.

Without having a chance to stop herself thinking it, the thought floated into Maureen's head: What if they ripped out his vocal chords?

In the kitchen, she sat with her father at the dinette, waiting and fidgeting. Her mother filled the percolator with water then stood there staring at the useless electrical outlet, the cord dangling from her hand. She wiped the counters and scrubbed the sink and folded the tea towel. She rubbed lotion into her hands and took a pitcher of tea out of the refrigerator and put a tin of oatmeal cookies on the table. Maureen shuffled the cards and thought about dealing out a hand of Go Fish, but then put the deck down and shoved it to the middle of the table.

Her brother came into the kitchen, more himself in a T-shirt and jeans, except for the flattop that stuck up in jagged spikes like the hair on a dog's back after rain. She didn't remember Billy's ears being so big, and she wondered for a second if a mistake had been made. A silent stranger wandering into the wrong house. Before he left, Billy kept his hair long like John Lennon's on the cover of *Revolver*. Maureen poured this new version of her brother a glass of tea and put an oatmeal cookie on a flowered saucer in front of him.

"Thanks, Mo," he croaked, like someone who still had vocal chords but had not used them in a long time. He nibbled the tiniest fraction of his cookie. Maureen wanted to stop looking at the fever blister all yellow-edged in the corner of his mouth.

"We didn't know you were coming home," their mother said.

Somebody swallowed. "I wish I could have known—I would've made a celebration meal!" Katherine had that cheerful upturn in her voice to hide the quivering. She held her eyes wide open so nothing would spill out. Watery globs pooled under her eyelashes. Maureen chewed her cookie so fast that she bit the inside of her cheek. It was unnerving, watching her mother act this way.

"It's good to see you, son. Have you home in one piece." Their father's voice didn't shake but his hands did. Maybe her dad was thinking of the other boys who had also come home not in one piece. Maureen wished her parents would act normal. They were obviously making Billy nervous.

"Well, it wasn't exactly my idea," he said. "Getting out, I mean." Billy broke the oatmeal cookie into pieces. "I got into a fight."

"Curly's dead," Maureen blurted, but nobody looked at her. She watched Billy's Adam's apple move up and down while he drained the tea from his glass. She sat on her hands and waited for him to speak again.

"I was drunk." His fever blister broke open. If Maureen were Billy she would stop talking so the sore didn't split wider and have all that yellow liquid run out. Their father's breathing seemed to be the loudest sound in the world. Maureen pictured the hairs in his nose vibrating and wheezing like a gang of teeny old men.

"I, for one, think we should *all* go to *all* the funerals," Maureen said. Her mother and father looked at her but neither of them spoke.

"I let some coon have it pretty bad."

"Willis Theodore Juell!" Katherine hissed. Their father glared at him. Maureen sucked in a breath. She was pretty sure that in the house where she and her brother had grown up, that word got you a whipping you would not soon forget. The Juells had all watched news of Selma and the fire-bombings. The little dead girls in their church outfits. They had followed the March on Washington together, their whole family, Billy included.

"Stupid fight." Billy's knee bounced under the table. "I don't even remember what it was about."

Katherine blinked fast and patted the corner of her eye with a Kleenex. Everybody stared at the cookie crumbs spread in front of Billy.

Billy said, "Fucker almost didn't make it." He seemed to be trying for a laugh but it came out choked, a *khar-khar* sound.

Their mother let loose that kind of inside-out sob that sucks up all the air in the room. Maureen felt on the verge of fainting or bursting out laughing, she couldn't predict which. She wished Billy would keep his mouth shut for a second and let her catch up with what was going on. Had she heard right? Had he really almost killed somebody?

Katherine and Willis appeared to have been struck dumb.

"Jink Riley killed Paco," Maureen said, only because she was going to split wide open if someone didn't say something. "Halloween night."

"Idiot had a heart condition even he didn't know about," Billy said. "Shouldn't even have been in the goddamn army. Don't worry, I still get my GI." He glanced at his father and shoved half the cookie into his mouth at once. "It's a discharge, but it ain't a dishonorable one. Discharge don't mean shit these days anyhow." A pink line of blood marked the corner of his mouth now.

"Discharge *doesn't* mean—" Maureen started to correct, but she couldn't make herself say S-H-I-T, not with their parents sitting there. And—ain't? *Ain't?* Their mother had to be dying a thousand deaths.

Willis stood up. "I might've left the windows down on the truck." He went out straight into the storm. Maureen watched through the kitchen window as he disappeared into the barn. Their father was in Korea back when.

Katherine and Billy and Maureen sat there in the kitchen like graveyard statues for an eternity. It was quiet as a tomb and very nearly as dark. Maureen moved her eyes toward the clock on the wall and saw that it had stopped.

They all three jumped when the electricity suddenly cut back on and the lights flashed and the refrigerator clicked and began a low-screaming hum and the radio on top of the fridge blared to life with the deejay shrieking, *It's wacky! This is W-A-K-Y Radio serving Greater Kentuckiana with the latest news and up-to-the-minute weather information!* Their mother yanked the radio's plug out of the wall. Maureen thought for a second that the radio might go flying across the room.

But Katherine Juell was not a woman who threw things. She turned the lights off and they sat in the dark a while longer. Maureen bit into a cookie. The crunching made her wish she hadn't. She shuffled the cards to hide the chewing.

Nobody said, *Go on and deal us a hand, Mo.* Thunder rumbled softly in the distance.

"The storm's moving off," Maureen said, trying for the same authority her father's voice had held. But she doubted the truth of it. The kerosene lamp hissed peacefully from the dead center of the table. Maureen was not fooled. People were not going to forget. There would be no stable full of horses, no bees or honey or maple syrup straight from the trees. The olden days were not coming back.

Billy pushed his chair out. "I'm bushed. Goddamn bus—must've got a crick in my neck—"

Katherine Juell shot from her chair and stood over him, an enlarged version of herself. "Filth will not be tolerated in this house!" Her nostrils flared out scary. "You are my son, and you will not be turned out, but you will use the English language as you were taught!"

Then her body telescoped down to its normal size. She flicked the lights on and pulled a roast out of the refrigerator and set the oven to 325° and began peeling potatoes. She did not turn back to her children when she said, "Supper at six."

Maureen sat very still and waited for Billy to whisper something sarcastic under his breath so they could share a secret laugh, or raise his eyebrows in that exaggerated way with his eyes bugging out in fake fear at their mother's snit. She waited for him to do any one of the things her brother used to do. Anything that would let her make sure it was him.

# THREE

She is in a dead coma Friday night when her mother calls at 11:58 to say, "Your cousin Donnie is gone." MaLou starts to say something flip: *Didn't that happen a long time ago?* But something in her mother's tone says this isn't just another of Donnie's usual sloppy binges, after which Aunt Martha and Uncle Rafe will track him down in some floozy's mobile home off Highway 68. Maria Louise Goins rubs her eyes awake enough to realize that *Donnie is gone* means Donnie is finally and irretrievably dead.

"What—how?" she wants to know, and in her half-sleep Donnie rises up over the handlebars of his banana bike, a bully with yellow spikes of hair who beat the crap out of her every summer for grins.

This couldn't come at a worse time. "Mother, I can't. My boss isn't going to let me drop everything and go down to Cementville right now. I've got a big story due tomorrow at noon." A fire at a local elementary school, suspected arson. She has been promoted from cub reporter to features—her mother knows this. That story is to carry her byline, damn it. Donnie has been courting death since he was nine, she doesn't say out loud to her mother, bouncing that trick bike over boulders in the rock quarry and climbing the water tower to paint his name in letters two feet tall. "The Toyota isn't running," MaLou goes on. "It hasn't moved from its spot on Tallahassee Street in nearly six weeks. There's probably crabgrass growing through the radiator by now." She doesn't dream for a minute her mother has already reserved a ticket on the Greyhound for her.

"Wake up and listen to me, Maria Louise." Her mother is using her I-don't-mean-maybe voice. "It isn't just Donnie. This thing is going to crush that poor town. A bunch of the boys from his unit are gone."

She does sit up then, asks her mother to repeat what she just said.

"Seven boys from right there in town. Fire Support Base Blacksnake was overrun. The bodies are to arrive home sometime early Saturday. Funerals throughout the week. We won't know when Donnie's is until Monday. I feel sure it'll be published in the *Picayune*."

MaLou had run with these guys every summer. Some she considered friends. Some of them she had even kept in touch with. She knew who had gotten married and which one had surprised them all by becoming a dad last fall. FSB Blacksnake was their last known location, a hillside supply base people said was at best foolishly located, at worst a death trap. There is a name she is afraid to say. But, "Boyd?" she says, holding her breath. *Defenseless* was the word he had used to describe the base in his last letter. Wide open to the enemy.

Across the phone line comes the whispery shuffling of newspaper. MaLou can hear her mother's lips softly going over the words as she reads to herself.

"Read it out loud, Mother."

" . . . 138th Field Artillery unit, which was attached to Battery C in support of the 101st Airborne division stationed at Phu Bai—is that how you say it? Phu Bai?—took heavy casualties as North Vietnamese overran—oh, MaLou, don't make me do this."

"The names, Mom."

"Let's see. Brandon Lee Miller, Mitchell Kidwell—oh, there's Donnie—Donald Raphael Goins III, Malcolm T. Spalding, Boyd

Farber Jr.—isn't that the boy who was sweet on you in high school?—Charles Gordon, and Richard Welch. That's it. Seven."

MaLou breathes, clears her throat, and tries to sort out from the jumble in her head what to say. This is exactly what was not supposed to happen.

"I don't care how you do it, but you are getting your patootie to the bus station at four thirty tomorrow morning. I'm down in my back again," her mother tells her. "You're the only person we have to represent our side of the family. Your Aunt Martha is going to need you."

Now here Maria Louise Goins sits, fifteen minutes into the five-hour bus ride from Cincinnati to Cementville, snugged up-close and personal next to a man she definitely wishes she had never laid eyes on. She knew the second he boarded the bus that he was going to do it, fold himself into the seat next to hers. She pretends to read the paperback she brought for the trip as he slips out of a thin jacket. Exactly what it is the stranger smells of takes a while to discern. Ritz crackers soaked in turpentine? Oil-based house paint and waterless hand cleaner? No, it's the greasy dirt floor of Uncle Rafe's garage. Specifically, it is the deep pit dug in the center of his shop, where her uncle slides daily on a little wheeled trolley under the belly of whatever wreck he's disassembling. MaLou is almost certain she can smell on the man in the seat next to her the exact concoction of yellow clay dust mingling with the fluorescent green antifreeze leaking from a crack in Uncle Rafe's plastic dishpan. The stranger seems to occupy less space in the seat than she does. She had her eyes fixed on her book when he sat down, so she can't be sure how tall he is. She looks out of the side of her face at the length of hip joint to knee and decides maybe he is taller than she thought, that's a long thighbone there, and skinny too. And his fingernails. Lined with black grime. Must be a mechanic of some sort. She can only hope he won't try to strike up a conversation.

As a proscription against such a notion she cranes her head to the window, propping it against the cold glass, and closes her eyes. The man rifles through a filthy backpack and produces—judging from the soft crinkling paper sounds, for her eyes are shut tight—a homemade sandwich that must be wrapped in wax paper. Her nostrils flare a bit as they take in the smell of peanut butter and banana.

She feels a tentative tap on the sleeve of her jacket and opens one eye. But she must be mistaken, because no, apparently he did not tap at all. The man is not offering her half his peanut butter and banana sandwich. Staring straight ahead, he chews politely with his lips closed, no smacking, which she'd almost expected. MaLou watches him lift the sandwich to his mouth, a gesture she would not have thought could contain diffidence, and imagines touching the rough knuckles, brushing a finger over the pale fluff of hair curling over the back of his hand. She tries to drift off.

"I have an extra apple."

She jumps at the sound, fakes a startle, pretending to have been asleep. She inhales audibly and sits erect as if shaking off an unpleasant dream, her eyelids flickering in an exaggerated manner.

"Sorry. I thought you were awake." The stranger leans deferentially in his seat away from her as if trying to respect MaLou's personal space.

"Oh, no problem," she says. "I need to wake up anyway. I don't want to miss my stop. Do you know where we are?"

"We not five miles back passed Walton."

At least four hours to go.

He reaches a hand over her side of the armrest and she flinches. But when she looks down, a small green apple settles in her lap, the kind she and Donnie collected as kids. They had ranged far and wide over the countryside, exploring abandoned farmhouses where daffodils or peonies bloomed faithfully in the spring as if they expected their people to come back. Sometimes she and her cousin came upon whole orchards, deserted and spooky, laden with fruit. MaLou picks up the apple in her lap. Black wormholes speckle its surface. She pictures the young man next to her gathering apples on the side of the road this morning in the gray dawn. But it is May, apple season months away.

"Thanks," she says, biting in with relish, surprised at the disappearance of proper reserve. She is hungry. She is on a Greyhound bus at five thirty in the morning. Who is she kidding about reserve? Peanut butter and banana would have gone good with this. "Where'd you get these?"

"My landlady. She calls them October apples. Stores them in her cellar, each wrapped in its own little paper collar."

"I didn't know you could make them last so long."

"Oh, she's a wizard all right." They sit in silence for a while. "Where you headed?" he says.

"Funeral."

"Aren't we all." He finishes off a second apple and wraps both cores in the wax paper from his sandwich. "Say, you're not on your way to Cementville, are you?"

"Cousin," she says, nodding, too surprised to lie, and what good would it do anyway?—they will be getting off the bus at the same place. Her heart might as well be lodged in her ears, as loud as it's banging there inside her. A desolation she doesn't want to feel and an odd attraction to this raggedy traveler skirmish for her attention.

He holds out the open lunch sack and she drops her apple core in.

"Brother," he says.

MaLou isn't ready for this conversation. For all her familiarity with catastrophe—indeed, she has lately become concerned at the way she nearly craves the tragedies of strangers—she does not hanker to hear another story of family loss in this war.

"I'm sorry," she whispers and leans her head toward the window and lets herself drift again. But the stranger doesn't seem to mind this, and when he starts talking, she doesn't mind either. She is in that half-present hovering state, one foot on this side, one on the other. MaLou doesn't open her eyes, listening like a child playing possum. His voice is the way she remembers her father's, soothing with that backcountry lilt; he could be singing, for all the melody in it. It's doleful, that honey accent, mountain-thick—*dulcet* is the word. But she suspects he somehow knows her secret, that she is a promiscuous borrower from the stories of other people's calamities.

"Daniel," he says. "He hadn't even started high school, last time I saw him. He's the first of us to do that. Graduate high school. And boy, don't you know a week later that government letter arrives."

MaLou sits up, checks her soft drink can to see if there's anything left. "He wasn't in the Guard unit with the others?"

He shakes his head ruefully. "Guard's filled up with everybody who's somebody. People like us get the draft, pure and simple."

At Christmas dinner her uncle had talked about the National Guard, how it had gotten more difficult to get in. People saw it as an honorable way to serve your country without getting blown up for nothing in Vietnam. Donnie and Boyd and the others were in their third year in the Guard when word came that the unit was heading to Texas for intensive training, and shipping out in a matter of weeks. Uncle Rafe wasn't sure which was worse, the sense of betrayal or the complete and utter bewilderment. Some of the parents had all piled together into Buck Farber's real estate van and driven to the capitol to protest. The governor couldn't see them, but they crowded into their congressman's office and gave him what for. "And what for?" Rafe had ended the story, his face red, as he attacked the Christmas turkey with his carving knife. "Nothing." It was the first holiday meal their only son had ever missed. Aunt Martha had to remind Rafe they hadn't yet said the grace.

A pale heat sneaks over MaLou's left shoulder; the sun is coming up. The bus glides southwesterly. The stranger's head has dropped back onto the headrest and in this naked moment when his eyes are closed and hers are open she examines his features. The shock of persimmon hair over his forehead. It is longer than that of other young men she has known. It curls softly around his neck like the tail of a fox kit. The profile dominated by a cliff of a brow, the fine orange hairs curly above deep eye sockets. She has not been able to gain the color of his irises yet, but given that fair skin, she imagines them close to the cerulean of her Aunt Martha's morning glories, the ones that climbed the porch rail in late summer, big as salad plates. MaLou shifts slightly toward him.

"He was cleaning fish behind Mama's trailer," he says. "Daniel. I had tied a few things in a pillowcase and was heading out. Didn't see him there at the edge of the woods. He called out to me, 'Where you off to, Byard?' I said, 'I'll be back directly, little brother.'"

"Where *were* you going?" That hunger is up in her now. MaLou would swallow his story whole.

"Where any draft-age man with half a brain in his noggin was going. Canada."

"You've been on the run all this time?"

"Going on five years. Take a look at the regular Army these days. It's pretty much the poor kids and the coloreds, and them few that enlist of their own free will. I don't know why I'm blabbing on like this to you. You could be Selective Service for all I know, hunting my sorry ass down." He does not sound as if this is a prospect that truly worries him.

"And you came home for your brother's funeral." She watches the tiny throb in his neck, willing him to speak again. He nods, his eyes still closed.

"Mama got ahold of me. I had taken a little place in the Bow Valley. Fellow that runs a hunting lodge let me get my mail there and use his telephone from time to time."

"You aren't afraid? Of being arrested?"

Her traveling companion surveys the sleeping forms up and down the aisle of the bus. MaLou is wedged in the corner, the back of her head pressed against the window glass, and now it is she who is protecting the space he needs to empty his grief. His hands rest in his lap, palms open as if in supplication. He turns to her. His eyes are blue.

"You sure you're not SS?" he says and smiles broadly. He rolls up the leg of his jeans. His knee is a mangled lump of purple, red, and white.

"My God, what happened? You didn't—you didn't have someone do that to you, did you?" She had heard the stories, young men literally shooting themselves in the foot.

"I didn't want to be killed in some stupid war, but no, I am not crazy enough to request something like this. This pretty thing came by tripping over the edge of a mountain."

"You don't think the draft board will be looking for you? Won't some patriotic kook be waiting for you to come home now?" MaLou had seen an article about a guy who came back from Toronto when his own father died. The FBI arrested him at the funeral.

The stranger, whose name she now knows is Byard, taps a finger to his temple. "Psychogenic fugue state," he says, grinning. "I got me papers that say so. Up in Saskatchewan, see, you don't have to be anybody special to avail yourself of a doctor."

"Fugue state—what's that mean? You've been out wandering?"

"That's the idea. Stranger in a strange land, don't even know his own name." His face clouds over.

"What was he like? Your brother?"

"Hmm. Well, Mama always said if she didn't have any more babies, she'd always have a child in Daniel. I'm not saying he was a retard. Just slow. Teachers held him back in first grade. I remember Mama crying after they summoned her to the school for a meeting. They said he was classifiable as a moron. Wanted to see about shipping him off to Eastern State. But Mama pitched a fit and said over her dead body, and they let it drop. After that they passed him on through the grades whether he'd learnt anything or not. You would of thought that would steer the draft board away from him, but you would of been wrong." Byard's jaw is working hard and MaLou cannot stop looking at the tendons straining across it. The journalist in her isn't ready to rest. She needs to change the subject for a bit or she will lose him to his grief and anger, those twinned emotions so rich in story. There might be a way to use this later.

"When I think of Canada, I always think of expanses of timber and log cabins buried to the windowsills in snow," she says.

There's a long bus ride ahead, and she might as well make the most of it. When she asked for time off, her boss suggested she write a story about the town's tragedy. If it was good enough, he'd consider front page.

"There is that. Toronto is where most resisters go. I started out there. But look at me. I've got 'country' written all over me."

MaLou laughs and lets down muscles she hadn't realized were clenched.

"Wasn't long before the city got to me, and that first spring thaw, I hitched a ride west to the Canadian Rockies." He pulls a wax paper bundle from his pocket and offers her what appears to be a homemade cinnamon roll. MaLou's eyebrows shoot up in question. Byard shrugs. "My landlady is partial to me." They eat in silence, licking sugar and cinnamon off their fingers. "I'd gotten there a few years before the big wave of resisters started, so when the government let us apply for immigrant status, I had a front-row seat."

"So you have legal status? But that still doesn't stop authorities here from arresting you, does it?"

Byard's mouth is full. When he finally swallows, it's he who changes the subject. "What about your cousin?"

"Donnie? Meanest bastard you would ever want to see."

"Oh, I doubt that. You don't know what all I've seen."

"Well, mean enough for me." MaLou stops herself. "He wasn't always that way. Once—we were probably ten, eleven—I fell out of a tree and had the breath knocked out of me. All I could think was, I am going to die. Donnie sat there and held my hand and told me to just give it a few minutes." She laughs. "The second I was all better and we knew nothing was broken, he stuffed a fistful of crabapples in my mouth. You have other brothers and sisters?"

"Yep." There's a sudden set of the jaw, so subtle that if she hadn't been studying the lines of his mouth, MaLou would have missed it. She waits.

"I have a little sister. Augrey. She's—let's see—she's fifteen, I reckon. Doesn't seem possible," he says after a long silence. "Tony's thirteen. Little Nate would be seven now, but he passed on. Long time ago. House fire." Byard stops again, but MaLou senses that he isn't finished. And again, her training as a reporter tells her to wait it out. Her traveling companion takes in a deep breath and with a long exhale says, "And then there's Levon."

"Ferguson? You're Levon Ferguson's brother?"

"You've heard of my brother. You don't sound like somebody raised in Cementville."

She shakes her head. "Cincinnati. My dad was from Cementville. He told me once that he drove like the proverbial bat out of hell away from Cementville the very day he graduated high school."

"A sentiment shared," he says. There is something of the old mountain eloquence in his speech, the inheritance of generations of Bible-reading ancestors.

"I was the city mouse visiting her country mouse cousins. Every July my parents shipped me off to Aunt Martha and Uncle Rafe."

"Not of Rafe Goins Auto Body?"

"You know them?"

Byard's face breaks open. "They're good people." He shakes his head. "I'll be damn. Old Donnie Ray, dead," he says, more softly. "Mama said a bunch of them were killed over there, but she didn't give names." He stares at his hands as if he is searching out something written there. "Wait a minute, I remember you . . . what was your name? . . . Don't tell me. . . . "

She does. "Donnie's the one who started calling me MaLou. It's really Maria Louise." She shakes her head and stares at him. "I can't believe you are the infamous Levon Ferguson's brother."

"I can't believe his reputation has spread as far as Cincinnati."

"Are you kidding? We were terrified of him when we were kids. I have seen him torture small animals with my own eyes. That must have been a trip, growing up in that shadow."

"That's one way to put it." Then, "Who else?"

She looks at him blankly.

"Who else got shoveled into a garbage bag over there?"

MaLou's eyes are blinking fast. "I . . . " She buries her face in her hands. The words come out muffled and strangled and thick. "There were seven. All National Guard. They'd only been there a few months." She is gulping air, but control escapes her. "Ricky Welch. Bran Miller. Mac Spalding. Chuckie Gordon. Mitch Kidwell. And Donnie." She saves one, the one that cannot be real, for last. "Boyd Farber."

"Sorry." Byard takes her hands away from her face. "I'm an asshole. You knew all of them?"

MaLou nods. "I had a letter from Boyd two days ago." She should have known better than to put mascara on this morning. It must be all over her face by now. "He said they were assigned to a firebase on the side of a hill. He said they were sitting ducks." She turns her face to the window. She could sleep for a long, long time.

"I've been up way too many hours," Byard says. "I bet you have too."

"A nap sounds good."

"Shall I awaken you when we arrive?"

She had not wished to be charmed. Not by this handsome and filthy wanderer who is holding her hand now, not by anyone. When she closes her eyes, her cousin's lopsided grin occupies the whole of her mind until she manages to shake his image and conjure Boyd Farber. Her first heat, who let her bury her nose in his wavy brown hair that always smelled like rain. Boyd's mother had held on to some of the country ways and made the whole family rinse their hair in rainwater every Saturday night. MaLou wasn't a real girlfriend—they were just kids together. She and Boyd. Donnie. All of them.

In the old days, women married their childhood sweethearts. And when the tragedy of war struck, they were meant to compose lyrical elegies and place tiny braided wreaths of their own hair on the graves of departed lovers. She wonders what she might do to make sure it will not ever be as if Boyd Farber never lived. Any ideas that come are no less morbid than those of the Victorians. At

PAULETTE LIVERS

twenty-three, Maria Louise Goins has gone to too many funerals, the result of belonging to a family whose web of begats rivals that of Jesus. She gives another cynical shake that becomes a shudder, and the strange young man seated next to her squeezes her hand.

"Miss? You feeling sick?" The smell of Uncle Rafe's greasy black garage, oddly comforting, mingles with the tart green apple of his breath.

Homesick, MaLou starts to say, maybe.

# FOUR

Martha Goins has come over early to help Evelyn Slidell with her bath, lifting her in and out of the tub as if she is nothing more than a dried husk of skin, which she isn't really. At the vanity table Martha does what she can with the hanks of wispy gray hair, a dab of rouge, a new shade of lipstick she picked up for Evelyn at the drugstore. She slips the beige dress over Evelyn's old bones and fastens the matching jacket at her neck. Chanel. Not that any of the hayseeds at the service are going to notice.

"Don't you look pretty, Mrs. Slidell."

"I look like Bette Davis in that dreadful movie where she tries to kill Joan Crawford," Evelyn growls when she finally works up the gumption to glance at the mirror. "I hope you told Judge Hume I don't intend to say a goddamn word at this thing."

They are skipping the parade ("I just don't think I'm up to it," Martha had said yesterday when she and Evelyn talked about the schedule), and will arrive at Legion Park in time for the speechifying. Evelyn Slidell hates Memorial Day. It reminds her every year of the burden that accompanies being what she refers to as a *goddamn pillar of society*.

"The Judge has his marching orders," Martha assures her. "Listen, we need to swing by the house and collect Rafe and Maria Louise. Remember, I mentioned our niece came down from Cincinnati last Saturday? I can't believe she's already been with me a whole week. Got here when . . . " She stops talking for a beat.

Evelyn knows: Martha's niece arrived by bus from the north the same day the funeral cortege drove into town from the south.

"I am so glad to have her. She's been a godsend." Martha's chatter will not save her. Her voice trails off again, and this time the tears, though silent, will not be refused.

Bless the woman's big, broken heart. Evelyn had found the thing that connected her to her nurse: They each had birthed a near-worthless son. Now the tie might be even stronger, given that the lives of both young men were cut short under circumstances of abominable waste. Evelyn had never liked Martha's Donald Ray; a snotty, mean boy who gave Martha and Rafe no end of torment. Still she hopes the grenade, or whatever it was that flew into his bunker as he slept that night, hit before he woke up. She cannot let herself think what pieces of him—twenty-three years old at the most, poor lout!—lay in the box they put in the ground this past week. Her Stanley hadn't even been that old. But that was a long time ago, and her grief is a tiny dead coal compared to Martha's bright, burning fury.

"Let's get on with it then," Evelyn says, not unkindly, handing Martha a linen hankie from the top drawer of the vanity. She leans on Martha all the way down the staircase and across the broad hall, and can almost feel the big woman's anxiety pulsing off her. On the front porch Martha goes ahead without asking and picks Evelyn up in her strong, fat arms and carries her out to the car.

Honestly, this life. Sometimes Evelyn really does wish she had the courage, not to mention the physical wherewithal, to just get it all over with.

Martha's husband Rafe is waiting out front when they pull up to the Goinses' house.

"Shouldn't you be dressed, honey?" Martha calls to him from the car.

Rafe struggles from the porch swing and calls something into the house through the screen door. The girl steps out. Pretty thing. Evelyn remembers her now. She was a handful, couldn't stay out of trouble at home in Cincinnati, so her mother had to send her to her Aunt Martha's every summer for some old-fashioned discipline. Everybody knows everybody's business, one of the few available means of staving off boredom in a town this size. Maria Louise was around Donald Ray's age, if Evelyn recalls correctly. Today the girl looks ready to murder anyone who tries to get friendly. Right behind her comes a red-haired young man Evelyn thinks she ought to recognize. Wait—Martha wouldn't allow Levon Ferguson onto her property, much less in her house, would she? No, this boy is handsomer than Levon. But a Ferguson, Evelyn feels sure. The two young people climb into the backseat and Rafe slams the car door on them.

"Aren't you coming?" Martha's voice threatens to go shrill.

"You all go on. I got things need doing in the shop." Judging from the blur in his eyes, Rafe has already spent time in the shop this morning. Nipping, Evelyn thinks. Rafe had once been something of a hellion; got mixed up in some kind of infraction, a ring of automobile thieves or some such, and did time at the state penitentiary. Came home a different man. Evelyn took him for a teetotaler all these years. Nobody was going to begrudge him for tippling a bit, what with his loss. But he really ought to be there at the service today. For Martha.

Nobody speaks as they make the short drive through town. Finally Evelyn turns around and stares at the young man and notices for the first time that his hair has been drawn into a small curly ponytail.

The girl gathers her wits from wherever they have scattered and says, "I'm sorry. Mrs. Slidell, this is Byard Ferguson."

He nods, his startling eyes almost hurting her, they are such a crystalline blue. Thank heavens Evelyn has worn her large sunglasses.

So he is that other Ferguson brother. Where in the world did he tumble in from? People said he ran off to Canada a few years ago. Draft dodger, some called him. Evelyn called him smart.

"Charmed," Evelyn says, and over the seat she offers him a white-gloved hand. When he does not take it, she lets it fall to her lap.

At the Legion Park, MaLou tells Martha they will meet her at the car after this thing is over, then MaLou and Byard disappear into the crowd. They have arrived in time for Father Oliver's Benediction. Martha guides Evelyn up the rickety steps to a scaffold construction that makes Evelyn think not of Memorial Day festivities but of public lynchings. People trickle in from the parade, and as Evelyn settles into her seat behind the podium, Lemuel O'Brien and his wife Lila clamber onto the stage. Behind them comes their son Harlan, newly freed from a Vietcong hellhole where they did a messy job of sawing off his gangrenous leg. He is awkward with a fancy new cane. Evelyn would lay down money that Harlan O'Brien wasn't a bit sorry when the parade in his honor was postponed last weekend. The storms saw to that, power out, trees down everywhere. Poor fellow only got a reprieve. Made to ride through town on Freeman's black nag today like some kind of clown. She hopes his parents didn't insist he attend those funeral Masses. Seven of them, spread over this whole agonizing week. Evelyn couldn't bring herself to go to all of them, not after the exhibition of grief on display at the first one. Honestly, when did it become acceptable to shriek and carry on that way? In her day, a person grieved in private and with dignity and it was understood that one was not to be disturbed in her mourning. No, after that first Mass for the Farber boy she stayed home. It strikes her now that a lot of the racket at Boyd Farber's funeral was coming out of Maria Louise Goins.

Of course Evelyn sent a large tasteful basket of lilies to each of the families and made a substantial donation to the Holy Ghost Altar Society in the dead boys' names.

From her vantage on the platform (if you could call it that—plywood and two-by-fours and a handful of nails, from what she can tell), Evelyn Slidell looks down into every single face that belongs to this town. She knows what they are all thinking: Why hasn't she died yet? They see a desiccated old woman hiding behind a pair of dark glasses large enough to cover half her face. She had selected these sunglasses this morning with particular care, the better to intimidate the populace. Heavy tortoise-shell frames and lenses so black she can stare without people being certain whether she is looking at them or someone just over their shoulder. It has become a prerogative of age, as far as she is concerned, to stare.

Benediction done, Father Oliver steps aside for Judge Hume. "Good people of Cementville," the Judge starts, and the secular portion of the invocation begins. Freeman Hume's rumbling baritone shushes the crowd as the pastor's tenor could not. The speech will go on twice too long, every word predictably patriotic pap. Praise be for whatever it is out there that passes for a divinity, Evelyn thinks, that the day is not hot. Last weekend's storms, in addition to delaying the parade, broke the strange spring drought, and now her valley is lush and green. The air is cool and she is glad for her jacket. Not that she would take it off even if she were steaming—and what?—reveal the shriveled arms that refuse to do as she bids them anymore? Dresses for old women ought not be made sleeveless.

Everybody is here at the new Legion Park, the memorial patch of crabgrass created by unanimous resolution at the emergency meeting of the City Council. After news of the war dead broke, right off they stormed Evelyn asking for money to throw the whole thing together. Levon Ferguson and his scrawny little brother Tony were hired to whack down the wild privet that had taken over the vacant lot north of the distillery. Stick a few sad-looking box elders in the ground, something cheap, fast growing. But weak wooded—oh, how people have lost the long view of things! Evelyn believes with all her heart that this place, historic district designation or no, will wither into a ghost town, and sooner rather than later.

The Altar Society women at Holy Ghost joined with the Presbyterian Women's Auxiliary (will miracles never cease!) and stitched together a bit of bunting for a grandstand, the brilliant red, white, and blue stripes highlighting the fact of this acreage being little more than a cinder dump abutting Taylortown. Evelyn still has to stop herself calling it Coloredtown. Not that she isn't glad for Civil Rights. She is, she really is.

> —*I am humbled to stand before you on this consecrated day, a day to reflect on those who serve in the defense of our land. Those of us who have heeded the call can remember that first haircut, or the mystery meat served up in the chow hall. We dwell on those memories that do not fade.*

"Stop it!" It is a girl's voice that has interrupted Freeman Hume's blather, and he and everyone in attendance turn heads together toward the peals of tinkly laughter. The giggling and commotion continue, some pushing and slapping of hands, until finally Evelyn can make out where it's coming from. A girl, a child really, with that blaze of hair, and she's half-heartedly fighting off the playful advances of a couple of skinny young bucks right there at the corner of the stage for all the town to see. *Who is that?* Evelyn mouths to Martha, which question only elicits a roll of eyes and a shake of the head.

> —*My four years at the United States Naval Academy in Annapolis, the football games, the times my buddies and I went for a dip on a dare in the icy Chesapeake Bay, and of the day I learned I would be going to Navy Flight School . . .*

It's that Ferguson girl. Stepped into the role of town strumpet as if it was written for her. What on earth made Arlene Ferguson hatch such a name for a baby girl? A name that calls up portents of bad things to come. Evelyn shivers again, watching Augrey Ferguson bat away the probing hands of three or four boys.

Evelyn gives the crowd another once-over to see how Freeman's speech is playing. Most of the blacks have left by now, knowing the

Judge is not talking to them—but not old Nimrod. Poor cuss thinks this Memorial Day ceremony includes him. Nimrod served in the Great War, one of the colored units. Came back a good many years later. Nobody was ever sure where he stayed in the interim. Evelyn Slidell can still remember Nimrod's mother, who stomped on her thick brown legs into Evelyn's mother's kitchen almost every dawning day of her life. Evelyn and Nimrod chased each other around the orchard when they were small, until they both got old enough that her parents made her stop. Maybe she will get Martha to drive her out there to see him one of these days. Better do it soon, she thinks, before both of us croak! And she chuckles so loud Martha looks at her with concern. Evelyn realizes she has laughed at an inappropriate time. Freeman Hume is rattling on about mourning and the call to liberty.

Evelyn had considered herself Nimrod's friend, and wonders whether he did, or does, the same. She cannot remember when they last spoke.

At the back of the crowd, Levon Ferguson and a couple of his hoodlum friends sneak off toward the distillery. Pretty soon they will have no doubt sawed the lock off Warehouse D, farthest from the road, and will have tapped a barrel and stolen as much bourbon as they can carry down to the river.

> —*I remember the heartbreak of leaving my wife and my young niece, Katherine—you all know Katherine Juell, her husband, her pretty little daughter, and their boy Willis Junior, whom the Lord has seen fit to return to us, praise be. Ah, I remember the joy of homecoming after a long deployment. And I remember the men lost.*

And blah-de-blah-blah, Freeman, you pompous ass. Evelyn Slidell observes the proceedings from the edge of the stage. The Judge checks her immobile expression now and again to see if his words are meeting with her approval. Evelyn dabs at her face with the hanky she keeps in her pocketbook. *You remember exactly nothing!* she wishes she could scream—how her throat burns with indignation. Hume sat out the First World War in law school, running panty raids on Radcliff girls.

Also on stage are the parents of the other boys. Rafe's seat on the other side of Martha is empty. The Kidwells and Farbers and Mitchells are there. The widow Welch. And Happy Spalding, whose wife ran off, leaving him with small children and a restaurant to run. Even the Gordons are there, though they moved away recently, him lured by one of the Tennessee distillers, Jack Daniels, she thinks it was. Evelyn's late husband Lewis had groomed Charles Gordon Senior for a good position at his own distillery here in town. Evelyn can't say why, but she is glad Charles Junior's body will rest here rather than in Tennessee, so far from home.

> —*The men we buried this past week took no part in the burning of draft cards. They did not flee the borders of this great country to avoid serving. They did not hold with celebrities protesting injustices done to the enemy. They saw their duty to God and country.*

Evelyn stops listening. There's poor, obese Arlene Ferguson, mother to Levon and that bunch. Arlene and her sister Bett prop each other up like two Pisas slammed together at the top. Maria Louise Goins has followed Byard Ferguson to stand with them. Evelyn glances at Martha to see if she also notices that MaLou's hand is twined in the hand of the pony-tailed young man. Wouldn't it be nice if the girl stayed with Martha and Rafe for a while? Maybe she can fill Donnie's empty room. Find work here.

They are a handsome couple, Evelyn thinks, and there is a stirring in her, of something perhaps tired, but not moribund, as she watches the way MaLou Goins looks at Byard Ferguson.

> —*As we mourn our war dead, this sadness is eclipsed by the joy of welcoming back into the fold one of our own who has suffered the loss, not of life but of limb. We stop to give*

*thanks to our Maker, not only for the glory and luck of being
born Americans, but to stand before these mothers and
fathers who have contributed to something they considered
priceless—the defense of our country.*

The Judge gestures broadly behind him toward Lemuel and Lila
O'Brien and tries to catch Harlan's eye. Weak applause peters out.
Nobody is sure whether clapping over the dead, not to mention Har-
lan O'Brien's artificial leg, is appropriate.

Evelyn spots the Asian woman Jimmy Smith brought home
with him. For three years now, Cementville has had its very own war
bride. Giang Smith is staring into the Judge's face. What she is thinking is anybody's guess. She might swallow everything he's saying.
She might see a fool.

*—Lieutenant O'Brien comes home to us today as a man
who can be counted on to be true to his word. He has proven
himself so in the two years he spent in a Communist prison.
America deserves men and women of honor and character,
who do not have to make excuses for their past or current
actions, who have earned the name "hero."*

He sits like a starved saint at the far end of the stage. That
O'Brien boy, or man, really—what—twenty-nine, thirty now. Confetti from the parade still litters the shoulders of his uniform like
colored flakes of snow. Lemuel and Lila O'Brien look like they don't
know whether to weep with joy or run for their lives. They are eyeing
their son as if they are not convinced he isn't an imposter.

*—We must have the courage to live as a nation under God,
as our founders did when they forged our country nearly two
centuries ago. And so let resound the rallying cry: Long live
God's great democracy, the United States of America!*

THE CROWD PARTS DOWN THE middle, Red Sea–style, to let pass the families of the fallen, trying but unable to keep their heads down, compelled to stare into the wretched faces as if hoping for inoculation against sorrow. Evelyn will be the last to leave the stage, and while she waits her eyes trace the horizon, the cleft where her ancestors, and the forebears of most of the people here at this scroungy park, scrambled across the Appalachians and into this valley. The history of this place, and the name into which she married, is like the weight of a great ugly bauble hung about her neck.

He was a Baltimore man, that first Slidell, and the people milling about below Evelyn now are the direct descendants of the men and women William Slidell dragged here with him, a retinue of masons, craftsmen, and servants. (Not slaves, Evelyn's late husband would have noted, but freedmen of color, decorated with new liberty on the eve of the journey, a source or a product of the pomposity against which William Slidell is said to have struggled.) Also a wife, three daughters, and a son, and two thousand in silver. The state's first governor had signed over to William Slidell the better part of this stretch of river basin, one of many deep cradles hanging in the ragged breaches of the Mississippian seabed. This entourage formed the front flank of the Catholic exodus out of Maryland, descendants of Jacobites who had fled England. The land was beautiful, if a bit hillier than the newcomers might have wished. Dense with woods and full of game. Rocky too, being a quilt of deposits from the ages, riddled with shale and limestone, petrified mussels, corals, and trilobites, the fossilized remains of sea creatures. Every square foot of alluvial bottomland they freed of stone yielded not just good farmland but the building blocks for walls to separate cows from crops, kitchen garden from a sheep or goat's unceasing appetite. Those walls still stand, most of them, lining the roads that have not changed routes in two centuries.

"Won't you let me buy you all lunch?" Evelyn says as the four of them make their slow way through the crowd to Martha Goins's car. Martha nods, wiping her nose. Maria Louise and her companion are silent. "Say, did you see that child down front flirting with those boys? If I were her mother—" Evelyn stops short, remembering that Byard is a child of that same mother. No doubt the others in the car are now busily imagining how someone of her standing and age and wisdom would handle such carnality in her own child. None of them offers a rejoinder. Evelyn swivels around toward the two in the backseat, ready to offer an apology. She is startled to find Byard Ferguson glaring at her.

"Happy's or Hungarian Gardens?" Martha says. Evelyn has not yet heard an opinion on this new place. That Cementville would have a Hungarian restaurant of all things—this world has not ceased to surprise her. Her vote is for the devil she knows.

MaLou blurts suddenly from the backseat, "I have to say I think it's terrible how there was not a single mention of Daniel."

"Daniel?" Martha says sweetly.

"Byard's brother Daniel died last week in Vietnam too. He was on night patrol in a whole other part of that shitty place. Where do they get off not even reading his name in the roll call? How do you think Arlene felt, came out today expecting the support of her community, and all the other parents there on the stage—sorry, Aunt Martha—and Arlene has nobody but her sister there by her side? The fucking government drafted him—didn't even give him a choice! God, how I hate this place!"

Martha keeps her eyes on the road. The girl cannot stop herself.

"They haven't even buried him yet," she wails. "Duvall said his funeral home was all booked up."

The boy folds the girl into his arms and she is sobbing into his clean white shirt—or Rafe's shirt, more likely, Evelyn thinks; it swallows this lanky young man.

"Shush now. We'll bury him this week," the Ferguson boy says. "Mr. Duvall is doing everything he can. It'll be all right."

Evelyn does not know MaLou well enough to know if she is always this dramatic, but if what the girl says is true, she makes a solid point. Evelyn will have to get Martha to dig out last week's

*Picayune* to see if there is mention of a dead Ferguson. She thought she had clipped everything related to the war. Her own personal scrapbook of atrocities.

The restaurant parking lot at Happy's is packed. The parade and memorial service seem to have created something of a weirdly festive atmosphere in town.

"You know, Byard and I might go on," MaLou says, tipping her head toward Pekkar's Alley down the street. Evelyn cranes her neck and sees some of the local youth already malingering around the door of the vile joint. Levon Ferguson leans against the wall with a plastic cup in one hand, cigarette in the other. Evelyn is glad Lewis is not alive to see this place. Yes, he made whiskey for a living, a very handsome living, but to his death her husband considered bourbon the drink of gentlemen, not something to be consumed till a person groveled in the road, vomiting and retching and behaving in ways to which no civilized human being should ever stoop.

But MaLou is not her niece. Evelyn keeps her lip buttoned.

"I think I'm out of the notion too, Mrs. Slidell," Martha says. She fishes a Hershey bar out of the glove compartment for Evelyn, but Evelyn shakes her head. Martha opens it anyway, breaks off several squares, and lays it on the car seat between them.

What Evelyn had wanted was to walk into that restaurant and let people see her sitting rod straight, enjoying herself over a hearty lunch with the handsome young couple and the well-liked Martha Goins. She would have taken off her sunglasses and smiled at everyone so they could see that she is very much alive, and she is a person who still knows what it means to be a goddamn pillar of the community. And just as quickly there is a little caving in, right there behind her breastbone, with the surprising knowledge: She does not want to be forgotten. Not before she is dead anyway.

"Let's drive out a ways," Evelyn says to Martha after they drop MaLou and Byard at Pekkar's Alley. Evelyn doesn't blame the kids for craving a drink, after that speech of Freeman's. Her own mind wanders to the crystal decanter on the sideboard at home.

"I can't think of a thing I'd rather do," Martha says, and Evelyn believes she means it. She is surprised almost every day that Martha Goins, whose heart is big and innocent as a child's, is actually fond of her. Evelyn can feel it in her nurse's voice when she blusters in through the front door and sings her arrival up the stairwell, or when she makes a simple lunch for them to share on the screened porch. It is an undeserved grace that has been conferred upon her, that Martha left her job as school nurse and wanted to come take care of an old woman for several hours a day.

"Where shall we go?" Martha says. Her voice is sunny enough to almost hide the tremor in it. Evelyn sees that she is silently crying. She doesn't know whether to offer her nurse another hanky or let the woman grieve in peace. A tear rolls down Martha's quivering chin and onto her shelf-like breast.

"I haven't been out Crooked Creek since I don't know when," says Evelyn.

They pass through the center of the distillery's sprawling campus. Its big windowless warehouses flattened against the sky always remind Evelyn of blank-faced prison barracks. Stanley's father enjoyed parading out-of-town visitors through the grounds. He started what he called the Tourmobile, charged them a half-dollar apiece to be driven around town in a fancy wagon with a tasseled awning, pulled behind a tractor piloted by some high school boy or other. She can still hear the slow, comforting murmur of Lewis's voice (God help her, how it would melt her from the inside!) welcoming the tourists as he dipped a cup into the tank of sour mash and sniffed its earthy aroma as if it were nectar of the gods. "Smells like money!" Lewis would say, and it always got a laugh out of the group. The tour ended at the sampling room, where the ladies would roll their eyes at their husbands and warn them not to overdo.

In a blink Martha's car is well up Crooked Creek Road and entering Taylortown. Local lore had it that, after a first rough winter, William Slidell's ragtag band of pioneers began to prosper, and Slidell saw his way to apportioning to the people he referred to in his journals as *his* Negroes their own corner of land behind his bur-geoning distillery at the south end of the new settlement. The road narrows here, crowded on both sides with honey locust and arrow-wood scrub and the stinking ailanthus trees that threaten to colonize the whole valley. Their weedy limbs are strewn about the road, casu-alties of the recent storms.

Evelyn glances up where Adelaide Ricketts's place still haunts the ridge. What was it Faulkner said? The past is never dead. It isn't even past—something to that effect.

Adelaide. Now *there* was old. The woods around the two-room shack have grown even thicker, if that is possible, and Evelyn won-ders if someday they won't find Adelaide cold and dead in there, strangled in vines, her bony spine bent over some cauldron of herbs. Adelaide averred that her people were here before any of the rest. Claimed to be Cherokee, although everybody who cared about tracing such things knew she was some percentage blend of Negro and plain old English. When people called Adelaide a witch, she never failed to put them right. "Root doctor," she would lisp with a gummy smile. Then she'd hold out a hand that resembled more a bundle of twigs and wait for the few coins she required to tell a fortune. Evelyn herself had spent time and money, years back, at Adelaide Ricketts's shack.

They pass the stooped figure of Jesse Greathouse trundling down the road. Martha slows the car to let a mangy hound struggle out of the middle of the road and creep into the ditch. Is everybody in Taylortown ancient now? Evelyn wonders. But there is Bett Fergu-son, unfazed by being one of several whites living in what most still think of as the Negro section. Bett is sitting out on her front porch with that passel of children, one crying on the steps, another in a tree, two or three more running around the yard in dirty drawers. She and her sister Arlene must be well into their late forties by now, which to Evelyn is not old anymore. Bett is still wearing her nice dress from the parade and service, but she has kicked off her shoes and is rubbing one foot, her big white thigh gleaming. It's a good thing Civil Rights came along and they could stop calling this place Coloredtown. Bett's brood is probably the youngest lot here, as so many of the younger blacks have shoved off to parts north where jobs might wait for them in Chicago and Detroit.

Bett waves as they pass by. At Martha, Evelyn is sure.

"Stop the car," Evelyn says suddenly, and Martha pulls over so close to the brushy side of the road that limbs scratch against the window glass. She follows Evelyn's gaze to the porch of Nimrod's house, where he sits dozing in the shadows, his downy head resting on his chest. He probably got a ride home with Bett.

"Did you want to pay him a visit?"

"Oh, no! No," Evelyn says. Although wasn't that the reason she wanted to drive out Crooked Creek to begin with? Surely not, because now, seeing the old man—who is a stranger to her, really—Evelyn cannot imagine she actually believed they would sit together and have a nice long chat, that he would take her hand and pat it and they would spend the afternoon exchanging remember-whens. The top of his silver head almost glows in the shade of the porch.

"I'm sorry, Martha," Evelyn says, "I thought for a minute I left something back there on the stage, but I must have been mistaken." She stares straight ahead as Martha pulls slowly into the road. She does not let herself turn to look at him, or wait for him to raise his head.

AT HOME, SHE LETS MARTHA help her out of her things. She watches the woman hang her dress in a zipper bag. Evelyn has taken to keeping everything zipped—moths were so thick last summer, they would have eaten her out of house and home if she weren't vigilant. The day has taken it out of her, and Evelyn asks Martha to bring lunch up, rather than eating in the dining room. While the nurse is downstairs, she pulls a box out of the bureau and opens it onto her bed. It is stuffed to bulging with crumbling papers and photographs she hauled down from the attic last fall when she still had her strength. There are things she needs to see today.

At the top is the Slidell family Bible, the same allegedly carried from the shores of England across the ocean by the first to come to Lord Baltimore's wild Maryland shore in 1690. Who is there now to question the mythology surrounding those early ancestors? Her boy Stanley was the last of them, and he cared nothing for dusty history. Look who he married, running off to Gatlinburg with Johnny Ferguson's girl, Loretta.

Oh, how Evelyn had raged when she learned what Stanley had done! It physically hurt her, him throwing everything away. If there was anything to the transmigration of souls, the comings and goings of the dead and the reborn, her boy came awfully close to running into the soul of his homely infant daughter, skinny squalling thing of two or three weeks when Stanley fell into his permanent sleep in the backseat of Buck Farber's coupe. That Wanda. It was as if the girl was born to intentionally irk Evelyn. Her granddaughter is a spinster, rocking her way to early decrepitude there on Johnny Ferguson's scrap of land.

Evelyn rubs circles around the spot on her breastbone where her breath is always catching. She flips through the front pages of the Bible where three hundred years of names are recorded in faded ink. She pictures the joyous occasions, all the different hands that scrawled across the page the names of newborns. Some occasions were not joyous—for too many, the days between birth and death can be tallied on one hand.

The name right above Stanley's at the bottom is her own little Eugenia. The baby was so perfect, on the outside. The doctor said he did not know how Evelyn herself had lived through the horrific birth, and Evelyn said, when Lewis was out of the room, that she wished she had not.

The old names were beautiful though. Her favorite is Jacoba Clementina, first-born daughter here in the New World, named for the deposed James II. The story goes that Arnold, that original Slidell to make the passage, was such an ardent Jacobite he tried to incorporate some variant of the king's name into the names of all his children.

One of the Slidell women somewhere along the way had tried to write it all down, how Arnold Slidell had fled with other supporters of the Catholic Stuarts and had gained the patronage of the High Sheriff in Maryland, Lord Henry Darnall. Arnold was probably responsible for that entrepreneurial spirit that kept the Slidells on top of the heap down through the generations. Evelyn must locate the journals where all that was recorded. She hasn't seen those volumes in a long time, but they must be somewhere in the attic. So much junk—clothes and jewelry and more moldy books and papers. Mice and snakes too, harmless black snakes who've found shelter and a steady supply of food. Evelyn no longer minds knowing they are up there.

Something slips from the pages of the crumbling Bible, and when Martha comes into the room carrying the lunch tray, Evelyn is in bed reading the original yellowed front page of *The Slidellville Picayune*, which had first come off the press in April of 1861, in time to announce the secession from the Union of neighboring Virginia.

"Will you look at that!" Martha says. "Where in the world did you come across that old thing?" She pulls down the folding legs on the bed tray and sets it across Evelyn's lap.

"This family throws away nothing." Evelyn hands Martha the fragile clipping, already cracking where it has been creased for a century.

"What I always wondered was why they'd name a newspaper something so silly."

"Oh, I think they had in mind the nickel price. They certainly weren't thinking the news they published dealt in the trivial," Evelyn says, buttering the cornbread Martha made yesterday. She feels bad that Martha has taken just one day off since she received news of her Donald's death. Evelyn told her to take as much time as she needed, that there were other women around town who would fill in for her. But Martha insisted that sitting at home alone was the last thing she wanted.

"If there's nothing else, Mrs. Slidell, I'm going to go on home and see about Rafe."

Evelyn waves her off, but at the bedroom door Martha stops.

"I know it's going to take time, but other than the funeral I don't think Rafe has left the house in six days." She looks at the floor. "You've walked this walk, Evelyn. Is there any advice you can think of? Anything I can say to Rafe? Or do for him?"

The look on Martha Goins's face is of such wretchedness, Evelyn's mind goes blank for a moment. What is it Martha is asking of her? Surely she does not expect Evelyn to say: *You will be all right. Your husband will become again the contented man you knew. You will return to enjoying his company across the supper table and card games with your friends.* Evelyn Slidell is not given to platitudes, knowing from experience that most of them are lies other people will tell you for their own comfort. She may be the town's ogress, but she is not a liar.

The cornbread in her mouth is dry as dirt, and she gulps at her tea to get it down. "Mr. Slidell was long in the ground before our Stanley passed."

"Oh, I'm sorry. I forgot. You went through that all alone. I am so sorry."

Evelyn is about to let her leave, then, "No, no, Martha, it's me who is sorry. I have not said all week how sorry I am about Donnie Ray."

"Yes, you did—"

But she stops her, stops this large-hearted woman's protestations, and Evelyn Slidell gives to Martha Goins the lies she needs.


AFTER THE DOOR IN THE hall downstairs clicks shut, Evelyn sets the dinner tray aside and returns to her box. She riffles through several diaries and disintegrating albums of snapshots until she stops at a large, blurry photograph. It is a spring day, the weather not unlike what swept through the valley last weekend. A blustery wind plasters the women's long dark dresses to their legs. The sky behind the buildings looks ominous. There she is, Evelyn herself, at five or six years old, near the front, partly obscured by her father. She is wearing a white pinafore, and Lewis, holding onto her hand, is beside her in a dark suit with short pants. They glare out at the camera together, Lewis and Evelyn versus the world. The men all stand with their hands clasped behind their backs or arms folded, all their faces pointing in one direction. It is the beginning of a new era for the town. Evelyn's father, the Vice President of the new operation, has stepped aside to make way for Melburn Slidell, Lewis's father, who is cutting the ribbon on the gates of his spanking-new cement plant. For the next century the main ingredient for modern building would be churned and ground and belched and breathed into the very lungs, powdering the pores, clothing, food, and even the roots of people's hair. To celebrate the town entering the industrial age, they changed the name to Cementville in an extravagant ceremony meant to sanctify it with prosperity. It is this that the photograph documents. All the men not engaged in farming or whiskey-making found jobs with Slidell Cement.

But this photograph is not what Evelyn is looking for. More digging, and there it is at the bottom of the box, something that had flitted through her mind as she seethed on Freeman Hume's rickety stage this afternoon. A yellowed tract from Twain—a piece he composed in the midst of the Philippine War—torn from a magazine. Was it Lewis who had found its bitter irony so appealing, and intended to hang onto the clipping, maybe to pass it down one day to a son or daughter? Stanley had been spared ever knowing conflict. Born after the First World War, dead before the Second. How Lewis had loved Mark Twain. Still, he had left her to go off to the Great War. Such things he saw over there. Such things he brought home with him.

Maybe some long-lost version of Evelyn herself had clipped the article from *Harper's*. She runs the tips of her fingers over the slick page, feeling the impression of the type. Evelyn can imagine her own younger simulacrum, thin and already embittered, cheated, though she was not quite sure how, stealing into the library and ripping out the page and folding it to fit in the bodice of her dress, keeping it there like some kind of talisman against war ever blighting their home again. She reads the whole story now, her dry lips whispering each word. In it, a preacher delivers a fiery exhortation to the God of war to deliver an obviously deserved victory. Then a hoary stranger ascends to the pulpit and cautions the congregation to be prepared to accept the consequences of what they pray for. He holds forth to their stunned ears what he says are words given him by God. It is this portion of the story that Evelyn needs.

> *O Lord our Father, our young patriots, idols of our hearts, go*
> *forth to battle—be Thou near them! With them—in spirit—*
> *we also go forth from the sweet peace of our beloved firesides*
> *to smite the foe. O Lord our God, help us to tear their soldiers*
> *to bloody shreds with our shells; help us to cover their smiling*
> *fields with the pale forms of their patriot dead; help us to*
> *drown the thunder of the guns with the shrieks of their*
> *wounded, writhing in pain; help us to lay waste their humble*
> *homes with a hurricane of fire; help us to wring the hearts*
> *of their unoffending widows with unavailing grief; help us*
> *to turn them out roofless with their little children to wander*
> *unfriended the wastes of their desolated land in rags and*
> *hunger and thirst, sports of the sun flames of summer and*
> *the icy winds of winter, broken in spirit, worn with travail,*
> *imploring Thee for the refuge of the grave and denied it—for*
> *our sakes who adore Thee, Lord, blast their hopes, blight*
> *their lives, protract their bitter pilgrimage, make heavy their*
> *steps, water their way with their tears, stain the white snow*
> *with the blood of their wounded feet! We ask it, in the spirit*
> *of love, of Him Who is the Source of Love, and Who is the*
> *ever-faithful refuge and friend of all that are sore beset and*
> *seek His aid with humble and contrite hearts. Amen.*

With scissors from her sewing basket, Evelyn clips out the tract, refolds the paper, soft as silk, along its creases. She fits it into an envelope that she will slip into the mail slot of his front door tonight while the Judge and his wife are gone to dinner at the country club.

"We always fight ourselves, Freeman," she says to the empty room, the empty house. Why hadn't she been able to say that to him as he handed her down from the platform today, instead of giving him a vacant nod? Evelyn imagines her friend's confused face tomorrow, opening the morning mail. Unable to help herself, she feels her mouth draw up in the rictus of a wide grin.

# FIVE

When Lieutenant Harlan O'Brien comes home from two years in a bamboo prison, dead eyes sparking an ice fire, his stiff shoulders square and strong—they have their man. And they decorate their manikin, a purple medal directly above the heart. They fling flakes of colored paper as he straddles the mayor's black-as-midnight mare in full dress blues, Irish eyes unsmiling at his hero's welcome.

If the young lieutenant cannot imagine the life stretching in front of him, it may be that the howling jungle he recently left has so cleanly swept away his past. The town's desperate insistence on the life they need him to have holds him upright in Judge Hume's good leather saddle, squeaking now beneath his meatless buttocks.

They take down their big toy soldier and fold him into a metal chair in the church cafeteria, his medals clinking rin-tin-tinny. They shove him up to the table groaning with German potato salad steaming with vinegar and pink-singed bacon; kale greens in brackish pot likker; white navy beans glistening with bloated chunks of fatback; banana croquettes and banana cream pie and banana pudding built of layers of yellow puffy cream and wafers and more wafers; blackberry cobbler, crust bruised blue; tender catfish flayed and fried; sliced tomatoes and mounds of legs and thighs and necks and breasts and backs and hearts crisped brown and crunchy the way he remembers.

*All you want! All you can eat!* they sing. All he wants, shoveling it in right then, is his clay bowl of gray rice speckled with twitching legs of grasshoppers, headless, wingless bodies lolling, lidless eyes clinging to the sides of the bowl and mingling with the browner grains of rice. (*Brown is better for you,* his mother had always stressed, *being whole food straight from the hand of God.*) He misses that crunch between his molars, now unfortunately loose.

He rides home with distended belly in the backseat of his mother's Pontiac, to the future they have imagined for him, to the house of his father. Harlan O'Brien stretches out that night beneath the rigid tin roof, rain beating a Taps tattoo. He stares, sleep-starved, at the ceiling memorized in boyhood, blood beads leaking from under his thorn crown.

* * *

AT THREE, THE PAIN AT the small of her back snakes up to the base of her skull. Giang Smith rolls onto her left side, but it won't do. Her husband, a warm rock in the middle of the bed, produces sonorous booms, letting go the tissues in the back of his throat, his arms and legs thrown wide on her side and his. Jimmy Smith has slept harder and longer lately since the Phenobarbital. Some nights Giang sleeps through the racket coming from her husband's mouth. Others, she lays staring at the brown stains in the ceiling, raggedy islands in a dirty sea.

She tries to put her finger on when the aches started. The persistent twinge between her shoulder blades came from swinging the sickle in her father's lowland rice fields. She remembers a burn lower, in her hips, after she and her sister went to work in the city, from legs spread too wide, too long.

These new aches have their own source.

Giang rises from the bed and downstairs makes strong tea, folds herself into her husband's big chair by the wood stove. She fishes a diary from under a pile of *Field & Streams*. She doesn't worry about her husband reading her private words.

*Looks like a chicken danced over the page*, Jimmy always says of the wild characters and diacritical marks swimming across the leaves of her cloth-covered book.

*Zzhhaaang*, he drawls at night, drawing it out to make her laugh when he's feeling good, the Phenobarbital coursing through his blood. An office boy for a general, Jimmy was lucky to not see real combat, unlucky to be driving an explosives-rigged jeep, a bomb meant for his boss. *Read me some poems*, he'll say. Several times a day, Giang rubs sweet oils into the skin where tiny scraps of metal still freckle his ribcage and back; she is grateful for the training Saigon gave her. She and the drugs and the occasional poem give him some relief. It's the least she can do, considering what he did for her.

She lights a candle each morning at the little Buddha altar she has made here in this strange country. And each morning she calls to memory the day Jimmy Smith came for her, how he appeared at the brothel door with a fistful of money, intent on buying her way out of there. She lays flowers before the statue of Quan Âm, the bodhisattva of compassion, and marvels at how her simple obligation has become comfortable habit, how the duty and debt to one's savior, fed and watered, ripens to something like love.

He came home from work on the second shift at the cement plant last night and woke her. "It's the summer solstice, baby, get up!" he said, and they had stayed awake until one in the morning trying to make eggs balance on end, laughing like children at the kitchen table. "Why won't it work?" Jimmy guffawed as one rolled to the floor. "There goes breakfast!" She does so love him at times like this. Giang tells him about *Ha Chí*, the name for summer's apex; today, June 21, is the middle of summer in Vietnam, the time to make offerings to the god of death so that loved ones will be safe from malaria-bearing mosquitoes. *Tet Duon Ngo* is the time for "Killing the Inner Insect Festival," she tells him, and this makes him burst with laughter all over again. She does love him. She does.

Jimmy has tried to correct the *Geee-ang* his bumpkin friends call her. He brags that Giang's mother was *boi tai*, a high servant in a French household, fluent in both Vietnamese and French, governess to the sons of a Parisian diplomat. Years later she would teach her twin daughters to form the words for both languages.

Restless day and night, Giang has taken to walking along the river at all hours. She returns to find her untouched tea cold and throws it down the sink. Hours still before she will pad upstairs to draw Jimmy's bath. From the dark of the kitchen window she watches the eastern sky, its tinge of blood seeping from the bottom edge. A cloud is on fire.

Giang bends over the kitchen sink and, stretching an arm overhead, lets the muscles pull sharp at the waist. She breathes into the pain at the base of her spine, imagines herself an arabesque, pliant and muscular, a tight coil ready to spring. She reaches her hand into the fruit bowl and draws forth a plum, rubs a thumb over the skin's powdery bruise.

The floorboards creak overhead and Giang knows her husband will stumble down the hall soon. She should go and draw his bath. She keeps her eyes closed for a minute more, a finger holding the page where yesterday she copied a few lines. Beneath the *nôm*, the traditional Vietnamese characters of that watery land, an ancient poem flows. This one tells of the river and its inhabitants, and of lost love: *Stepping into the field, sadness fills my deep heart. / Bundling rice sheaves, tears dart in two streaks. / Who made the ferry's leaving? / Who made this shallow creek that parts both sides?*

Giang tries to write a poem per day, from memory.

There are poems that cause a startle—in them she sees a double of herself, whether she reads them once or a hundred times. The first time it happened she was thirteen, the last year her mother was alive, the year before their village was relocated. The words drifting around her, she was both the fish and the river. Like the promise of her given name, the river constantly keened toward the sea, struggling against the crags and banks and the men who tried to hold it back for their own purposes.

Her father keened and crashed and grieved like a crazy person for his dead wife. Came the day he placed his twin girls, Giang and Suong, on a riverboat. He told them to wait, he would return with tea and food. But he did not come back. The riverboat carried them away, down to the city, to the five black years.

When she thinks of the brothel, she sees a pair of matching strung playthings in the vague shapes of herself and her sister. Tangled puppets, dancing to the rigged fate of a fickle and careless god, collapsing into each other's arms, sleeping through whole days.

She wonders whether her husband is right. Would she be less sad if she let the poems go? Simply toss all three of the little cloth-bound books—one for each year she has been in this place—into the Papa Bear wood stove? They could curl up the chimney with the smoke of the rotted crabapple Jimmy split and stacked into a neat rick last August.

She should listen to him. He had saved her, after all.

*I WANT TO DANCE WITH my wife,* Jimmy says, breaking the spell. He has been teaching Giang the contra dances in anticipation of the big annual barn dance. He won't hear her protests that it's too early for dancing. He lets the diamond needle down on the record player and he spins toward her across the wooden floor of the living room.

Twirling in her husband's arms, Giang tries to dislodge from her mind the specter of Suong floating away from her. Watching her sister plunge into the filthy river below their Saigon bedroom that night, Giang had dug her nails into the windowsill.

She thought she had swallowed for good that old companion, despair. But closing her eyes and resting her chin on Jimmy's shoulder now, her twin is forever falling from the window, her arms cartwheeling, her black eyes sparkling in the muddy current.

Suong had yelled to Giang three times, *Jump!* before the river carried her away.

Jimmy and Giang Smith make a lovely pair, the townspeople will say, the china doll in the arms of a burly farm boy, wheeling around the room to the Spanish Waltz.

\* \* \*

"HARLEY, GET UP! GET UP, Mr. Harlan Wilder O'Brien! There's the fences want mending, and holes in the roof that want stoppering from the rain, and there's the barn dance, Harley, the barn dance coming soon, where Analisa Frasier wants dancing, dancing by the light of the moooon."

Lieutenant Harlan O'Brien lying board straight on the wood floor, under a storm-strewn sky, under his father's roof, under his mother's wedding quilt, tries to recall: Is he a good son? The son who mends fence and roof and who mows and gathers hay into great round bales? The woman singing at him up the stairwell, a crazed meadowlark, seems to think so.

His mother's laugh sprinkles the air with birdsong and confectioners' sugar. She tousles the head of her boy on whom the sun has cast the brilliant light of bravery—or would as soon as the sun cleaves the black-clouded sky. She shoves at her sweet stranger the plate of turnovers she has made for him.

She is anxious to show him off again.

After breakfast, he works alongside his silent sentinel of a father, the older man's stride certain, the younger's half-pained, stretching new wire across the breaches where bawling animals have scratched their massive sides, mashing down the fence. The two men work through a persistent drizzle until finally a wan sun rolls up the storm sky like a window blind. The two do not speak, but walk toward the house and the smell of lunch rolls. The roof will not dry enough to mend this day.

The noon meal would be a silent affair but for the meadowlark voice of his mother. "Analisa, Analisa," she keeps saying, "you remember Analisa, Molly and Leonard's girl a few years behind you in school? She'll be calling you directly. Everybody's saying she has her hopes pinned on you." The annual barn dance, to which the girls invite the boys, is this weekend, a vaguely pagan festival ushering in the summer.

The men stare into their Dutch blue dinner plates, gradually revealing the windmill design in the center by scooping up the navy beans with hunks of lunch rolls, light and flaky, washing it all down with buttermilk.

# SIX

When the Duvall Funeral Home got a window in its schedule, Malcolm Duvall drove his hearse to the county morgue to pick up the body of Daniel Ferguson. Arlene Ferguson was still a mess, and it seemed urgent to her that someone from the family accompany the boy, whose embalmed body had been kept iced, so to speak, in the hospital basement for ten days. It fell to Byard to ride along with Mac Duvall. Levon was unreachable, and who else was there? Not their no-account grandfather. Nobody could remember when Angus Ferguson had last drawn a sober breath.

"I feel bad this took so long for us to get to, Byard. You understand, with the sheer number of funerals here lately, something had to be put on hold." The mortician kept his eyes on the road as he spoke. He was a rather wooden man, something Byard reckoned was the result of all his years managing other people's grief. "And Reverend Aiken agreed to the delay. I had no idea he hadn't conferred with your mother."

Aiken was the traveling Presbyterian minister who passed through town once a month or so and preached to the few of his flock that called the predominantly Catholic Cementville home. Byard was not about to give Duvall the satisfaction of an answer, even though he did understand perfectly—he understood that his clan, his kind, would always be the ones at the bottom of any list. He also understood that the undertaker was trying to apologize. Leaving the hospital, the long black car rolled almost soundlessly through town, cut down the alley, and pulled in behind the funeral home.

Roddy Duvall came out to help his father unload the gurney from the back of the hearse. Byard remembered him as a sweet-natured kid who was chummy with Daniel. Roddy and Daniel had been in special ed together at the county high school. Roddy appeared to recognize Byard too, and he dipped his head in a respectful nod and mumbled something Byard couldn't catch. Evidently Roddy's draft deferment for low IQ, unlike Daniel's, had gone through without a hitch. The mortician and his son rolled the gurney across the loading pad, and Byard followed them through the funeral home's back door.

"We'll take good care of him," Mac Duvall said. He stuck a hand out to Byard. "You can bring your mama over about four this afternoon. We'll have time for a private family viewing before the wake starts at seven this evening."

As if anybody other than family is going to care about coming to see Daniel off, Byard thought, knowing he oughtn't. The undertaker was trying to be kind, and little kindnesses warranted acknowledgment. Byard was pretty sure the price Malcolm Duvall quoted them for the entire funeral service and burial arrangement was half the usual cost.

"We appreciate it," Byard said. "Everything." He shook Duvall's hand and reached for Roddy's, and the boy seemed surprised. "Daniel always liked you, Roddy."

"Daniel was my friend," Roddy slurred. He was more profoundly retarded than Byard had known, and Byard was ashamed for his close-heartedness of a moment ago.

He headed out on foot toward Rafe and Martha Goins's house. He and MaLou had moved into the empty bedroom where Donald

Raphael Goins III had slept for all of his twenty-four years, until he left for training at Fort Hood, Texas. Martha claimed that MaLou and Byard staying with them would help her and Rafe move on, that the house felt too empty. Rafe had kept silent on the matter, as seemed to be his way about anything having to do with his son's death. Byard intended it to be a temporary arrangement. He and MaLou would get a place together, something cheap, save enough money to get out of here. He was prepared to go back to Canada, and MaLou, amazingly, seemed ready to follow him.

It was still a mystery to Byard that MaLou had wanted to stay here at all. That she made him stand there in her Aunt Martha's kitchen while she called the newspaper in Cincinnati and informed them she wasn't coming back to work. That she rode with him over to Travelers Grove and, in the living room of the Justice of the Peace, in the dress she'd worn to her cousin Donnie's funeral, said she would have and hold him—*him*, Byard—all the days of her life, while Martha and Rafe stood witness.

What had gotten into the girl? Into him, for that matter? He had come back to Cementville against all common sense. Selective Service would catch up with him sooner or later. He was as good as a criminal already. But he couldn't have stayed away, not when his mother needed him. Not when his little sister Augrey was becoming more of a hellion—okay, a tramp—and more unreachable. Bile rose in his throat, thinking about it.

God he was thirsty.

He reversed course and headed upriver toward Pekkar's Alley, knowing it was a bad idea. He'd managed to avoid the place since he and MaLou had gone together to raise a glass with most of the town after the Memorial Day parade and the judge's bizarre speech. They'd both needed a drink then. But the place gave MaLou the heebie jeebies—or rather, Levon's presence there gave her the heebie jeebies—and they hadn't stayed long.

Byard stepped into the bar's dim interior, his eyes watering a moment against the stench of soured grease. He slid into an empty booth. He didn't recognize the girl who took his order. Five years was all it took to lose track of a place. Was she Happy Spalding's girl? She had that round face, the big surprised eyes.

"What you got on draft?" Byard asked.

She told him. "You want anything to eat with that or you doing liquid lunch today?"

Byard looked at the wall clock and saw that it was already twelve thirty. "Pekkar Burgers still as bad as I remember them?"

"If you order extra onions, we'll throw in the heartburn for free." She said it with a flat voice, as if she'd been trained to make banter with the customers and had used the line a hundred times too many.

"Aren't you one of the Spalding girls?" Byard said. She moved her head slightly in what passed for affirmation. "Why did Hap let you come over here and work for Roger Pekkar? Seems Happy's joint is pretty hopping these days."

"Wasn't a matter of *letting* me," the girl said. "I do what I want."

"Hey, don't get all het up. I'm all for women's lib." Byard grinned, but it did little to warm her up. "I'll have the burger, hold the onions. Fries. Forget the beer. I'll take a shake. Chocolate." He was already thinking of kissing MaLou, and he didn't want her tasting onions or beer on his breath.

"One Pekkar Platter Deluxe and a shake," she said and vanished into the kitchen.

Ever since they'd come into Pekkar's last weekend, when MaLou had seen Levon drunk—and a good portion of the other men in town fall-down drunk too—she had been after Byard, just slightly, but after him in a way that made him uncomfortable. Byard had shared highballs with Rafe one evening and MaLou wasn't happy about it. And Levon had come by the next afternoon to ask Byard if he wanted to pick up a little part-time work with him, and MaLou nixed the idea. They'd had their first fight after that, and he had come right out with it: Did she think he was some kind of alkie? That he was a loser too, just like Levon, just like his grandfather Angus, just like every other goddamn Ferguson? He hadn't meant to yell, but there it was. The generational self-loathing that seemed to be a third corpuscle in Ferguson blood.

They had made up, of course. MaLou curled herself around him that night and they made love in Donnie Ray Goins's bed and she was as tender with him as anybody had ever been in his life. He lay in the dark later and wondered if it was time to stop thinking of himself as an unlucky man.

"You are a good man," she had said out of nowhere, as if some gentle spirit had been listening to his thoughts and chose to speak through her.

Now Byard doubted the magic of it, and he played his wife's words over and over, trying to remember where the emphasis had been placed. You are a *good* man. You *are* a good man. As in, she would talk herself into it. As in, no matter what people say, she believed in him. As in, she would argue for his decency, and perhaps would continue trying to convince herself, even after all the evidence was in and he had proven himself otherwise.

He waited for the Spalding girl to bring out a plate of food that would sit heavy on his gut the rest of the day. Waiting, he tried to imagine MaLou learning what is really inside him, the kinds of things he is capable of. Could she insist on his goodness then, once she knew the worst of the things he had done? Years had passed since that awful night, years that he had hoped were enough to create real distance. But what constituted enough time? Eight years, nine? Could the young man he'd once been—weak, corruptible, barely the agent of his own life—could he have been replaced by the good man MaLou believed in now? The Canadian doctor had pinned that night, nine years ago, as perhaps the start of Byard's "fugue state." The beginning of his wandering, if not of his secrets.

Byard jumped at the sound of a Pekkar Platter Deluxe clattering on the table in front of him. The Spalding girl tallied his check and tore it from her pad. She didn't thank him or wish him happy eating. She didn't check on whether everything met with his satisfaction.

She took up a sentry position behind the bar and gazed distractedly out at the otherwise empty restaurant.

He knew that people assumed he ran off to Canada to get away from the draft and, as long as he was hiding out in the Canadian hinterlands, it had never been in Byard's interest to disabuse them of that notion. Other than Byard himself, his big brother was probably the only person in town who knew that what he had been running from all along was Levon.

* * *

THEY STREAM TOWARD THE DUVALL Funeral Home by various means: On foot if they live nearby; in taxi cabs if they are from out-lying communities or are too old or drunk to drive; by Greyhound if they happen to be of the original mountain stock who chose to stay in Appalachia; in dilapidated trucks borrowed from neighbors, the cargo loads of which consist of children, most of whom wear shoes scrounged from somewhere and an outfit suitable for the occasion. The extended Ferguson clan is impressive, if for nothing but its size, numbering close to a hundred.

The women wear the dresses they save for the weekly grocery trip, their hair done up high on top and sprayed into unyielding helmets. Adolescent girls slink around in miniskirts and fishnets and bored looks that avoid the taciturn, barely caged scrutiny of the men. Young boys hide their diffidence behind swaggers and spit, taking turns pulling a comb from a back pocket and running it through their flawless and gleaming hair. They have not adopted the new style of collar-length locks or longer, they are no hippies, no studious sensitive types. They brook no trade with the anti-war talk that lately flavors the air. They have come to pay respect to their fallen brother, cousin, friend, to one of their own cut down for God and country and to stay the yellow horde.

Arlene Ferguson in a Valium haze is guided up the front steps of the old house that Malcolm Duvall and his wife converted to a mortuary some years ago, an antebellum behemoth set off to the east by the Slidell mansion and by Judge Freeman Hume's Victorian manor to the west. Like a house herself, Arlene is similarly bolstered, each elbow held by a son. Levon, the older, on his mother's left, has this afternoon grudgingly put on a suit of blue serge purchased for him by his beleaguered wife Virginia. (Three days ago, Ginny had gone back to Levon—yet again, and against the advice both of her cousin and of her neighbor, Katherine Juell—but it is Ginny's dance, not theirs, Byard thinks.)

Byard holds Arlene by her right arm. His own gray suit hangs on him, belonging not to him but to Rafe Goins, a considerably larger man. Behind him the assortment of relatives have finished greeting one another and, still mumbling last bits of family news and expressions of sadness, assemble into something of a procession to follow the wretched and drugged mother into Duvalls'.

The retinue, once inside, is reduced to stunned quiet. The dark elegance of the parlors on either side of the great hallway, the sweeping staircase that recalls glamorous Civil War movies, only serve to call attention to their motley clothing and brassy hair. Eyes adjusting to the dimmer light, they discern which room contains the casket. The other room appears to be for less formal sitting and visiting. The men pointedly look through Byard and filter off from the women and head toward the latter, a paneled parlor where, after an appropriately respectful interlude, thin bottles will appear from back pockets, the ubiquitous half pint that, once empty, has the power to shear in two a grieving man's heart. But as soon as one bottle is gone, another is produced, and after a while the soft drone of the men's voices gets loud enough that someone from the office comes to politely suggest they move to the broad veranda where they'll be more comfortable in the numerous rocking chairs and gliders. It is suggested that the men can enjoy a smoke without discomfiting the women across the hall.

Arlene and her sister Bett are squeezed together on a velvet settee near Daniel's coffin, two large and uncomfortable women clutching their purses on their laps. Arlene's grief bestows upon her a rare grace. Levon stands behind his mother. When Byard and Levon catch each other's eye there is a cautious hatred that Byard knows is kept at bay only out of respect for Arlene's public moment. The brothers have not been alone together since Byard's return, and he dreads that moment coming. Maria Louise has made clear she would rather it not happen at all. She won't come to the funeral home until later tonight, insisting that Byard have this time with close relatives, an excuse to delay her having to face the sobering fact that she has married a Ferguson. He wouldn't blame MaLou if she showed up as drugged as Arlene.

Mac Duvall cuts silently through the space of the bereavement room, nodding at one woman, touching the shoulder of another. His years in the business have honed him to a fine shining blade of reserve. He accomplishes an elegant gloom in his trim black suit, knows all the right expressions for the situation, what to murmur, when a simple nod will do and when a pat on the back is appropriate. The man makes of anguish something that is handsome and noble.

Levon steps forward. "War's been good to you, ain't it, Mac?" he blares, and the women all look up from their sniffling.

Mac Duvall's arm reaches out for a handshake, a motion that must be instinctual for a man in his position. "Levon," he says, but Levon keeps his arms locked tight across his chest, rocks on his heels and nearly loses his balance.

In the deep pockets of Rafe's gray suit, Byard clenches and relaxes his fists. Clenches and relaxes and glares at Levon. But Levon's attention is already engaged elsewhere, busy with his own dark judgments. Byard follows the line of his brother's scrutiny and realizes that Levon's eyes are trained on their sister Augrey.

Her hair a careless tangle, her skirt impossibly short, she leans against the jamb of the enormous door to the parlor, the strap of a straw purse dangling off the shoulder from one hooked finger. Her other arm is tightly wrapped halfway around her, articulating the tiny waist and still-boyish hips. Their mother had asked Byard to talk to Augrey. "She's acting up," was how Arlene put it, "and it can't hurt to have a man talk to her, I mean, a man who don't want something from her." Arlene didn't need to say anything else for Byard to sense the deep worry, that his mother saw her girl following the same path she herself had taken, an unthinking child reckless with what little she owned of herself. He looks at his sister now and tries to imagine what other men see, but he can't. Augrey's skinny hips, the fishnet hose that sag at the knees, make her look like a little girl playing dress-up, only instead of the glamour of mom's classy heels, she's borrowed her role from a fifty-cent novel.

He'd tried to talk to her last week, ran into her on Council Street, bought her a Coke at Happy's. She had thrown back her head and laughed and then pinned him with a way-too-old look that said she found it both flattering and funny that he wanted to save her, that he thought he could tell her a goddamn thing about the dangers of this world.

The way Levon is staring at her now, it's obvious he has a thing or two of his own he would like to tell his sister. Byard can only hope Levon will keep it to himself long enough to spare their mother more suffering today.

"Do you want to get out of here for a little while?" Byard asks Augrey. She shoves the strap of the purse onto her shoulder and follows him out to the parking lot. There's a tree at the far corner, a patch of lawn next to some ditch lilies, their orange blooms harkening summer with bright abandon. Byard sits and leans against the tree and pats the grass next to him. Augrey sprawls on the grass several feet away and slips off the cheap T-strap heels and rubs her toes.

"These things are killing me," she says.

"Come here," Byard says, but she doesn't move.

He has no right to expect her to trust him. She was so young when he left Cementville. He hears the discordant trills of a pair of woodpeckers and his eye follows their gangly flapping in the tops of pines across the way. Their red crowns bob comically as they hammer for bugs. When he turns to tell Augrey—Look! Pileated woodpeckers! (because it's not every day you get to see those)—she has scooted closer to him. She leans toward him now and he shrinks from her, but she puts her head on his chest, and in seconds he realizes she wants only comfort.

"Danny was the easiest of us to love," she says. "Mama's not going to get over this one."

He gives her hair a tentative stroke. It is softer than it looks, long and gently wavy. He looks down at the top of her head, her small nose with its wash of freckles. She is quite beautiful, her lips parting to let go a labored sigh; he hadn't known her to be capable of crying. She's like their mother in that, stoic. He looks out over the parking lot. Only a lattice fence separates it from the formal gardens of the Slidell mansion next door. Through diamond-shaped holes Byard can see the rows of manicured boxwoods, the carefully placed statuary, the orderly brick walkways. A nice place to sit, he imagines. In Canada, in the Bow Valley, he had found places to sit, wild places that would put this tamed garden to shame. His landlady, a rich-girl, free-love hippie who'd left Montreal to open a remote refuge for American war resisters, had taught him how to meditate. TM she called it. By the time he left Canada, he could sit for nearly an hour straight.

"Levon—" he starts to say, but Augrey goes taut, as if a volt of electricity has shot through her. "If you ever want to talk or anything." But why would he think he's equipped to handle whatever it is that has happened to this girl, that he can help her? Strong as the pull of shared blood can be, he doesn't know her either; she is another sad, pretty girl whose life is going to get steadily worse. Byard has neither the wisdom to guide his little sister nor the courage to save her, and truth be told, if he could walk out of this place right now, he'd do it.

Augrey's breathing is steady. The rise and fall of her against his chest and the slackening of her shoulders, the weight of her head, tell him she has fallen asleep. Byard continues to stroke her hair. Can you do more for the people you are supposed to love, he thinks, than to wish them well?

THE FAMILY SCATTERS BETWEEN THE funeral wakes of the afternoon and evening hours to find something to eat. They trail off to Happy's or Pekkar's Alley, or buy a loaf of bread and a heel of bologna and assemble sandwiches by the river. A number of them gather in Bett's front yard for hot dogs. Someone has brought a watermelon, and the smaller children are stripped to their underwear for a slice, the juices dripping down their unembarrassed bellies. Their mothers will wash them at the spigot, button up their good clothes, and get them ready to go back to Duvalls'.

MaLou comes into the funeral home with Martha and Rafe Goins. She walks toward Byard, near-angelic in the navy-blue dress she wore to marry him. He takes Augrey's hand (she has stuck close to him all afternoon), and pulls her toward his new wife. When he introduces them, the two females blush and stammer and he thinks for a minute that both might begin to cry and after a moment they do. MaLou takes Augrey into her arms and they go out together into the hallway. There is a quiet lounge adjacent to the Ladies Room, and Byard imagines MaLou there, making over his little sister, washing the girl's face.

He pulls a chair to his mother's side.

"I am glad you're here," she says. Her face is immeasurably older, this woman who is not yet fifty. She had been almost pretty, with a buxom figure, the kind French painters loved to paint a century ago. He had never thought about whether his mother was smart, whether she expected things of herself. She might have hoped to get out of here, build a life somewhere else. Once he left home, he had not thought much about any of them. "It means a lot to all the family," his mother was telling him. "You coming back. How long will you stay?"

"I don't know, Mama. Long as you need me, I guess."

"Careful what you're saying," she says, almost with a laugh.

And then Levon is standing above them, looking at them with those flat, blank eyes. "Yeah, careful what you're saying, little brother."

"Levon, honey, fetch me a glass of water, will you? I expect it's time for me to take my pills." Arlene's voice turns into a whine around Levon, as if she must become helpless to temper his cruelty in advance, to keep him from running her over. It was a habit that developed when he was still an adolescent. Levon purses his thick lips at their mother now and Byard, unsettled, wants to hit something.

"How many of those have you had, Mama?" he says when Levon has gone for the water.

"However many it takes." Arlene pats his hand.

## SEVEN

In the Pontiac's plush interior and hush of sealed windows Harlan's father drives them, like sophomores on a first date, to the barn dance where "Old Joe Clark" and "Soldier's Joy" threaten to burst the boards of Judge Hume's black barn. The Judge is magnanimous in his hosting, standing in his white seersucker at the flung-wide barn door, greeting his fawning guests. He has personally paid for an eight-piece band this year, bragging that some of the musicians were Grand Ole Opry regulars. It is an annual event, the highlight of summer, the place where all the townspeople are welcome and for one night can pretend there are no divisions among them. Country farmer and town lawyer, cement worker and shopkeeper, all are there for the square dancing and music, for the lime sherbet punch and mixed nuts and fancy pastel mints. The nuns at Holy Ghost School have always eyed the dance with suspicion, its concurrence with the summer solstice feeling a mite chummy with pagan brouhaha for their comfort.

The Judge stops the music and drags Harlan to the stage. The microphone squawks and squeals as Judge Freeman Hume pontificates to a crowd itching for the quadrille.

"Our hometown hero has been back with us for near a month now—"

He bumbles on, but no one is listening. He is talking about things they want to forget, the young men they are all too aware are not among them, the ones who are not here milling about and flirting with pretty young women, but should be. The people here tonight, the living, breathing people, are grateful to the Judge for throwing this party, but right now they just want him to shut the hell up. The humming and prickling energy of the room finally force Freeman Hume to cut short his oration and the band strikes up with "Turkey in the Straw."

All the girls have come prepared to dance by the light of the moon, as Lila promised, smiling faces with white teeth, bright for their anointed beaus. Will they all get to dance, with so many of their young men gone? They know all the square steps and two steps the caller calls. Harlan cannot seem to remember. He sits trying to tap his one cooperative foot and apologizes to Analisa that although he cannot dance, she should; after all, they are at a dance.

But she sticks by him in her new eyelet peasant blouse and seems to want to dance right out of her chair next to him, squirming in her white skin that smells like paper narcissus. The copper of her POW bracelets clinks up and down her white arms. A few other girls wear one of the memorial bands bearing the name of a missing or captured soldier, but Analisa is the only girl wearing five. She shakes them like a tribal talisman when she moves, and she bares her teeth at all the swirling couples. She has snared the catch, the decorated and paraded Lieutenant Harlan O'Brien. For her, he is not a broken man.

When she gazes sideways at his tapping toe, lets her eye travel up the long leg to that soldier's profile, she sees not a death mask but rather the square jaw set to stand the tests of time and matrimony and the childbearing bed.

For they would have many children—she pictures it—and he would be a man of God. Not that he would wear his god on his sleeve, all preachy and holier than thou. He is nothing like the cheap and predictable pups slinging their stuck-up girls around to the tune of "Star of the County Down." Finally it is the "Spanish Waltz" that lets the pretty girl convince her man to usher her around the room in simple circles, Analisa's skirt a swirling cloud that makes his peg leg seem to float.

\* \* \*

LILA O'BRIEN GLOWS BEHIND THE punchbowl, seeing her mutilated boy dance. Truthfully, she has worried; she has heard his anguished cries in the night, how many times over these four weeks since he came home to them. She had wiped his brow when he didn't know who she was. Tomorrow she will drag out the family albums in the quiet of the afternoon and remind herself: This is indeed her boy. This is no stranger come home from war. The men will catch her dabbing an eye when they come in for early supper and to get out of the unceasing rain.

Mr. O'Brien will mumble, *Are you all right, Mother?* so softly she can't be certain he has said anything at all.

\* \* \*

THIS IS THE SIGHT BEHIND Harlan's curtained eyelids each night, the scene of a long-running play: He carries on his back the legless girl, her purple stumps smooth as eggplants. She is ageless. The years of thumping across a dirt floor fall from her when she shrieks with laughter. They are getting out. Carrying the child is a favor to the girl's mother, who'd been so kind to his unit in the Duc Duc Resettlement Village. Washing laundry. Offering a hot meal.

They laugh through water swirling hip deep where they are joined like one human sprouting from his pair of strong legs, amphibious. Little boats crowd around them through the flood and the girl waves to her brother, who hangs from the bow of a sampan like a monkey clinging to its mother. In the mist above hangs a canopy of trees, verdant mosquito netting. Lieutenant O'Brien hears a swarm of choppers whump across the sky in the distance.

Harlan feels through the water with his bare feet—the legless girl carries his boots high over her head. Her arms are strong. He praises her for keeping them dry. He steps gingerly through the water, sensitive to anything that should not be there.

But he cannot contain, for all his care, the concussive blare that sends his stumped-off girl flying from him. In that long silence when everything is aloft, he sees flash by—not his life at home, the sad or smiling faces of his mother and father, his room under the eaves of their red tin roof—but the tumbling procession of the dead in the here and now, their arms and legs waving in a kind of whole-body sign language as if they would communicate with him, beckon him to join them, until Lieutenant O'Brien does land in a hillside wash already corpse-crammed. Their bloated skins have taken on a uniform gray, and it is no longer possible to separate yellow from white. A tangle of limbs, arms seeking a mate to pray with. He is webbed in.

A tree bends over him, its roots clinging impossibly to a scrawny ledge. From the nearest limb hangs another limb, the fingers of which graze his cheek as if trying to soothe him. He can almost hear a voice saying, *Shhh, shhh.*

It is a match being struck. His nostrils fill with the smell of kerosene. He calls out a single word that might save him: *No*, he says out loud in their language. And he thinks he hears them respond with the word for *savage* or it could be the word for *no*—are they mocking his poor accent?—and he is being pulled from the ditch screaming for the foot that refuses to come with him.

He knows he is the one screaming, that the pitch and wail belong to him, and it is comforting to own the howling, given the cold desertion of the left foot. The lyrics accompanying his screams go like so: *This is my body / this is the arm / this is the neck / the trunk the thigh the calf / the no-foot.*

He feels better, having figured out a name for it and where its absence fits. They drag him, toss him like a rag doll onto a truck bed. He thrashes his head this way and that, searching for his precious charge. There, at the edge of a ruined mango orchard, two lovely eggplants peek from the mud. The laces of his boots wrap themselves around and around her mad-apple knees in love knots.

\* \* \*

AT THE SOUND (always a light sleeper—she has "nerves") Lila O'Brien's eyes burst open as if spring-loaded. Propped on a bird-elbow, she lifts a corner of the curtain by her side of the bed and spies the erect tin soldier crunching lopsided down the gravel road. In the dark, it is her son.

\* \* \*

THE LIEUTENANT HAS TAKEN TO walking out at night with the moon in his face. Phantoms rise from the Raggedy Robin roadside and curl like cats round his shuffling limbs. He goes to the place where the dead are buried, stones lined up with truncated elegies etched across their faces (*Beloved Son*, or *Brother Gone Too Soon*, or *On the Wings of a Dove*). Peace might wander here, if it weren't for the silent crowd straining from behind the stones, open-mawed like overgrown baby birds, insatiable.

There are seven fresh mounds of dirt, all littered with shriveled mummies of carnations, gladioli, baby's breath. Atop each temporary marker, tiny American flags—already fading and torn—tremble in the night breeze.

*What do they want from us?* he asks the white stones. Their response is but inconsolable bleating. This place the people kept calling home is an ignoble place, scraggly and scrabbly, nothing like he remembered or hoped for. It makes a person want to go off and look for somewhere to practice dying. Having seen the walls of huts fall around screaming babies, having kicked rice bowls into the dirt so that any foolish enough to survive will have nothing, he is past being horrified. It was all about order, the war. In the middle of the unfathomable disorder, there was always the order. The order: They must all be shot, every one.

This is what the stones tell him: Never again will you rest your head in the warm nest of home, never will you count on the managed life that once lay spread in front of you like a promised picnic. You, fed once on sweet fruit, remembering the way its juices ran down your chin, you will find the seeds and juices burn like ash till the skin melts from your face, napalm makeup. You, whose silent father taught you the art of stalking and hunting, will find you cannot lift a gun. You will writhe in sleep, dreaming of your guts spattering the Milky Way.

He craves to lie down at night without these apparitions worming their way under his fingernails. Half a blood-red eyeball on the eastern ridge steals a look at Harlan O'Brien. From behind a dewy stand of cedars advancing up the hillside like the mantled Birnam Wood, dawn comes. In the early light, he makes for the river.

He sees her there on the bank, her ocher reflection. Her hand floats in the water like a separate living thing seen to by a small god she might stow in a pocket. From his distance, Harlan imagines multiple courses of a long meal with her. He sees her placing a blue plum in his mouth, chased with ambrosia, a stream of fruits whose names he does not know. The blade of his unused voice parts the air between them.

Her name means river, he will learn.

\* \* \*

SHE TURNS, STARTLED, LETS DOWN her shoulders. She recognizes him from the barn dance. *Their new latest hero,* Giang thinks, *the one they had all been waiting for.* The one who came back alive. She'd seen him across the room at the dance earlier tonight, had read his brokenness and considered: This one could be dangerous.

In the brothel she had seen many like him. Hybrid animals of wild confusion, looking at once to crawl into her sex and to knife her as the enemy. There were stories of girls found in pieces after their callers left.

It had been three years, these good years with Jimmy, since she had encountered such a face.

The moon peeks at her over his shoulder, fashioning for him a kind of nimbus, a hazy crown. Instinctively Giang begins speaking into the vacant face hanging above her, soft words from her own tongue, words he might have learned over there. (That language of poems always works on Jimmy when shadows rip into their bed in the night.) She puts on the blank countenance of a mind reader in an effort to glimpse what this damaged man sees looking down at her: a yellow woman squatting by a river. She rises, and her eyes are level with his chest. He is taller than Jimmy by a head.

Her smile loosens something inside him. What his face gives back is a grimace, a smile unpracticed.

They walk the length of the river together for an hour. His stiff prosthesis over rocky ground makes the going slow. When he speaks, Giang knows from the stitched-together phrasing that she is the first person he has talked to about these things. He draws images in the air before her, the same ones she has conjured against loneliness when she despairs of ever seeing home again. In his harsh tongue sprinkled with the sounds of her own language, Harlan O'Brien talks of the emerald forest, of farmers conspiring with the wet soil and a stubborn cow to make the rice grow fat, of children laughing and begging candy.

For her he is holding back the darker images. The stumps of palms stripped of foliage; the jungle paths swollen with long files of the displaced; the malnourished babies, black hair fermenting to the color of papaya.

She knows he was in a prison camp. This is the central image around which he hobbles. She is not a stranger to the ways this soldier's nights and days unfurled in that camp. She hopes sweet opium smoke was there to help him as it did her. She walks the riverbank and feels beside her the swinging arm of another bundle of damaged goods, the cargo traded in any war.

\* \* \*

GIANG LOVES HER HUSBAND, AND has told herself this every time she has gone to the river and waited for Lieutenant O'Brien to come through the gray veil of early morning. She has met him for many nights now. She steals out on nights when Jimmy Smith has taken twice the prescribed Phenobarbital, which he seems to do with increasing regularity.

When she is not with Harlan, the cells of her keen dangerously toward him. It is three weeks since she first met the lieutenant, and since then she has moved through her days as if floating weightlessly through an alien atmosphere, washing Jimmy's clothes, washing the floor, washing the windows of the small sturdy house Jimmy built for her. Through these windows she can see clear to the river.

She had been with so many men. She and Suong counted them at first, a silly contest between girls, something to make it not real. The sisters compared the men's private parts and giggled, foolish children playing dangerous games.

Then the first girl was murdered; things changed. Soon Suong and Giang rarely spoke when they brushed past each other in the brothel's hallway, terror a knife between them. During the black period, between Suong's leaving and the coming of Jimmy Smith, opium helped Giang to lay still, to stop measuring days or nights. Opium made the men into not men, more like bed clothing grown too heavy to fling aside.

Sometimes she wishes she had not said yes, if yes was what she said, to Harlan O'Brien. Another in a string of a thousand yeses the opium once allowed her to give away. Sometimes she imagines her husband's truck swerving in the dark road in the middle of the night, and sometimes she wishes she could be an opium eater again.

But then Jimmy climbs into her bed and she melts into his scarred backside where she has rubbed jasmine oil. She murmurs bawdy phrases of the poetry that women such as her have always whispered to their men; a lyric vanishes into the angel wings of his shoulder blades, and she disappears in there with it.

This time, waiting here for Harlan O'Brien to come, she knows she cannot leave her husband.

\* \* \*

I DON'T BELIEVE YOU, HARLAN says when Giang tells him tonight that she cannot meet him anymore, that she can no longer walk with him by the river.

They lay by the water on a soft bed of storm-tossed leaves, corpses starved for each other's clinging, and what had been a closely guarded seed in their blackest corners swells and grows to a writhing choking vine. They couple fiercely at the edge of the river, drifting out upon its surface, their bodies rising and falling together, white and yellow intertwined. At the easternmost bank, the limbs of a downed elm grasp the lovers in a terrible embrace.

In the dream, he studies his hands as if they do not belong to him. Black and rotted, they belong with the left foot somewhere on the other side of the so-called peaceful ocean. He had heard stories of the Poles carrying boxes to the graves of loved ones lost in the Second World War. Through English sheep pastures they bore boxes of Polish soil to sprinkle on the hundreds of unnamed graves, marked only by white crosses.

Is there a person somewhere in that far land to sprinkle his blackened foot? They will know it by its scar, sickle moon–shaped and curving along the arch, from where he ran across a broken bottle when he was ten. Will some kind stranger sprinkle his foot with the soil of his homeland?

For his anguish and his sudden fever his mother wrings a cold towel, soothes his forehead. Such is the nightmare that awakens Harlan O'Brien from his first deep sleep in three years.

\* \* \*

AND SUCH BEGINS THE NIGHTMARE from which Giang will not awaken. She watches him walk away from her, and she turns to the river's gloomy murmur and closes her eyes. She sees Suong floating among the debris of the ragged people below the brothel window. Her sister's gown billows around her, a dirty sail filled with water. This waking dream allows Giang the knowledge that Suong is dead, flung out that night like so much refuse. A red ribbon, a garrote of blood, circles around her sister's neck and blends with the river's mud.

Giang opens her eyes and her lips part to say the word. "*Vang*," she tells the water. Then, "Yes," because this is an American river.

She does not feel the blow from behind, does not even have the chance to say to her assailant, *Cam o'n ban. Thank you.*

# PART II

*The land mourns. Joy is withered away. Sun and moon darken, and when the stars withdraw their shining, the menace shall run up your walls and through your windows like a thief. Your old will dream dreams and your young will see visions, wonder in heavens and earth, blood and fire and pillars of smoke. This day is near in the valley of decisions.*

—PROPHETS: JOEL REDUX

So many have come back. The dead, the wounded, the incarcerated. The insane. People remark how the blacks are acting odd—and wonder privately whether the riots in the big cities could possibly spread out here, infecting our peace—because the women too are not the same, their quiet natures flavored now with a rare new anger. Then too there are the strangers streaming into town, trying to take all our jobs at the new paper plant. People are fractious.

A man took a walk on the moon the other day, "a giant leap for mankind," he called it. But we walk around our own town like we don't know the place, as if body snatchers might have snuck in overnight and replaced all of us with replicas. There are black wreaths on too many doors, broad ribbons of yellow plastic around oaks in almost every yard. *Come home, come home,* the yellow ones say. *Go back,* say the black ones, *go back to where you came from and send my real baby home to me.*

Mothers do not take their eyes off their children now. No use in arguing. Jimmy Smith's war bride is dead. A killer is on the loose and people look in the eyes of neighbors they've known all their lives, and they wonder. Everybody on the street is a stranger.

People talk. When did that one get here? I wouldn't let my sister or daughter out of the house with him. Heard they beat a fellow after the graveyard shift the other morning, dragged him off into a field and left him there. Argument over a lunchbox or something. Warning words scribbled across his forehead, words you wouldn't want your mother to see. Poolroom squabbles turn into blood matches.

The Bible's Lamentations have got nothing on us: The Lord was as an enemy; He hath swallowed up Israel and hath increased in us mourning and lamentation. Our gates are sunk into the ground. The children and the sucklings swoon and their souls are poured out onto their mothers' bosoms.

Our covenant is with a two-faced god of forgiveness and vengeance. Yes, He has led us and brought us into darkness all right. His hand against us is turned all the day. It is hard in times like these to remember that the Lord is good to them that seeketh him.

# EIGHT

Billy Juell leaves his father's house, passes through the broad meadow, and crosses over the wooden stile into Lemuel O'Brien's pasture. The ancient stone wall separating the two farms has long since crumbled into a low, serpentine heap, rambling over the land like the ruined tunnel of an enormous drunken mole. Billy is overdressed in a green camo vest and long sleeves so that perspiration soon pricks the skin of his neck. The sky stretches over the valley white and even like a taut sheet, its bland cloud cover doing nothing to break the summer heat. Three boxes of number seven and a half shot protest with soft rattling against his chest. It is a half hour after dawn, and by the time he reaches the edge of the woods, a rivulet of sweat makes its way down his spine, clear to the waistband of his jeans.

The path through the woods is much the way he remembers it, but narrower, dark and littered now with shards of yellow light that make the trail seem to slither along like some living thing in pain. The quiet swells in his skull, broken by the occasional despondent *hoo-ooh-who-who-who* of a mourning dove calling from the glade ahead. Reaching the clearing, he stands still in trained reconnoiter, barest movement of eyes and head, the gun hanging stiffly from his shoulder, a Remington 870 that marked his fourteenth birthday. Beneath the cedars at the clearing's edge is a battered paint bucket, a crude bench for watching. Billy situates himself there with a good view of the stand of wild sunflowers and elk thistle where he's seen the doves feeding.

He has been home for a while now and still he and his family circle around one another like strangers thrown together randomly into a boarding house. Early on after he came home, he tried to take most meals with them, but his sister always watches him across the table. He catches her staring as if he is somebody she might recognize but isn't so sure. His mother hovers over him and he is pretty sure his father hates his guts. Willis has all but quit talking to Billy. And once Uncle Carl arrived on the scene Billy can't tolerate being in the house at all.

He's been sleeping late most mornings, and when he wakes he lies upstairs in his bed and waits until all sound fades in the house below and everyone has gone about their day. He makes toast or a bowl of cereal and gets out of there fast. He was glad when old lady Slidell hired him on to keep the grounds at the mansion, but now she's near-dead and he's afraid he won't know what to do with himself in the afternoons, once she croaks. This whole place seems festering with death. Cutting across the hillside a few minutes ago, he could see the cemetery below where the graveyard crew's backhoe still sat beside a new-dug grave. They must be going to plant Jimmy Smith's dead gook wife this morning.

When he rose before the sun today his hope had been that he could steal out before the family stirred, get in a little hunting, try to see if he couldn't find his old self out here. God, what was wrong with him? Talking about finding himself and such—it was that counselor his mother dragged him to at the VA in Louisville. He'd agreed to one visit to get her off his back. Hopefully none of the guys at Pekkar's would find out. Last thing he needs is them thinking he's spending time with a shrink. Not that he'll ever darken that fucking doctor's or any other's goddamn door again. Anyway, he thought he'd be safe getting out of the house early, and he tiptoed downstairs and filled a Mason jar with water. He slapped a slice of baloney between some bread and put it in a baggy and left the house, closing the door behind him without even a click. He almost screamed when he turned around and there stood Mo, right in his face. *Sorry!* said Mo. *Sheesh!* And the way she looked at him, as if she knew everything about him, all he's done and seen— Billy tried to shake it off, but right there, just like that, the tremor took over his hands and now the day is probably fucked in terms of hitting anything. *Don't be sneaking up on people*, he hissed at her. But then she grabbed his hand and held it in front of her face and when she saw the way it was shaking, she pressed it hard against her chest, staring at him the whole time, as if she was trying to grab something inside his head. He jerked his hand away from her and laughed and said, *You little freak!* And then he rubbed her stupid pixie haircut to cover for how bad he was shaking.

*You want to help me with my memoirs?* Mo had said then. She had dragged him over to the picnic table where her papers were spread out, little rock cairns holding them in place. *I'm interviewing people,* she said. *You can be my first one.* Billy shrugged and sat down. Most people in town have been taking one look at him and turning right around and heading in the other direction. He wished somebody would explain to them the difference between an honorable and dishonorable discharge. He hadn't done anything almost every other grunt did at some point over there. Nobody had sure as shit asked to interview him. So, *Shoot,* he said to his sister, *Ask me anything.* And she took the cap off her cartridge pen, all serious, her mouth so bunched in a tight little *o* it nearly broke his heart.

To save his life he cannot remember the questions she asked. Fragments of the things he said rattle around in his head now as he sits in the glade watching the doves feeding on thistle and wild sunflower heads. *First,* he told her, *people need to get it straight: I was separated* with honor. *The other day Alden Wilder saw me a half a block away and he crossed the street. And him Uncle Judge's best friend.*

He told her about flying out on a medevac, the way the nurses made him lay on a stretcher. He yelled at them, he remembers the yelling, telling them he wasn't some Section 8 nut job, and the way they looked at him with their wet, tired eyes. They told him they didn't think he was crazy, that everybody on the plane had to be on a stretcher. So Billy had lain in the back of that hospital. *Yeah,* he told Mo, *those C-141s are like a big-box hospital with wings*—all the way across the ocean. He was back there with some bad cases. One guy had both legs gone, both arms. Another one's eyeballs fried straight out of his head, stone blind. Burns all over his face, breathing through a plastic tube. Rows and rows of them. *Then there was me.* Mo didn't get the joke when he told her that if they'd had Dr. Frankenstein on board he could have assembled one good whole body out of all the parts that were somewhat intact. Nobody talked. All the way to Los Angeles.

His sister must have asked him what he remembered most about the place, because now he is thinking of the flies. Flies over there big enough to carry off a chicken leg. *Imagine what three or four hundred of them working together might do,* he told her. That's what he said to a thirteen-year-old girl. Her face got all blurry and not like the face he knew, but he couldn't stop himself, and he said, *Oh, yeah, and I guess you don't forget the smell of the bodies.* Billy and his friends called it hamburger meat. *Hey,* somebody would say, *sure was a lot of hamburger meat out on the road today.* Because that's what it reminded you of, when they'd been laying out there in the sun and the heat for six, eight days.

He hadn't meant to tell her about the dream, how over and over again when he closed his eyes, he found himself captured during a night patrol. The gooks always took him to what everybody called the Hanoi Hilton. And in the dream, when he got to the prison, his little sister was already there. *They had you there in the room next to mine, and whenever they came in to question me, they would start working on you. Trying to make me talk through your screaming.*

She must have asked him about the black guy. The one with the bad heart. *Oh, DeAngelo,* Billy said. *DeAngelo Blessing was his name.* He was Billy's friend. DeAngelo wasn't afraid of gooks, and Billy was. Billy wasn't afraid of snakes, and DeAngelo was. They had worked out a system to save each other's ass. He had no recollection what the fight between them had been about.

And maybe Mo said something then like, *Was it worth it?* Or was he glad he went? Glad. After that about the road meat and the torture and the flies? Glad to be part of defending his country? she had said. Who feeds these kids that kind of bullshit? Billy wonders, watching the doves peck devotedly at the seeds. *They're not going to be able to recall this one with pride, the way they've talked themselves into for every other war,* he told her, as if she would know what he meant. They're not going to know what to do with this one. Not for a long time.

That was when he looked up and saw his father standing in the kitchen doorway. How long had he been listening with that disappointed, unmoving face? Billy had stood up from the picnic table and flung the rifle over his shoulder and walked toward the ridge.

A GRASSHOPPER CLICKS AN ARC in front of him, and Billy thinks of Paco snapping his teeth at empty air, the dog forgetful that already and always he would never catch the voracious things, but never failing to try anyway. Maybe Billy should check with Levon Ferguson, see about that bloodhound bitch that was about to whelp. Maybe one in the litter has Billy's name on it. A little girl this time, maybe. Say what you want about Levon—and Billy wouldn't trust him any further than he can throw him—but the man knows hunting dogs.

The doves are joined at the stand of thistles by three crows, darkly comical in their shiny black suits, compared to the doves' soft colors and gentle demeanor. One of the crows scratches at a low hillock on the ground, and Billy remembers suddenly that this is the site of the O'Briens' sawmill. Lem's father operated the mill in these woods in the thirties, forties, on into the fifties. It was said that the wood for framing the new church came from this forest. The skeleton uprights and roof trusses of the old mill's open-air pavilion stand guard over the clearing. Billy spots the long, low tracks of the power train that carried cedar logs to the saw blade. He remembers watching men shove logs toward the blade, and how he cringed with fear that one of the workers would lose a hand or an arm, that the spinning wheel of the blade would jump the track and take on a will of its own, and fly off to carry out its mayhem all over the county. If you weren't careful, even now you could stumble on the half-buried wheels and rusting gears of the steam tractor that powered the operation; you could find in the weeds the rotting piles of hickory slag, shaggy bark riddled with curving trails of beetles. The crow was pecking and digging in the conical heap of sawdust Billy had kicked and wallowed in as a boy; it's now a low, breast-shaped mound, hairy with dry wild grass. When Billy was younger, he and Willis and Lem O'Brien would crank up the tractor now and then. Cut a few boards, maybe build a playhouse for some neighbor kids, or repair a decrepit outbuilding. Nostalgia, mostly. Lumber is a thing gotten cheaper these days from some far off, manmade forest, single species of trees planted in sterile rows. Birds dare not live, much less sing, amidst such bald fakery.

A rustling at the east corner of the clearing cuts through the quilted silence, and the doves take wing, chirring softly toward a grove of locusts. Billy creeps around the perimeter of the glade, just inside the darkling edge of the woods. It is a man, crouching over the spring that bubbles from the roots of a sycamore. Billy watches the man lie down on the leafy ground and drink, his mouth directly kissing the water like an animal.

It is Harlan O'Brien. There is nearly ten years between them. When Billy wasn't yet eight, Harlan had gone away to West Point.

Billy's parents are longtime friends of Mr. and Mrs. O'Brien and have allowed no gossip or innuendos of murder in their home. Such nonsense is the bailiwick of ignorant folk in whom his mother has never put much stock. Katherine Juell is still the outsider, a citified stranger to the natives.

But there is talk aplenty in town. At Pekkar's Alley, Billy has heard them wondering why an arrest hasn't been made. He does not remember people being so restless and, well, mean. Are they bored, he wonders, so many laid off from the cement plant? Resentful of the unfulfilled promise of more jobs at the new paper products factory? Some of the guys, when they get liquored up, say outright that they are tired of pretending they don't know there was something going on between the dead Vietnamese woman and this big-deal hero.

When Harlan's head makes a slow swivel, the younger man flinches. The eyes too are those of an animal. Billy pushes the Remington further behind him and clears the phlegm gathering in his throat.

"Dove hunting," Billy says, and pauses. "My dad talked to your dad. It's all right." He remembers the lieutenant riding through town at the Memorial Day parade, mounted on Uncle Judge's black mare, Harlan peering out through narrowed slits of eyes at all the confetti floating down around him. Billy hadn't had difficulty imagining what it reminded Harlan O'Brien of: ashes. The way, over there, the air filled with gray flecks of burning buildings and flesh.

"I was so thirsty." Harlan struggles to his feet now, or his foot, and Billy salutes. But Harlan swats a hand through the air and stares at the ground. The two men begin to walk in the listless and aimless way people will when time has appeared to stop. They don't converse about being back here, about how they'd both rolled into town that day with the seven dead. Seven—a mere handful when you thought about it, compared to the mounds and mounds of bodies they both had seen. Billy and Harlan do not discuss these things as they cross the same land they tramped separately as boys. There is no clapping of shoulders, no hail fellow well met, no nostalgic sighs. Periodic need for statement, rendition, interpretation arises and is dispensed with by utterance of a few small words that drift to the ground like brittle, stubborn leaves from a water oak, always the last to let go. For a long while, neither speaks. Then Harlan.

"Mother said you'd gotten back. When was that?"

"May. Same day as you," Billy says. "I was with the guys on the bus. Behind all the funeral cars." He tries for a mordant chuckle but lets it peter out when it becomes obvious that the lieutenant doesn't share his sense of—well, he could hardly call it humor anymore. Irony, is that what you called it? Not that Billy saw it as ironic that Harlan had come home alive. Harlan O'Brien was the mythical quarterback of the Holy Ghost Shamrocks, who led the football team to the triple A championship in '57, the handsome and aloof heartthrob stared after by every girl in town.

But Billy himself? Any god who'd seen fit to spare him was a fucking sphinx.

"I heard Carl's home," the lieutenant says.

It strikes Billy that Uncle Carl and Harlan would have grown up together, about the same age, here on their fathers' neighboring farms. He cannot imagine the two having anything in common, Harlan O'Brien being a war hero, and Uncle Carl being a certified loony with papers to prove it.

"Sure enough," Billy says and laughs nervously again. He needs to get control of himself. They walk.

"Back before, a lot of folks would pile their kids in the car after Mass on Sundays, go out visiting," the lieutenant says suddenly. "Go see their old people who lived deep in the hollers. I remember my Aunt Fern—she was my grandmother's sister—hobbling out onto the porch, shading her eyes with both hands. Uncle Bud right behind her, both of them wobbly stacks of bones. You got the feeling you were waiting for you. The way they gathered you in their arms."

Harlan falls silent again, and Billy is too stunned by this long string of words to speak. The few times Harlan has come into Pekkar's, he sits at the bar nursing a bourbon straight up for an hour or more without speaking to a soul. People tried to get friendly with him when he first got home. Lately they steer clear.

The two of them continue to footslog across one stream after another, and Billy becomes aware that he has taken on Harlan's halting gait, his back straight and stiff. Limp arms swing at their sides, counterweights to the ponderous ballast of some unspeakable apprehension, stones rattling in both their heads.

"Or we could hit the new toll road, making a clear shot all the way to Louisville. Whatever road you picked there was sure to be a haul of cousins at the end of it waiting for Sunday company, or people that weren't cousins, but might as well be," Harlan says. "We always stopped in at your granddad's place on the way home. And there Carl would be."

So that's it, Billy thinks, Carl is what inspired this ramble.

"Old Carl," Billy says, hoping Harlan has not finished. He wants to know why, *really* why, his uncle went away.

"Carl always had some new project, something he was building, some new animal he was raising. Fancy chickens. Peacocks. Goats. Chinchillas, of all things. He even talked his father into letting him get a pair of Percherons. There would always be a handful of other kids from town who had walked to the Juell farm, late on a Sunday afternoon. I swear, I believe those kids would have walked twice as far to get to spend time with Carl. Best entertainment around."

"Did everybody know he was nuts back then?" Billy says, and instantly regrets it. There is a slight hesitation in Harlan's pace next to him. Billy can feel the man looking at him, feel his own blood rush to his face. He continues to stare at the ground in front of him, aware he has made some sort of grave error.

"For most of us, Carl Juell was as close as we were going to get to an adventurer, a soldier of fortune, without ever leaving home. You know what a bagworm is?"

Billy nods. "Sure. Bunch of them hanging on the cedars right now." He looks around to confirm that he knows what he's talking about and plucks one from a tree, fingers its intricate brown sac of shingled twigs.

"We could sit for an interminable time, watching Carl cut those bags open with his pocket knife and pop those things into his mouth," Harlan says, and when Billy grimaces and throws the moth case aside, Harlan laughs. "We'd help him gather eggs—Carl knew how to blow an egg dry without breaking the shell, poke a pinhole on either end with a good-sized needle—and he'd hide a couple of empties in his mother's egg basket for a joke. I once saw him tie himself by a single foot to a tree branch hanging out over the river. He scooped water in his hand as he swung, then let the water fall through his fingers like liquid pearls."

This is a Carl Billy does not know. A Carl before his and Willis's mother had passed. Before Willis had left for Korea. Before Carl's and Willis's daddy went into the barn and hung himself. Before they found Roy Stubblefield with his head caved in.

Billy had heard versions of the story, outlandish tales that had reached the proportion of myth by the time he was in high school, the way kids will make up a story in the absence of the truth. He could remember being at the homes of friends, overhearing the adults talking, whispering usually, in another room, the women making the little sucking sounds with their tongues over their teeth, the sounds of nonjudging judgment that serves mostly to distance the lucky from the judged. While his friends bragged about imagined exploits with girls, Billy would be listening to see if the adults would talk about what had happened to Carl, if they would let their guard down enough for him to get the real story, or some semblance of it. What he wanted was something along the lines of relief from the uncertainty surrounding his uncle, the fate he sometimes worries might be also closing in on him, a hereditary curse.

He gathered from people's whispers that after his mother's death, Carl had taken to loitering at the depot with a bunch of lowlifes and hobos who drifted between a rooming house and the railroad tracks, pretending to wait for work to open up. Willis was already off in Korea by then. Carl quit going to school—the nuns sent him off the grounds at Holy Ghost every other day anyway, due to his outbursts. And then a drifter named Roy Stubblefield—Billy pictured a filthy man more than twice Carl's age, all covered in creeping eruptions with a Lucky Strike hanging off his bottom lip—Roy Stubblefield had taken to lingering around wherever Carl was. People were always seeing him standing close to Carl, closer than seemed right for an unrelated man and boy. None of the mothers Billy heard whispering at night in his friends' kitchens ever came out and said it outright, probably out of respect for Mrs. Juell's memory, but Carl was maybe funny in more ways than one. Then Stubblefield turned up dead and all those no-accounts got hauled in and questioned, and somehow Carl's name didn't make it on the list of those present, though people said, low under their breath, of course (by then Billy had come to understand that under the breath is the only way things of this sort can be discussed), they said, *Everybody knows Carl was there . . . those tramps likely were fighting over him. You know. As if he was a girl.* The details and the timing were fuzzy, but Billy had pieced together that, one day, his grandfather had gone into the barn and tied himself a good strong noose. Uncle Freeman must have gotten word to Willis, because he came home from Korea. In no time, Carl was whisked off to one of those places where people go to "rest." Apparently a person could be so tired it was a long, long time before they let him go home again.

Walking in silence beside Harlan O'Brien, Billy wishes he could work up the guts to ask whether the story he has assembled is anywhere close to the truth. Harlan would know; he had been there. But Harlan is finished with talking.

They are both sons of Cementville after all, where good people raise good kids and even in the face of tragedy go on about their lives, strong where it counts, and knowing right from wrong. Billy follows the lieutenant across the last stream, wondering whether the artificial leg minds the water, whether the stump carries memories of fording this creek in the past. They mount the hill and finally reach the rock wall that divides their fathers' lands. They shake hands, part ways.

Walking toward his father's house, the unopened boxes of birdshot chatter softly against Billy's chest.

# NINE

Wanda Slidell sat up late knitting a cap for her friend June Cahill's cousin who had the Big C and had lost all her hair.

"Rats," she whispered, not wanting to wake her mother. There was a monkey wrench in the cable pattern twenty rows back. That meant ripping out an hour's work, minimum. It reminded her of the old days, learning to knit, picking out the crooked little rows. Her mother had taught her. Tried to teach her to spin, too, but she never got the hang of spinning, and after Loretta was diagnosed with lupus, they sold the sheep, and the spinning wheel got pushed further and further in among cast-off furniture and mountains of canning jars in the old meat house.

Wanda's mind wandered to thoughts of having to leave Hanging Valley, drive down the hill, walk into the hospital in Travelers Grove, and hand the red cap to a sick girl she barely knew, and her heart flipped and flopped around her chest. In her head, she rehashed the words to the argument she and her mother were having—again.

"How about the one Doc Carruthers recommended," Loretta had said. "You don't have to commit to anything long term, just see what he has to say." It seemed that the sicker Loretta got, the more she insisted that Wanda needed a doctor. She wouldn't say the word "psychiatrist." Thinking about driving into downtown Louisville, Wanda broke into a sweat.

Agoraphobia, the *Diagnostic and Statistical Manual* said. She had looked it up at the library, pinned it down. Naming a thing did not make those assaults any easier, Wanda discovered. Whatever was wrong with her, she figured she could handle it as long as she stuck with what worked. Namely, staying home unless life's necessities sent her out.

But she did struggle against it, this agoraphobia, and mightily. Forced herself to do the grocery shopping, for instance, ever since the lupus had made driving excruciating, not to mention unsafe, for Loretta. And Wanda allowed June to drag her to the movies once or twice a year, until the Arco downtown closed and the only theater within seventy or eighty miles was the new eight-plex on the edge of Louisville. Crowds gave her hives.

To show how hard she battled her condition, as her mother had come to call it, Wanda had even competed for a scholarship to college in her senior year of high school, and won it. Reading was the only thing that ever sparked a fire under her. Discovery of the English department at Saint Brigid College was a magical thing: the only place she had found where she wouldn't stick out. Nobody marked it as strange for a person to go around with her nose pressed in the gutter of a book all day, or if they did, they never said it to her face. The English Department was a safe little cocoon, a couple of classrooms and offices tucked on the tiptop floor of the Saint Brigid College Library. There she could move from class to the stacks and to the next class with practically no extraneous contact with gangs of marauding college students. She had come home after college graduation with a double major in literature and linguistics and had not found a compelling reason to leave Cementville since.

Her father's life insurance policy kept them out of the poor house. Loretta Ferguson Slidell was not going to make her daughter go to work at the cement plant, much less at the distillery, since Wanda had been half-orphaned by the effects of liquor. Whenever Wanda thought of looking for gainful employment beyond the county line, thrusting herself out there into the wide open land past the knobs whose profiles she knew by heart, her chest muscles clamped a vise around her rib cage and she had to fetch a paper bag to breathe into. She would be ever grateful to Charlene Cahill, who had convinced her to come and work part-time in the college's library, where she could again hide in the stacks without fear of aggravating her condition. Dusting, re-establishing order in the card catalog, lining the spines of books on the shelves. It made her feel like somebody.

And now here was Carl Juell, returned to them.

"'Because I do not hope . . . I no longer strive to strive towards such things,'" Wanda recited out loud. Her Eliot had not left her, nor her Hardy, her Woolf—for all the good they did her. And yes, Mrs. Dalloway, she thought now, with Carl's round face before her in her mind, you are right: Perhaps the reward of caring for people is that they come back.

Wanda's head leaned against the little cervical pillow behind her neck. Falling asleep in her grandfather's easy chair wasn't so easy anymore. The springs were sprung and the upholstery on the arms was pretty much nonexistent, leaving a bare wooden frame where a person could set her tea. Loretta talked about sending it to the dump now and then, but Wanda insisted it would leave a hole in the house.

"You know how many naughas died for this chair?" her grandfather used to ask several times a week, and she would have to laugh, because his feelings were hurt when she didn't.

She might have been aware of the last flutter of her eyelids as her head came to rest against the wing of Poose's chair. Then Wanda was sitting at the feet of Death, meticulously unraveling the hem of his long dark cloak. She felt his frosty breath raise the coppery wisps of her hair. She knew, even sleeping, that the special feature of dreams is that bizarre goings-on can seem perfectly normal. Still, Wanda couldn't fathom what was compelling her to take apart the cloak of Death. Maybe she thought she could knit him a better one. Poose's theory had been that dreams were the sleeping mind's attempts to untangle the knots of one's waking problems. So maybe the twisted cable pattern in the red cap was begging for a solution. Stitch after stitch unlocked itself from the cloak's edge as Wanda rolled the crinkled black yarn into a ball.

She glanced up into Death's bloodless face to see if she was about to get clobbered. His mouth spread open and thinned the way the skin stretches wide over an old person's teeth when they're close to passing through the veil. When his lips turned up on the corners, Wanda could see he intended it for a smile—it wasn't unfriendly or evil. She had seen old people die. Too many people confused Death and the Devil, as far as she was concerned.

She felt his cold hand on her head. He smoothed the thick orange curls where they'd gotten all matted with napping. Wanda thought of her grandfather in his coffin at the Duvall Funeral Home. The last night of his wake, Wanda's mother had encouraged her to say goodbye, to touch Poose one last time before they closed the lid for good, and when Wanda put her hand on Poose's plastic-looking one, she immediately wished she hadn't. Strangely, she did not mind holding Death's hand now; he seemed in need of companionship, comfort of some kind.

Wanda stood and the two of them proceeded down the main hall to the front door, which they passed through as if it were nothing but air. They strolled around Loretta's perennial beds in the dark. The full moon made the peonies glow like big white bulbs, lighting up the path in an accommodating way.

Wanda murmured, "Really, I ought to wake up," but the dark figure next to her said nothing. Part of her did not want to wake up, not yet.

"What brings you here?" she asked after a polite interval.

"Eet's your *grand-mère*," he wheezed.

She let go his frigid fingers.

"Hold on, hold on." Wanda looked at him with a skepticism some might have found rude. "I never knew Death had a French accent. And besides, my grandmother has been dead thirteen years."

"*La mère de ton père,*" he clarified. "*Le Mort,* he speaks all zee languages, Mademoiselle must know that." He flicked his long cape over his shoulder.

Wanda was not a fan of the melodramatic. She had learned from her mother never to trust pretension in any form. "So old Evelyn Slidell's passing on, is she? I never met the woman, not officially. She refused to have anything to do with us after my father kicked the bucket." Wanda reached down and deadheaded a handful of poppies, throwing the withered blooms onto Loretta's compost heap. Wanda reminded him, as if Death needed reminding, how her father had passed on during the same bitter winter she was born. "I can't even remember getting a birthday card from her."

"*Elle n'a pas une famille,* or no family to speak of, but you," Death intoned mournfully. "When her only child died—*ton papa*—Evelyn shut herself off from the cruel world." He plucked a heavy-headed peony blossom and tweezed the individual petals, letting them fall like snow from his long fingers. He sighed deeply. "There are people who do that, you know, hide behind doors, don't venture out, except for groceries or the occasional movie. They quit trying."

The French accent had waned as he spoke, but Wanda didn't appreciate the preachy tone that replaced it. She stopped in front of a shrubby vine, its dingy purple blooms writhing over the path.

"Look! Deadly Night Shade—one of your favorites," she said to change the subject. She yanked the plant out by its roots, knowing Loretta wouldn't want such an invader in her garden. Could he know about the agoraphobia? Was it possible Evelyn Slidell suffered the same condition as Wanda?

"She wants to see you, *ketsele.*" Death put his long cold arm around her shoulder and pulled Wanda closer.

"Wake up," Wanda whispered, pinching herself. The reek of his breath reminded her of something she couldn't place. An old bouquet of roses, maybe, that should have been thrown out weeks ago.

"Last wish of a dying woman," he said. "That *altercocker* husband of hers—may he rest in a peace he never allowed her while he was alive—wouldn't let her make a single decision on her own. Even the rich have regrets." His bony hands flew around the air in front of him as he talked. "*Bubbeleh*, listen, it's one of the six hundred mitzvoth: When someone asks forgiveness—love, hate, hate, love—you can't refuse them, no matter how *meshuga*." And he raised his flapping cold hands in a hopeless shrug.

"Hold on, hold on—now Death is Jewish?" It was better than the French accent, but still. Cementville's only Jewish family, the Kirshbaums, ran the clothing store on Council Street. The narrow aisles between dress racks and shirt boxes and lingerie provided another place for Wanda to hide, and she sometimes lurked there for the pleasure of listening to the Kirshbaums holler at one another in the stock room. She had picked up a few handy Yiddish phrases of her own, but rarely had the opportunity to put one to use.

"And call me Wanda, *oy gevald*," she ventured.

"Wanda, she's asking for you. Please do come tomorrow at four for tea. Nurse always lays it out proper." The dark stranger clasped his hands under his long chin like an English schoolgirl. "Cakes, crumpets, and lots of sugah!"

"I don't think people in Cementville eat crumpets. Biscuits, yes. Scones and crumpets, no. Do you always get involved in patching things up between people?"

"All part of the job."

They strolled like old companions back to the house and Wanda couldn't help noticing how similar their frames were. They could have been cousins to Oz's lanky Scarecrow. Death left her at the door and she watched him fade off down the road toward town. He looked lonely, stooped, yet at the same time somehow tireless.

She woke in Poose's easy chair around five with a stiff neck. There was a knot in her back and when she reached behind her, she half-expected to find a ball of scraggly black wool. Wanda laughed when she pulled out the familiar red yarn still attached to Valine's little cancer cap.

Out the kitchen window the rising sun lit up Juell Ridge. She put water on to boil for the coffee and before long heard her mother stirring at the top of the stairs. Loretta's lupus was flaring up again, badly this time. Loretta refused to move to the downstairs bedroom, so Wanda held her breath each morning while her mother gripped the banister and crept down the steps sideways like a crab. She thought about not mentioning her plan of calling on Loretta's nemesis of a mother-in-law. But who was she kidding? Lying to her mother, even by omission, was out of the question.

"I think I'll go into town this morning," Wanda said over a bowl of oatmeal. She avoided Loretta's eyes and focused on the cloud of hair. The notorious Ferguson red never quite disappeared. On Loretta, it had become a swirl the color of ripe cantaloupe riddled with silver wire.

Loretta had been a looker in her day, generous of figure and fair in the old Scots way. Wanda's favorite rainy afternoons were spent perusing musty albums stuffed with snapshots, lingering over pictures of her parents on their honeymoon in the Great Smoky Mountains. Even in the black and white photograph, Wanda could see Loretta's long strawberry tresses trailing over Stanley's shoulder as he pressed her in a kiss, his shiny black hair glinting in the sun. It was a secret she kept from her mother, the nearly operatic version of her parents' brief and flaming passion, Wanda's prized creation. She imagined the stranger they asked to click the button on their Brownie Flash, pictured the stranger's smile warmed by Loretta and Stanley's fire, up there in the Smokies. They had run off on Loretta's sixteenth birthday and been married in Gatlinburg, a transgression beyond all forgiveness as far as the bluestocking Evelyn Slidell was concerned.

"Town?" Wanda's mother was a woman of scant words, masterful at getting everything out of her daughter by employing as few syllables as possible.

"Fryers are on sale at the A&P," Wanda said now, "so I was going to stock the freezer. I thought I'd spend a little time at the library, pick up a new novel, some knitting books, maybe. I'm bored with these patterns I've used a jillion times. I'll work my shift while I'm there—Charlene no doubt has several cartloads of books that need reshelving. She never manages to get to them all on her own, you know. Can I get something at the library for you? Oh, and I heard Mrs. Slidell has been sick. I thought I might drop by and see her. And of course I ought to run by the Cahills' house and give June this cap I made for her cousin—remember Valine? Whose hair has all fallen out from the chemo and radiation? You remember Valine. She was two years behind me at Holy Ghost?"

"Mrs. Slidell?"

Wanda knew it wouldn't slip by her mother. Nothing ever did. "I heard she's pretty bad off. I don't know any details, but she's a lonely old woman and I didn't figure it would hurt to let her know somebody cared enough to stop in and say hello. Now that she's going downhill."

"Why?" Loretta set her cup in its saucer without a click.

"I know what you're driving at, Mother. As a grandmother, she has expressed no interest in me, and there's never been any love lost on my part either. But I look at it this way—I could be in her shoes someday. Let's face it, I am no prize. The likelihood of me living out my days alone grows greater with each passing moment. When the time comes that I find myself in Evelyn Slidell's position, you will please pardon me for hoping somebody out there might bequeath a minute of their time to visit a lonely woman passing out of this plane and on to the next."

She helped Loretta get situated with her books and pillows in the front room. Wanda pulled on her summer sweater, a favorite despite the fact that it had shrunk in the sleeves, leaving her wrists gangling a good four inches from the cuffs. "You didn't say—do you want anything from the library?"

"Maybe some Virginia Woolf," Loretta said, and then, in the way she always began sentences of a cautionary nature, "Wanda Ferguson Slidell, that woman is mean."

"For somebody who professes such disdain for the upper classes, you sure are fond of your blue-blood Brit-lit." Wanda grabbed the keys to the Plymouth Fury off their hook by the kitchen door. "And I will don my evil deflectors before entering the dragon's castle, Mother, not to worry."

WANDA SQUEEZED INTO A NARROW parking space at the library, right behind the dumpster, and sat for a good five minutes before the mad rabbit of her heart stopped its thumping. She tied a scarf over her head and pulled a pair of sunglasses out of the glove compartment. It was childish, thinking they protected her. But when she was having a really bad spell, the sunglasses did seem to help. She slipped through the back door into the Saint Brigid College Library and almost ran across the marble lobby to the wide stairs leading to the upper stacks. Charlene Cahill, her friend June's mom and Cementville's lone librarian, waved as Wanda flashed through.

Wanda set aside two lace-knitting books whose patterns she hadn't already plundered, *Best American Short Stories of 1968*, and *The Waves* for Loretta. She busied herself with reshelving until Charlene closed the library at four, then followed her home to the Poplar Bluff subdivision.

Wanda had grown to enjoy visiting with her friend's mom before June's shift at the cement plant ended. Charlene Cahill was a good friend to Wanda in her own right. She was as extravagant with words as Loretta was frugal. Conversing with Charlene required no expenditure of energy or concentration on the part of the other person, so Wanda always brought along her knitting. She got the cable straightened out in Valine's little red cap while Charlene recited the catalog of what all she was planning on putting up from the garden this summer. Wanda pictured the Cahill cellar already bursting with ten years' worth of jarred tomato juice, sauerkraut, and pear butter. June and Charlene lived alone now that Mr. Cahill was gone, so who was going to eat all that? Wanda couldn't find fault with it though. Her own knitting was no different from Charlene's canning. It was what they measured time with. Three afghans, five sweaters, four or five shawls, countless mittens and socks—for Wanda that was a year. For Charlene, a year was thirty quarts of vegetable soup, twenty of grape juice, umpteen pints of apple pie filling.

Wanda had to admit it—they were the same woman. But Charlene Cahill had managed to get married and appeared to be immune to panic attacks.

Half-listening to Charlene, Wanda worked her way to the crown of the cap and thought back to a time when she didn't even know what a panic attack was. She had just turned sixteen and had watched Mem take her last breath.

The night before Mem's funeral, Wanda was in the kitchen putting away leftovers. Loretta and Poose had gone to bed, worn out with the waking. All Poose's and Mem's old friends had gone home, and every surface in the kitchen was covered with casseroles, endless loaves of home-baked bread wrapped in tinfoil, and frosted jam cakes on crystal cake stands. Wanda wondered why people always brought so much food to wakes, when the last thing a grieving person wanted to do was eat. She turned on the radio and waltzed to the table, singing softly with Johnny Cash. She was scraping the last glob of scalloped potatoes out of Charlene Cahill's CorningWare and into the slop bucket when a movement on the other side of the room caught her eye. She turned to see a grisly shadow in the doorway.

"Uncle Angus—" Wanda tried to keep her voice even.

"Sorry about yer granny, girl," he slurred and opened wide the screen door and lurched into the kitchen.

"Everybody's gone to bed. The funeral's tomorrow."

It was general knowledge that Angus Ferguson in his younger days had blacked the eyes of his wife Maddie and daughters, Bett and Arlene, on a regular basis. Broken bones. Other things, never mentioned, in Wanda's presence at least, above a whisper. Her grandparents kept mum regarding the stain of generational violence on the Ferguson name. In fact their connection to the clan was rarely discussed at all, and Wanda was for the most part content to remain ignorant. But a person couldn't help hearing talk in town. She had caught a glimpse once of Angus's hunched-over wife at the Kirshbaums' store. Maddie Ferguson lurched down the narrow aisles with the demeanor of an adolescent girl who'd been suddenly turned into a broken-nosed troll by some witch's curse.

That night in the kitchen, the unkempt old man staggered toward Wanda with his arms spread wide as if gathering in the cloud of his whiskey breath.

"Ah lof yoo lil gurrl," he blubbered, throwing his bulk at her. He fell on top of her, his skull banging loudly against the wall. He pinned Wanda's flailing arms above her head with one big paw and jerked up her skirt with the other.

Suddenly Poose's shotgun divided the narrow space between them, the gun's barrel pressed to his brother's temple. Wanda could see the throb of his blood there.

"Git, Angus," Poose said softly.

Angus Ferguson slammed the screen door behind him and stumbled off into the dark.

Then Mem's funeral. When Wanda fainted at the graveside, people took it as the grief. In the silence around the house over the following days, Wanda began to wonder if it had happened at all, the thing with Uncle Angus, except for the bruises along her knobby spine. She would steal glances at Poose, waiting for him to mention it to her in private, to say something that would ease her fear. He never returned her looks, never mentioned what had happened that night.

Over and over again in the following days she grew dizzy over seemingly nothing. She worried she was losing her mind—the fluttering in her chest, the sudden unbearable perspiration, the pounding in her head. It was months before she could bring herself to tell Loretta about it.

With the help of her mother—and Charlene and June Cahill—Wanda finished out high school, dragging herself through each day in a violet cloud of anxiety. She made it all the way until Poose himself passed on, and then it was as if her last protection was gone. From there, things had only gone from near intolerable to worse.

Wanda sat in the Cahill kitchen with Charlene now, listening to the woman's comforting litany of domestic accomplishments, envying her homey pleasures. June sagged in around four thirty covered in gray dust. Wanda's friend had been lucky—or unlucky, depending on your point of view—to land a desk job at the cement plant. June had been almost pretty once. The walls of the drab Slidell Cement office did not prevent the lime and grit from finding its way into every pore, every fiber of her clothing. She grabbed a Pabst Blue Ribbon for herself and a Grape Nehi for Wanda out of the fridge. They went outside and sank into the swing under Charlene's grape arbor.

"I hear that crazy fuck Carl Juell has been let out of the nuthouse," June said. The smoke from her cigarette curled its fingers into Wanda's nose.

Wanda felt her face flush. This was not a subject she was prepared to discuss. "That was so sad about Jimmy Smith's wife," she said.

"Awful," June said, and pulled long at her bottle of beer. "You think Harlan O'Brien did it?"

Wanda looked at her friend in astonishment. "Of course I don't think Harlan did it! Why on earth would you say that? The poor man can barely string a sentence together, June."

"I heard the DA wanted to arrest him, but Judge Hume put the kibosh on it. War hero and all." June inhaled deeply on her cigarette. "Strictly hush-hush."

"I'm sure the DA wants no such thing." Wanda rolled her eyes, but her friend wasn't looking at her. "Rumor loves nothing so much as filling the void where no story exists." Wanda had her own theories about the Vietnamese woman's brutal slaying but wasn't sure now was the time to mention it. June had stuck by Wanda, in her way, through all the permutations of her condition, had driven her every day of that last miserable year of high school, had encouraged her to apply for the scholarship to Saint Brigid and to finish her bachelor's in linguistics. She had been trying lately to draft Wanda into what passed for a social life in Cementville, which as far as Wanda could see consisted of drinking at Pekkar's Alley, which was no doubt where June got the ridiculous idea that Harlan O'Brien had murdered Giang Smith.

"I should think they'd be looking at Levon Ferguson before anybody else," Wanda ventured.

June stood suddenly and stamped out her cigarette, too close to Charlene's zinnias.

"What?" Wanda said with fake innocence, thinking: So it's true. June's been sleeping with that bucket of scum.

"People need to lay off Levon," June said.

"All right!" Wanda whispered. "Christ on a bike. Somebody would think you were in love with him or something."

"He's not the way everybody thinks he is. He's had a life you wouldn't wish on Satan himself." June sat down and lit another cigarette. She puffed furiously and the swing pitched back and forth with vehemence. "Angus Ferguson, he's the one that ought to be locked up. I can't even repeat the things that pus-bag did to those kids growing up."

"June, you know I don't butt into other people's beeswax, but I wish you'd stay away from Levon. You know he's been two-timing and beating tar out of Ginny since the day they got married, if not before. Besides, I've already got Mother to worry about, I don't need to add you to my list."

"He's getting divorced, for your information." June at thirty was still given to pouts. "Arlene was a fool, letting a man like Angus Ferguson around her children, when she knew good and well—first-hand, in fact!—what he was capable of." June pushed the swing harder and grabbed a fistful of zinnias. As the swing moved forward, she tore off every blossom within reach. She put out a foot and the swing lurched to a stop. "Sorry. Just remembered—they're your relatives. Sorry, Wanda."

"Don't worry about it. Hey, speaking of badly behaved kinfolk, you won't believe where I'm going when I leave here, much less why." Wanda was trying both to change the subject and to recapture the conspiratorial urgency with which she and June used to tell each other things when they were twelve and thirteen, letting it out in a single long breath.

"Go on."

"I'm going to visit old Mrs. Slidell."

"Get out."

"Dead serious!" As soon as she said it, Wanda knew she could not tell June why she was going to visit the grandmother to whom she had not spoken in her entire life. *Oh, Death came by last night and invited me over to my rich evil granny's house for a quick tea party.* June had been her best friend—admittedly, her only friend. There was a time when Wanda could tell June just about anything. Just about. But sharing hallucinatory dreams with another human being is shaky ground, even if you were not already an agoraphobic train wreck.

Of course, Wanda didn't believe it herself. She had waited all morning for the uncanny pull of the dream to leave her, the urgent sense that she was supposed to go and see her estranged grandmother. Estranged would have been putting it mildly. What she felt was a kind of second-hand hatred. The last time they'd laid eyes on each other, Evelyn Slidell had spotted Wanda in the parking lot of the A&P. The old lady turned straight around and hobbled back to her car on Martha Goins's arm, forgoing groceries altogether rather than speak to her granddaughter.

"Why, pray tell?" June sank into her more customary cool indifference.

"Well, I heard she's really sick. She's probably dying, and I'm her only blood relative. I feel bad for her, all alone up there in that big moldy house."

"And there may be some money involved . . . " June rubbed her fingers together and squinted hungrily out of the corner of her eye.

"Don't be absurd. I heard she was sick, that she might want to see me. I am not going to begrudge a simple kindness, June."

"And this juicy lowdown came from . . . ?"

"Talk around town. You know, the kind of thing you overhear in the checkout line."

"You overheard people at the A&P saying that Mrs. Slidell needs her granddaughter—whose existence she has not acknowledged for thirty years—to come hold her hand while she trundles on home to Jesus?"

"Oh, shoot—look at the time! Give my love to Valine." Wanda tossed the little red cap into June's lap and left her in her mother's porch swing, pushing herself with one foot, shaking her head.

THE SLIDELL MANSION WOULD BE imposing in a city of any size. In Cementville, it was a castle. Wanda puttered up the boxwood-lined driveway in Loretta's '61 Fury. The peal of the doorbell echoed from deep in the center of the house. Martha Goins, the nurse from Holy Ghost School, opened the door.

"Wanda! I didn't know Mrs. Slidell was expecting anybody today. Well, isn't this nice. I was just getting her tea tray ready. Come on in, sugar." Mrs. Goins huffed and panted the way big people do with the effort of a string of words.

Wanda stepped into the foyer. A breeze rushed through the front door as though snatching a rare opportunity, setting the crystals in the chandelier tinkling. The familiar smell of old people roused itself, then settled into the corners like a cat declining to be disturbed. She thought of Poose and Mem, the way their clothes, the furniture, the house, came to smell of stale saltines and tea left sitting too long.

"You must think I'm awful, Mrs. Goins. Here it is July, and I never told you how sorry I was to hear about Donnie Ray."

"So horrible, what happened to the little Vietnamese girl, wasn't it?" Martha Goins clasped her hands in front of her and gave the barest hint of a nod to acknowledge Wanda's condolences. She seemed to be staring at the air over Wanda's shoulder as she burst forth with, "And how is that mother of yours?" She turned to the tea tray sitting on a table near the front door, rearranged the cup, the teapot, the budvase, letting Wanda know that grief was a thing one ought not tempt into getting the upper hand.

"Mother is, well, Mother—you know her. Maybe I could pick your brain sometime about how to get her to behave. She won't move to the downstairs bedroom no matter how clearly I outline all the reasons she should. We'd love it if you came by for lunch some afternoon."

"Name the date! I'm always looking for something to do." An unspeakable sadness flitted across Martha Goins's broad face before she pushed on. "Oh, say! Rafe's been talking to Carl Juell about coming on with him in the shop. Weren't you two an item for a while when you were youngsters? I always said it was a shame the way that boy got shipped off to that awful place."

Wanda brushed her finger along the petals of some daisies on the tea tray. "Pretty!" she said, taking her own turn at being cagey.

"Lunch with you and your mother would be nice. Speaking of which, I better not let this tea get cold. Mrs. Slidell hates that. Let me put a second cup and plate on for you. Why don't you go on up. Visitors are not a regular occurrence, as you might imagine. Judge Hume calls every now and again, but even that has dropped off. Poor thing has only me to talk to!"

"I'll wait for you." Wanda followed Mrs. Goins's broad backside out to the kitchen where she fetched an extra teacup, a chipped Limoges, probably once exquisite.

The staircase was one of those broad, carved, mahogany extravagances. Wanda's carefully chosen outfit of khaki skirt and pink blouse was suddenly Eliza Doolittle–shabby. They were halfway along the wide upstairs hall when she heard the furious tinkle of a bell. The rabbit in Wanda's chest thumped a frantic alarm.

"She always seems to know when somebody else is in the house," Mrs. Goins whispered as she swung open the door of Evelyn Slidell's bedroom.

A tiny figure sat in the middle of a four-poster, her gray skin blending with the faded bed clothing, her nearly colorless eyes alert to the intruder. Loretta's stories of the woman's cruelty and arrogance flashed through Wanda's head.

"Look who's here! Somebody has come to see you, just in time for tea!" Martha Goins seemed too cheery, a little too singsong. From everything Wanda had heard, Evelyn Slidell was not the kind of woman who handled condescension well.

"Hello," Wanda croaked, and cleared her throat and hollered, "I don't know if you remember me! I am Wanda Slidell! I am your granddaughter!" She suddenly felt every single one of her seventy inches, a giant freckle-faced tree towering over this dainty bedridden lump of humanity.

The old lady didn't respond; she had eyes only for the tea tray being rested across her lap. She brushed her nurse away as if the two-hundred-pound woman were a bothersome fly. Martha placed the second cup and a plate of biscuits and jam on a Chippendale table that appeared all set to skitter away on its spindly legs. She indicated a brocade chair next to it where Wanda should sit.

Martha Goins mouthed a silent "Good luck," and Wanda was suddenly alone with Evelyn Slidell, who immediately assaulted the tea tray like a ravenous vulture.

"You probably find it odd, me showing up here this way—" Wanda began.

"Stop yelling," she snapped. "*He* sent you, didn't he?"

"He—who?" Wanda tugged at the sleeves of her sweater where her naked wrists kept jutting out.

"Old Man Time," Mrs. Slidell mumbled around a mouthful

of biscuit, "The King of Terrors. Hell's Grim Tyrant. The Reaper. Whatever they call him these days."

Wanda rubbed tight circles around her temples and tried to breathe deeply. She looked at the desiccated human being in the middle of the bed, remembering a superstition that cautioned against speaking the name of Death out loud. This was a mistake, pure folly. The woman was batty.

The crone shoveled jam through her thin slit of a mouth and plunked four or five cubes of sugar into her teacup, gave it a perfunctory stir, and swallowed the whole thing at once. "I've been thinking about it," she said.

Wanda watched a couple of the sugar cubes travel the length of the old woman's craw as she crunched her tea. She cleared her throat to keep her voice from quavering. "I'm sorry—'it'?"

"It. You. You're all that's left, Wanda, sad as that is to admit. You're not much to look at. I was stunning when I was your age. Your parents were handsome people, too. What happened?" She stopped and seemed to be pondering the mystery of Wanda's plainness. "There probably isn't a lot of time left, and some things are best cleaned up for whatever's to come. Now, I understand you're something of a shut-in—"

"I get out. I'm here now, aren't I? I just came from the grocery and the library and—"

"You're a shut-in, Wanda." Evelyn Slidell lifted the cracked teapot. "There's not a lot left, but it's enough to make a difference to someone in your position. The house, of course. Some stocks—a few unfortunately in that worthless junk heap, Slidell Cement. The distillery went public a long time ago—some fellow in Japan probably owns controlling interest now, for all the difference it makes to me. There's some cash. Saint Brigid College is taken care of, of course—although for the life of me, I never did understand why they saw fit to name it after the patroness of milkmaids and bastard children. Prescient, I guess, hmmm?" She stopped and squinted at Wanda. "I suppose I could leave more to charity, but it's been so long since I participated in any of the local causes, much less cared. You can't tell who's crooked these days. I might as well leave it all to you."

"I don't know what to say."

"You don't have to say anything. And besides, it doesn't come without a catch."

"Of course." Wanda forked open a biscuit and slathered it with butter and jam.

"You were an innocent baby, and your poor mother was unfortunate enough to lose her head over my son, bless his drunken soul. I probably shouldn't have taken my grief and disappointment out on the two of you." She waved a limp hand. "Bygones. We're all entitled to a few bygones, wouldn't you agree? And that was a long time ago."

"Excuse me—disappointment?"

"Your mother was a Ferguson. Johnny Ferguson wasn't ever going to amount to anything. Old crooner. The man sang in *lounges*."

"My grandfather was the finest tenor in the county. And he couldn't just sing, he was a fine man, too. He and Mem saved up and bought that farm. With their own sweat. They weren't handed things." Wanda felt the perspiration beginning to prick around the ginger fuzz of her hairline and tried to catch her breath. "He gave the Ferguson name any polish it now has."

"Exactly," said Evelyn Slidell. "You can't polish a turd. But you're missing the point here, girl. You are to be my heir."

"Is this supposed to be some kind of warped apology, Mrs. Slidell? Because my life has been good. Please don't get the idea that your severing all ties with my mother and me has affected my happiness—" A thin trickle of sweat rolled in front of Wanda's ear.

"I make no apologies. This is an amends. Big difference. Didn't they teach you anything at that pathetic excuse for a college? Is that tuition money another total loss?"

"I beg your pardon, ma'am, but I attended college on a full scholarship."

The older woman looked at her with the fake patience people display while waiting for something to sink into the head of a dunce. Wanda shifted on the stiff cushion where she perched like an overgrown bird.

"And you are *Anonymous Donor*, aren't you." Wanda felt thick as a stack of bricks.

"Wanda, I have money, and there's no question it belongs to you. Now you can make this easy or you can make it difficult. When the time comes, you're to go and see my attorney, Alden Wilder." Evelyn Slidell busied herself with what remained of her afternoon snack and seemed to forget Wanda was in the room. A smoky draft wafted from the fireplace. Could the blood in ancient veins really slow to such a pace that a person needed a wood-burning fire in the middle of summer? A mantel clock ticked away at lost time, it too apparently unable to keep up with its immediate surroundings. Wanda looked at her wristwatch and was about to make an excuse to leave when her grandmother became aware again of her visitor.

"Or—" the old woman squinted at Wanda for an uncomfortably long spell. "You can rot out there on Johnny Ferguson's sheep farm and keep that stick up your you-know-what."

"What is it you want from me exactly?"

"Get the hell out of this place, Wanda. Surely there are places you've always wanted to see. I married your grandfather when I was eighteen, and your father came squalling out from between my legs nine months later. I've been withering in this mausoleum ever since."

"So I'm supposed to live the life you didn't."

"But not for me, of course. You're not a hopeless case."

"Well, thanks. I think." Wanda chewed on the inside of her right jaw, screwing her mouth to the left. It was a habit that drove her mother crazy. "What about Mother? She can't get along without me."

"You'll be able to afford a nurse. Martha's schedule will open up before long." Evelyn Slidell laid her head against a tatted pillowcase in practiced exhaustion. "Think of Paris, London, the moors of—where was it the Brontë girls were shut up at—you were a goddamn English major, weren't you?"

"Haworth." Wanda took some needles out of her handbag. "Yorkshire." She cast on twenty-seven stitches in a pink elasticized cotton, soft, not itchy.

"What's that?" The old lady feigned disinterest in the activity in Wanda's lap.

"Creaky house—probably gets drafty," Wanda said. "I can whip out a pair of fingerless gloves for you in no time. Keep your hands warm and still let you hold your tea."

"So. You'll take me up on my offer?"

"This sort of decision requires thought. Knitting helps me think." She was aware of her grandmother studying her. Wanda wondered if the old woman was searching her profile for some trace of her beloved and worthless Stanley.

They let the silence settle around them for a while.

"Hunh. You didn't get *that* from my son. Only kind of thinking he did was with the Little Head." If she was waiting for a reaction from her granddaughter, she got none. "You're not saying you would actually walk away from a fortune that's rightly yours." The old woman appeared to be growing smaller in her bed.

"I'm not saying anything particularly. You haven't paid me any attention for almost thirty years, so it won't kill you to give me a while to chew this over." Wanda finished off the cuff ribbing for the first glove.

"It might," Evelyn Slidell said, and laughed hard enough to make herself cough.


WANDA VISITED THE SLIDELL MANSION several times a week after that. Their chats grew less combative with every meeting. She put off making an answer to her grandmother's offer for as long as possible. The idea of any quantity of money—much less the blurry nightmare images of Wanda herself wandering the dark and winding streets of some medieval city across the ocean—engendered in her chest a sort of breathless excitement and caused a patch of eczema that crept from Wanda's bony ankle to her knee.

But each time she drove down the hill into town, Wanda met with less anxiety. She thought about the mocking dream of the black-caped scarecrow, a specter she almost wished would come back. She wanted him to see her walk right into the grocery store on a whim now and then to pick up a surprise dessert—one of multiple odd little things she found herself doing to placate Loretta, who had grown even more laconic, if that was possible, as Wanda's visits to the Slidell mansion became more frequent. She tried to ignore her mother's pouting, not wanting to be drawn into an impossible quarrel in which she rambled on defensively while Loretta got by with a few precious syllables.

One morning, this was probably after she'd been to visit Evelyn Slidell six or seven times, her mother stopped her as Wanda was heading out the door.

"Leaving?" Loretta said disinterestedly.

"I have some errands in town. Do you need anything?"

"Taking the Fury again?"

"It's the only car we have, Mother."

"I might need it today." Loretta shuffled over to the stove and lit a burner.

"You haven't driven in over three years. Is this about Grandmother Slidell?"

"You're calling her grandmother now?"

"Sometimes. Most of the time I don't call her anything." Wanda waited, one hand on the doorknob, the other on her hip. Her mother didn't respond, and when Wanda raised her eyebrows in question, Loretta waved her out the door. Wanda went out and turned the key in the Fury's ignition. The engine grumbled, then hummed.

Wanda turned the car off. She couldn't drive away knowing Loretta was more than a tad hurt by what must have felt like disloyalty, what with the two of them skinning by on practically nothing all these years while the old dragon sat there in town on a pile of God only knew how much cash—money she intended to leave to them someday anyway. Wanda crossed the side yard and poked her head in the kitchen door.

"Do you want to come with me?" she said as Loretta broke two eggs into a skillet.

Wanda jumped when her mother spun around. "Fetch my sweater," Loretta said.

MARTHA GOINS WAS THRILLED AT the sight of Loretta crabbing up the front steps of the mansion. "Loretta Ferguson! If you aren't looking beautiful as always!" Martha took Loretta's hand and pulled them both toward the huge kitchen that spanned the back of the house. "I have been meaning to get up there to see you all, but it's one thing and then another—oh! But you haven't heard, have you—"

Martha paused and fussed nervously with the pans on the stove, clearly ready to burst. She grabbed a tea towel and hid her face with both hands, weeping quietly into the cloth. "Mrs. Slidell took a bad turn yesterday evening . . . oh, I should have called . . . but I was here until late with Doctor Carruthers, and just dead on my feet when I got home . . . "

"Martha." Loretta put a hand on the woman's arm. "Martha, we don't have a phone."

"I ought to know by now, this happens to old people—I mean, what are you going to do?" Martha shook out and folded the tea towel. Women like Martha were raised to believe there was always something you could do. You got out of bed in the morning and put the best face on the day.

She patted her hair and straightened her skirt, her voice still tremulous when she said, "We lose people . . . "

Loretta rubbed her shoulder. Martha covered her mouth and looked away.

"A bad turn, as in . . . ?" Wanda set on the kitchen counter the jar of apple butter Charlene had given her to take to Evelyn. Everyone in Cementville seemed to know about the town granddame's sweet tooth.

"Doctor Carruthers thinks it may have been a stroke. Mrs. Slidell has given us strict orders—" Martha paused again, her face pinched and red, "—no hospitals. The only other trip she intends to make out of this house is feet first, straight to the Duvall Funeral Home. You all won't mind carrying lunch up to her, will you? She has to be encouraged to eat. Tell her I've got chores . . . "

She let Wanda take the lunch tray. Upstairs, the old lady's reaction to Loretta was more restrained than Martha's had been. Seeing her daughter-in-law's face after so many years seemed to cause Evelyn Slidell to lose her bearings. She allowed Wanda to feed her a few bites, then glared at her to stop, and in minutes nodded off without a word of acknowledgment to Loretta. When she woke, her eyes wandered between Wanda and Loretta.

"You're Stanley's Loretta, aren't you?" she asked Wanda. Her speech was halting, soft and faraway, as if she were trapped inside a box.

"No, Grandmother, I'm Wanda."

Evelyn stared at Loretta vacantly. She looked at Wanda again. "You're Stanley's Loretta, aren't you?" she repeated.

"This here is Loretta, Stanley's wife." Wanda nodded to Loretta, and her mother stepped forward. "You remember her. She's my mother." Wanda had noticed Evelyn repeating herself more lately but had not seen this kind of helpless disorientation.

"Maybe I shouldn't have come," Loretta said.

"No, I think she just needs to sort things out." Wanda took her usual seat on the skittish Queen Anne chair and motioned her mother to its mate on the other side of the bed. The two sat for a long while that afternoon. It was a mostly silent visit, but not unpleasant.

Evelyn Slidell lingered, mute and still, through July and August. Her eyes roved the room, lighting on her few visitors, flashing a startled recognition and just as quickly blinking out. Doc Carruthers said her body had probably been peppered with tiny strokes and grape-like tumors that orchestrated a gradual cutting off of thought and air and blood. Loretta came often with Wanda on her now daily visits to the mansion. Her mother sat on the side of the bed, rubbing lotion into the liver spots on the wrinkled hands, her ancient nemesis rarely conscious in that last week. Several times Wanda came into the room, having gone downstairs to make sandwiches, and found Loretta deep in a one-sided conversation.

The night before her grandmother's death, Wanda dreamed she was standing in the cupola atop the Slidell mansion watching Evelyn's last stroll with her gaunt companion. The two were fading down the street when Death looked over his shoulder at Wanda, his lips contorted in the expression she understood as friendly, perhaps even kind. His long fingers gave a toodle-loo wave. More a gesture of familiarity than a real goodbye.

When Evelyn passed away, Loretta Ferguson Slidell buried choking sobs in the tatted pillowcase next to the old lady's head. Wanda could only imagine that her mother's grief was for unsaid things—not the things Loretta had never spoken to her stone-cruel mother-in-law, but the other way around—that she had come here longing for a few words from Evelyn that would wash away the years of bitterness. In the gulf between the two women hung the memory of a dashing young man with brilliantined hair. Wanda stared out the window while her mother wept for him.

Most of the town turned out for the funeral, not for a surfeit of affection—and certainly not to enjoy the weather, as the August heat had settled into the valley, the long, rain-drenched spring having morphed into a muggy summer—but to pay respects to the end of a line, the last of the small-time robber barons, as close as Cementville was likely to come to having a tycoon of its very own. Led by O'Donahue's patrol car, the cortege snaked its brief way from the Duvall Funeral Home to Holy Ghost Church for the Mass. Malcolm Duvall and his wife and son moved silently about the sanctuary, beckoning in turn to various speakers who rose to the podium to besaint the town's First Lady. Then with a few deft hand motions, Mac herded the crowd to the walled cemetery beyond the church doors.

The cemetery lawn, carefully tended for a century or more by the Knights of Columbus, had been trampled to within an inch of its life by this summer's melancholy parade of traffic. There'd been the seven Guardsmen. Danny Ferguson was buried in the southwest section that nobody called the Potter's Field, though that's what it amounted to, where the poor and the non-Catholic and the unplaceable were given their rest. Jimmy Smith's wife, whose attacker had not yet been found, had been allowed burial in the main cemetery only after Vera Smith, Giang's outraged mother-in-law, threatened to write the *Courier Journal* to expose the town's treatment of her. Even last night, at Evelyn's wake, Wanda heard the whispering, that everybody knew the Vietnamese woman was a Buddhist.

*It's 1969!* Wanda wanted to scream. Perhaps there was something to her grandmother's wish for her; maybe getting out of Cementville, at least for a while, would do her some good. Under a dark green canopy Wanda, in the dress she'd worn beneath her college graduation gown eight years before, sat in the front row of folding chairs draped in black sashes. The heft of Martha Goins's thigh buttressed her on one side, Loretta's brittle frame on the other. Evelyn's coffin lay before them on the contraption that would lower it into the hole, a green cloth tastefully draped over the mound of excavated dirt. Several men who did odd jobs around town had been engaged to fetch the flowers from the funeral home and now the earthen mound was buried in great heaps of gladioli, lilies, and roses. Wanda's unweeping face bloomed crimson then blanched ghostly pale then went to crimson again with the dawning awareness of her new position as official heir. Father Oliver's somnolent voice was reading to them about ashes and dust. The priest seemed to have been rendered listless by the summer's repetition of tracts from the Books of Wisdom and Job and Lamentations. Wanda let her eyes drift over the cemetery lawn studded with stone tablets in shades from white to deep onyx.

She thought once that she saw the lurking figure of Angus Ferguson behind a clump of wild bittersweet, and she shut her eyes. When she opened them again, whatever it was, phantom or pariah, was gone.

# TEN

He had nearly forgotten what it was to be outside on those nights when a person can just about read the newspaper by the light of the moon. And here now Katherine Hume Juell lets him sleep on the screened-in porch that runs along the side of the house, same as he used to every spring, all the way until fall, or until he couldn't feel his feet. Best is when a full bladder wakes him before dawn and he'll stumble out into the yard and stare at the sky all filled with swirling red angels and powdered with a thousand stars. Naturally the Big Entire sees to it that the moon doesn't light the place up every single night of the month, its very preciousness making it the best time of day or night, because that's when the voices in his head settle to soft whispers and seem more concerned with naming planets and stars and nocturnal creatures than with ordering the likes of Carl Juell around.

He has long since quit apologizing for the voices, but he doesn't go around talking about them very often either, since mention of it runs the risk of people jumping to conclusions: Oh, he's psychotic or schizophrenic or what have you. Carl doesn't waste his time or theirs, trying to disabuse people of that notion. At least his voices take turns. It can be crowded in there, but it's reasonably orderly.

"Write it down, Uncle Carl," his niece Maureen is always saying, "maybe these characters have stories to tell." But Carl knows he would be doing nothing but sitting around writing stuff down all the time, once he got started. Maureen knows crazy and not crazy. "You just have a creative mind," she says. Maureen is very smart for thirteen.

Carl is beginning to be glad his brother's wife said yes, at least he is pretty sure she said yes, when the people at Eastern State Hospital suggested that Carl come live with them. Carl lived at the hospital a long time—not for as long as he can remember, as some people say, but only since right after his and Willis's father went off to the barn and swung himself on a rope over to the Big Entire, which is plenty long enough ago.

The people at Eastern State, now *they* were crazy. The ones that could not perform chores on the hospital grounds drooped in big circles around the walls of the Day Room, forgoing the tables of bead stringing and jigsaw puzzles. When they managed to steal outdoors they continued with their circling. They could be found wandering in the woods barefoot at the very edges of the hospital grounds, as if they were being paid to measure out the tall chain-link fence. Carl does not often allow himself to think about them wandering the borders of the property that way, because it makes his feet hurt to remember his own wandering. He does not like to think about walking the blacktop over near Shakertown, miles from the hospital, with feet so cold he may as well have had knives laid blade up inside his slippers. When his feet went from violent hurting to being free of all feeling, the hills around him began to fade, and the air went so white there was nothing but the absence of all color crawling down his throat and suffocating him from the inside out. He was sitting on the sheer limestone palisades overlooking the Kentucky River when they found him. The hospital people said he was missing four days, although Carl believed they exaggerated.

For Carl it ran together into one single long white night with black edges that curled in like bony fingers, like Cathy Earnshaw scratching on the window glass, crying *Heathcliff! Heathcliff!* It was the harshest December on record, the hospital people said. They said it was a miracle Carl did not die of exposure. After that it took a long time for things to get right again.

But now he lives out here with Willis and Katherine and Billy and Maureen, and he is good. Forty-two whole days he has been here and not a single episode. He won't wander again because he does not want Willis to decide he is crazy. He does not want Willis to decide this is all a bad idea, allowing Carl to sleep here in the same house with his and Katherine's children.

Oh, Carl does thank the stars that he is not crazy.

They had tried to teach him to pray in the hospital but he chose not to pin down an Almighty, because Carl did not particularly want to draw the attention of anything powerful enough to hold all this flotsam together. He secretly believed most people were foolish to assign names to such a force. As far as Carl was concerned, it was a thing too large to fit inside a name, although in his head he called it the Big Entire.

The day Carl was dismissed, Doctor warned the family that schizophrenia is a disease your mind keeps telling you you do not have, which is why people stop taking their medication. He spoke to Carl and Willis and Katherine very slowly, as if they were children. "It's more common than you might imagine," Doctor said. "We think perhaps one in a hundred people have the disease." Which Carl thought was pretty scary. You could bump into any of these nut jobs at any turn in the road. Carl knows he is not supposed to call sick people nut jobs. They were always reminding him of that at Eastern State. Doctor said that scientists thought maybe it had to do with a person's dee-oxy-ribo-nucleic acid. Then too there was a study that said if a woman had the influenza when she was pregnant, that might be what caused the illness, or if she took too much aspirin or if— But what was the sense thinking about the odds of all the stuff that can happen to you when you haven't even been born yet, that's what Carl was thinking—and perhaps Willis was thinking the same, because he interrupted Doctor and said that it didn't matter now what caused it, we are family, end of story.

Now Carl has a job, a real job, not just raking and sweeping, although sometimes sweeping. He started last week with Rafe Goins, part-time three mornings a week with the A-number-one best auto-body shop in all of the county, maybe even the state if you believe the Yellow Pages. It was a job Rafe had been saving for his son Donnie Ray, but now Donnie and his dress uniform are rotting in the ground over at Holy Ghost Cemetery, his name on a brass plaque at the new veterans' park next to the distillery.

Last Monday, while Carl and Rafe extracted parts and pieces from Willis's Hupmobile that got ruined when a tree fell on Willis's machine shop, Rafe told Carl his life story.

"Everybody's got a story, Carl," he said. Rafe said he had started on at Slidell Cement at sixteen, when the plant still employed a couple hundred people. "Everybody said how lucky I was to get on, seeing as they were cutting people right and left. Robots." Rafe made a disgusted face. "Robots'll ruin this country, Carl, you heard it here. Let me tell you, I was a caged animal. Got drunk every weekend. Started to have run-ins with the law every time I turned around. This was before Martha, of course."

Rafe quit talking and after a long silence, Carl decided that story-telling was not Rafe's strong suit. He watched Rafe move in and out of the guts of the Hupmobile like a surgeon set on cleaning the cancer out of a human being, even talked to it every now and then, half apologetic, as if the car was an elderly lady he was trying to make comfortable. Carl stood by with plenty of rags and a bucket of naval jelly and cleaned the parts as Rafe handed them to him.

They stopped for lunch and Carl ate the sandwiches Martha Goins would have been making for Donnie Ray if he had come home from the war breathing instead of in pieces. Carl had all but forgotten the thread of Rafe's life story, when Rafe started in again.

"Well, after one particularly bad scrape with the law, I landed in the state pen. You probably remember that, Carl, you were still around then. Three years stamping out license plates. Heh heh, there you go buddy, you and me both can relate to that locked-up, bat-shit feeling. You know what I'm talking about!" He jabbed Carl in the ribs, and Carl realized Rafe was drunk. "Anyway, I got out, and my daddy sent me to a trade school in Tennessee. Eventually I came home, opened a little shop." Rafe looked around him at the orderly, if a bit dank and greasy, building. The expression on his face was one of mild surprise. "And I commenced to build a name for myself. This here is a business that is the envy of many a local man." He handed Carl a chrome-plated wheel disc. Carl polished it until he could see his own ungrinning face. He thought briefly about his father stand-ing in the barn whistling, saying he never thought he would see the '33 Victoria looking so fresh. Carl's father and his uncle had maneu-vered the Hup around gravel roads and up and down Council Street when they were young men on the prowl.

Carl and Rafe catalogued and labeled each piece of the auto-mobile, and Rafe took out an advertisement to sell the parts in the *Hemmings Motor News*. The money didn't mean near to Willis what the car did. But Rafe Goins delivered the Hupmobile Victoria a death with dignity, improving upon the death-by-lightning ending to the car's own life story.

"It is service that really makes a business," Rafe told Carl. "Don't ever forget that. Customer satisfaction."

Carl had to agree. Not every auto-body man knows that. People trust somebody that would take particular care with what other folks might regard as another useless heap.

Take Harlan O'Brien, Carl thought as he polished the parts. The town hero had not come home in quite the shape people needed or expected him to be. People didn't get Harley. The only person who seemed really comfortable around Harlan O'Brien was Carl himself. It was a puzzle for a while, why he and Harlan got along so well. Carl could see how, when Harley first came back, everybody was in his face. Naturally they meant well, people trying to get him to talk the way they will. *How had he been caught? Did the gooks torture him? Was there really such a thing as phantom pain when you get something cut off? And what about the rescue, the Special Forces' blazing guns, and all that?* They thought they were just being sociable and concerned, kind of a mixture of pity and hero worship. Carl recognized the looks on their faces, from long stares to secretive glances to bald scrutiny. The same way they looked at him. Behind the scrim of friendly curiosity, people were fearful Lieutenant Harlan O'Brien might pull a knife on them or commence with maniac shrieking at the drop of a pin. They had heard all about shell shock and were waiting—hoping?—for something big to happen. But Harley had neither use nor need for their compassion and their flattery. They caught his drift quick enough and eventually did leave him alone.

Now, some of them had gone so far as to suggest Harlan O'Brien was capable of worse than flying off the handle. Willis's son Billy has told Carl of big talk at Pekkar's. *He's too good for us,* people said. Some were throwing around accusations. When they got drunk enough they made loud demands for an arrest. *Gook woman or no,* they said, *murder's murder.* Some of them wanted to see blood. Levon Ferguson egged them on.

Carl and Harlan had been in school together, but they weren't what you would call friends. Things felt different now though, and Carl burned with a tiny flame of hope that he had finally found someone to talk with about his theories.


Last Sunday Harlan showed up at the Juell house in his father's truck, wondering would Carl want to go for a drive with him. As the two of them rode deep into the forest covering the eastern part of the state, Carl got the sense Harlan O'Brien was looking for something. Before long he figured out that it was big trees, the ones old enough and tall enough to dwarf the rest of the forest canopy.

Carl admired Harlan's knack for picking the finest specimens. Harlan said sitting under big trees helped him leave behind all the noise.

*What noise is that?* Carl wanted to say, but he was pretty sure he already knew. Carl suspected he wasn't the only person with a boatload of blabbering going on inside him at any given moment. It was quiet there in the hills under the trees, but he wasn't sure whether any place was quiet enough for minds the likes of his and Harlan's. He did not care whether Harley's voices were the result of a shitty prison camp in a faraway jungle or if they were the kind that might be located in a fancy psychiatrist's notebook. He had not an ounce of envy for Harlan O'Brien. At least the voices in Carl's head spoke English.

They located an obscure trailhead deep in the woods. Harley pulled his father's farm truck off in a pillow of dust and turned off the ignition, keys jangling. Lemuel O'Brien had paid Rafe Goins to rig the farm truck with hand controls for his son so that he could operate the vehicle, what with the special fake foot and all.

Carl read the Forest Service sign. LOST MAN TRAIL, it said. They had traveled seventy or eighty miles and were at the northwestern edge of Daniel Boone National Forest. *Lost Man Trail—what are we doing here?* was what Carl wanted to know, but that was not the kind of question you asked somebody like Harlan O'Brien. Carl kept his face blank—a skill he had perfected at the hospital—so as not to give away his trepidation. Harley squinted at him, regardless of Carl not having said a word, and swung his stump down. He reached around and pulled his left foot off the jump seat behind him and strapped it on. They commenced walking.

They maintained silence a good distance up the trail, stopping occasionally to reconnoiter. Turkey vultures circled the cloudless sky over the valley. Carl cleared his throat, a bit too loudly. He swallowed big.

"I don't always trust what I see in Nature," he said. "It's worth taking the time to make sure what you're seeing is Nature making the choices, and not some A-hole from Texas draining Her blood and trying to pass it off as 'stewardship' or 'conservation.' Daddy taught me about that kind. He said you might as well accept there has always been greed, people stripping this and that out of the Earth. All of us share the guilt. The metal it takes to make a car, for instance, or wood for a house. But that doesn't mean I have to like it. I accept that. I am not stupid. I went to school, not as long as some, but I know some things." Carl glanced over at his companion. There was no way to tell if Harlan was getting the drift. He sucked in some more air and went on.

"Take a for-instance. Doesn't it wrench you to watch a starling pester a downy woodpecker to death and finally throw that poor thing out of her nest and then stomp her eggs and throw her bald-headed babies on the ground to rot by their mama's carcass? Some will say, *Well, that's Nature for you!* But starlings are not natives to this place. Man in his infinite wisdom imported those thieving winged rats here from England." He shut up for a bit, huffing some with the increasing arduousness of the climb. They rounded a bend. Before them lay a vista that made them stop. Carl put a hand on Harlan's shoulder and spread his other arm, an embrace of the desolation below and about them, a fresh clear-cut hacked into red-brown hillside ripped and ridged by rain. Laid out wide like a young girl left behind by a gang of rapists.

"All that soil will soon run into the creek and off to the ocean far away from here. Those red roads you see slashed across there like streaks of blood," Carl whispered, "they cut across the state. I hear they're hauling off the tops of whole mountains." His voice had taken on the tone of a so-called man of the cloth he'd heard under a tent once when he was a boy. "You don't have to look too close to see the difference. You wonder: Is it Nature doing the damage to herself, or is it fellers in some big skyscraper in Houston looking for coal or sometimes what they're calling shale oil, or is it—" This was the part Carl hated. "Sometimes you got to look in the mirror and ask, *Is it us?*"

Harlan, silent, had his eyes pinned on something straight ahead, which Carl took as a motion to continue.

"That's preaching though, and I'm no preacher. I don't go in for God and the hereafter and whatnot, and whether or not we get multiple cracks at this mortal coil. I just know things. Harlan, I'll say this about that and then I'm done." Carl swallowed hard again and licked his lips. "There are all these highways everywhere out there in the air, see, layers upon layers of them, all at once going in every direction, connecting all our heads. Whizzing through every time and every age. In the top of all our heads there's this invisible hole, tiny as a pinprick. Once in a while, some soul pulls off the highway and takes a sharp left-turn detour down the hole. The soul didn't choose you necessarily, although sometimes I wonder about that part. Maybe I've got a flashing neon sign saying, *Eat at Carl's!! Stop in for Good Food!! Last Chance!!* The soul pulls off. Me, I've come to expect these visitors. Everybody's bound to have them, the way I figure. They just don't talk about it. Afraid of people thinking they're crazy. So mostly I keep my mouth shut too."

And for the moment, Carl did. He'd gone on longer than he intended. He would keep his mouth shut and let this information sink into his friend's poor addled brain and hope it gave him some relief. They walked for what to Carl seemed an eternity, even with his two working legs. A red-tailed hawk swooped across the trail not two feet in front of them, and they sucked in a breath at the same time, then laughed and shook their heads.

When Harlan was ahead of him by several paces, Carl heard him say, "Roy Stubblefield had it coming, Carl." A minute or two went by, and Carl began to think that perhaps it was not Harlan who had said it at all, because the sentence repeated itself in his head several times.

They broke for bologna and tomato sandwiches under a white oak maybe seventeen feet around. Three men holding hands in a ring would have had a hard time encompassing it. Harlan took a parcel of wax paper out of his knapsack and unwrapped a handful of Oreos. The two men grinned when both of them twisted the black cookies apart and scraped off the white cream with their teeth.

"You're wrong about that last part," Harlan said. Carl was taken aback by the tone of certainty in his newfound friend's voice. "I don't think everybody hears them."

They spoke little the rest of the day except to mark a particular plant or bird or track.

"Skunk cabbage," one would say.

"Solitary vireo," the other would say.

"Polecat."

"Yellow warbler."

"Dogtooth violet."

They managed the entire drive home in a comfortable hush. Music rolled over them from the car radio as they headed into the sun that evening. It was good having somebody that understood you. Best thing for people like Harley and me, Carl thought, is to get out where the voice of the Big Entire, or whatever the hell it is out there, gets louder than all the ones inside a body's skull. Find the tallest knobs with the tallest trees where the only voice we can hear is the one that says, *You don't belong here! Go on back to your ridiculous crackerjack box with its power lines and its refrigerator hum and its doors closing one room off from another.* A voice that lets you know there's no such thing as making sense of it all.

Carl decided to say one last thing when he got out of the truck that night, lightning bugs flaring off and on over Katherine's vegetable garden.

"Nature talking to me doesn't make me grind my teeth," he said. "She has a right to her opinion. And as for the voices, well, they mean no harm."

"Hard to tell sometimes though, isn't it?" Harlan said as he shut the door.

Carl watched Harlan's taillights disappear across the narrow ridge road over to the O'Briens' place, where he imagined his friend stretching out on the floorboards, dreaming himself back to his little bamboo box in the jungle.

# ELEVEN

Dusk. Nimrod Grebe floats near the ceiling, circling like a hound that cannot find a resting place, watching the blood pour out from a hole in the shoulder of the broken-down mess of a man sprawled on the floor below. He had not thought things through. Had not counted on missing his head, big old thing, head so big it was hard to find hats to fit it. Most of all he had not counted on Bett Ferguson's children being the first ones to run up on his porch and look in through the screen and find him there, his blood mixing with the spilt cup of Heaven Hill. Worse, he has soiled himself.

In the years since Nimrod returned to Cementville (it was Taylortown he was returning to, really, not to put too fine a point on it) to live in his dead mother's house, he has watched the neighborhood go downhill, from a reliable bunch of hardworking colored sharecroppers to successive clans of white trash who hollered and fought one another all hours of the day and night. Recent years, Nimrod watched from his front porch as Bett Ferguson's five, six, seven children (he could never be sure how many there were) ran around the yard in their altogethers, white moon bottoms shining, lawless innocents climbing his crabapple trees and terrorizing God's creatures with the hard green fruits. Sweet, really, but wild, just wild, having no daddy. Bett Ferguson, she's all right though. How often Nimrod has stopped to visit when, at the end of the day, Bett props her swollen feet on a raggedy ottoman on the front porch. She has been nothing but kind to him, giving him rides to town, sharing big hunks of government cheese and whatnot. All he has to give is a few eggs from his banties, knowing full well she's got chickens of her own.

"The kids love them little banty eggs," Bett always tells him. She asks after his health. It's been a long time since anybody else did that.

"I got a dirty liver, Bett," Nimrod tells her, shaking his big head.

"Here's some tomato juice I just put up," she'll say. "I got too much. It'll spoil if you don't take it off my hands."

Nimrod brooks no judgment for poor Bett, daughter of that scoundrel Angus Ferguson who rode with the Klan. Her nephew Levon, now he is another matter entirely. Hellhound. And Nimrod knows from hellhounds.

It galls Nimrod that Levon's face is the one that comes into focus now. Galls him so badly that the part of him floating against the ceiling drops suddenly to the floor and nestles itself, glove-like, back into his body, like some kind of charism inhaling the hot breath of God.

Levon rips the blue tape from Nimrod's left hand and sniffs at the sippy cup. "I tell you what, boys," he says to the silent children, their eyes wide, "that is one bad-smelling highball." And Levon throws Nimrod's cup out the window.

O'Donahue pulls up in his cruiser, big hell-colored light swiveling round on top like an evil eye. Bett must have got ahold of him. Sheriff figured on finding a dead body, because he picked up the coroner, Tommy Thompson, on his way out here to Taylortown. Malcolm Duvall from the funeral home pulls in behind the squad car. Duvall's long black hearse doubles as the only ambulance for miles around, always rolling onto the scene whenever there's trouble of a potentially mortal nature, its nearly silent V-8 engine gliding in like a vulture.

"Get back, kids," O'D says. "Levon, what the hell you think you're doing? This here's a crime scene. Get those children out of here." Malcolm and Tommy finagle the gurney onto the porch and through the door.

"He dead?" somebody says.

"Naw, more's the pity," Levon says. "What's that blue stuff?"

"Blue?" Tommy says. Tommy Thompson has been county coroner so long that when he kicks the bucket himself, people will not be able to fathom anyone else filling the slot.

"All over his hand there . . . "

"Holy Mary," O'Donahue says and lets out a long whistle. From Nimrod's hand he wipes off blood that has already begun to thicken and turn black. Nimrod watches the sheriff's face change as he figures out what is strapped to his hand with bright blue tape.

"I bet that's his old war pistol." Tommy whistles too. "I always took Nimrod for a happy man," he says, as if Nimrod is indeed dead and not laying right there staring up at him.

"We cannot know a man's insides," Duvall the undertaker murmurs profoundly.

Well, if that isn't divine revelation, Nimrod would say to Mac Duvall, were he not too weak to speak. Sheriff O'Donahue and the coroner and the undertaker all seem to receive his thoughts, the way that woman on television talks about reading minds, because they all look at him at the same time.

"Nimrod, what on God's sweet earth were you meaning to do?" the sheriff whispers with that familiar mix of condescension and magnanimity and tired patience, as if Nimrod is a child and not a soldier once, of the 369th Infantry of the 93rd Division, who had received France's Croix de Guerre for holding a line west of the Argonne for over a month, all before Mickey O'Donahue was even born.

"Can you tell us who taped this pistol into your hand?" O'D is hollering at Nimrod now, assuming as so many do that the old and the helpless are also deaf.

Nimrod looks the other way while the three men hold their breath against the stench and, *With a one, and a two, and a—*lift him onto the gurney they have dragged in through the door. Mickey O'Donahue, poor excuse for a sheriff, forgets and leaves Nimrod's old World War I pistol lying under the overturned lounge chair.

"If he needs finishing off," Levon starts to say outside, where he is leaning against the hearse. He shuts up when O'D glares at him. Levon squints at Nimrod lying there on the stretcher and smashes out his cigarette on top of Nimrod's mailbox. The hearse is gliding away, and Nimrod cannot stop staring—it is as though Levon Ferguson has, with his dark gaze, snared him in some evil thralldom.

Nimrod closes his eyes and hears his mother praying far off for the Lord to have mercy on her wretched son.

IF A MAN SUCH AS Nimrod kept a diary, a little hardback book with fake leather binding, if the sheriff and the coroner and the undertaker had come across such when they found him, it could have told of what led to that day. Show them what they know about happy.

What they found instead was a shoebox full of palm-sized notepads, the kind that always end up with a wire crooked out from the corner ready to gouge a hole in your breast pocket. A person doesn't necessarily think, jotting down Scripture or recording a prayer he hopes might save his sorry soul, that such entries will be gazed upon by others as the writings of a man hopeless enough to commit (and worse, fail at) the final sin of despair.

Mac Duvall had it right: One person can't know the things another person is wishing for, the dull little stones clutched under his rib bone, trusting they will turn to pearls someday. There are people who will borrow your hopes, thinking maybe they can turn your straw into gold. You can never be sure what's guiding such people.

*—In the evil land, please stay Your hand, give us righteousness that we might stand. Your hand shall wave from sky to*

*sky, when You come to claim the apple of Your eye. When the evil one marches on the land, marches to deceive, who will stand?*

Madeer, Nimrod's own mother, mumbled such prayers through the steam rising from her ironing board. Thump, thump, the iron would complain over white shirts, piles of them that never grew smaller. She prayed into a cloud of flour while her big brown arms flung their flesh above a rolling pin. She prayed while she cut round hunks of white dough and threw them into the bacon grease. She squinted and prayed into the sizzle and pop.

The two of them would recite the grace and eat in silence, the lamp flame flickering on the wall. Then she would tell him the Bible stories in the dark. This was when Nimrod was small.

She told him about Nimrod the warrior rebel who came from the seed of Noah. He was a filthy wicked man, she said, a mighty tyrant.

Nimrod the boy lay on his cot straight as a stick and pulled his cover to his chin. "Why you name me after such a wicked man, Madeer?" he asked her.

"So you never forget the sin of Adam you carry, just like old Nimrod. I name you that so God keep His eye on you. I name you that so you wake up every morning and ax Him to rain His grace on your wicked soul. His grace is out there, boy, and He give it to those that ax Him for it." His mother rocked back and forth on the end of Nimrod's cot and sucked at her bottom lip and looked off beyond him as if considering what ghosts lurked there in the dark. She said, "Your name make the Lord nervous. He don't forget that other Nimrod, who built the Babylon tower. He watch you, and He want you to be good. He don't want to have to divide all the languages into seventy-two pieces again. We can't halfway understand each other now, when we supposed to be speaking the same language." Her shoulders shook with a laugh that had no sound. She would always end the night goo-goo-gah-gahing at her boy same as she had when he was a baby, hoping to make him snigger after she scared the drawers off him with her Bible stories. She would tickle his feet under the covers and say, "Don't worry, boy, God got His eye on you. You the apple of God's eye, Nimrod."

Which was small comfort in the dark with a broken-hearted whippoorwill mourning lost love through the shivery glass of the window by his bed.

Nimrod never did forget what Madeer told him. He asked for grace to rain on him, and when he found himself in flood, he sang His praise. And when he found himself in drought, he examined his conscience for what slight he might have committed.

As a young man Nimrod went off. He wandered the land, worked for his food. He served his country without ever once killing a man that didn't need it. And he was never hungry.

Got to where he was always thirsty though, rain of grace or no. At night alone in whatever four walls made home, Heaven Hill rained down his throat and the closest he came to wickedness was to laugh in the face of God. He swam in John Barleycorn's pond and felt the same rapture the saints felt when they were tied to the whipping post.

Last job he had was hod carrier. His bricks built a bank tower in the center of a big city up north. It might have reached Heaven, for the ones who had the most money piled inside there. Nimrod worked until his spine hunched and ripped and burned, and when he learned his Madeer had passed through the veil, he crawled his way back to the place he was born. Knees all turned to gravel and stretched out rubber bands by then.

Most days found him after that on his porch from midday till the sun slipped behind the knobs looming over him like a pyramid made up of God's minions, and him no more than a decrepit student of the Bible, clucking and acting the old woman, quoting Job and Numbers, Esther and Judges, same as if Madeer haunted his insides. Sundown, he closed the brittle leather cover on her Bible, placed it on his bed-side stand, and took up his rock and his friend, his Heaven Hill. Just a smallish tumbler-full, he told himself each night, knowing there was not a soul around to give him Hell when he lost count.

Things went that way till the girl showed up.

THERE WAS MAYBE A QUARTER hour of light left. Fingers of sun glanced off the knobs to the west, the kind that stab at your eyes and make a person think of angry red seraphim lifting the hills and flinging them at their adversaries, the foot soldiers of the Evil One, like in that Heavenly battle, where God told Lucifer, *Go then, my bright and fallen son!*

That was when she first came. Nimrod heard her before he saw her, a tinkly voice circling around her like a body of bees. First she was a silhouette far up Crooked Creek Road, her boy hips waltzing with brazen importance. Then he could make out her finely muscled arms twirling a stick around her head, tossing it in the air periodically, her knees kicking above her belly as she high-stepped up his road. He squinched his eyes at her, a warning. She stopped in front of Bett Ferguson's and called out.

"Aunt Bett!"

Out came Bett on her porch in a swarm of children and the two bantered back and forth. Nimrod cocked his head at an angle as if to catch the June breeze, but it did nothing to aid him in making out their words. He fastened on Bett's smoky drawl. She seemed glad to see the girl.

In his head he hollered out to Bett, *Don't!*

She was some kind of snake charmer, with that high tinkle voice. Nimrod did not trust that girl. Nor did he appreciate her cutting through Crooked Creek to get from the Chaney Farm, where she did odd jobs and looked after those sickly boys, over to her granddad's trashy trailer. No reason she had to cut through this road when there was a perfectly good path, and shorter. Bett ought to tell her dirty little niece to jump in that creek, that's what Nimrod thought, maybe wash some of the trashiness off her filthy young soul. She came closer and he could hear the song she sang, one of those terrible songs they play on the radio. He scooted his chair back all cattywompus, upsetting the notepad where he recorded highlights of Scripture. The corner of his eye caught the glow of her white ankles clomping up and down in cheap tennis shoes all smashed down at the heels. She high-stepped straight at him, twirling that stick like it was a sterling silver baton.

She slowed down and called out, "Hey, Mr. Nimrod, how you doing this afternoon?"

He dipped his head close to the Scriptures in his lap and ran his hand over his forehead beaded with salt pearls. *You pretend not to hear,* Spirit told Nimrod. Galatians 4:14: *My temptation, which was in my flesh, ye despised not, nor rejected; but received me as an angel of God.*

Rex, the yellow cur belonging to the Ferguson children, had been sleeping in the middle of the road. He got up and slinked off to the woods. Rex is a superstitious dog, wise to evade her. She stopped square in front of Nimrod's house, and all lazy, brushed the top of his mailbox with her stick till he felt it crawl across his own skin. He couldn't help it, he had to look.

She up-arched one tweezed eyebrow, a crooked twig flicked toward the sky, and she said, "We been given another beautiful spring day, ain't we, Mr. Nimrod?" like God had made it that way just for her.

Then she did it. She let her head fall back between her shoulder blades—that girl could not care less if it fell plumb off—and she opened her mouth and let out a laugh from the bottom of her gut, rumbling all the way up her white neck. No reason, nothing funny, no good reason at all to laugh. Nimrod dipped his face low. When she gathered her head onto her shoulders and got her breath again, he could feel her looking at him. He knew without taking his own two eyes from the Good Book that she was studying the top of his silver head.

"You have a wonderful rest of the day, Mr. Nimrod." Then she commenced to hum, threw that stick high in the air, end over end. She caught it, perfect.

The laugh-out-loud girl went on, calling out to Jesse Greathouse and the other old people. Nimrod stood from his chair to stretch, and when he leaned out over the railing he was able to watch her progress down Crooked Creek Road. She would come this way tomorrow. And the next day.

AND SHE CAME BACK, AND was soon passing this way every day except Sundays when her granddaddy, old Angus Ferguson, made her pull three Plymouth Rocks from the coop behind his trailer and wring their skinny necks. She chopped off their heads and let those chickens run in headless circles till they couldn't. After the slaughter she dipped them in a scalding bucket and plucked them and cut them up and rolled them in salted flour and fried them in the same manner her granny had before Angus lamed that poor woman's arm. Their neighbors would smell the chicken shit and the blood and the horrible boiling feathers all week while Angus Ferguson gnawed on the chickens' bodies from one Sunday to the next.

"Mr. Nimrod," the girl would say, "in my fifteen years I've wrung too many necks." These are the kinds of things she told him, standing at his mailbox.

She had been coming down Crooked Creek Road for three weeks, stopping and talking to everybody in that tinkly voice. Each time she stopped in Nimrod's yard she came closer to his porch. Finally, up she came on the middle of three steps to where he could smell her girl smell. She took off one of those stomped-down shoes and shook it till the insole fell out all filthy and wadded up and he couldn't help it, Nimrod said, "You need to throw them things away."

He should not have opened his mouth. Because she drew that stinking wad to her nose and said, "Pee-yooo-weee!" And threw her head back all crazy again, making him think it's going to fall straight off her long chicken-white neck and roll out into the road. Even though he knew by then it wouldn't, having seen her laugh in that fashion twelve, thirteen times already. She took off the other shoe and pulled out the insole and threw both of them over her shoulder and she said, "Mr. Nimrod, I been thinking, I been thinking you might need you a cook."

Revelation 3:10: *And the Lord said, I will keep thee from the hour of temptation, which shall come upon all the world.*

"Maybe somebody to clean your place," she went on. "Sweep, odd jobs, whatnot." She came right up onto the porch and peeked in through the screen door. "It's a nice place you got here, Mr. Nimrod."

Then she walked, by God, into his very house. He sat there on the porch, a stone figure. He could hear her moving around inside. She was in there a long time, clanging things around, scraping chair legs across the floor, whistling like a man.

He got up and went to stand at the screen door, looking at her moving about among his things.

"If you looking for money, you barking up the wrong tree," Nimrod said.

She spun around on him and her smile was so big it hurt.

Nimrod sat heavily in his porch chair and opened his mother's Bible and flipped through the filmy pages looking for the line about suffering the children. The girl came out humming a song he thought he recognized.

"Long as you not expecting anything," he said. But she skipped down the steps and proceeded up the road. Only that tinkle of laugh as an answer. He went inside and checked to make sure, but nothing was missing.

Thursday was the day she settled on as cleaning day, as if it was a thing upon which they had reached agreement. She would greet him and Nimrod would bury his face deeper in his reading. Before dark she would come out on the porch and say, "Well, she's good as new. The place is clean as a baby's powdered butt." She would put both arms round his shoulders and squeeze hard enough to stop up all the air in him and then clomp down the steps in those smelly stomped-down shoes. When Nimrod was sure she was far away, he would look around him as if some spell had been lifted, and he would go inside the clean house where she had left for him a plate of beans and that scent of cinnamon and sweat.

What kind of name is that anyway, he would think to himself. Augrey.

Fourth Thursday she came and he was already inside his house. He had latched his screen door against Bett's ragamuffins annoying him. Nimrod sat eating yesterday's greens in front of the television set. A man moved across a stage with a microphone, telling sick people to stand and be healed. The laugh-out-loud girl tapped on the window screen.

"Mr. Nimrod, I'm here to sweep up, dust."

He startled up and lightning shot across his eyes and he fell not unlike a great tower himself, straight to the floor. A light like a blast at the temple, his body suddenly all rigid, then just as quick, numb. Through the screen door, Nimrod could see her feet outside on the porch and she pulled and screamed like a banshee at the door. She smashed that screen straight through with her fist and lifted the latch and came in. She pulled him out straight as a board, cradled his head.

"Don't you worry, Mr. Nimrod, I'll get somebody to help us."

Maybe his ears, like his legs, were failing him, but he thought he heard the girl sobbing.


WHEN THEY HAULED HIM HOME from the VA, there she was in his house. Two orderlies carried him inside and Augrey Ferguson pointed them to an aluminum chaise lounge she had unfolded and placed by the window. They laid Nimrod down in it and she messed about, covering him with a light summer quilt he recognized as one Madeer had pieced for him when he was a boy. It was freshly laundered and gave off the smell of new-cut grass. When Augrey turned to deal with the blue-uniformed lady who had followed them in, Nimrod noticed flecks of dried grass scattered over the quilt. The girl must have hung it on the porch rail to dry, then mowed his patchy dirt lawn. Borrowed her Aunt Bett's lawn mower, no doubt.

"Sure is nice your *niece* can sign the papers for you to go home, Mr. Grebe," the VA lady hollered, staring down at Augrey's bare white feet. "Looks like she believes she can take care of you."

That was when Nimrod spotted the pallet she had fashioned for herself in the kitchen corner.

"Welcome home, Uncle!" Augrey said, loud, like if she could say it with enough volume and conviction, the VA lady would believe this little tramp was related to an old black man.

Nimrod worked his lips around a few syllables but could not make words come out correctly. The VA lady leafed through a folder of yellow and pink papers.

"Mr. Grebe may regain some bits of his speech," she said to Augrey without once looking her in the face, "if you're willing to work at it with him. The outlook on the paralysis is a bit less rosy." She handed the girl a stack of papers and silently indicated the lines where Augrey should sign at the bottom of each one. It was supposed to be proof she understood how to take care of a stroke victim, how to lift and bathe and feed.

HE WAS A PAPER HUSK of a man, him a strapping hoddie who once built towers to the sky, light enough now to be lifted into his chair by a girl. She grew stronger every day, it seemed, grabbing him full around the chest, grasping him close to her and hoisting his body like a half-filled sack the way the VA lady showed her.

She had borrowed from her Aunt Bett the aluminum lounge chair, the kind with the little teeth in the arms so a person can sit up or recline. She arranged Nimrod in this chair by the window, no more free will left to him now than a big play doll. His legs had turned into lifeless things, hanging like ravelings off the bottom of an old coat. She propped his head on a pillow so he could see out the window to Bett's garden.

"Gobby supple," Nimrod said.

"It is pretty, isn't it," Augrey said. "Zinnias in every color." She kept up a stream of conversation, and she did get better at translating his efforts. When he grew frustrated, she wiped his eyes.

Every afternoon she did this: She put two fingers of whiskey into a plastic cup, the kind you give a child so he won't spill, with a cap and built-in straw. This she placed in his right hand, taping his knuckles around it so it looked like a bandaged claw strapped with bright blue painter's tape she had gotten from the Ace Hardware. Last she opened the Old Testament on his lap, turning to one of several favored tracts of Prophets.

"There, now," she would say, getting him settled.

She never went back to the Chaney Farm, nor to Angus Ferguson's trailer.

ONE NIGHT THEY WERE WATCHING a western on television. Some gunslingers promised to protect a village of poor, frightened Mexicans and were shooting it out with the bandoleros who had been terrorizing the villagers. After the fighting ended on television, the sound of gunfire continued.

Nimrod and Augrey looked at each other and realized at the same time that the shots were not part of the movie. Augrey used the pliers to turn down the volume. She stepped out on the porch.

Levon was using the bird box in Nimrod's crabapple tree for target practice. Nimrod could not see her from his lounge chair, but he heard Augrey speak with her older brother. He struggled to get to his feet and nearly tipped the damn thing over.

"Go on home, Levon." There was something Nimrod had never heard in Augrey's voice, something that was part anger and part fear.

"I *am* home, little sister. I'm staying with Bett."

"Why ain't you staying with Ginny?"

"Bitch kicked me out again."

"Good for her. Maybe this time she'll haul your mean sorry ass into court and get shut of you once and for all," Augrey said. "Well, anyway, keep your goddamn gun off our property."

"*Our?*" Levon said, and spit.

Augrey slammed the door, came inside. "Mr. Nimrod! You about fell out of your chair!" She pulled him upright and tried to make him comfortable again.

"Guh," he said, nodding toward the chest of drawers.

"You need something from the dresser?" Augrey pulled open the top drawer and looked at him. Nimrod rolled his eyes at the bottom drawer.

"Guh," he said again.

She knelt and rummaged through the drawer, holding up various articles for his inspection: some of Madeer's worn garments, candles and matches for when the electricity went out, dingy shirts he had not seen in a long time. Augrey reached into the back corner, then she froze. It was a long moment before she turned and looked at him.

"Mr. Nimrod, what do you want with a gun?"

"Shoo Leef."

Augrey replaced the gun and closed the drawer. "I'm not going to let him hurt you. I won't let anybody."

Nimrod looked out the window toward Bett's house. Levon was sitting on the porch rail smoking a cigarette, squinting at Nimrod through the window screen.

"He hur *yoo*," Nimrod said.

"No. Not anymore." Augrey took the pliers from the top of the TV and turned up the volume.

*Villages like this, they make up a song about every big thing that happens,* the young hothead gunslinger was saying. *Sing them for years.*

HE WOULD NOT HAVE BEEN able to say with any degree of certainty—his useless hands had long since refused to write anything down in the little spiral-bound memo pads, and he had never been crazy for wall calendars as Madeer was, measuring time instead by the cycles of egg-laying and gardening and the lengthening days—but for two months, maybe three, things proceeded in that fashion. Her feeding him in his wretchedness.

Bedsores blossomed, new ones overnight, it seemed. When feeling returned in the right leg, he was sorry it had. He had begun soiling himself in the night. How he hated for the girl to have to give him a sponge bath under those, or any, circumstances. But to complain would have been rank ingratitude. Madeer had raised him better than that.

One day, it came to him.

"Kill me," he said, and she almost missed it, so interleaved was it into Nimrod's mumbled Psalms.

"You know I can't do that," Augrey said, bending close. "Religion calls that a mortal sin, Mr. Nimrod. I love you too much to let you go. *God forbid, thou shall not die.*"

He rolled his eyes at her, tried for a smile. Her using the words of Samuel 20:1.

DUSTING SEVERAL WEEKS LATER, SHE lifted the lid of the jewelry box on top of the chest of drawers. The tiny ballerina inside spun on one pointed toe to a tinny melody.

"Madeer," Nimrod said, jerking his head toward the box. "Necklace."

In the mirror, Augrey held to her neck the gold chain with a tiny pearl that Nimrod had carried home at the end of the war, a gift he never got to give his Madeer. He caught Augrey's eye in the reflection and gave her a nod. She clasped it under her flaming hair. He saw that the girl's blue eyes were swollen and red and he realized he had not heard her laugh out loud for a week or more.

That afternoon she bathed him and put on him a clean shirt. She scrambled and fed him three banty eggs. Then she taped his cup in his left hand, filled it with Heaven Hill, and screwed on the top with the sipping straw. She took from the chest of drawers the single-action automatic pistol Nimrod had carried in Europe, and she wrapped it in his big blue claw of a right hand.

Before she left she asked, all business, was there anything else. Nimrod rolled his pair of dried-out eyeballs toward the window and she pulled the drape so he could admire Bett Ferguson's black-eyed Susies.

She closed the screen door behind her so it didn't make a sound. There was the soft flutter of her tennis shoes across the porch. Nimrod heard her brother Levon, sitting on Bett Ferguson's front porch, holler out to her as she passed. She did not stop to answer. Did not pick up a stick to toss. From his window Nimrod watched her walk up the road.

Just walking, walking, straight as the line of a slow bullet.

# TWELVE

It didn't take long for Billy's room to start smelling like him again. Like the air outside, like goat and the woods with sweat mixed in. What was odd and unsettling was that his smell was the thing Maureen was most aware of, as an actual sighting of her brother was rare. Life was the opposite of what Maureen thought it would be. She had expected that Uncle Carl would move home from the nuthouse and hole up in the attic, the only hints of his presence being occasional spooky footsteps on the floorboards overhead. But Uncle Carl was always around, underfoot, if it were possible for a two-hundred-pound man to be underfoot. He seemed to be everywhere at once.

It was Billy who was nowhere. *Nowhere man*, like John Lennon sang about. She found excuses to walk past his room, hoping to catch him tinkering with some electric gizmo or sorting through his enviable collection of record albums from all the British bands he was so crazy about. (So far, thank heavens, he hadn't missed the Led Zeppelin album Maureen gave Augrey Ferguson in exchange for the confiscated Ouija board.) But Billy was rarely there. He slept through breakfast. He grabbed lunch at a mysterious hour when nobody else was in the kitchen. Katherine was either involved with her vegetable garden or visiting people in town. Willis was always working. Maureen would be out on her research errands or writing outside at the picnic table with her new permanent shadow, Uncle Carl, never far away. By suppertime, her brother was already gone out for the night. At most meals now Uncle Carl, not knowing better, had taken to sitting in the chair that used to be Billy's before he went to the army.

Willis and Katherine sometimes argued about which of them should do something. *Talk to him!* Katherine's voice would rise from their bedroom late at night, and Willis's, deep and hesitant, would fall silent. Her parents were always arguing now. They did not seem to have adjusted to the new family configuration any better than Maureen had.

Not talking much was common for Willis, but Katherine too had gone strangely silent that first week or so after Billy got home in May. Over the next few months, Maureen tried to decode the blurry blank spots between the words coming out of her mother's mouth and the body language that vibrated off her whenever Billy was around. The words were the equivalent of, *Glad you're home,* but the nervous energy was, *Who are you?*

It reminded Maureen of the days surrounding her brother's signing up to join the Army last year. At seventeen, he had needed a parent's signature, and their mother begged and pleaded with their father not to let him go. But Willis did cave, and once Billy was gone, Katherine cried for days and finally quit talking at all, except to Maureen. Maureen she treated like a three-year-old. Katherine made her snuggle with her on the couch and watch old Loretta Young movies. "I have homework," Maureen would say. "I ought to go to bed." Her mother just blew her nose and threw the Kleenex into the snowy heap on the coffee table and tightened her grip on Maureen.

Willis would stretch and say, "Well, I'm going to hit the hay!" as if everything was fine as frog's teeth. And Katherine would burn a hole in the television screen with her eyeballs and squeeze Maureen's hand under the afghan until it hurt.

Then one Sunday they had all gone to Mass, and when Katherine came home she made chicken and dumplings and four different vegetables for dinner, all spread out on the good damask tablecloth. After they ate she said, "Maureen, go get your father's newspaper for him." And they never talked about Billy being gone and whose fault it was ever again. Maureen knew everything was going to be okay after the first letter Katherine wrote to Billy. She asked her mother if she could put a note of her own in the envelope. When she went to slip it in, even knowing it was a federal crime to look at someone else's mail, she read her mother's letter. *Dear Billy,* it said.

> *Well, you're gone now and there's no sense crying over spilt milk, as your Uncle Judge does not cease to remind me. Young men must serve their country, he says, it will put hair on his chest. And I could smack him. It would be ridiculous for me to say it's already high time you were coming home. I am not angry with your father anymore, although I maintain this could have waited. This war is not going anywhere.*
>
> *But I am done with fighting. If you get yourself blown up, you'll have me to answer to, mister. Maureen is, I am afraid, turning into a wild animal, and needs a big brother to rein her in.*
>
> *Oh heck, I have to say it. Come home. Lie if you have to. Tell them your mother is dying. Which is only half a lie since I am dying to hold my boy in my arms again.*
>
> *—Your loving Mother.*

Eventually Katherine was cuddling on the couch with Maureen's father instead of Maureen, and watching *Dragnet*.

Maureen knew the truth of it: Nobody hated *Dragnet* more than Katherine Juell.

Even with the tension around the house now, there are still, once in a while, good moments. Take this evening, before supper. Billy is sitting in a kitchen chair, slipping out of some boots all muddy from tramping in Lem O'Brien's woods, and Katherine comes up behind him and rubs his neck, and he stretches like a cat. Maureen watches them from where she's standing at the sink rinsing garden dirt from some radishes. For a few brief seconds, it feels like the old days. Like before. Almost.

Then in walks Willis. "Don't tell me his majesty is going to grace us with his presence tonight?" their father says.

Their mother, who is not naturally given to smoothing over, does just that. "Well," she says, and Maureen wishes for Katherine's sake that it could come out less forced, "I do happen to be making spaghetti and meatballs." And all three, Willis, Katherine, and Maureen, seem to hold still like characters in stop-motion on a stage, and they wait for Billy to decide. It's one of those permissible white lies, Maureen supposes; Katherine has the ground beef already shaped into meatloaf. But it was spaghetti and meatballs that always made Billy take seconds.

"Sounds good," he says. He sets the muddy boots outside the kitchen door and walks in his socked feet upstairs.

Katherine and Willis and Maureen stand there and listen for the sound of the shower overhead, the trickle of water as it rains down the drainpipe in the walls. Then all three break pose and go on about their business, Willis peeling out of the coveralls that are his second skin during work hours, Katherine breaking up the meatloaf with her bare hands and working in some oregano and forming it into balls. Maureen chews on a radish.

Later Willis will grumble about his son spending all his time at Pekkar's, blowing what pittance he earns from yard work on Millionaires' Row. When Billy first got home nobody thought much about the frequency of his visits to Pekkar's Alley. He was catching up with friends, he deserved some time to relax. They watched as it went from a few times a week to every night.

But for now, the five of them, this newly reconfigured family, sit together and pass the platters of salad and garlic bread and meatballs and spaghetti, and the conversation skims above the surface of the table. Katherine's lips tremble with fragile contentment. Maureen expects any second for Willis to fuss at Billy for coming to the table shirtless. But her father instead asks Billy how it was working for the late Evelyn Slidell. Did she trail after him, ordering him around? Did she have him trim her boxwood maze with fingernail scissors, as rumor had it?

"Not after she took to her bed," Billy says. Since the old woman died, he's been doing yard work for Uncle Judge and the Duvalls and anyone else who will hire him.

Katherine continues to smile. None of her family's uncomfortable conversation matches her face.

Carl, seeming to note the effort the family is making, injects something barely audible into the conversation and Maureen asks him several times to repeat it. She snorts when her uncle grows agitated and turns over a glass of milk.

"Maureen!" Katherine says. "If you can't be civil, please excuse yourself." This is mother-speak for *Go to your room.* They both know it, but Maureen tries to pretend that the order is lost on her. She doesn't want to miss anything. Under her father's glare, she finally pushes her chair from the table and leaves the kitchen.

Upstairs, instead of going to her own room, Maureen sits on Billy's bed and waits. She runs her fingers across the spines of the LPs lining the shelves he assembled from bricks and two-by-twelve planks. They form a U-shape around his bed, walling it in like a cave of hard rock. The records are perfectly alphabetized, from the Beatles, the Jeff Beck Group, and Cream to the Rolling Stones, Steppenwolf, the Who, and the Zombies. She picks out one she's never seen before. The name of the band, Iron Butterfly, calls to mind some bizarre combination of medieval torture device and mechanical insect. She holds the vinyl disk by its sides, her fingers straight, the way she's seen her brother do, and places it gently on the turntable.

The volume is all the way down, and she turns it up just enough to hear the words, deep and thrilling. *Oh, won't you come with me,* says the scary voice, so male and strange it runs a current through her. The song keeps going, seemingly without end.

When he comes in, she thinks at first that her brother doesn't even register her presence. Billy yanks a fresh shirt from his dresser drawer and pulls it over his head. He cranks the stereo to ten. Maureen can feel the vibrations of her eardrums—matching the beats of the drummer, now playing alone. The song, amazingly, is still "In-A-Gadda-Da-Vida."

"Man, I am getting *wasted* tonight!" Billy shouts over the music without looking at her, and slaps cologne on his cheeks. His hair has grown over his ears. She watches this stranger in her brother's body and can't think of a thing to say.

Then he is gone.

"*Wasted!*" she repeats to herself, and she wonders what that feels like.


APPARENTLY CARL HAS DECIDED THAT Maureen is his favorite Juell. He has taken to following her around all day, and whenever he starts to get on her nerves, she reminds herself that he has lost all the friends he had at the nuthouse. He wanders around the yard, the house, an odd shoe looking for its mate.

She set her alarm this morning to start working early on her memoirs. She has taken to working outside at the new picnic table they bought with the insurance money from the May storm damage. She tiptoed past Billy's room—not that he would hear her, dead to the world till noon anyhow—and she stopped in the kitchen to smear peanut butter and molasses on a couple of last night's biscuits before heading outside. And who was already out there?

Uncle Carl, of course, standing at the very tip-edge of the bluff hanging above the valley. It wasn't even all the way light yet. Maureen cleared her throat and he jumped and she realized too late that he wasn't just admiring the last stars or the twinkling lights on the cement plant but was privately peeing, him all rushing to put his thing away. She pretended she didn't see diddly-squat.

After a polite minute, "I love dawn," she said.

Carl said, "I love the red angels best." He talked in this mysterious whisper without a lot of ups and downs in his voice, which Maureen judged the best thing about him. "We had lots of those at Eastern State."

"That's good," Maureen said, nodding. She found herself nodding at most of what her uncle said, because often it was hard to tell what was crazy and what was just really smart. People said smarts were what drove him crazy, but her mother calls that nonsense.

Carl went on studying the sky, moving his eyes in a circle like he was following a moth's path. Maureen headed to the picnic table, knowing he would follow her. She spread her papers out. She was writing on loose leaf now. When she and Katherine went to the store to replace the diary that had been ruined by the storm, she had decided at the last minute that cute diaries with a lock and key were for little kids. She picked out instead a serious-looking three-ring binder and a thick pack of college-ruled paper and a Sheaffer cartridge pen with three prefilled cartridges in blue, black, and red. It was in that moment, standing in J.J. Newberry's, that Maureen realized childish scribbles in a diary were not what she wanted to be writing at all.

She was a girl who'd been "touched," Adelaide Ricketts had told her. Katherine would be horrified to learn that Maureen and Eddie had been sneaking off to visit the root doctor. They always dismounted their bikes and pushed them up the steep woodland path, hiding them in the dense growth near Granny Ricketts's falling-in cabin. Maureen got a queasy feeling in her gut remembering how, after she had told the old woman about the lightning strike and the death of Curly, everything went blank and Maureen's hair seemed to be newly electrified from the roots out. That had to count for something, didn't it, being touched? But that seemed ages ago, since

Granny Ricketts put the blessing on her, and Maureen still waited for her special powers to make themselves known.

At the top of a new clean page she wrote: *Chapter 3*.

Carl stood behind her, breathing the same way her father did, stiff little hairs wheezing and complaining at the brink of his nostrils.

"You can't stand back there, Uncle Carl," she said.

He sat across the table from her. "What are you writing?" he whispered in the creepy voice that she hoped none of the popular girls at school would ever hear.

"It's a combination memoir and history of Cementville."

"Why?"

"Because I find life interesting, my life, I mean. At least I plan for it to be. Someday. If it goes on this way much longer I am going to have to off myself." Maureen figured her personal life could not become duller, although thus far the only special power she had been granted from the lightning bolt appeared to be the ability to make her uncle stick to her like gum on the sole of a shoe.

But she was heartened by the thought that Cementville was getting more interesting and stranger every day. First, not long after all the soldiers had been buried, people were in a thrall of gossip about Augrey Ferguson who, so the story went, had begun working as a maid, which would not have set off any alarms in itself, except the person whose house was being cleaned and whose food was being cooked was an old colored man, Nimrod Grebe. And that's not all, people said; near as anyone could tell, she was doing it for free.

Then something way bigger happened, two weeks ago. Jimmy Smith's wife had allegedly been murdered. Maureen asked her mother why the *Picayune* still said "allegedly" when everybody in town knew about the gash in her skull and the purple bruises all around her neck (thanks to the big mouth of Roddy Duvall, who had seen the body before Tommy Thompson's autopsy). But instead of answering her, Katherine had snatched the newspaper out of Maureen's hands and thrown it in the trash.

Rumors were thick as pokeweed around town. Levon Ferguson had been questioned after several witnesses reported him making belligerent statements about the dead woman both before and after the discovery of her body. The sheriff had also picked up some of the GIs who came home in the last few months, as well as a few strangers who had been hired on at the new factory. Somebody said they even took Jimmy Smith in, which Willis said was ridiculous because a blind man could see he was nuts about his wife and torn to pieces over his loss. Willis said he would sooner believe the mother-in-law, Vera Smith, had done it before he would suspect Jimmy. Katherine swatted him with the classified section and rolled her eyes across the breakfast dishes at where Maureen sat scraping the last of the scrambled eggs from her plate.

Between what Maureen got from Eddie Miller and from eavesdropping on her parents' conversations and the rare snippets Billy brought home from Pekkar's Alley, people were behaving like a bunch of bees whose honeycombs had been ransacked by an enormous bear.

"Yes, I will just off myself," Maureen repeated now, looking at her big uncle across the picnic table. She reddened, suddenly remembering the newest secret she had uncovered: Her grandfather really had offed himself (this being the new term she had learned for suicide). Her parents would have been shocked to find out Maureen was aware of this dark family secret. Who knew that her family even had dark family secrets?

Ginny Ferguson had accidentally told her all about it the other day, when Katherine made Maureen walk Ginny home from the latest crying jag in their kitchen. This tearful episode was brought on by rumors that the clodhopper Ginny was married to was a suspect in Giang Smith's death, which Maureen would not have doubted for a second. "Ain't Mizriz Ferguson already had enough heartache?" Ginny sniveled as Maureen escorted her down the Juell driveway to the tenant cabin where Ginny and Levon lived, occasionally even at the same time. "What with burying her boy Daniel and all? And what about me, 'bout to drop this baby—I don't know how much more of this stress I can take!" Maureen reminded her that she had vowed three times since Easter alone to leave Levon for good, and Ginny came close to slapping her. "It ain't like you Juells got nothing to be ashamed of!" Ginny said with a hot vengeance that seemed to surprise Ginny herself as much as it did Maureen. And in the fluster that often was the only way Ginny could communicate, she spilled it all, some confused rigmarole that took Maureen a few minutes to unravel, about Carl and some dead hobo. "And that's what caused your granddaddy to tie a rope around his neck and string himself up in y'all's barn!"

Maureen wasn't sure whether her heart skipped a beat or sped up. She was both thrilled and appalled that such a thing had happened in her own family. She thought back to the middle of May, before the dead boys had come home, when her red diary was brand new and she had a hard time coming up with two sentences at a time that were exciting enough to put down there. She'd been resigned to the fact that nothing of an astonishing nature had ever or would ever occur to anyone in Cementville, much less to her own kin. And now she was the granddaughter of an actual suicide! Before this, Maureen had known only that Willis was off in the Korean War when his father passed away. She asked Ginny in a hushed voice if it was Carl who'd found him hanging from the rafters. "Oh, Lord! Please don't tell your mama I told you!" Ginny cried and hurried into her house and slammed the door. Maureen had stood a long time in the middle of the road. Was that what had driven her uncle off the deep end all those years ago? Coming across his father swinging at the end of a rope? It certainly sounded like the sort of thing that might end up with a person getting locked away in an insane asylum.

Here her uncle sat, staring at a curving line of ants making their way across the picnic table between them.

"I thought somebody should write a history of Cementville, you know, because of what a nice place it is," Maureen said to Carl now, and did not add, Or *was*, until this bizarre summer. In truth she wasn't sure if she was writing a history or a novel or a memoir or what, only that big things were happening, and it did not appear as if any of the adults around this town were capable of making sense of it all. She tried to rub out the sharply alternating mental images of the crumpled form of a woman lying on a rocky riverbank and a dark shape (someone she only knew from faded photographs) swinging from a hayloft. She wanted it both ways: the breathless excitement of strange events and the good place she knew too, like an old coat that fits right and belongs to you.

"Don't you think people ought to know about what a good place it is, Uncle Carl? The story of how our town got here and everything?" she persisted, unsure whether she was trying to convince her uncle or herself of the truth of it.

"What if nobody wants to know about what a good place it is. What if they already have their own good place and they're afraid knowing about another good place will make their place disappear?" Carl asked.

"Well then, they shouldn't read anything if they're so afraid of having their minds changed," Maureen said. What she had started to say was, *This book will be for normal people, Uncle Carl.* Her mother had reminded her several times since Carl's arrival that it pays to think before you speak.

He wiped his eyes. Small sucking sounds came from the back of his throat. Maureen was learning it did not take much to get her uncle going. She really should not have mentioned offing herself.

"Maybe I'm writing it for us," she said with a cheer she did not feel. "Just think. When it gets published, it'll be like a version of home you can take with you if you ever have to leave again. Say you're living in Indiana, or Paris, and you start to feel homesick. You can pull out my book and flip to a chapter and say, Oh, I remember that!"

"I'm a native of Cementville, too."

"I know, Uncle Carl." She pretended to study a brochure about Mammoth Cave that she had picked up the week before on a research run at the Cementville Tourism Bureau, which was basically a folding table at the bus station where Vera Smith sat behind a rack of brochures about things to do when you were visiting the area. There was a brochure about the distillery, and the Palisades on the Kentucky River, and one about the Tourmobile. But most of the things to do were in other parts of the state. She offered a biscuit to Carl.

He took a tiny bite, wiped his fingers on his pant leg, and opened one of the travel brochures. "Since the day I got taken away I've been a visitor here forty-five times," Carl said.

Maureen glanced up. "Forty-five?"

"Thirty years old now, minus fifteen years when I got taken away, equals fifteen years I lived at Eastern State, times three visits a year—Thanksgiving, Christmas, Fourth of July—equals forty-five visits."

Maureen remembered Uncle Carl turning up at certain times and was vaguely aware that the relatives took turns having him sit at their holiday table. He was the hot potato that had to be passed around and couldn't stay in anybody's hands too long.

"What about Easter?" she asked.

He made a face like he could not believe what she had said. "And miss the Easter egg hunt."

She nodded. "So you were a little older than me when you moved away."

"I didn't move away." Carl wiped both eyes at once with his big fingers.

"When you were taken away." Maureen tried to picture herself bundled in a white straight jacket, her parents loading her into a van full of strange men, Katherine and Willis and Billy standing at the top of the driveway, waving goodbye to her. Or taking her to spooky old Eastern State Hospital themselves and walking out the front doors without her, then driving home singing along to Pee Wee King on the radio, no different than if they had just hauled cast-off clothing to Appalachia for the annual Holy Ghost Charity Drive.

She filled one sheet of loose leaf and set it aside. Carl picked it up and looked it over and placed it exactly as he had found it.

"Did you put in about the murder?" he whispered.

"Mother said I need to stop dwelling on what happened to Giang Smith."

"The other one," Carl said.

"She says I have a morbid sensibility, and if I don't stop it, she's going to take me to see a doctor." Maureen's work would get nowhere today if she indulged every crazy idea clattering around inside her addlepated uncle. That was another new term she had learned. Addlepated: being mixed-up. Confused.

The two of them sat out there at the picnic table, Maureen writing, Carl squashing ants with his big fat thumb anytime one ventured near her stacks of papers and brochures. To give him something productive to do, Maureen handed him a red pencil and let him read over the first chapter. All the while he made little throat noises she could not decipher as agreement or disapproval.

When she studied her notes later, she found not red pencil marks, but a parade of ant bodies scattered across the pages like tiny pressed flowers.


THE NEXT DAY, WHILE KATHERINE was lying down for a rare nap, Maureen fastened her book bag onto her handlebars. Her mother had been acting more protective than Maureen could remember, hesitating to allow her to ride her bike to town or even over to the Millers' house. Maureen knew it was because of Giang Smith's murder and the fact that the sheriff had been questioning people but no actual arrest had been made. But she had been cooped up on their ridge for six days in a row, and she had work to do, and summer was slipping away. She wasn't sure which was stronger, the twinge of guilt at sneaking off while her mother napped, or the fear of what would happen when she got home.

She was a third of the way down the driveway when Uncle Carl came barreling behind her on foot. Maureen skidded her tires to a halt in the gravel.

His face said, *Where are you going?*

"Today's a research day." She explained that she had already covered as much as she could from home and memory and her own imagination about the dead soldiers, their families, this war, and other wars that had sent dead soldiers back to Cementville. "There's some stuff I need to look up at the library. Some stuff about the Army. About how the National Guard came to be something different from what people thought it was."

Carl squeezed the bridge of his nose hard.

Maureen remembered Billy's old five-speed in the barn. She pushed her bike back up the hill. They brought her brother's bike out into the sun and checked the chain and tires. Willis squirted it with WD-40 and spun the pedals to get the chain oiled. The tires were low, but not dry-rotted, so he thought they could make it to town all right, if Maureen and Carl promised to stop at the filling station and put air in them.

"Your mother knows you're taking off, right Mo?" Willis said. She nodded. Lying was getting easier. "Carl, you behave. Mo, keep an eye on him."

Which seemed to Maureen a ridiculous thing for her father to say regarding a grown man. They flew down the hill, gravel pinging crazy tunes against the spokes of their bicycle wheels.

Mrs. Cahill always had things picked out for Maureen in advance, books and articles that might add something interesting to her research on Cementville or help her improve her prose. Maureen would vote Mrs. Cahill the Best Librarian in the World, even given that she is the only librarian Maureen has known, except for Miss Wanda, Mrs. Cahill's part-time assistant who was not a real librarian but basically just a haunter of the library stacks who never talked to anybody and probably would have made a good librarian if she were not so afraid of people. Maureen would not have been surprised if creepy Miss Wanda was snooping around the stacks right now, peering out at them this very minute between *Billy Budd* and *Moby Dick*.

"This is my Uncle Carl," Maureen told Mrs. Cahill, who was already checking him over like she was trying to figure out whether he was the kind of person who could pass muster. The librarian dabbed her eyes with the wadded tissue she kept in the sleeve of her green cardigan and came round to the front of the desk. She was a small woman, and when she tried to gather Carl into her arms as if he were her own lost child, she looked like an elf attempting to tackle a large mammal.

"I heard you were home, you handsome thing, and you haven't stopped in to see me before now! How is my favorite researcher?" She glanced at Maureen. "I mean my two favorite researchers?"

Maureen picked up the stack of books Mrs. Cahill had set aside at the front desk. Carl followed her to the table by the microfilm viewer. He flipped through her notes about everything interesting she had learned so far from old *Cementville Picayunes*.

"You still don't have the murder in here."

Before Giang Smith, people did not get murdered in Cementville, except maybe in the Civil War days, when Confederate raiders roamed the hills, shooting people at random and stealing their farm animals. When kids told ghost stories at church weenie roasts, some of the boys swore that renegade guerrillas ate whole calves raw like bloodthirsty vampires. But it looked as if Maureen was going to have to pander to her uncle's obsession with *somebody's* murder or he was not going to let it go.

"Okay, what murder?" she said.

Carl rifled through the drawer of film canisters and pulled out July–December 1954. He dragged a chair next to Maureen at the microfilm viewer and inserted the film and whirred through the frames.

"How do you know how to do that?" she asked him.

"Why do you think Mrs. Cahill likes me so much?"

Maureen leaned in and read the clipping he had centered in the viewer. "Police Probe Slaying. Man Found Dead Behind Council Street House. Coroner Rules Homicide," Maureen read aloud. Then silently down the narrow column. *"Roy Stubblefield bled internally from being beaten with a blunt object, possibly an ax handle found near the scene," the coroner said.*

She pushed the chair away from the microfilm viewer. Her heart pumped furiously like it had the day Ginny blabbered out her angry story. *Hobo, rope, grandfather, barn.* The words swarmed around in her head. 1954. Fifteen years ago. Fifteen years since Carl Juell had been locked up in the nuthouse.

"Nobody's going to want to read that," she said, afraid to look at her uncle. "Besides, I wasn't even born then. It doesn't have anything to do with me."

Carl glowered at the microfilm viewer as if it had let him down. "I thought you wanted to write a history."

"Well, yeah, but—"

"Dead people are part of history. Murderers make history."

They had covered some gruesome events in school. Hitler and Mao. Genghis Khan. The guillotine. The Salem witch trials. Maybe her uncle's line of reasoning wasn't all that crazy. Maureen peered into the viewer again. "What does 'home-at-large' mean?"

"Means you don't have one."

"Everybody's got to live somewhere, Uncle Carl." She couldn't stop reading. The article gave the names of men who were there when Roy Stubblefield was killed. Two Fergusons. A Goins. A few names she didn't recognize. An unnamed witness. "Wonder who the mysterious witness was? Did they ever figure out who did it?"

But Carl was squeezing the bridge of his nose, lost somewhere once again.

Virginia Ferguson sat in the Juell kitchen. The weeping this time was over the whereabouts of her sister-in-law. None of the Ferguson clan had seen Augrey for weeks.

"Bett was in regular touch with her all that time while Augrey was taking care of Nimrod Grebe—you know she been staying there with him for going on three months, but ain't nobody seen her since he tried to shoot himself." Ginny shrugged a shoulder to wipe her nose on her blouse.

Katherine shifted uncomfortably and nudged the box of Kleenex closer. She told Maureen to go up and clean her room, but didn't seem to notice when Maureen parked herself on the stool by the refrigerator.

"Levon tried and tried to get that girl to go home to Arlene. He's that way, you know, always looking out for family," Ginny sniffed. Levon had moved in and out of the little tenant house at the bottom of the hill three or four times since the beginning of summer, generally leaving Ginny behind with a new shiner.

"I expect she'll turn up." Katherine got up and began whipping egg whites for the meringue pies. Uncle Judge and Aunt Mary Frances were coming for supper and she preferred to get some of the work done ahead of time so she could put her feet up and rest before her godparents arrived. "Maureen, didn't I tell you to go upstairs? Start your bath."

Maureen remained in the corner, pretending absorption in *The House of the Seven Gables*, which she had renewed ten million times at the library already this summer. If something had happened to Augrey Ferguson, she needed to know.

"Virginia, did you want Maureen to walk you home today?" Katherine said.

Ginny and Maureen glanced warily at each other, then away.

"Oh, I'll run on home," Ginny said. "Levon likes me to be there when he gets off work."

Maureen was about to say, *Levon works?* But Ginny was out the door.

She watched her mother closely to gauge whether it was a good time to spring an idea on her, an idea that would require Katherine's permission. She took in a good breath and said, "What would you think about me doing some interviews?"

"Interviews?" Katherine dabbed a finger in the egg whites to see if they were stiff.

"Maybe with the mothers of the dead soldiers."

"Absolutely not," Katherine said, stopping the Mixmaster and looking at Maureen, clearly appalled. "Chop the celery and apples for the Waldorf salad, would you?" She flipped the mixer on.

"Well, which is it, Mother?" Maureen hadn't known she was going to yell until she did. "Clean my room, take a bath, escort Ginny, or chop apples?"

Katherine switched the machine off again. "I—"

Maureen braced herself for a good fussing.

But, "I'm sorry," Katherine said.

*Sorry?* What on earth had gotten into her mother?

Katherine started to speak, seemed to think better of it, tapped a finger on her lips. "Then again—the effects of the war. I can see where you're going."

This was the moment for Maureen to stay quiet. She could almost hear the cogs clicking in her mother's mind. Katherine was a self-described pacifist, had become stridently so after a series of photographs published in *LIFE* magazine showed anguished children running naked down dirt roads in rural Vietnam, that faraway place that now seemed to turn up in every other conversation. Tiny Cementville had lost so many sons, all by itself. With the escalating death toll Walter Cronkite tallied up for them every night, and images that stayed in people's minds long after they turned off the television, there seemed to be no end to the amount of things Katherine and Willis could find to argue about behind their closed bedroom door. Maureen suddenly saw her mother as a woman whose own son had gone away and come home a stranger.

"Lila O'Brien maybe . . . " Katherine said. "After all, she's been watching her boy try to recover from the most extraordinary experience imaginable. And Lila is the loveliest person. She's nervous, of course, you would have to go at it obliquely, gently, try not to pull anything out of her too abruptly . . . "

It was Maureen's turn to be horrified. Harlan O'Brien, the weird one-legged son of their neighbors! She'd had nightmares about the artificial foot in which it scrambled on its own across the field toward their house. "Some people say Harley was the one who—" she started, but Katherine cut her off, holding up an index finger, a dollop of egg white on the end.

"Don't. I will not hear a word of that horrible gossip in this house." Her voice was angrier than it needed to be, in Maureen's opinion. "Lila was nursing Harlan's fever the night Giang Smith died. She told me so herself. He was in bed for days."

And before Maureen could make further objection, her mother was dialing the phone. Lila O'Brien shrieked, loud enough for Maureen to hear from across the kitchen. Now would be the perfect time for her to come on over! Right away! She was just pulling brownies out of the oven!

"I didn't promise you the calmest person," Katherine said, hanging up. "One of Lila's brownies may be just the thing to pull you out of this mopiness. Carl can walk over there with you."

"I am not a mope." Maureen finished chopping a stalk of celery and threw it in the salad bowl. "I just never expected all this obfuscation."

Katherine looked up from the chicken she was trussing. "What sort of obfuscation have you experienced, Miss Webster?" She knew good and well that Maureen hated when adults acted like certain people don't have the right to use certain words.

She decided to ignore her mother's condescension for now. "I thought you wanted me to take a bath."

"It's only Uncle Judge and Aunt Fan," Katherine said. "They don't care if you have a smidge of summer dirt behind your ears."

"I can't so much as go to the library anymore without Carl breathing down my neck!" Maureen threw hunks of apple into the bowl. Hot tears rushed to her eyes. "Did you know he used to help Mrs. Cahill? I might as well have been invisible yesterday at the library."

"Chop those apples fine, Maureen. Aunt Fan will make those cow eyes and run her tongue around her dentures the way she does."

Maureen bit into an apple. "Who knew everybody would be so

crazy about him? You should have seen Mrs. Cahill, falling all over herself. It was all: *Carl, are you settling in okay? Carl, have things changed much? Oh, Carl, I'm so glad my best researcher ever is back.* He must not have been all that loony."

"Watch it, missy." Her mother did not even have to stop trussing and look at her when she said this for Maureen to know she was on razor-thin ice. It was plunge in now, or lose her chance.

"Well, what happened, then?" Maureen said.

"What happened when?"

"When you all shipped Uncle Carl off to the loony bin."

Her mother's shoulders tensed, just a little. Katherine finished stuffing the roasting hen and wrapped it up to rest on the counter. "He just—got *sick.* . . . Your grandfather died suddenly, and with your father getting back from Korea and us trying to get on our feet, and Billy was a baby then—we couldn't take care of him, Maureen." Katherine looked at her as if to gauge whether her daughter was satisfied with this.

She wasn't. "Sick how?"

"Nervous. Strange," Katherine said. "Carl was, I guess you'd say, unpredictable."

"What about Roy Stubblefield?" Maureen kept her eyes on the apples she was mincing to a fine paste on the chopping board, then glanced up in time to see her mother's face go from surprise to that vacant look adults get when they're pretending not to have the slightest idea what you are talking about. "The murder?" Maureen persisted. "1954? Right before Uncle Carl went off to *rest*?"

"Oh, that drifter, you mean. He was in the wrong place at the wrong time, poor thing. Some vagrant nobody knew."

"I get the feeling Uncle Carl knew him."

"I don't think so. That man wasn't from around here. I can't see it has anything to do with the history of Cementville." Katherine started humming and took some eggs out of the refrigerator. "I'm thinking deviled eggs. Uncle Judge loves deviled eggs."

Nobody could tell Maureen she didn't know obfuscation. But she had pushed her mother as far as she could for one day.

Billy walked past the kitchen window dragging the lawn mower. Katherine ran water into the Dutch oven. She placed the eggs in, two at a time. "What about your brother? Interview him. What it's like to be home. The war. All that."

"Already tried." Maureen followed her brother's movements, watching through the window as he coiled a garden hose around his arm and stared off toward the O'Briens' pasture. "It's not hard to picture him killing somebody," Maureen said.

"Your brother didn't kill anybody."

"He was in the war, Mother. Shooting people is sort of part of the job? Plus there was that black guy in his platoon—"

"That boy had a freak heart attack. It was coincidence that he and your brother were in a tussle when it happened." It was the tone meant to stop the conversation in its tracks. "Now, shoo. Go see Lila. Make her feel good. Eat some of her brownies," her mother said. "Carl!" she called out the window toward the picnic table, where he sat like a misshapen lump of clay.

Maureen gathered her notebooks and papers and slung the strap of her book bag over her shoulder.

Katherine put some new potatoes in a paper sack and tucked them into Maureen's book bag. "Tell Lila I just dug those. Tell her to boil them twelve minutes. And they're sweet enough you don't even need butter."

LILA O'BRIEN WAS LEADING HER son out to the yard like a blind man when Maureen came across the pasture, Carl panting behind her. A card table in the front yard was decked out with a white table-cloth and checkered napkins and lemonade and the brownies piled in a neat pyramid in the center.

"Maureen, you remember Harlan, don't you—although you were a baby when he left for the service, gracious, what two or three or something—Harlan, Maureen Juell, you remember Willis and Katherine's little girl, and her brother Billy, he was in the war too!" Mrs. O'Brien sang, capable of long strings of words unpunctuated by breath or rest.

Maureen started to introduce Uncle Carl around, but Mrs. O'Brien reminded her that Carl Juell was no stranger in Cementville, and she tucked napkins into both men's collars. Maureen tried to keep her mind away from the artificial foot. In her whole life she had never been in the presence of a real live amputee.

Mrs. O'Brien lowered her voice and said, "Now. I already had to give him his evening pills, they help him sleep, you know, so he's in a sort of quiet mood now."

"But it was you I wanted to interview, Mrs. O'Brien," Maureen said, pulling out her notebook.

"Oh, pshaw! As if somebody like me could know anything about war! It's Harley you want to talk to," Lila said. She bent over her son and straightened a lock of hair that had fallen over his brow. "Harley, you help Maureen with her paper now, she's writing a paper about the war."

Before Maureen could argue further, Lila O'Brien flitted across the lawn and into the house. Maureen turned back to her uncle sitting lumpen and smiling next to the soldier. She was suddenly glad Carl had come with her.

"Well," she said, and laughed nervously. She stuffed half a brownie into her mouth at once, then realized she was the only one eating. She opened her binder to a clean page. *Lieutenant Harlan O'Brien*, she wrote at the top of the page in cursive that looked nothing like her own, it was so shaky and ragged. She had the strange feeling the person sitting across the card table from her wasn't really there. She could see him there all right; but what she was seeing made her think of the eerie costumed mannequins her class had seen in a Civil War museum. She wondered, if she tapped Harlan O'Brien's chest, whether she would hear a soft empty thud.

*Question #1*, she wrote, like this was the interview she had prepared for, and begged her mind to stop repeating *Wooden leg, wooden leg, wooden leg.*

"Lieutenant O'Brien, people are curious about what it was like—they had a special about POWs on television? About a deserted prison camp they found over there in the jungle? Maybe you could describe a typical day for a prisoner of war. Those pens, sort of bird-cage-looking things? I mean, every day, day in, day out—"

Carl put his hand on her arm, and Maureen sat back in her chair. Maybe the soldier's blank stare meant he was trying to process her question, or questions—she hadn't meant to ask so many at once. Maureen was able to put the fake foot and the museum mannequin out of her mind, but in their place now was the dark hollow space inside a milk chocolate Easter bunny whose marzipan eyes can't see a thing.

A spray of starlings lifted noisily off a tree behind him so that it looked like birds were flying straight out of Harlan O'Brien's head.

"So, Harley, I was thinking we might go out this Sunday if you're up to it, maybe head toward Cumberland Gap this time," Carl whispered in his creepy mental-institution voice.

The soldier's vacant face melted slightly, the marzipan eyes blinked. It was as if, with a single sentence, Carl breathed him to life. If you could call it life, the way Harlan O'Brien sat there blinking, blinking. But the two men did begin talking about the times they'd gone camping in the woods when they were boys, her uncle's soft whisper restoring Harlan O'Brien to what Maureen thought might be a feeble version of the person he once was. She listened as they talked, or Carl talked, mostly. Since her uncle had moved back into the house where they had both grown up, to the hometown where he had maybe killed a man, to the barn where he'd found his father swinging, Maureen had quit trying to figure out which thing took up a bigger percentage of her uncle's brain, the crazy or the brilliant.

The two men talked and the light faded and she felt herself fading too, into the waning afternoon. She remembered the new potatoes in her bag. Neither of the men appeared to notice when she went into the house carrying Katherine's offering.

Maureen did not find Lila O'Brien in the kitchen. She followed the sound of a voice up the stairs. Lila was probably in her bedroom, talking to someone on the phone. Maureen glided past the bathroom and glanced into a bedroom that she guessed must be Harlan's. She pushed the open door with one finger and stepped in, leaving the door ajar enough to hear Lila's voice so that she would know when her phone conversation was ending.

It was a typical boy's room, a lot like Billy's, painted a dusky blue, with blue and brown and tan curtains and matching bedspread in some woodsy print of trees and animals. Someone had arranged the soldier's medals in a neat row across the top of his dresser, and Maureen bet it was not Harlan.

She ran a finger across a complete set of Britannica and spun the globe on the walnut desk. Her mother would be ashamed of her, snooping around like this. She traced the spines of several books, some Twain, some Defoe, a worn copy of *Johnny Tremain*, the last book she had read at the end of the school year. There was a long set, eight or nine books, all of them about someone called Tristram, with a title that said it was his "Life and Opinions." She made a mental note to consider that title for her own book: *The Life and Opinions of Maureen Juell*. She turned to head back out to the hallway when she spotted something sticking out from under the bed: a thickness of several blankets folded to a neat rectangle to make a sort of pallet. So it was true. People around town had said the lieutenant slept on the floor, couldn't get comfortable in a bed again. She knelt and reached under the box springs, ran a hand over the worn flannel blankets. Maybe he had a bad back, the fake leg throwing him off balance; she'd heard of that, how a limp could cause your body to lose its sense of symmetry. And before she knew what she was doing, she had crawled in and stretched out there beneath the coils of springs under Harlan O'Brien's bed. She breathed carefully in the tiny space. What was he thinking about when he lay down at night?

But surely Lila's phone call was over. Any minute she could come trilling down the hall. Maureen scooted out from under the bed and, taking a last look around Harlan's room, stepped out into the hallway. She walked toward the bedroom at the other end, and as she got closer she was pretty sure that the sound she heard wasn't Lila O'Brien gossiping on the phone. It was muffled weeping, the woman's birdlike voice transformed to that of a child with a very particular heartache, and nobody to tell. This was the kind of moment when her mother knew exactly what to do, how to comfort the grieving and the frightened and the bewildered.

Maureen waited at the end of the hall, watching from the second-story window as Carl talked with Harlan O'Brien on the lawn below. Her uncle gestured broadly with his big hands and galumphed across the grass for a bit, miming some lumbering animal, at which the soldier nodded, maybe even smiled. Maureen suddenly saw why people loved Carl. He made them feel lucky.

She jabbed a finger in the pocket of her shorts and stroked the rabbit's foot she had found in the field behind their house at the beginning of summer. She'd been carrying it ever since. It could have once belonged to Billy, or even Uncle Carl, years ago. A tinge of color remained under one of the tiny claws. It must have been dyed green when it was new, the kind of dime-store novelty all the boys at Holy Ghost carried in their pockets for luck. The rabbit's foot had not brought her luck. Then again, neither had her uncle. But people seemed to like shooting the breeze with batty old Carl, so maybe she was lucky to have him following her around. They might loosen up and talk to him in a way they couldn't or wouldn't with a kid like her. Maybe the only way she was ever going to get any scoop on what had happened, what was happening, to her town was if people thought they were just passing time with Carl.

When Maureen had originally told Mrs. Cahill about her project, the librarian had suggested she talk to Giang Smith. Mrs. Cahill said Giang probably looked at Cementville with a different point of view, coming from so far away. But Maureen had never worked up the guts. Now Giang Smith was dead, and Maureen could not put a finger on why she had never arranged an interview. She didn't want to think she was afraid of the Vietnamese woman's way of speaking, of the almond eyes so different from those of anybody she knew. War probably looked different, viewed through those eyes, when the place you lived was suddenly overrun with guns and helicopters and strange voices flying everywhere. Mrs. Cahill said that Giang Smith had come into the library often, looking for poetry. Listening to Lila O'Brien weeping at the other end of the hall, Maureen remembered finding a slip of paper in a library book a few weeks ago. Poems by Edna St. Vincent Millay. The last person to check it out had been Giang Smith. The slip of paper was covered in curly letters with tiny dots and dashes and carat marks floating over them. Maybe it was a translation of the poem on the page next to it. In that poem, a woman was wiping away tears and imagining another woman named Penelope doing the same thing. There was something about weaving all day and undoing the weaving all night. The woman in the poem sounded tired and lonely, and maybe with a whiff of disgust.

Suddenly Lila O'Brien burst out of her bedroom and chirped, "What! Are the boys all out of lemonade? Well, we girls better get cracking then, hadn't we?" And she laid a feather-light arm across Maureen's shoulder and they went down to the kitchen for more refreshments before rejoining *the boys* on the lawn. They sat around the card table, Lila coaxing everyone into more brownies, and Maureen trying to figure out how to extricate herself from the failed afternoon. She remembered that Uncle Judge and Aunt Frances were coming for supper and was finally able to graciously (she thought with satisfaction) excuse herself and Carl.

They were hoofing it across the pasture for home when Maureen saw Ginny Ferguson emerge from the little house at the bottom of the hill and light out for the Juells' as if trying to outrun a swarm of yellow jackets.

"Oh, for Pete's sake," Maureen said. "Wonder what she's crying about now."

But there was something different in Virginia Ferguson's voice. Ginny caught up to them and threw her arms around Maureen and blubbered crazily into her hair. Maureen took hold of Ginny and shook her.

"What, Ginny? What—I can't understand you!"

"They found her! Oh, Maureen, they found her."

"Found who?" Maureen wanted to be angry with the pregnant woman. She'd seen in movies how people slapped someone in the throes of hysterical fits in order to bring them to their senses, but Maureen just stood there, a bad feeling crawling into her stomach. She didn't want to say it again. "Who did they find, Ginny?"

"It's Augrey. Oh, Maureen. Little Augrey is dead."

# PART III

*But only return to me and repent and rend your heart;
and rain will come, and milk and wine. I will restore
to you the years that the swarming locust has eaten.*

—*PROPHETS: JOEL* REDUX

WE ALL KNEW THE FERGUSON KIDS LIVED A LITTLE TOO MUCH like wild animals, eating ravenously of canned pork and beans and headcheese made in their own barn lot. They bathed as the notion took them in a sort of massive serial ritual, filling the rusted cast iron tub behind the trailer with scalding water, and one by one soaping several weeks' grime into the tubful of darkening gray soup. Augrey was *of* them, yet she was separate from—and if possible, more frightening than—the rest of Arlene Ferguson's brood.

Mothers were leery of girls like her. Augrey Ferguson was lean and strong—not the stringy, sinewy strong of most country kids— but thick and muscular, handsome as the finest hunting dog pup. Her skin was white against that orange-peel hair, even in summer, a sprinkle of persimmon freckles across the bridge of her round Scots nose.

Even when she was small she was capable of grotesque feats. She could hold on to an electric fence with both fists, her pelt of thick hair lilting in a crestfallen halo above her shoulders. She once stuck seven darning needles into the palm of her hand and held the hand straight out in front of her like a trophy for all the neighborhood kids to examine for a quarter apiece. She seemed always to have several mangled cigarettes in the pocket of her shorts and could perform on demand the stunt that was a particular favorite of her audience: Augrey inserted the lit end of a burning cigarette into her mouth and let the smoke flow out through her amazing flared nostrils.

Skills at which many country kids were proficient she elevated to an art form. Masterful tree climber. Fearless bareback rider—even of Trigger, the furious and starving stud kept locked in a neighbor's ramshackle paddock. In baseball, spot-on, first chosen for every team. The girl appeared to have been born immune to the usual dangers that stalked rural children. A boy pulled the rearing Trigger over onto himself, rupturing his spleen. A girl fell from a grapevine swing into a ravine, the breath knocked right out of her; she limped home with a fractured tailbone. Augrey's younger brother jumped from a hayloft and missed the haystack by eighteen inches, cracking three ribs. But Augrey emerged from the woods or the barn or the crow hunt with little more than the odd scratch.

Kids would have followed her anywhere, and usually did.

She got older and the feats were no less masterful and certainly no less physical in nature. At thirteen, she could fill out a pair of fishnet hose better than most women and she traipsed down Council Street every Saturday like she had someplace to be. At fourteen she had bedded more of the male faculty at the consolidated high school than—well, there is no fitting metaphor. At fifteen she was making better than egg money offering T&A shows after hours at Pekkar's Alley. Great little dancer, Augrey, hunting dog muscles all grown up. Her mother kicked her out of the house—or the trailer that particular branch of Fergusons were calling home at the time—after finding Augrey compromised under Arlene's new beau. Consigned her to Angus's care, if care is what you want to call it.

Then she seemed to just disappear. Nobody could decide where she went. She quit showing up at Pekkar's. Weeks went by without her coming home to Arlene's or Angus's place. Word got around the way it will: She was sleeping on a wad of blankets behind Nimrod Grebe's woodstove. Her brother Levon had seen it with his own eyes when he took the old man some fresh eggs. People shook their heads in astonishment but eventually ran out of ways to be appalled.

There was more than a bit of shame in the fascinated sadness we all felt when Levon's hounds came across Augrey's body in shoulder-high thistles behind Judge Hume's black barn, cheap gold necklace tight around that pretty white neck like a garrote. It didn't take long for the coroner to declare the trail all but cold. That didn't make us stop speculating.

Nobody said out loud that she had it coming—what kind of people would we be? We had seen Nimrod sitting there day in, day out, where she had arranged him by the window, grizzled head staring out into nothing, making some of us expect all the sons of Noah to come charging over the knobs gathering two of every kind. We privately thought of them, the young girl, the old man, cleaving as one to save the race there on the ark. We didn't say these things, of course. We are not that kind of people.

Mothers keep their children home and long for this summer to end, for the doors of the school to open wide and take them in. Maybe for those six or seven hours each day their children will be safe from whatever it is that's out there.

# THIRTEEN

Maureen sat at the kitchen table shuffling through the pages of the memoir that had tried to become a history but now looked like nothing more than the pitiful efforts a younger, stupider version of herself would have scribbled into the red diary. Where were the words that could tell this story right now, that could describe what was happening, that could make time stop long enough to stanch the flood of awfulness threatening her town? They weren't flowing from the end of her cartridge pen, that much was obvious.

She watched out the window where her father and Uncle Carl worked on the driveway gate at the top of the hill, hammering and oiling and coaxing the hinges to cooperate after years of idleness. Carl used a shovel to level out the peaks and valleys that had developed in the gravel over time, hindering the gate from swinging easily across the driveway. Maureen could not remember the gate being closed, much less latched, ever. Her father couldn't possibly think a chain and padlock were really going to make a difference. If a killer was intent on murdering them all in their sleep one night, no gate could keep him out. Maureen watched them work. Her mother, sitting at the table with the *Picayune*, was watching them too.

"I'm not sure how much longer your uncle will be staying with us," Katherine said.

"I've gotten used to him though," Maureen said, and was dismayed at how unsurprising it was, hearing her mother say this, as if it was something she knew was coming. There was dismay too at the secret tremor in her own voice.

"Well. It's not working out," Katherine said.

"I don't agree."

Katherine had been staring out the window during this exchange, and she turned and looked at Maureen as if seeing a person she was not sure she recognized. She opened her mouth. She closed her mouth. She looked back at her midweek edition of the newspaper.

And Maureen understood what Uncle Carl had tried to tell her in his weird whispery way without saying it outright. She wasn't getting the whole story. Now the deeper truth hit her full in the face: It wasn't likely that she was ever going to get it, not from the adults around here, and not from a bunch of stupid, pointless research. She wadded her neat stack of notes into a tight ball. Her mother glanced up from the *Picayune* in time to see Maureen march across the kitchen and throw the big white wad of paper in the trashcan.

"Hold on, hold on," Katherine said, rescuing the crumpled pages. She flattened them on the table. "Do you have any idea how proud I am of you—taking on a huge project—"

The set of Maureen's face stopped her. Maureen had been unable to look at her mother, to *look*, really, at anyone, for the last twenty-four hours. That was when official word came. A new murder. Not some drifter from fifteen or twenty years ago who everybody but Uncle Carl and some flimsy microfilm at the library appeared to have forgotten. Not some foreign war bride from far across the ocean who kept so close to herself that few could recall ever having an actual conversation with her.

Augrey Ferguson was dead. The word kept pounding in Maureen's head as if it had taken over the job of her pulse. Dead. Dead. Dead.

She hadn't gotten to know Augrey, the girl about whom everybody claimed to know everything. For Maureen, Augrey was the fascinating bad girl who would cadge things for you, particularly things that kids from respectable families weren't supposed to have. The Ouija board. A forty-five of "Louie Louie" that Maureen was pretty sure had been shoplifted from Newberry's (*This is* so *dirty*, Augrey had promised Maureen, pulling it out from under her blouse). Even a cigarette once. Now each time Maureen thought of Augrey, which felt like every minute of every hour, what flooded through her was not the dread of a lurking killer that appeared to have settled into Katherine's very bones. What sank in and wouldn't leave Maureen alone was an overwhelming sadness at the final and complete loss of any possible chance to ever know Augrey Ferguson. Augrey had walked through a door and it had closed behind her, and it was never going to open again.

Katherine broke into the thick murk. "Want to help me make some bouquets?"

Maureen took the basket Katherine thrust at her and listlessly followed her mother out to the cutting garden.

"They've organized a flower drive at Holy Ghost. We're supposed to drop them off at the cafeteria, then somebody will get them over to the funeral home. Evidently the Altar Society has come up with what they think Arlene Ferguson really needs."

There it was again. The barely concealed disdain Maureen was beginning to suspect her mother held for everything about their town. "You don't like Cementville much, do you?"

Katherine knelt before a row of gladioli and clipped a few and laid them across the basket. "What's gotten into you, Maureen?" she said without looking up.

"Do you think you'd ever just, you know, leave?"

Her mother stood and rubbed her hands down her skirt and as she was about to answer, there was Carl, looming out of nowhere the way only Carl could.

"Could I have some flowers?"

"Sure," Katherine said, handing him the clippers.

He gathered an assortment—lavender globes of Stars of Persia, white and yellow snapdragons, deep purple angelonia, and long stems of fragrant lilies, all gently swaddled in his big arms. Maureen and Katherine silently watched.

"What do you plan to do with them, Carl?"

He looked around him for a bit, as if Katherine might be talking to someone else. "I thought I'd take them to Miss Wanda," he whispered to the ground.

"Oh. Oh, right. She and Arlene are cousins or something, aren't they? That's a wonderful idea, Carl," Katherine said.

He held the clippers out to her, and after the tiniest flinch, Katherine took them. Carl disappeared into the house.

"Mom," Maureen said.

Katherine busied herself arranging the flowers in the basket by size, longest on the bottom.

"Mother."

Katherine looked up.

"You're afraid of him, aren't you?"

"Of course not." Her mother pursed her lips in a laugh. "You really are too dramatic for words sometimes, honey."

In the house Maureen found Carl at the kitchen sink filling several canning jars with water. "You've got more than you can carry," she said. "Mind if I come along?" Without waiting for an answer, she helped him distribute the flowers into four jars.

Katherine met them coming out the back door. "Where are you going?" She looked at Maureen, not Carl.

"Carl can't carry all this by himself."

"Let me drive you."

"No." In memory, she had never said that word to her mother, not in that way, not with that tone. To her surprise, Katherine stepped aside. Maureen followed her uncle across the yard, each of them hugging two Mason jars stuffed with flowers.

When they reached the head of the driveway, Katherine called out. Maureen backtracked to where her mother still stood at the kitchen door.

"Are you sure you ought to be going up there? Wanda's mother has been sick for a long time." The basket of flowers they had cut for the Altar Society hung at Katherine's side. She tried to give Maureen her listen-here look. She lowered her voice to a whisper. "I'm not sure Mrs. Slidell's health will support an outburst from Carl. Plus there's Wanda herself, with that condition of hers. Carl is likely to send her into one of her attacks." She was about to launch into the standard lecture about how to behave, but Maureen cut her off.

"Carl has not had an outburst since the first night he came home from the hospital," she reminded Katherine. "That was in June. And it wasn't even an outburst. He was just nervous from not being used to us and from missing all his crazy friends who he had only lived with for his entire adult life." Maureen was surprised and angry and confused all at once and didn't know why she couldn't stop herself. "And, Mother, I am not some kind of feral cat that has never been inside somebody else's house before."

"Okay," Katherine said. "Okay." She gave Maureen a quick hug and carried her flowers into the house. Maureen walked the whole length of the driveway without once looking back to make sure her mother hadn't changed her mind.

THEY WALKED THROUGH TOWN WITH Carl's flowers. Maureen glanced at her uncle, her big hulking shadow. Katherine used to call Maureen "Daddy's little shadow." She didn't follow her father around much anymore, and she didn't really know when she had stopped. Willis seemed to have caved in on himself somehow, as if something inside him had been scooped out, something that wasn't required for you to keep on breathing, but the absence of which left you no longer the person you'd always been. Not that he'd ever been a big talker. But he had always been present, Maureen always knew where he was.

She knew the smell of him by heart. He was sad about something, that much was clear, and it wasn't just an old car. But could he ever be sad enough to—

No, she couldn't let herself think that. Willis Juell would never, ever . . .

Maureen looked at Carl again, at his thick arms and big plodding feet. He'd been a little boy once, a motherless boy with a very sad father. He probably adored Willis, probably followed him around everywhere. Maureen could imagine how hard it was for Carl when his big brother went away to the Korean War. Had he gone to look for his father that day? Maybe there were chores he'd been meaning to finish, and that was what sent him into the barn where his father . . .

She had gotten used to Carl, to having him follow her up and down hills and around town, huffing along, trying to keep up. Today it was Maureen who trailed behind, weighed down by the bleak mood that had set in last evening when they heard about Augrey. After Giang Smith's body was found, her mother would only let Maureen venture off the farm if Carl went with her. Now with the news about Augrey, Katherine appeared not to trust even Carl.

So much had changed in the span of one summer. The world was becoming a place where she might never feel at home again.

They clopped over the last bridge in town and began the slow climb up Crooked Creek Road. Maureen felt the slightest shiver as they passed Nimrod Grebe's house, dark and deserted since his cousins moved him to a nursing home in the next burg. Nimrod may have been the last person to see Augrey alive, other than the killer. Bett Ferguson's yard, normally crawling with raucous children, was empty and quiet.

Johnny Ferguson's farm was perched almost straight across the valley from the Juell farm, on the opposite side of the river. The house on Buckskin Ridge was one of the last places left in the county without a telephone. Carl and Maureen were going on the assumption that Miss Wanda would be home. What did Wanda Ferguson do, living up there on that windy knob with her grandparents' ghosts and her ailing mother for company? Maureen had not been to the Ferguson farm since she was little. The house was smallish, nicely kept up, peony bushes all across the front, the vegetable garden immaculate.

Carl knocked. Maureen didn't know she was nervous until her knees went watery. From inside came the sounds of somebody making their slow way to the door. She and Carl seemed to agree to an unspoken pact right then not to look at each other. The door opened and Loretta Ferguson Slidell stood before them, leaning on a cane.

Maureen would not have considered herself shy, so when no words came out of her open mouth she had to chalk it up to the flat-out beauty of the woman. Not beautiful like a movie star. She was more of a see-through, floaty vision, like the ghost of beauty. Where Maureen had pictured a decrepit and shrunken invalid, Loretta Slidell stood straight as a statue. Her pale skin held a few phantom freckles, as if some trace of the young girl she had once been was trapped inside and was being gradually erased. Her Dreamsicle hair floated in a loose twist, orange sherbet blended with vanilla ice cream. Maureen wanted to reach out and dip in a finger and taste it.

They followed her into the kitchen. Loretta directed Carl and Maureen to sit at the table. She took a dipper off the wall and ladled out two glasses of water from a metal bucket sitting on the drain board of a long plank cabinet. A smell came off the bucket, cool rocks and watercress, and Maureen remembered hearing that there wasn't running water in Johnny Ferguson's house. Willis had said Rafe Goins had offered his Ditch Witch to lay the trenches and pipes to pump county water into the house after Johnny died. Loretta Ferguson Slidell had quietly thanked them and told them spring water straight from the earth was what she had grown up drinking, and the last day of her life she wanted nothing but to drink a tall cold glass of its pure freshness. From the looks of things, Mrs. Slidell must have dipped her drinking water out of the very same beat-up tin bucket sitting on that same old drain board her entire life.

Without a word, Loretta vanished behind a flowered chintz curtain. Maureen and Carl heard a low exchange and some more shuffling, and when Miss Wanda parted the curtains, Carl stood up. Wanda and Carl appeared to be scanning each other's insides top to bottom. Maureen was embarrassed on behalf of them both for their lack of manners. She set her flowers on the drain board near the old tin bucket. Carl stood mutely holding his bouquets. Maureen lifted them from his hands and gave them to Wanda, which seemed to break the spell. They all looked at the flowers.

Wanda seemed unable to find her voice for a bit and when she finally did the words were barely above a whisper. "They're so pretty. Thank you."

Wanda Slidell was slender as her mother, but where Loretta was statuesque, Wanda was a gangly heap of bones, nearly as tall as Uncle Carl. The two women shared the trademark Ferguson red hair, but it was as if Wanda's had sucked all the color from her mother's and in the process the top of Wanda's head spontaneously combusted into a raging flame. She tried to keep it under control—Maureen had seen her fuss with her hair at the library when Miss Wanda thought nobody was looking, tugging and pulling it into a tight bun that sprung open like a fiery touch-me-not when she let go.

Maureen tried to make eye contact with her. Wanda began striking matches on the old black stove. She finally got one to light and held it under a teakettle so the burner hopped to life. With her back to them she said, "Well, Carl, I haven't seen you since I don't know when."

The kettle started with a low hum that quickly rose to an awful screaming whistle. Wanda took a box of Lipton off the shelf. She whipped around with two steaming cups in her hands and set them before Maureen and Carl.

"1954," Carl said and searched the bottom of his cup for more words. He took a careful sip, apparently oblivious to the absence of a teabag. Or maybe he was being polite; it was impossible to tell. "You and me were about to turn sixteen."

1954, Maureen thought, when the hobo got his head caved in.

"That sounds about right." Wanda took a butcher knife to a big loaf of black bread and put a few slices on a plate in front of him. She stared at the surface of the table as though a cryptic message at any second might arise from the wood. She kept her long slender fingers folded in front of her, laced so tight her knuckles were white.

"You're looking well, Miss Wanda." Maureen tried on the opening lines she'd heard her mother use dozens of times. Wanda turned her surprised attention upon the girl sitting at her kitchen table as though just realizing Maureen was there.

"Why do you kids all call me 'Miss'?"

"Beg pardon?"

"You never hear of anyone else my age being called 'Miss' anything anymore. So I wonder, why me? It's so old-fashioned, isn't it?"

Maureen wished she could say, *Old-fashioned? Look around you! Abraham Lincoln could walk into this kitchen and be right at home!* But Maureen saw her point. Miss Wanda was not all that old. She just acted old.

Maureen sipped at her steaming cup of water and made appreciative *mmm* noises. Wanda continued to look at her as if waiting for an answer. "I'm really sorry about your loss, Mi—Wanda."

"My loss?"

"Augrey. Augrey Ferguson." Maureen glanced purposely toward the flowers waiting on the drain board. It dawned on her that Wanda had taken them not as a condolence offering but as some sort of romantic gesture on Carl's part. Maureen tried on the look she had seen adults use when speaking to the bereaved. "I hope they find whoever did it."

"Oh. Yes. Horrifying. I didn't know her."

"Isn't she your cous—"

"But having grandfathers who were brothers doesn't mean I knew her. In fact, I seriously doubt we ever exchanged more than ten or fifteen passing words." Wanda sliced more black bread and pushed it toward Carl, even though he was still on his first piece. Whatever the condition was that made this woman so withdrawn and panicky about talking to people at the grocery store or the library, it seemed to be somewhat less of a problem here in the antiquated comfort of her own home.

"Do you think whoever did it was angry about her being, you know, friends with Nimrod Grebe?" As soon as it was out of her mouth, Maureen saw it—the line that wasn't to be crossed—and she was standing wide of it, on the other side. Wanda bored a hole in the table's invisible Ouija board with her eyes.

"Will you attend the funeral tomorrow?" Maureen said.

Wanda narrowed her eyes at her.

Carl fidgeted. "I sure am glad it's summer," he whispered. Wanda looked at him, and her shoulders sagged a good two inches when she sighed. "I prefer summertime. Give me hot weather any day." Maybe Carl *was* trying to court Wanda Slidell.

"I bet you know all kinds of interesting things about Cementville's founding fathers, Wanda," Maureen said, "since they were your very ancestors."

"My ancestors are dead, Maureen, except for my mother, who I believe you've met." Wanda looked into the clear contents of Carl's cup and her face reddened. She grabbed the Lipton box from the stove and plunked teabags into both Carl's and Maureen's cups. She shoved the sugar bowl closer to Maureen and scooted the plate of bread toward Carl. "I just baked that today. I can get jam, if you want it?"

Carl took a large bite. "Not necessary."

Wanda jumped up and took the jam from a shelf and slammed it on the table. She sat again and placed one hand on her chest and swung her long leg in nervous arcs. She reached behind her and grabbed a spoon from the drain board and clanged it onto Carl's plate of bread, then stared at the table some more.

"Have you ever been inside the Slidell mansion?" Maureen tried, but Wanda didn't bite. Maureen already knew the answer. Everybody in town knew the answer. Wanda Slidell's grandmother had made her a very rich woman.

"Are you getting used to Cementville again, Carl?" Wanda uncrossed her legs and crossed them again so they were pointing in Carl's direction. "Things have changed a lot since you lived here."

Maureen decided to go for broke. "How does it feel to be the last Slidell, now that Evelyn Slidell has passed on?" Katherine would have died a thousand deaths if she heard her daughter ask such a thing.

Wanda and Carl were unflummoxed.

"Long as they don't change the street names on me, I'll do all right," Carl said.

Wanda laughed and poured more hot water into their cups. The afternoon wore on, the two of them making awkward small talk and staring into their watery tea as if they were reading a future there that didn't look half bad. Miss Wanda ignored Maureen and her questions in a rude way.

Maureen found herself feeling sorry rather than mad, walking down the steep gravel road from Buckskin Ridge, although she couldn't say sorry for what.

She wasn't lying when she told her mother the next morning that she wanted to go to the library. Maureen fully intended to go to the library, to start with. She sat at breakfast behind the cereal boxes.

"The library, huh?" Katherine said.

Maureen shoveled Cheerios.

"Are we meeting someone special at the library?"

"Mother." But Maureen had to admit, she *was* looking pretty good. She had pinned her baby-fied bangs over to the side with a tiny lady bug hair clasp and borrowed some of Katherine's mascara, which made her look at least fifteen. The lipstick was being smeared off with each bite of Cheerios. She sighed. "Eddie Miller and me might go get Cokes at Happy's." She tried to keep her eyes on Katherine's forehead. "I mean, Eddie Miller and *I*."

"I'll drive you."

"Fine." Maureen drained her glass of orange juice then stared at the clock so she would have somewhere to look besides her mother's face. Twenty after nine. She needed to get Katherine into the car. Her mother hadn't let her ride her bike into town since they found Augrey, and she seemed to have lost her enthusiasm for Carl as bodyguard. "I promise to call you when we're done."

Katherine stared at her daughter for a few yearlong minutes with that X-ray vision mothers have that slices around inside a person, then she said, "Your hair looks pretty styled that way. Maybe it's time we let those bangs grow out. You're getting a little old for a pixie."

"*Thank* you," Maureen said. "I hope you'll remember that the next time you go waving your scissors around."

"You and Eddie walk together from the library to Happy's. And stay on Council Street. I mean it, Maureen. I don't want you going anywhere alone. And call me when you're ready to come home."

"Yes, ma'am." All these years, she had no idea lying was so easy.


KATHERINE DROPPED HER OFF IN front of the library. Maureen felt her mother watching as she climbed the steps. She waved Katherine off and went inside and without thinking pulled *The Outsiders* off the shelf and took it to the checkout desk.

"Haven't you read this twice?" Mrs. Cahill said.

Minutes later Maureen was walking across the Slidell Bridge carrying *The Pigman* and *Mr. and Mrs. Bo Jo Jones,* along with strict instructions from Charlene Cahill that Maureen make it clear to her mother that the books came *without* her recommendation.

Maureen ducked into the alley behind the Duvall Funeral Home and snuck around front. Roddy Duvall had hoisted the flag at half-mast in the middle of May when the dead soldiers came home. Now, three months later, it still hung there, limp and faded, the red washed to a pale pink. A few men stood in a circle near the flagpole, smoking and doing that low-talking thing men do in groups, hands in their pockets, eyes on the ground or pinned on a thing in the distance that nobody else sees. She hid behind the wrought-iron railing where the broad veranda jutted from the corner of the building and scanned the group, hoping Levon wasn't there. The men all carried that family resemblance, same hair on fire, same big eyebrows. They could all be Augrey's brothers, as far as Maureen could tell, standing around in sport coats that seemed to have been grabbed at random out of a bag, and nobody had ended up with one that fit. They huddled, round-shouldered, as if protecting their hearts from a cold wind. But it was a hot August day and at ten o'clock in the morning the air was thick and still. A few cupped their cigarettes in a half fist and brought them to their mouths so they looked like they were about to tell a secret no one was meant to repeat. She didn't see Levon, but the other brother, the one Billy said was a draft dodger, burst out onto the veranda and sat heavily in a rocking chair only a few feet from the railing where Maureen was hiding. The men were blocking the entryway to the funeral home. Maureen sucked in a breath and drifted nearer. She sat on the low stone wall, hoping they would break up their little party soon.

*Mumble mumble*, one of the men said. He spit on the ground and they all looked over at her at the same time. A boy broke off from the group and came to where Maureen was sitting. He stood there a while, the smoke from his cigarette curling around his face and making him squint.

"Maureen Juell," he said.

She didn't know where to put her eyes.

"Ain't you Mo Juell?" He was staring at the top of her head in a way that made her reach up and touch her hair. The ladybug hair clasp slipped into her hand. She tried to smooth her bangs over but could feel them sticking straight out from her forehead like a hat bill.

"I thought for a minute you had a bug in your hair," he said. Another of Augrey's brothers—Tony, she thought he was called. The cigarette didn't disguise the fact that the boy was close to Maureen's age, nor did it hide his red-rimmed eyes. "You know Augrey?" The tone in his voice said nothing would convince him that could be true. He sized her up. "You come to gawk, didn't you? Don't worry, you ain't the first."

Straight into her face he blew three perfect smoke rings at which Maureen silently vowed not to blink or cough. She waited for him to turn away, bored with her, and rejoin the men.

"Well, come on then," he said. "I'll take you to her." He cut through the circle of men and headed up the steps and into the Duvall Funeral Home. She slinked after him.

She had been inside Duvalls' only two times before, and that was years ago when she was just a kid. Her mother's second cousin had electrocuted himself rewiring his house. A little girl she didn't know had contracted tuberculosis from her own daddy. The dad recovered at the sanatorium in Glasgow, but his child did not. Tiny coffin, all pink satin and lace. Maureen had not forgotten that spooky combination of sounds unique to funeral homes. Weird quiet music of no particular tune that comes out of invisible speakers in every corner. The muffled ruffling of a couple dozen Kleenexes being removed from and shoved into pocketbooks. Women's cut-off sobs buried in the shoulder of somebody's Sunday suit, the wind seizing in their throats, catching and gasping like something being tamped into a soft hole. Maureen followed the boy and those sobbing Kleenex sounds. On the left was a room filled mostly with older men she'd never seen before. They looked up when she and Tony passed. One man handed a small, flat bottle to another. Maureen had seen Uncle Judge bring such a bottle out of his inside coat pocket sometimes after supper and tip it to his lips. The men stared at her with their long faces, their jutting chins and tall slanting brows telling her without using words: She was interrupting.

"In here," Tony said, and he directed her to a doorway across the hall, a parlor outside of which stood a pedestal with a white guest book waiting for people to sign in. The boy handed the pen to her and pointed to the next open line, his dirty fingernail leaving a little black half-moon scar on the page. Maureen signed her name, then stepped across the threshold and into Augrey's parlor.

Heavy velvet drapes floor to ceiling, deep burgundy walls, dark woodwork, brocade settees positioned in angles near the casket. This was probably the fanciest room Augrey had ever been in. On the couch nearest the front of the room sat two large women, enough alike to be identical twins. Maureen wasn't sure which was Arlene Ferguson, Augrey's mother, and which was her Aunt Bett. Both of them looked pretty well cried out, their faces matching wrung sponges. Several rows of white folding chairs were lined up for the service. Maureen picked a chair in the back row, and the boy who'd shown her in sat beside her, as if he didn't trust her to be around his sister's coffin.

One after another, people bent toward the larger of the two women. They clasped Arlene's hand in both of theirs and murmured. Maureen couldn't make out what was being said. She was going to have to walk up there and give her condolences to Augrey's mother, and she had no idea what she was meant to say. Maybe if Katherine had allowed her to attend Brandon Miller's wake, she would have had more experience with these things and she would have known. But Bran's mother Raedine had talked Mr. Duvall into letting Bran have an open casket, despite the fact that her son's neck had been gashed by a satchel charge thrown into his bunker as he slept. Katherine understood Raedine's thinking: She wanted people to see what war had done to her boy. It was not, however, something Katherine thought Maureen needed to see, not with her own brother newly returned, and not with several other local boys still there in battle. So it was Katherine's fault that Maureen didn't know the appropriate sorts of things you were supposed say to a grieving mother. People generally whispered in the presence of the dead; she remembered that much from when she had been here as a child. She was wracking her brain for a simple comment or greeting for Augrey's mother when Ginny walked in. Maureen melted with relief at the sight of someone she recognized.

She practically ran to greet Ginny. "I'm so glad you came!" Maureen said, realizing at once that she'd blurted it too loud for the circumstances. It wasn't as though they ran into each other at a party or something. What on earth was wrong with her?

But Ginny appeared not to mind. "I'm glad you came too," she cried, and embraced Maureen so tightly they had to lean awkwardly over top of Ginny's pregnant belly. Ginny didn't let go for what felt like a very long time. She hugged and wailed into Maureen's neck until Maureen could feel tears rolling down the inside of her collar. When Ginny finally came up for air, they stood and held hands and inspected the swirling pattern in the carpet.

"Well," Ginny said, and turned toward where her mother-in-law sat watching. Maureen followed Ginny to the front of the room. Maybe listening to Ginny's words of condolence would help her figure out what to say.

"I am so sorry, Mama Arlene!" Ginny crumpled to the carpet and buried her face in Arlene Ferguson's lap. She cried so thoroughly and loudly that someone was sent across the hall to tell Levon to come get his wife. Maureen backed up a few steps and made way for that scary man she had so long despised. But it wasn't Levon who helped Ginny to her feet. The other Ferguson brother, Byard, cupped Ginny's elbow in his hand and once she was standing, put an arm gently around her shoulder. Maureen and everybody else turned to watch them go out to the hallway. She heard the rough slur of Levon's voice. There was the sound of a scuffle, and a high shriek from Ginny, and everyone craned their necks to catch a glimpse of the scene between the two brothers.

In the midst of the melee, Maureen turned and looked into the waiting face of Augrey's mother. She bent over stiffly and thrust her arm toward the woman's thick hand. In a sealed box not five feet away lay the body of a wild girl who drank and smoked. People said she danced for men for the cost of a cheap glass of whiskey at Pekkar's Alley. It was more than a rumor now that she had moved in with Nimrod Grebe this summer and took care of him after his stroke. People said Augrey was a trashy little loner who, yes, had drawn a fistful of short straws; but she had willfully broken that final straw, living with an old colored man that way. When she had finally worn out all of her town's possible forgivenesses, someone had been angry enough to hurt her. Someone had hurt her to death.

But the girl in the wooden box was fifteen years old, and she was the daughter of the big woman whose face was tilted up at Maureen now, no doubt trying to place who, exactly, Maureen might be.

For a long moment in that mental blank spot, Maureen forgot what it was that made her come to the funeral home. In the next, what she could remember about her motives turned her face hot with shame. She had come to stare into the maw of grief, to see if she could grab hold of something there, something she could use, swallow it like a magic potion that would provide her with instant understanding. A kind of medicine for the fear, a sticky balm that might seal the hole being bored through her gut by the raw guilt she shared with her town for Augrey Ferguson's death.

She looked into the face of the dead girl's mother, a face newly drowned, eyelids full up, floodgates all ready to let go. What came out of Maureen's mouth were the words of an idiot.

"She. She was. Very popular."

Arlene Ferguson patted Maureen's hand and said with shocking grace, "I thank you for that, honey."

Maureen followed the line of people waiting to pray in front of the sealed coffin with its spray of red gladioli draped over, a pile of bloody spears. Augrey's school portrait sat atop the flowers like an icon of the Virgin in a scarlet shrine. In the photograph, that stunning hair fell over one shoulder as if she had gathered it all to the side to show off her long white neck. Maureen leaned in to study the photograph. Her face went hot again as she recognized a chain of purple blotches there. Cheap makeup hadn't quite covered up the unmistakable hickeys. Augrey's crimson lips were an exact match to the gladiola spears darting from beneath the picture frame. In spite of herself Maureen pictured a boy, or a series of boys, heading into a closet or a darkened room by turns to kiss those lips, passionate kisses that moved from her lips to her neck—and then what?

The nuns at Holy Ghost School had taught Maureen plenty of prayers. But when she bowed her head, what popped into her mind was *Now I lay me down to sleep . . .*

She tiptoed through the sniffs and sobs that sounded like dozens of tiny strangulations, all the way to the back row of folding chairs where she reclaimed the seat next to Tony or whatever his name was. He was holding *Mr. and Mrs. Bo Jo Jones* open to its middle, and it was obvious he was only pretending to read. Maureen glanced at the words under his finger: *. . . when he got in bed beside me I found I was still feeling hurt . . .*

Maureen felt the heat rise up her neck, an instant mortification that vanished when a drop of water fell on the page of the open book. And another. She looked at the boy's wet face, silent, motionless, flowing with tears. Maureen reached over and closed the book but kept her hand over his for half a minute, until he jerked it violently away and scowled at her.

Mr. Duvall floated through the mourners, an imitation shepherd in a polyester suit, tending his flock, patting a shoulder here, holding a hand there. He owned his position at the lectern to the right of the coffin. His practiced undertaker's voice did exactly what it was supposed to do, lulling the mourners off to a counterfeit valley of peace, all green pastures and milk and honey where they could pretend for a while that a forgiving god had gazed upon a sweet girl and called her home. The funeral director led the faithful in prayers Maureen did not know. *He is my light and my salvation. Whom shall I fear?* His droning voice was comforting, and she felt herself grow sleepy.

Her head jerked up when Levon Ferguson strode to the lectern, setting off the soft flurry of a new round of whispers. He stood with his hands folded in front of his groin and he closed his eyes. His big flat mouth opened in song. It startled the room, and after half a minute of shocked murmurs the gathered mourners calmed down enough to listen.

*Love's own tender flame warms this meeting*, he sang, and Maureen was glad his eyes were closed, because she would not have

PAULETTE LIVERS

wanted to look into them. *And love's tender song should sing. But fly away little pretty bird, and pretty you'll always stay.* This haunting melody, clear as mountain air, couldn't be coming from the mean drunk whose battered and bruised wife lived in the tenant cabin below the Juells' house. His song pushed against the walls of the old mansion, and even the men from across the hall left their pint bottles and came to stand in the doorway and listen, bleary-eyed and weaving on their feet.

The draft-dodging brother squatted at Arlene's feet and glared at Levon. Maureen could see his face only in profile, but that did not prevent her from reading the amused bitterness in Byard's expression. The Ferguson clan had come together to mourn their loss. But there was something wrong here, and not just the men's drunkenness or the dagger gaze of one brother to the other, or Tony's refusal to openly cry for his dead sister.

Maureen hadn't known it was possible for family to hate family.

She looked at the glowering boy next to her but he wouldn't look back.

"Thank you, Tony," she whispered. He continued to stare at his hands, pulling at a hangnail until a bright bead of blood popped onto his filthy thumb. Maureen gathered her library books and slipped out of the Duvall Funeral Home the same way she had come in. She walked down the alley and out to Council Street. She used the phone at Happy's to call her mother.

"Did you and Eddie have fun?" Katherine gripped the steering wheel at ten and two and stared straight ahead, but Maureen could see she had the single eyebrow arched, the sign that she meant to be sharing in whatever mischief Maureen was up to.

"I might be coming down with something." Maureen let her head fall against the window. "I just need to be home." She made herself keep her eyes open, made herself watch her town pass by on the other side of the car's window glass, committing to memory what remaining things she knew to be true.

# FOURTEEN

Wanda had put off meeting with Alden Wilder as long as she could. It had been weeks since her grandmother's passing—could it already be September? Given all that had happened this summer, there had been plenty of excuses to postpone getting together with Evelyn Slidell's attorney.

When first she had taken a seat at the old woman's bedside, Wanda had assumed it was a gesture of kindness on both their parts, an obligation of blood bond. In some strange way, spending time with Evelyn was like a traded penance for Wanda's failure to attend the funerals of this grisly summer. She really had meant to attend at least some of the services for the Guardsmen, but as the appointed day and hour for each funeral loomed, she found herself laid low with intestinal difficulties, arrhythmia, the sensation of numerous tiny screws being driven through her skull, et cetera, et cetera. She was so weary of herself.

Nor had she gone to the funeral of Giang Smith, or her audacious little cousin Augrey only last week. At no time would she have said out loud that her grandmother was *working* on her. But that must have been it. Getting to know Evelyn Slidell, a helpless and lonely elder, during all those visits into town had wrought something of a change, a *translation* of the woman Wanda was.

Now she sat in Alden Wilder's office. Loretta had declined to come along, having rarely ventured far from her bedroom since Evelyn's funeral.

"You're aware that Mrs. Slidell has left everything to you." Mr. Wilder carefully placed his half-eaten fried egg sandwich on top of a wedge of paper towel on his desk, its runny yolk and faint sulfur smell creeping toward her. Wanda struggled to keep her eyes off it. Packed and labeled boxes sat stacked against the office walls, ready and waiting for their owner's retirement.

"Yes," was all Wanda could manage at first. The threat of arrhythmia lurked in her chest, the slightest flutter of stamping feet, that sure marker of an oncoming panic attack. But as quickly as it threatened, it diminished, as if some stronger part of her had come out of hiding and yelled *Boo!* to the frightened rabbit in her. "But I'm not sure I know what that means."

"Well, there's the house. I don't know if you'll want to list it for sale, auction it off, or move into it. I can give you as much or as little help as you wish on any of those options."

That was a lot of information. She tried to create an outline in her head. Roman numeral one. The House.

Capital A. List it.

B. Auction it.

C. Live in it.

"May I have a piece of paper and a pen?" Wanda said.

The lawyer rummaged through an open cardboard box on his desk and pulled out a yellow pad. He slid an elegant cup of pens to her side of the desk. "I apologize for the condition of my office. I'm afraid this box is my temporary supply cabinet. I'm supposed to retire next week."

"Oh, don't mention it. I can't begin to say how much I appreciate you helping me out."

"Now. There are several accounts," he said. "Eight fifty in Farmers Bank right here in town. The mutual fund, which we might want to get out of—the thing is tanking right now—my man tells me this bear market isn't likely to move for a while—your mutual fund is worth about six and a quarter. I'll have Mrs. Slidell's accountant calculate the value of the stock portfolio, and you can decide how you want to handle that. No rush."

Wanda scribbled the figures in a column. She relaxed and let out a pleasant exhale. "So there's about fourteen seventy-five, plus whatever the stocks are worth," she said. She wondered if it was the first time she ever used the word *stock* as a noun to refer to anything not on four legs.

"Fourteen hundred and seventy-five thousand dollars, yes, that's right. A million, four hundred and seventy-five thousand. The portfolio is probably another million. Give or take."

The last thing Wanda saw before she lost consciousness was the top of Alden Wilder's shiny head as he reordered papers in the fat file representing Evelyn Slidell's earthly possessions.

THE LAWYER COULD NOT HAVE done a single other thing to make the execution of her grandmother's will go smoother. He routed the paperwork through the bank to combine the myriad accounts her grandmother had set up. He put Wanda in touch with a financial planner in Louisville who would personally drive out to Wanda's house and help her sort through the stock portfolio, all the buying and selling and what not. He arranged a trust that would issue a modest check on a regular basis.

All of Alden Wilder's paper shuffling uncovered the circuitous ways the old woman had helped Wanda and Loretta over the three decades since Stanley Slidell's untimely death. The full ride to Saint Brigid College, which Wanda had been led to believe was from some nebulous foundation, was only a portion. Wanda remembered times when Kirshbaum's store in town notified them that there had been a mistake and there was a credit on their account, usually around the end of the year—the only way Evelyn could secretly manage a Christmas gift for her grandchild. Then there was the money that had appeared every month—the bank called it a "death benefit" from Stanley's life insurance.

"Why couldn't she have just come out and said to my mother, 'Here, let me help you'?" Wanda wondered out loud. Alden Wilder had no ready answer, but Wanda imagined they had similar thoughts about it. Evelyn Slidell couldn't feature such a public connection with Ferguson blood.

When the last pesky pieces of paperwork had been stuffed into their manila envelopes, Mr. Wilder reached into a desk drawer and brought forth a pocket-sized silver flask. He pulled two cone-shaped paper cups from the dispenser above the restroom sink and he filled one with bourbon and handed it to Wanda. He filled his own and tapped it to hers with a muffled chink. Wanda had never tossed back even a thimbleful of pure liquor before, but she mimicked Mr. Wilder's fluid motion that ended with a decisive flick of the head. The gag reflex she expected never came. The bourbon trickled down, its fiery honey warming her tonsils and esophagus and her entire chest. Wanda smiled.

She pulled the Plymouth Fury up to the farmhouse and sat there for a while in the idling car, trying to figure how to tell her mother about the unfailing kindnesses Evelyn Slidell had secretly thrust into their lives. She cut the engine and went inside.

None of Wanda's mental preparations included a provision for Loretta breaking down altogether. Her mother kept her spine straight at the kitchen table while her face came apart like a crushed box. When Loretta's silent weeping was done, Wanda helped her to bed. She fetched tea and a paperback her mother had tried to read the day before. Loretta, propped on pillows, feigned reading from the middle of *Pride and Prejudice* then let her head fall to the side.

Wanda closed the door behind her and went downstairs to take care of the lunch dishes. Then she took a bowl and a knife and went to the garden to cut kale.

Loretta stayed in her room all that day. An hour before suppertime Wanda tapped on her door and stuck her head in. "I'm going to fry those catfish Carl Juell brought over here this morning. How does that sound?" There was nothing her mother preferred over fresh fish. Loretta began struggling wordlessly to extricate herself from the bedclothes.

"Pete's sake, Mother, it wouldn't kill you to ask for help now and then," Wanda said.

Loretta rolled her eyes. They had always related most comfortably in this chiding way. Everything was right between them again; they were past whatever riffs Evelyn's interference in their lives had caused. The money wasn't going to change anything.

"That young man is still sweet on you," Loretta said. "Look at how he pitches woo. Catfish."

"Mother, Carl and I are thirty years old."

"You're not saying you're too old to be romanced."

"Stop it now." Wanda felt herself blushing.

Supper was simple: Carl's catfish dredged in cornmeal and green onion-flecked hushpuppies. Sliced tomatoes, the kale braised with a little bacon. Wanda offered her mother some ice cream. She had picked it up after leaving Mr. Wilder's office, popping a Certs in her mouth before heading into the A&P. The last thing she needed was to add drunkenness to the buzz about her that had Cementville in a subtle quiver. But Loretta said no, she'd skip dessert tonight.

"Have to watch my girlish figure, you know."

Wanda, surprised and delighted at this rare foray into humor, let loose a horsey laugh. A breeze ruffled the edge of the curtain. They played Crazy Eights a while. Her mother was in bed again before the sun went down.

Wanda went out walking for a bit before turning in. It was already cool. A gibbous moon warped itself into a lopsided ball of yarn, lighting up the fringes of three clouds snagged on Juell Ridge. On the limestone slab that marked the beginning of their driveway she sat down and folded her long legs under her. She leaned into the mailbox post. She considered how all the things that had happened over the past few months were bearing down and threatening to topple her into an impossible future. Wanda tried to see herself traipsing through London or the Louvre, sketching in the details of the mad fancy that Evelyn Slidell had indulged on her behalf. She thought of the poets who lay under stone slabs in Westminster Abbey. She could walk the places where they had walked, the landscapes of dream-country, as Hardy called it.

She remembered walking their road with Poose at night, frightened by the haunting shapes of fence posts and trees. The memory of Death's little visit floated in the space around her, wavering, vaporous, his friendly grimace transmogrifying like an out-of-focus snapshot. *When I was a child, I thought like a child*, she recalled from Paul, Corinthians. She would claim to have long ago put away childish things, but then again, it was only a few months earlier that she'd actually entertained the notion of Death's little visit being more than what it surely was, the product of a dream fog. Was that what Eliot meant, when he called life a *dreamcrossed twilight between birth and dying*? And what did it say about her, that the liveliest character of her dreams had been a needling Father Time, a polyglot Chronos with an agenda?

"Come on back here, you old troublemaker," she said to the fencepost across the road. Wanda shook herself and whispered, "Talking to shadows—what's next?"

She jumped when a voice answered.

"I'm not intending trouble." In the dark, in the middle of Crooked Creek Road, a thin form wavered.

"Are you drunk, Angus Ferguson?" She wasn't sure how or when it happened, but somewhere along the way Wanda had let go of being afraid of her great uncle, of his natural gift for hurting women.

Angus had to be—what, seventy, eighty?—after all. A shuck of his former dangerous self, any damage he might inflict already done.

"Reckon I've been soberer." He toed the gravel built up in the center of the road. "Though I can't remember when." He har-harred lamely, and in lieu of the old sense of peril Wanda felt nothing so much as pitying irritation.

"Truth is, Wanda Viola, I'm missing Johnny something fierce tonight." Old Angus sat down in the road and blubbered, out of which Wanda made a word here and there. "Little Daniel . . . blowed all to hell . . . nothing in that pine box in the ground but maybe a foot, little piece of ear . . . poor little Augrey . . . all chewed up by Levon's good-for-nothing hounds." Blubber blubber.

Angus and Poose hadn't spoken since the night before Mem's funeral, when Poose held the rifle to Angus's head. After his brother's death, Uncle Angus tried to ingratiate himself with Loretta and Wanda, the branch of Fergusons that had "done good" by marrying into Slidells. He showed up whenever he felt like it, never invited. Angus Ferguson represented the disreputable blood Loretta wished did not flow in her own veins. And now he had doubtless gotten wind of the inheritance. Wanda couldn't imagine there was a single person in Cementville who didn't have all the details of her recent fortune.

She stalked wordlessly into the house and came back carrying a plate of leftovers to where the old sot waited between two poplars out by the road. Loretta had forbidden him on the property after he tried in a blind-drunk stupor to climb into bed with her one night after Poose died. Although they hated to, they took to locking the doors at bedtime after that.

While he wolfed down the last of Carl's catfish filets, Wanda took the opportunity to say, "I am truly sorry about Daniel and Augrey both, Uncle Angus. They were too young. No family should have to suffer two such tragedies so close together." *Not even yours,* she did not say.

He polished the plate of fish with the side of his hand and licked his greasy paw clean. He handed the dish to Wanda. The moon cast his eyes in shadow under the wiry brows, white now with no trace of the famous Ferguson red. She hoped she detected a speck of gratitude there. But he wasn't a man to stand on ceremony. With the barest nod, he wobbled down the road in the direction of town.

"Git, Angus," Wanda whispered after him.

She thought of checking on her mother once before she went to bed but didn't want to risk waking her. In her own room, she threw a summer quilt over her legs and opened *Slaughterhouse-Five* to see what all the fuss was about. Wanda read late into the night, pulled to Billy Pilgrim's plight, to his time-traveling solution to the dilemma of free will, to his ridiculous optimism and acceptance in the face of war's outrages. She had to read the words of the dying hobo on the train several times.

*You think this is bad?* the hobo said. *This ain't bad.*

When she put out the light, the black sky behind the Juell house across the valley was touched at the horizon with pink, the last star fading.

SHE MIGHT HAVE ONLY SLEPT an hour by the time the sun warmed her cheek. Wanda woke to the odd sense that she was not in her own house. The forms of the curtains, the chifforobe, the desk and chair, things she had seen when she opened her eyes every morning of her life, might as well have been the furnishings of a strange hotel room. It caused a startle in her and, just as quickly, she knew: Her mother was dead.

She stood outside Loretta's bedroom for a long time before pushing open the door, and still she gasped on seeing the white profile, nearly the color of the sheets. Loretta's hand was still warm.

"I'll be alright, Mother." Wanda whispered her protest, even though her mother was giving no quarrel. "It's okay. You go on now."

IN THE WEEKS AFTER HER mother passed, Wanda found herself taking on Loretta's slow, deliberate habits as if some scrap of her mother's soul had been snagged on the briars of her own, a frail shred of cloth left behind, a fragment of a lost child's garment. Drawing a glass of water became an occasion to gaze out the same window where Loretta had hovered mornings, alternately sipping water from a chipped goblet and feeding the tiny tablets of prednisone and chloroquine between her dry lips. Wanda kept Loretta's wool sweater on a nail by the kitchen door and took to slipping it over her own shoulders each morning.

Outdoors, she put one tentative foot on the garden path in front of her, careful to measure the security of its purchase before the next step, the actions of a cautious invalid or an infant learning to walk. Sometimes as she tweezed the persistent lamb's quarters from between Loretta's clumps of borage and wild comfrey, Wanda was sure she could hear her mother's weary sigh behind her, that if she looked over her shoulder she would see the once generous figure standing, spine-arched, her hand pressed to the small of her back.

But no, Wanda was alone now on the old place Poose had christened Hanging Valley, in the house he called Maiden's Rest, the four walls she and Loretta had both grown up in. This occupation by her mother's ghost did not alarm her. That is, Wanda did feel unquestionably older, dragging herself around the house and what was left of Poose's dilapidated farm; but wielding the memory of her mother was less a drain on her than the weight of her grandmother's estate. Wanda had depended on Loretta to keep the crushing yoke of being suddenly wealthy from grinding her straight into the ground.

She heard voices, one high, the other soft, deep. Carl and his niece. Their heads appeared first as they pushed their bikes up the hill. Wanda rose to her feet, her hand rising instinctively to her throat. The pulse there was steady and slow.

# FIFTEEN

Katherine and Maureen were drying and putting away the supper dishes when the call came. Maureen answered the phone and was barely able to get out hello before the high-pitched squawk emanating from the ear piece made her hold the thing a good four inches from her face. Willis could hear Lila's screech from across the kitchen where he sat at the table sipping a cup of Postum. He claimed it was one of the few healthy habits he'd picked up in Korea—he couldn't handle caffeine at night anymore, and the grain-based drink seemed to help his digestion. They'd had a new phone installed, a wall unit with a long springy cord, and Maureen wrapped herself in it like a mummy.

"Mrs. O'Brien," Maureen mouthed to Katherine, her eyes wide in an exaggerated startle. She held out the phone and uncoiled herself from the cord. Her mother gave her a playful swat on the bottom with her tea towel.

"Lila, how are you?" Katherine said. "Hold on—slow down, Lila." She listened, nodding and glancing occasionally at Maureen and Willis as they waited transfixed to see what new excitement—or calamity—had arrived now. "I'll be right there."

Katherine hung up the phone and stood there a minute with her face to the wall. She breathed in, trying to put herself in Lila O'Brien's shoes. She pressed in place a strand of hair that had come loose, and she may have even prayed. When she turned to her husband and daughter, she must not have managed to smooth the apprehension from her face, because Maureen put a hand to her mouth and her eyes filled with tears.

"They've arrested Harlan O'Brien," Katherine said.

"Oh, thank God!" Maureen yelped.

"Maureen!" Katherine was about to slap her when she noticed that Willis, his face drained of color and his cup still suspended in the air before him, had deflated. He set the cup down carefully and put his face in his hands.

Maureen burst into tears.

"What—" Katherine looked in bewilderment from her daughter to her husband.

"We thought it was Billy," Willis said. "We figured Lem found him in a ditch somewhere."

"Oh. No. No, it's Harley. Sheriff O'Donahue has taken him in for questioning. I need to go over there. Lila is beside herself. Do you think we have any of those sedatives they sent Billy home with?"

"Seriously? Katherine, he probably ate that bottle in the first few days he was back." Willis shook his head as he smoothed and folded his *Courier Journal*.

Katherine glared at him. What had become of the sweet, compassionate man she married twenty . . . good God, they would celebrate their twentieth this winter. Where was her Willis, the gentle father who couldn't stand to see her spank the kids, even for the gravest of childhood offenses, who tirelessly read them bedtime stories after putting in a grueling day at the shop, so that she could put her feet up and just be, with no demands from anyone?

"I will remind you one more time: It was you who signed that form the recruiter sent home saying it was okay for a seventeen-year-old to run off to this idiotic and murderous vanity they are calling a war." She knew her voice had what Maureen called the "demon-possession" tone, and she knew the once private arguments between her and Willis had begun to spill beyond the bedroom.

"He can't use the war as an excuse to behave like a worthless drunk forever," Willis said.

Katherine shuddered, actually had to rub her arms to get the goose bumps to go down, from the chill in his voice. It was Willis who taught her what unconditional love—when truly lived—felt like. And now he seemed to suffer a physical revulsion at the very thought of his own son.

"He's been home four months, Will. Four. That is hardly *forever*." She had tried to get him to read articles about the new studies being done on war fatigue and stress and trauma. His response was always the same: It's not as though men have never gone to war before. But she couldn't deal with Willis now. She had to get over to the O'Briens' house. Lem was waiting till she got there before he drove to the jail, not wanting to leave Lila alone. Outside, the sun was already gone and there was a nip in the air.

"Maureen, would you get my sweater, the navy one with the pearl buttons?"

She watched Maureen run upstairs, knowing it would take her a few minutes to dig the sweater out of her closet.

"Will."

He looked up from the paper.

"Do you want to go over there with me? Lemuel would probably appreciate you riding to the jail with him. Maureen will be all right alone for a while. Carl will be home from Wanda's soon." Katherine tried for a smile; she needed to lighten the air in the room.

Will took the bait. "Sure." He stood from the table and at the same time they reached for each other. "I'm sorry," he said into her hair.

"I know," she said. "Me too." She was glad when Maureen came downstairs and caught them in an embrace. They hadn't done this enough lately, shown the kids how important family was, in good times and bad. Katherine nearly wept with the flood of relief, and her husband held her tighter.

\* \* \*

THE LAST OF THE SUN washed a ribbon of gold over the ridge across the valley. Willis could just make out the roof of Johnny Ferguson's old place, where Carl was probably wiping the crumbs of his dinner from his chin. He was glad for Carl that the meek flame he'd once carried for Wanda Slidell seemed to have been relit. In the least case, she would make a nice friend; a bit peculiar for his own taste, but probably perfect for Carl.

"Nice night for a walk," Willis said, his heart suddenly full with the realization of his unlikely luck, walking across the spine of land his family had called theirs for seven generations, including Maureen, and yes, Billy. They were bathed in this pink twilight, they were good people, a good family that was meant to be here, not the type who moved here or there whenever the slightest breeze blew them around. They would survive this—this thing, whatever it was—that had befallen their community; all of them, even Carl, would survive. Willis's wife strode along so upright and pretty by his side, her kind, strong face not minding the chill of the evening wind.

"There's a little bite in that breeze," he said. Katherine murmured agreement and held his hand and Willis wondered whether it was already time to light the furnace. He hated to, what with the cost of heating oil now.

They knocked on Lemuel's and Lila's door, even though they didn't really need to, being back-door neighbors all these years. Lem took them to where his wife lay on the couch in the front room. Lila started to struggle up, saying, "Let me get you all something, coffee, iced tea . . . " but Katherine was able to calm her down, and Lila fell against the arm of the sofa and daubed the wad of tissue at her eyes, trying for half a minute to be dainty, but then pulling several fresh Kleenex out of the box at her elbow and weeping freely into them.

"Now, Mother," Lemuel O'Brien said helplessly. He wagged his head at Willis and Katherine.

This was Willis's least favorite thing in the world to do. He was glad Katherine was comfortable offering succor, because he was woefully ill-equipped for the task. Not to mention, he had harbored thoughts of his own about Harlan, thoughts he never dared mention to Katherine, knowing where she stood on the subject. But Willis had seen Harley walking back up the hill in the dawn hours this summer. He had heard the stories, that people had seen Harlan O'Brien talking with Jimmy Smith's wife at the river, always before sunup. Which made the whole thing appear sneaky, when really they may have just been talking about things they had in common. Dalliances like that happened, Willis figured, people got entangled with each other, he understood it could happen without anyone ever intending anything bad. You could wake up and find yourself enmeshed or—or just as easily, separated or lost—without the first notion of how you got there. But objectively speaking, Willis wondered, could Harlan have murdered someone? Sure, he could have.

"Will, why don't you and Lem go see how things are coming along with Harlan?" Katherine said, and the two men lost no time heading out to the garage. Willis turned around once to see if he could spot her at the window, but the O'Briens' house sat stolid on the ridge, yellow-stained by the dying light.

"I expect Harlan'll be riding home with us," Lem said. "It's not as though they have anything specific on him. O'D said they're talking to a lot of men here in town, just gathering information."

"I'm sure that's so," Willis said. "They've got to gather information."

"I can't even recall when was the last murder in these parts." Lem kept both hands on the wheel, eyes ahead. Willis had known Lemuel O'Brien all his life. His friend was not a man given to provocation, so Willis didn't suspect him now of callously picking at old wounds. He wasn't trying to get Willis to talk about Carl, or the long-ago death of a vagrant.

"Me neither," said Willis.

But Lem was methodical, his years operating the sawmill and then working carpentry making him keen with numbers and solving loose ends. "Oh yeah, it was that Stubbs, or Stobbs . . . "

"Stubblefield," Willis said. "1954." He did not need to look at Lem O'Brien to know that the man was blinking into the windshield, aware suddenly that he had transgressed. The last two blocks to the jail rolled under them, the only sound the calm ticking of Lem's watch.

Mickey O'Donohue's new deputy waited for them.

"Lem. Willis." He shook both men's hands and directed them to the creaky church pew that marked the raw space as a waiting room. It was familiar, the walls bare but for a few Wanted posters. The rickety table with ancient yellowed magazines. The rough plank floors Willis had paced several times this summer, having driven here in the night to get his own son out of another scrape. The last time Billy was in for public drunkenness, Willis had left him in the tank overnight, and Katherine didn't speak to him for two whole days.

"Alden in there with them?" Lemuel said, and the deputy nodded.

Willis was drawing a blank as to whose kid the deputy was. Big ears; could be Pekkar's kid. That would be a strange turn—half the customers here at the jail probably got picked up wandering away from Pekkar's Alley three-quarters lit. Maybe the deputy was one of Hap Spalding's kids, there being seven or eight of them. If so, he'd lost a brother at Blacksnake. Willis wished he knew for sure, because he ought to say something, offer condolence. Lem might know who the kid was, but they were sitting too close to the desk, and even if Willis asked in a whisper, the deputy would hear. Willis glanced at Lem.

Lem was getting agitated, which was not a state one often saw him in. "Reckon they'd mind if we went in?" he asked. He hadn't taken his eyes off the closed door that Willis knew led to the kitchen. A kitchen that also served as the interrogation room.

The deputy looked up from his paperwork and gave a slow,

apologetic shake of his head. "Sorry, Mr. O'Brien. I'm sure they'll be out directly," he said.

Willis paged through a yellowed leaflet. *The Sunday Visitor*. June 1961. He threw it down. The door to the kitchen opened, and Alden Wilder came out. Lem stood up, the prospect of every possible outcome writ large across his face.

"He's—" Alden started to say. "Lem, Harlan is confused. I cut Sheriff O'Donahue off in his interview."

"Confused . . . how? What are you saying?"

"O'D thinks he ought to stay the night. I don't disagree with him, Lem. We'll call the VA and see if we can schedule an evaluation."

"You aren't saying you think he's dangerous?"

"Not to anybody else. But nobody wants to risk Harley hurting himself." Alden Wilder was solicitous and calm. He'd spent a lifetime being solicitous and calm. "They're going to let him rest, nobody's going to bother him tonight, no more questions. Why don't you go on home now."

"But what am I supposed to tell Lila?" Willis's neighbor, as sturdy a man as he'd ever known, stood there before the lawyer with his arms hanging limp at his sides. Lem swallowed hard and cleared his throat, but still his lips trembled. His eyes searched Alden Wilder's face.

"We'll let you know in the morning as soon as we hear from the VA. I'll give you a call myself, Lem, I promise."

Willis did not attempt conversation on the way home, which seemed to take much longer than the drive down. They found the women in the front room, much as they'd left them. When Lila saw that Harlan wasn't with them, she started in with renewed hysterics. Katherine looked questioningly at Willis. He raised his empty hands in a hopeless gesture.

"Oh, not to worry now, Mother!" Lem said with a cheer so hollow even a child wouldn't have been fooled. "Our boy is sleeping soundly. Ate a slice of cake and nodded off. You know how a full belly has always made him sleepy."

Lila frowned at her husband over a handful of Kleenex. "Cake?" she said.

"I think the Holy Ghost Sisters take a big cake over there to the jail once a week or so. Isn't that what they said, Willis?"

Willis pressed his lips together and nodded.

Katherine patted Lila's knee and stood to go. "You rest, too," she ordered.

Walking home, Katherine clutched her sweater around her, and Willis drew her near to share his heat.

"Cake?" she said. "Seriously?"

Willis chuckled. "I think Lem was more worried about Lila than he was about Harlan."

"Understandably. She's a rare bird, our Lila. I won't be surprised if this lands her back at Our Lady of Peace." Their neighbor had spent extended periods at the mental hospital in Louisville every few years for what she called her "spells."

It was midnight and Carl and Maureen were still up when Katherine and Willis reached home.

"To bed, you!" Katherine said to her daughter.

"What happened though? I've been waiting all this time!" Maureen wailed.

"Nothing happened. The sheriff needed to ask Harley some questions. That's all," Willis said, and when Maureen started again, "Sh-sh-shh! Everything's going to be okay. Don't worry, Maureen, you won't miss anything. Bed. Now."

And she did trundle off, complaining softly, tiredly, of the unfairness of every aspect of her life. She turned at the bottom of the stairs. "Oh, yeah. Billy came home."

"He's home now? He's upstairs?"

Willis detected a note of hope in Katherine's voice.

"No," Maureen said. "He went out again when we told him about Harlan getting arrested."

"Not arrested—" Katherine started. Maureen trudged up the steps.

"Did he say where he was going?" Willis asked Carl. He realized he was holding his breath.

"What happened though?" Carl said, his repetition of Maureen's words almost comically lacking inflection. Willis still hadn't gotten used to his brother's flat voice. He was ashamed of the uneasy feeling he got whenever he was around Carl. It occurred to him that, next to Maureen, probably nobody had spent more time with Carl than Harlan O'Brien. His brother deserved a better answer than the one they'd given their thirteen-year-old daughter.

"He was taken in for questioning, same as half a dozen other people. They need to find out who killed Jimmy Smith's wife. And the Ferguson girl," Willis said. "Alden Wilder was there to make sure the interview went okay. You know, see to it that Harlan was treated fairly, that his rights were respected, and so forth." Willis really wasn't very good at this, and he wished Katherine would step in. He looked at her to signal as much, but she was puttering at the stove, putting away the pans from dinner and getting out the skillet and coffee pot for tomorrow morning's breakfast.

"What are they going to do to him?" Carl said.

"Do to him?"

"Will they shock him?"

"No, Carl! God no. What—" Willis stopped. The only experience his brother had with someone being *taken in* was when he himself was taken to Eastern State Hospital, where his family proceeded to leave him for half of his life. Willis rubbed his face with both hands, suddenly overcome with exhaustion. Katherine was behind him then, running a cool hand across the back of his neck. She sat between the two men.

"Harlan is in good hands. He's safe. The sheriff is with him. Alden Wilder will make sure it all goes smoothly. We're all going to be okay," she said again.

How did she do it? How did she say such things with no apparent shortage of faith that this was true?

\* \* \*

ALDEN WILDER AVAILED HIMSELF OF the wobbly toilet at the jail, washed his hands at the porcelain sink hanging from the wall. The call summoning him to the jail had come as he and Jane were sitting down to dinner. He had polished off the last ounce in the bottle of whiskey left from his retirement celebration. The Judge's clerk started in with an apology for calling him at home. And then the Honorable Freeman Hume himself came on the line.

*A favor*, he said. Last one, he promised. The sheriff was insisting they had no choice but to bring Harlan O'Brien in for questioning, and could Alden please be there, as a precaution. Alden braced himself for Freeman's bombast, listening for the gist of his old friend's request. The bottom line was that if word got out that Cementville was the kind of place that would prosecute a decorated war hero, their prospects of landing another factory in the county would be shot. This was no time to be in the national spotlight again, Freeman Hume said, not after the scourge of the war losses and the pall of mourning and so forth. These murders would be ignored in the larger world, if they weren't so bizarre and non-normative for our town. *Non-normative.* Had the Judge actually used that word? Apparently the Fergusons had gone up to Frankfort about the death of the girl, even got an audience with the governor. *The governor!* Hume huffed with indignation. Who would have thought they could get themselves organized enough to file a complaint to the Commonwealth's Attorney? The judge rambled from one topic to another, clearly discommoded. That Vietnamese woman was some kind of geisha or something . . . Levon Ferguson was claiming Harley pulled a Bowie knife out from under the seat of his father's truck and came after him at Pekkar's Alley last week . . . oh, the suffering . . . oh, the sure-fire reaction of outsiders . . . temporary insanity, the Judge was thinking.

Alden wasn't listening anymore. This had to be all kinds of unethical, a sitting judge calling an attorney at home. But: *That's the ending I want to see for this story*, Hume was saying, and then he hung up.

Waiting in the jail's cramped kitchen for O'Donahue to arrive with Harlan, Alden rooted around the pockets of his coat for a cigarette, found his lighter, then remembered the pack of Camels lying on his nightstand at home. Holding the lighter up to the buzzing fluorescent light overhead, he read the inscription: *To AW, Worthy Adversary, Trusted Friend—FH.* Alden lifted his leather satchel from the floor and took out a yellow legal pad and three sharpened No. 2 pencils. He lined the pencils up then chose one to twiddle between his fingers, flipping and twisting it over his knuckles, a tiny baton.

When O'Donahue lead the lieutenant into the kitchen, Alden rose and shook the hand of each man. The deputy pulled out a chair for Harlan, greeted him familiarly—they were probably in the same class at Holy Ghost—then went out to the waiting room to meet Lem O'Brien when he arrived.

Harlan O'Brien sat, rigid as a man condemned, not by laws but by the jury crowding his tormented mind, a sentiment Alden conjured as he looked into the hooded eyes, the uncanted head rod straight. A line floated through Alden's mind, something from a half-remembered poem about the dead in war being more alive than the living.

Alden Wilder had never gone to war. In his years before the bar, he had never defended a murder suspect.

O'Donahue fetched a glass of water from the sink and placed it before Harlan. He engaged in one-sided small talk for five, ten minutes, and Alden realized the sheriff was the most uncomfortable person in the room.

"Mr. Wilder has come here to be on hand while we talk. He is willing to act as your attorney, Harlan, should it be decided you need one." The sheriff paused, waiting for Harlan to speak. "Do you understand why we've asked you to come in this evening?"

Harlan let out a deep exhalation, long and slow. "I don't mind. It's okay. We had to kill them all. That's how it works." He raised a hand to his chin, wiped it across his mouth, then pondered his hand as if it belonged to someone else.

"Are you talking about Augrey Ferguson?"

"Sheriff," Alden said. "Harlan, you don't need to answer that right now."

Harlan looked at O'Donahue as if just noticing his presence. "Who?"

"The Ferguson girl. She was found dead. Up near Judge Hume's barn. Do you remember that?"

"Augrey?"

"Yes. Augrey Ferguson is dead."

"I suppose we killed her too. We had to, you see."

"Giang Smith, too?" O'Donahue began, but Alden cut him off. "Well, Alden, for God's sake, what *can* I ask him?"

"Sheriff, all due respect, it doesn't seem as if Harlan is in a condition to talk this evening." Alden stood. "May I speak to you in your office?"

O'Donahue followed him out, signaling to the deputy to come sit with Harlan in the kitchen. And together the two men made a plan.

They went out to the waiting room. Lemuel O'Brien rose from the hard wooden bench. Willis Juell was there too, probably as moral support for his neighbor. Alden looked into Lemuel's face and assured this father of a lost man that his son was going to be safe.

"I promise you, Lem," O'Donahue said as he saw them out the door. "I'll stay up with him all night if I have to."

Alden Wilder left the jail through the back door and was walking up the alley to where his car was parked when a figure moved in the shadows. Billy Juell leaned against the old stone wall of the jailhouse, the lit end of a cigarette causing his face to glow for a split second.

"Billy? That you?"

The boy stepped forward.

"What are you doing out here, son?"

"Nothing," Billy said. "Watching. Waiting."

"For?"

Billy mashed the cigarette with his toe. In the dark, Alden heard him let out the last smoke.

"How about I give you a lift home, Billy."

"Nah, I'm all right. I'll be heading on home directly."

Alden Wilder eased his Lincoln out of the gravel lot behind his building, stopped, and rolled down the window to try and convince the boy one last time to get in the car.

Billy bent down and said, "You don't need to worry about me." His breath was a cloud of booze. "Everything's going to be okay."

\* \* \*

CARL IS FIRST TO WAKE. He shoots from his cot on the sleeping porch like a man on fire. In the same instant Katherine, recognizing the voice of her son, rises, tells Willis not to get up, that she will tend to Billy. She is relieved when he does, though, and he follows her down the stairwell to the kitchen below. Billy is sitting at the table, Carl already beside him, patting him the way you might a strange little boy you found lost and wandering. From Billy's mouth come the indecipherable whimpers, the drunken repetitions to which each of them have listened over the summer as the spaces between his binges decreased. Carl fetches a glass of water. They wait for Billy to breathe in the air of home, the only thing that works to calm him.

"Those guys who died. It's not like they died because of something they believed in. Not like they walked out in the street and got accidentally mowed down by some drunk coming out of Pekkar's Alley or something. They got swallowed up into the belly of some big nasty bird and carried off and brought back all chewed up and spit out. I'm the idiot signed up to go over there and they're the ones in pieces. It's not right, Carl." Billy tilts the water glass, gulps, and carelessly lets it dribble down the front of him. "Harlan O'Brien, now there was a soldier. He was their hero. And look at this shit, survives being captured over there, thrown in the gooks' hellhole—where at least they had the decency to get him some medical treatment, take care of that foot and all. He's suffered enough, sitting around here like a walnut hull, the insides of him picked clean. He didn't deserve this."

*Evil spirits*, Carl thinks.

*More drunken babbling*, Katherine thinks.

Willis takes a bottle of whiskey from the cabinet. He pours one for himself.

"They kept Harley at the jail to protect him," Katherine says. "They'll send him over to the VA hospital, get him evaluated so he can get the help he needs." She wouldn't mind pouring a little whiskey in a juice glass for herself.

"He's not charged with any crime," Willis says. "Not yet, anyway." And when Katherine shoots him a look, he amends it. "Nobody seriously thinks Harlan did anything, Billy. They're going to catch the real murderer. Eventually."

"They killed him, Mama. They've done killed him this time for good."

"Who? What do you mean, Billy?" Katherine still believes this is just another drunken tirade, more of the haunts that have plagued her son since they tossed him back to her from some far hell.

"Harley's hung himself." Billy grabs the whiskey bottle and tries to drain it, but Carl wrests it from him.

"Sweet Jesus!" Katherine hears herself whisper, a sound that seems to come from somewhere else. Carl rocks, patting Billy's shoulder.

"Too late to help their savior hero now. I think I'm going to be sick, Mama." Katherine can't move quickly enough, and Billy vomits on the floor.

She helps her son up the stairs. He vomits again into the toilet, then sits on the floor and watches her draw a hot bath. He lets her undress him and put him in the tub like a helpless child. She lathers a washrag, soaps him up. Here is her firstborn, leaning his head against the tub rim and closing his eyes while she shampoos his hair. She washed him with such care when he was a baby, and Willis did too, so tenderly, careful not to get water in his ears. How had they failed him? How had they let their boy go off and wade through a jungle full of people angry at an invading hostile force, people who would not hesitate to kill her son? He had avoided death only to come back to her unreachable.

His mother swaddles him in a towel and leads him to bed and covers his shivering nakedness. This may be the first, this moment of openness, when she really sees what has come home to her, a boy who is not yet a man but is already as broken as any man with decades behind him. She kneels by him. Night fills the whole window at the foot of his bed, the sky black and unlit by any moon. A darkness she could give over to now; she could pull herself and her loved ones out into nothing, like Peter Pan leading the children off to Neverland. It's no more a fantasy than the belief she has held onto the whole of this awful summer, the faith that her love is all the healing her son needs, that the practical tools of merciful time and patience and home cooking will whittle and mold and shape him back to the young man he was. There is no Neverland beyond that darkness. Outside the boundaries of their farm, outside the walls of knobs that divide their valley from the rest of the world, there are very real demons waiting to match wits with the devils who have taken up residence in Billy's mind. She kneels beside her son's bed, willing him to sleep, waiting for his breathing to even out. She rises, but he calls out, clings to her housecoat.

"I can't close my eyes, Mama. I see him hanging there, like some kind of Judas."

"Billy, why were you at the jail?"

"I wanted to try . . . nobody was there to take care of him."

She does not say to her son, *And you thought you could, in your condition?* She has run out of ways to beg him to stop destroying himself.

"I knew O'D would fall asleep, Mama. He always does."

Billy should know. Willis had refused to bail him out after the first two times he was arrested this summer, then insisted they keep him for a few days. Drunk and disorderly.

Katherine tries to remember the song she used to sing, before Maureen was born, when it was just the two of them. How did it go?

"Harlan already paid. That wasn't right, Mama. Something's gotta be done."

"We can't do anything for him tonight, honey." *Sleep, little baby.* It's coming back: *And when you wake, you'll have cake, and all the pretty little horses.* No, that was the song Maureen loved; she had wanted a horse. Why had Katherine and Willis never gotten her one? They had the land for it, after all. Another failing.

Then the thought fills her: Lem and Lila could do nothing for Harlan, and neither could she do anything more for Billy. She couldn't, but there might be others who could. Tomorrow, after she takes flowers and food to the O'Briens, she will call the veterans hospital and find out what she needs to do to get help for her own. Flowers. Food. A phone call. She can do this. She will.

She brushes Billy's forehead, sings the Pretty Horses song, even over his muttering. She stops when he says,

"Sometimes I wish I hadn't come back."


WHEN KATHERINE CRAWLS INTO BED next to her husband, she knows within a few minutes that he is feigning sleep. She curls around him and he relaxes into her. Things had been hard for both of them, father and son, since Billy came home from the war. Whatever anger she had held toward her husband, she wills it now to scatter, to leave her home and her family, to take its menacing pall and go. Something a Congregational minister had taught her as a young girl in Connecticut, when she still prayed, comes to her. *Let me sow peace*, the prayer went, or something along those lines. *Where there is darkness, light.* It comes to her, and she finds herself whispering the bits as they float in her mind.

"What?" Willis whispers back and pulls her to him and squeezes her hard.

"What's happened to us, Will? Maybe Maureen's right. It's as though this town has been invaded by something, like it's a different version of itself with the same tree-lined streets, the same quaint stores, the railroad, the picturesque river rolling through. But the old way, our way of seeing, it's all gone. I don't think we're ever going to get it back."

Willis inhales his wife's hair. "Our Mo is a smart one. But she's a child, Katherine. A little girl with a big imagination." He is wide awake now; Katherine can feel in his arms the strength, the contained love, the treasured and sometimes frightened part of him that he reserves for her.

"Our Mo starts eighth grade next week, Papa. She isn't a little girl anymore."

"You know what I mean. She lets her stories get away from her."

Katherine tries to lie still. Willis needs sleep. She needs sleep. It's no good.

"I hope Lila will be all right. This is going to be hard on her. She and Lem had nearly come to accept that they might not ever see Harley again, and then when they did get him back . . . " She feels her husband's breath on her neck as it returns to its even, low hum. She hears the whistling of the bristly nostril hairs, singing their blissful refusal to the day and its vicissitudes.

"Will," she says, one last time. "I will need you to go with me tomorrow. We're taking Billy to the hospital."

## SIXTEEN

MaLou does not wake when Byard stumbles in at two. He strips out of his wet clothes, washes his teeth with a finger, and gargles a splash of the nasty Listerine his wife keeps on the dresser, gagging softly and swallowing it, before slipping in next to her, careful not to jostle the bed. Her aunt and uncle, Martha and Rafe Goins, have been beyond generous, letting Byard and MaLou stay in their late son's bedroom. They'd intended it to be for only a week or so at the beginning of the summer; they would stay long enough to see Daniel buried, his funeral having been delayed on account of the run on war dead.

Then Byard and MaLou had surprised everybody, coming home one night with narrow bands of gold on their ring fingers. Martha and Rafe, even Arlene in her grief, were happy for them: it was obvious they'd fallen head over heels. Byard took on work at Gil Miller's tree-trimming business, just temporarily and for cash under the table, his legal status being precarious. The week after Daniel's funeral, MaLou picked up some freelancing at the *Pica-yune*. It was even her suggestion they stick around a while to help Arlene get back on her feet.

But lately MaLou has not taken time off from being pissed at him for one thing and another, most of it traceable to any time he spent with his brother Levon, or really, with any of his family. It has been a while since MaLou threw her arms around him the way she did at the beginning of this strange summer, when the two of them would be so drawn to each other's heat he feared he would break her ribs, he held her so tight. Even now there are times she forgets being mad and looks at him with a love he finds bewildering, and she says things like, "I want to know everything about you."

*No, you don't,* Byard thinks, staring at the psychedelic poster taped to the ceiling over Donnie Ray's bed. Jefferson Airplane at the Fillmore, the wavy type says. Donnie must have mailed off for it, because as far as Byard knows, nobody from Cementville ever made it as far as San Francisco. Other than Byard himself. He wonders if the day will ever come when he can tell MaLou the things he has done, the other reason he left, what really drove him to Canada. What would he say?

Byard had overheard Raedine Miller trying to talk sense into Gil a few days ago when she brought lunch out to where they were clearing trees for the new power line. Gil needed to open up, she was telling him, maybe go talk to Father Oliver. Gilbert Miller, who had not cried a drop since their son Brandon's funeral, was nearly bent over with the grief. He walked around at work like a five-hundred-pound chain was clasped around his neck. "Mourning is natural, honey," Raedine had pleaded softly with him. "It's not something weak that you have to hide. Remember what your mother always said: You're as sick as your secrets."

If there's any truth to that, Byard thinks now, he is terminally ill. He closes his eyes, wanting to believe that if he pretends at rest long enough, sleep will come find him, even here in Donald Ray Goins's boyhood bed.

His insomniac mind twists and spins until his eyelids flutter open to find the dead soldier standing over him, fading in and out like a television ghost. Byard knows it isn't real, but he whispers to the dark, "You want your old bed back, don't you, Donnie?"

Which bones in the bone closet have been rattling the loudest since he returned to Cementville? What secret, of all the secrets, should he tell his pretty young wife first? Can he tell her what he has done this night, before it becomes a secret too big to hold, another set of bones rattling louder than he can stand? Should he tell her about the stranger who had come to town, about the ignorant and gullible face of a veteran who was only guilty of the crime of looking for work and friendship?

Or maybe he should start from the beginning? Byard turns away from MaLou, hugs a pillow to his gut to stop the shudders of awful silent laughing. Because it is laughable, the idea of ever finding a beginning.

HE HAS TO THINK HARD to remember how old he was when it happened. Had he already turned eighteen? When he and Levon tripped up the flimsy step into their mother's trailer that night all those years ago, they stumbled into a familiar sight. The man was coming at her again. Byard and his brother banged open the trailer's flimsy door in time to see Dwayne Hodgister knock their mother to the floor. The man Arlene Ferguson referred to as their daddy stood over her, drunk and murderous. Byard and Levon didn't even have to glance at each other. Like two bodies with a shared brain, the brothers knew that if they let Hodgister get at her again there was a better than even chance he would kill her.

To this day, Byard cannot be certain whether it was him or Levon who pulled the trigger on the Baby Browning Levon had taken to toting with him everywhere, bragging how he bought it off a ruined preacher run on a rail out of Tennessee. Levon had been firing the damn thing behind Pekkar's Alley only an hour before, until Byard wrestled it from him and Calvin Pekkar told them both to shove off. And now Byard couldn't remember whose pocket the gun was in, or whose hand was holding it, when a bullet left its snubbed nose and lodged itself into the skull of their erstwhile father.

Hodgister fell on top of Arlene. Blood shot out his neck and across their mother's face. She stirred and moaned and that was how they knew she was still alive. Byard pulled the dead man off Arlene and helped her to the back room and put her under the covers. She was beat up and shivering even though it was late summer and you could cut the thick air with your arm. With a wet rag Byard wiped the blood off her as best he could. Blood of this man, one of however many who had put their seed in her over and over again till Arlene's body was worn out from babies.

Dwayne Hodgister had been making the rounds for as long as Byard could remember, showing up randomly two or three times a year in his piece-of-shit station wagon piled with cheap-ass kitchen appliances no self-respecting homemaker ever bought, and a back-seat full of even more cheap-ass presents for Arlene Ferguson's growing progeny. Byard remembered those visits, Dwayne hanging around their mother's house trailer for a week or two at a time, eating up their food and drinking Arlene's beer. No matter where in the valley she moved her brood, Dwayne Hodgister always seemed to find her. A parasite returning to its host. Byard remembered how, when they were little, his big brother ran out to meet Hodgister's car, how Hodgister pulled the scrawny Levon onto his lap and let him drive. The man would hand out ten-cent presents like a bogus Santa Claus, then he would hustle their mother into the back of the trailer while Levon and Byard and Daniel sat in the front room playing with their shitty flower pinwheels and Chinese finger puzzles and noisemakers that never made enough noise to drown out the grunting animal sounds coming from behind their mother's bedroom curtain. The next day, Byard and Daniel would watch their traitorous big brother go off with the man by himself, Dwayne's arm draped across Levon's shoulder, his obvious favorite. Levon would come back with new shoes, or a stringer of perch, or a straw hat from Fountain Ferry, the big amusement park in Louisville.

In Arlene's trailer on that killing night, Byard sat there with his mother until he could time her even breaths. When he came out of the bedroom, Levon was going through the dead man's pockets and coming up empty-handed, and Byard saw it for the first time: Levon was the spitting image of Dwayne Hodgister.

"Don't know what I was thinking, bum like him having anything," Levon said.

They became aware at the same time of their little sister, five years old, sitting up in the middle of the couch where she'd been sleeping.

"Blood," Augrey said, pointing.

Baby Tony woke too and started to bawl. Byard patted the baby's belly, those big eyes staring up at him, the tiny white face glowing from the moon shining through the window. Byard picked up the baby and took Augrey in his other arm and carried them both in to where Arlene slept. He opened the top of her dress to let the baby get at her milk. Augrey curled into her mother's other side and drifted off to sleep. Byard sat a while longer, trying to picture how this all must have looked to the little ones, him and Levon scrabbling in. The blast. The blood.

At eighteen, he did not consider himself a man of faith, but he did pray that night. Byard prayed that the little ones were not yet possessed of mind enough for creating memories. Their mother made soft noises, kind of a whimper, like a baby herself. Mother and babies blended into each other there in the bed, all one flesh. Byard was glad for them, even as he was envious of that temporary comfort, that pulsing warmth and sustenance, and he stood over them a while, watching.

He went out of the room, pulling closed the curtain that stood in for a door.

Levon was trying to drag the heavy body. Dwayne Hodgister was a large man, almost too thick to fit through the narrow trailer door.

"Give me a hand here," Levon said.

Byard picked up the dead man's feet and the two of them managed to pitch him into the mud below. The bare bulb of a floodlight atop a tall pole threw a buzzing halo of yellow onto the dirt yard.

From the trailer stoop it was not far to the dilapidated shed where Levon kept his hounds penned up. The brothers panted with the effort of their burden. Their hands glinted in the moonlight, shiny with blood.

Byard prayed silently for the second time: *God help me.* But not: *God forgive me.* He wasn't going to ask that.

In the shed, Levon's hounds became excited and commenced with their awful baying, the sound Byard thought held all animal mourning condensed into a single note. His brother always locked them up and starved them four or five days before he aimed to hunt so that the poor bastards would be rearing to go. Levon silenced the dogs with one sharp command, then took the hatchet from the wall.

Byard closed his eyes as the extraordinary quiet of the shed was sliced by the sound of a juicy thud. Levon worked methodically. The hounds lay in a mute row against the shed wall. Then, at Levon's signal, Georgie Boy, the granddaddy hound, walked over with his head low and licked one of the feet. He checked again with Levon, a questioning look—Was it all right?—before he carried the foot off to a corner.

Each dog after that came over and selected a piece. They lay together in a contented circle, chewing. Byard stood still in the dark shed as if cast in a salt pillar by a pitiless god.

"Unless you plan on sleeping in there, you best come on out," Levon said, and Byard realized his brother was getting ready to lock up. He joined Levon under the circle of light outside. Levon locked the shed door. He hung the key on a nail at the corner of the building.

"There's something rewarding about taking care of a problem once and for all, isn't there, little brother?" he said, and there was a chilling softness in his voice, a sincerity, as if he were giving to Byard a teaching, sharing a profound knowledge of something that had been long and arduous in the learning.

Byard tried to stand up straight but he was shaking hard and he braced himself against the wall of the shed. He bent over and retched into the crabgrass that fanned out from the base of the building. Levon patted Byard's back. Byard threw his brother's hand off. When he was finally able to stand on his own, Levon laughed in his face.

"Don't tell me you're actually shedding tears over that mother-fucker."

"We should have called the police," Byard said. "They might've hauled us in for questioning, but he was ready to kill Mama. Nobody would have blamed us shooting him."

"Us? You pulled that trigger, little brother. It was you."

"No."

" 'Fraid so." Levon raised his hands as if he was framing a headline and recited deadpan: "Teen comes home, murders father, chops him up in the woodshed like so much kindling."

"Your gun, Levon," Byard said. "Your ax. Your hounds."

"Your ass." Levon's lip curled with untroubled glee. "I saw it. Mama saw it. Hell, if they'll let a five-year-old testify, Augrey saw it."

Byard covered his face with his hands.

"Now, now." Levon patted him again. "I can keep my mouth shut. If you think you can."

When Byard removed his hands from his face, his brother was waving the gun in front of him. Byard batted at it and missed.

"Careful. Didn't anybody tell you to never play with guns?" Levon laughed, but his cheer seemed to have lost steam. He dropped the gun to his side and his expression went flat. He staggered over to Dwayne Hodgister's car and a second later the engine burbled to life, its muffler rumbling and coughing. Levon eased it over the shallow ditch and out onto the road, presumably heading to the reservoir, where the old station wagon would sink deep into the source of the county's drinking water.

Byard went into his mother's trailer. He stayed up most of the night cleaning the blood. Before dawn, he went out to the shed and let the dogs out and scattered new straw over the dirt floor. What bones he found he buried deep enough so the hounds wouldn't dig them up again. It would be as if the man had never lived.

If anybody in Cincinnati ever wondered what became of Dwayne Hodgister, nobody in Cementville ever heard tell of it.

Levon didn't come back for days.

But Byard awoke several hours later to the smell of frying fatback. He had fallen asleep on the couch, and his mother stood at the little two-burner stove. Baby Tony sat in the middle of the floor, beating a pan with a spoon. Daniel came in with a few eggs he'd cadged from a neighbor's coop.

"You want one or two?" Arlene said when Byard came over and gave her a peck on the cheek. She hid her blue-black face with a tea towel, as if wiping sweat.

"One'll do me, Mama." Byard sat at the table where Daniel and Augrey were drawing pictures on flattened grocery sacks. Byard offered up a thank you to whatever force out there had arranged for Daniel to be spending last night with his cousins over at Bett's house. He shook his head at the number of times he'd engaged in something that came awfully close to prayer in the last twelve hours.

"Where's Dwayne?" Daniel held a fat Crayola in the air and blinked at Byard with his sweet blue eyes. He was too old for coloring, Levon would have told him, too old for the sissy games he still played with Augrey. Daniel at twelve or thirteen years old was going on five.

Augrey did not look up from her drawing, which Byard could see was a house with a blue door and pink curtains in the windows and a stick figure family assembled in a neat line on the perfect green lawn. A big yellow sun tickled across the whole thing with jagged rays in every color.

"Reckon he must have shoved off again," Byard said.

Arlene cracked an egg on the edge of the skillet and it sizzled in the grease.

"Good," Daniel said.

"Good," Augrey said.

SLEEP DOES COME, IF ONLY for a while, a purifying fog he foolishly believes has done the trick. MaLou stirs next to him, waking Byard from the light doze he had finally managed. Standing by the bed is the figure again, a cartoon version of a lost soul.

"You can't stay here," Byard whispers, but Donnie's ghost responds only with his bland pose of mingled abjection and bewilderment. To prove his point, Byard stands and walks through the apparition to the window, which MaLou has left open. He shoves the sash down and turns to see if Donnie Ray Goins has gone, then clicks the latch in place.

*We will be okay*, he thinks, watching MaLou sleep. We will leave here. We'll go to Canada and make a life. He could crawl into bed now, could reach for her. He longs for nothing in this minute but to press her body into his, to tell her: *Baby, it's time*. Maybe the shudder of her breath, the warmth of her skin as she rises to him—

But no, he had made the mistake of letting it all back in, of falling asleep with the vision of Dwayne Hodgister's scattered parts, of his mother's blue-black face, of the bloodied trailer. The doctor in Canada had told him he had to get the poison out of him, the memories of his father's death. That night was possibly the real beginning of his fugue state, the doctor had said. There were several terms the doctor mentioned, and they'd been nothing but a confused swarm in Byard's head. Dissociative disorder, depersonalization, psychogenic amnesia. None of it made sense; and none of that matters now anyway. He has MaLou. What does matter is that he do something about Levon. Because this is what the night of Dwayne Hodgister's death did teach him: It was Levon. It has always been Levon.

Levon had made him go out tonight. If Byard had stayed home with MaLou, had watched another stupid, insulting episode of *The Beverly Hillbillies* and turned in early the way she wanted him to, none of this would have happened. Levon is the poison, and they share the same blood, and no amount of talking or "sharing," as the Canadian doctor tried to get him to do in group therapy, is going to get a man's blood out of him.

He closes his eyes again—*Sleep, sleep!* he tells himself, but there it is again, the insistent sound of the stranger's pleading whine, the man's thin legs shaking where he stood just hours ago on the bridge railing.

It is too early to be up, but anything resembling real rest is out of the question. It is as if the stranger has locked Byard inside an endless loop tape, and is making him live tonight over and over, punctuated at intervals by Levon's satisfied grimace. The poison. He has to get it out of him.

In the dirty half-light of dawn, Byard pulls on the dungarees still wet from tonight's rain. He closes the bedroom door soundlessly behind him. In the kitchen drawer where Martha keeps the phone book, Byard finds a pen and notepad.

*To Sheriff O'Donahue*, he writes across the top in block letters.

*Do with this information what you will.*

He has to put it all down before he explodes.


HE'D BEEN WATCHING OUT THE plate-glass window at Pekkar's Alley earlier tonight when the stranger wobbled up on that pathetic bicycle, the kind that makes you think of an old person with joints all loose and stiff at the same time, oxidized diarrhea-green paint job somebody knew was a mistake right after the spray can went empty. Everybody had seen this guy riding around town on a beat-up Ladies Huffy Cruiser the past week, had speculated as to where he came from, although nobody had actually conversed with the stranger, as far as Byard knew. Shit-green bicycle was how he got around—nobody had seen him driving a car, nobody had noticed a vehicle parked out in front of Mamie's Rooms-2-Let where people knew for a fact he had taken lodgings. It is not often you see a grown man ride a bike everywhere, not in this town, not in this day and age. This is a town where bicycles are strictly for the entertainment of children, things found by the tree on Christmas morning. Not the sole mode of transport for a grown man.

The stranger had a sober countenance when he dismounted—not drunk at that point, anyway. Levon stopped playing with his new gun for a minute, an old World War I semi-automatic he claims he picked up for nothing. He elbowed Byard and nodded toward the stranger, who threw down a nasty-looking backpack, strolled straight to the jukebox as if he owned the place, slammed in a pocketful of change, and punched in what must have been a dozen Howlin' Wolf songs back-to-back. He was one of those really thin guys, all cave-chested like he'd been chain-smoking since he was nine, the little treelike twigs in his lungs already shriveled up and shut down, and he shambled over and slumped into the booth kitty-corner to theirs.

Levon said, "Looks like he's ready to pass out or die. Maybe got the black lung. Could be from over there in Appalachia. Kind of looks Appalachian."

"How does a person 'look Appalachian'?" June Cahill said. She stood over them with two whiskeys on her tray. She waited for Byard to pay up, made change. "What're you doing in here tonight, Byard? I thought your wife forbid you from our doors. Especially with this one." She nodded toward Levon, who gave her the finger.

"Watch it, you, I'll bite that and more right off," June said. June Cahill always was a snarly type, but since she was let go at the cement plant and started slinging drinks for minimum wage at Pekkar's, what is supposed to pass for teasing comes out like fighting words.

"Promises, promises," Levon said and flashed the shit-eating grin that's been getting him laid since Mick Jagger made having a big mouth sexy. Levon has these big square teeth and a wide mouth that splits his face in a way people—male and female both—take as welcoming, the first time they see it, and sometimes even after they've been bitten.

"If you're lucky, maybe later on. If I can ditch this one," Levon told June, jabbing a thumb at Byard.

Levon had made overtures to Byard after Augrey's funeral, something that fell just short of apology. He said he wanted to let go the bad blood between them. They had gone out a few times together.

MaLou had even given a reluctant blessing to their efforts to make up. She thought it might help their mother to move through her grief if she didn't have to worry about her two eldest sons killing each other. MaLou had kissed Byard goodbye tonight and sent him off for a beer with Levon, saying not to be too late, she'd wait supper for him.

The stranger melted lower into the booth on the other side of the room. Levon got up, skirted the pool table, and sat down opposite him. Table legs scooted and wobbled and jostled the stranger out of whatever drowse he had managed amidst the racket of Friday night at Pekkar's Alley.

Byard could not hear what was said between the two, but he registered Levon's grin from across the room and saw in the stranger's relieved face that he'd fallen for it like an ugly girl asked to dance. Making a friend in a town like this isn't the easiest thing in the world. The fellow stood and picked up the mangy backpack, but Levon took it from him and slung it over his own shoulder, stopping along to introduce him to Benny and some of the boys. The stranger slid in opposite Byard. Levon sat next to him and flashed three fingers three times at June, who lined up nine shots on the table before Byard even caught this new fellow's name.

Above Howlin' Wolf's low growl Levon hollered, "Meet Virgil Grundy!" and raised two fingers to his forehead in a half salute.

The whiskey was performing its highest function as social lubricant before long, and that kind of banter that's general and vague and way too personal all at once was gushing around the table. Byard tried to remind himself of his tendency to blab things he would later wish he hadn't. They didn't know jack about Virgil Grundy, whether he had come to stay or was passing through. Levon ordered chasers, and Virgil said his gut was busting and headed for the head.

That's when Levon threw the backpack across the table and said, "Open it." The way he stared at it, it might have been full of rattlesnakes. But they found in the stranger's bag nothing unexpected. The cellophane pack of powdered mini-donuts, the thermos of thick coffee, the regulation Army knife, the bandanna. The raggedy billfold.

"Wilson Graves," Levon read from the driver's license in the billfold. "Probably one of those scabs taking our jobs at the paper cup factory. Hold on, hold on. What else he got in here?"

"Isn't a scab somebody who crosses a picket line?" Byard said.

Levon pulled from the bottom of the pack a sandwich bag of something white. Handling it like a gold brick from Fort Knox, he looked over his shoulder, untwisted the twisty tie, moistened a pinkie, and took a dip. Licked his finger. "Grade A," he said.

"Who died and made you Top Narc?" Byard asked, but knew there was nothing to be gained by telling his brother he doesn't know what he's talking about, that a neat baggie of heroin that size, especially pure, would be worth more than the likes of this bone-thin wayfarer and his crappy spray-paint bicycle would see in five lifetimes. Ever since Ginny left this last time, Levon's disability check has turned him into a cop-show addict. He's got it in his blood, ferreting out slimebuckets trying to spread their evil love in his town like a pestilence.

"I bet you anything he escaped from that narcotics farm the government's got up there in Lexington."

"What the hell are you talking about, Levon?" Byard wonders how long his brother's drunken ramblings here at Pekkar's will be ignored by this community whose grief has rendered it languorous. When Jimmy Smith's Vietnamese wife turned up dead, Levon practically cheered. Said it was about time somebody woke up to the presence of "enemy infiltrators." Levon has been bloviating all over town about how he finally figured out his purpose in life: That this place was changing for the worse, and it was past time for some cleaning up around here. Levon had always been a mean drunk, but now he was mean and pious.

Here he was again, sitting across from Byard and flipping through some unfortunate wayfarer's billfold and muttering about how there were people tearing the place apart, "dragging down a good town, till before long it will be in the same gutter this whole shitty country seems hell-bent on gushing down."

"Again," Byard said. "What the hell are you talking about?"

"You know, they got that drug addict prison farm in Lexington. Make them milk cows and whatnot, and in exchange for letting the doctors study their brains, they get paid off in drugs. Heroin addicts, most of them. All them colored horn players, junkies, they get busted up in New York City, and wind up milking cows." Levon whistled, like he couldn't believe he and Byard came so close to being bamboozled by this drug-dealing hillbilly, saved only by Levon's own quick thinking. "Bet you this Virgil's one of them."

"I thought you just said he was an Appalachian scab."

Levon dipped his finger in the baggie again. "I could identify that shit a mile away." His pronouncement sucked the air out of the place. The bad feeling that had been quietly circling in Byard's belly since the stranger parked his shitty Huffy outside nestled into his gut as if it planned on staying.

"Let's flush it," Byard said. "MaLou's got supper waiting."

"Last thing this town needs," Levon snarled into his beer, as though he was sad to have to share the news.

Virgil-Wilson-Grundy-Graves came back from the john, slid in, drummed on the table, and said, "You all Howlin' Wolf fans?"

"Don't you know it!" Levon flashed the grin. "Say, Virgil, you hungry?"

"I was planning to take a couple of Pekkar's Burgers home with me. Got an appointment with the television in Miss Mamie's living room later on. She's making waffles. That's how exciting my life is!" Grundy-Graves was too enthusiastic. "*That spoon, that spoon, that spoooonful,*" he sang with the Wolf and drummed his hands on the table.

"Now, we can't let you eat rotgut burgers when you're visiting our town," Levon said. "Isn't that right, little brother?" He looked at Byard for confirmation and winked. "What say we show Virgil what a real steak dinner looks like?"

"Shoot, I'm not visiting, I'm moving here! I appreciate it anyway, but Mamie sent me out to borrow a cup of flour. I've been riding all over trying to get somebody to answer the door. Mamie's no doubt wondering where the heck I've got to."

"You have to forgive them," Byard said, "people here are usually friendly. We've been trying to put ourselves back together again . . ." Levon's glare made him wish he could shut the hell up. Byard was suddenly very drunk, and they were all three heading for the door.

MAYBE IT IS HIS IMAGINATION, but in the slow-motion reel of this awful night playing in Byard's head, Benny and the guys playing pool seem to stop, then give a joint nod for whatever thing Levon was figuring to do, as if they are not only in on it, they give their blessing to the whole shit-storm unfolding. In grade school Levon had been the reigning king of practical jokes, fast thinking and witty, a great mimic. But the innocent pranks that began typically enough in adolescence had grown progressively nastier through high school until the other boys expended more energy trying not to make an enemy of Levon than they did trying to earn his friendship. So maybe Benny and the other poolroom hoods aren't so much nodding approval as they are failing to conceal their own longstanding fear of Levon Ferguson.

But it must be his mind playing tricks on him, sitting here at Martha Goins's kitchen table in the half-light with the wall clock ticking behind him and the pencil in his hand, hovering over the letter to Sheriff O'Donahue. Which is the story he will feed to the law? He needs to make sure Levon is put away and put away for good. Byard cocks an ear to the song of a nightjar—*Poor Will, poor Will!* the song goes—so close it must be sitting in the tree whose branches scrape the walls of Rafe's house.

In Byard's head the show goes savagely on, an unsilent film that will keep rolling, the mental reel that must uncoil itself and spill the night's events.

BYARD WALKED TO THE DRIVER'S side of the company truck, the keys to which Gil Miller gave him just last week. (In these parts, such a gesture is as good as giving a man a share of the family blood.) Byard would drop Virgil, or whatever his name was, at Mamie's to enjoy some late-night waffles. Then Byard and Virgil both can get a good night's sleep. And tomorrow, get the hell out of town.

But Levon said, "Here, lemme drive."

"He's awfully trusting for a scumbag drug dealer," Byard whispered.

Levon glared at him.

"Levon. It's flour. For waffles." Byard said this even as he handed his brother the keys.

"You never know, now, do you, little brother?" Levon said. "That's how they trick you."

MaLou, in Byard's head, said, *You promised me we were leaving here.*

The stranger threw his bicycle in the back of the truck and climbed up in the middle between Byard and Levon.

"You all know a Wilson Graves?" he said. "I found his wallet on the sidewalk. I bet he's wondering, *Now where the heck has that thing got to?*" The guy couldn't even let himself cuss. Virgil. Virgil studied the narrow cone of road in the headlights and kept up a steady chatter. "Sure do hope they'll take me on over at that new plant. You see signs everywhere: *Hire a Vet!* I sure do like this place. You all are some of the friendliest people a fellow could meet."

Levon would not return Byard's look. He drove far out of town along the river. The river was high, a wetter than usual summer after that early drought, a still wetter fall settling in, and Virgil Grundy was bouncing along, happy between Byard and Levon, smiling into the dark of the road.

Levon parked the truck smack in the middle of the bridge and all three got out. He put an arm over the stranger's shoulder and said, "This here's where all of us hung out in high school, after the football game or whatever."

"Those were the days," Virgil said. He almost had a twinkle in his eye, poor bastard. He was filling in memories he did not own, as if he were one of them. This bridge is where Byard's wife said *Yes*, or maybe it was, *Well, all right*. Like, what did she have to lose?

"Hey, Virgil, you ever bungee jump?" Levon said it as though it just occurred to him, and without waiting for an answer he was rooting around the bed of the truck. He pulled out the rope bag and started shaking all the equipment onto the ground, the clamps, grabs, foot ascenders, carabiners. The brand-new tree harness Gil just bought for the big job over at the city park, twenty sick elms that have to come down next week.

"That's no play-toy, Levon," Byard said, but Levon paid no mind. He started dressing Virgil up.

"This bungee? It don't feel all that stretchy," Virgil said with a giggle that made him sound like a ten-year-old girl. "I'm not much for heights."

The whine in the stranger's voice for a split second made Byard not sorry for what his brother was doing, and Byard recognized that thing he once believed he could hack out of himself, like a foul and useless organ. That thing he believed he could leave behind in Cementville, if he could get far enough away. And his foolish belief that Canada would be far enough.

Levon said, "Oh, you can't necessarily feel a difference, man, between bungee and plain old rope." He pulled Virgil's dirty bandanna out of his pack, started wrapping it around his head.

"Wait a minute," Virgil said. "This part of it?"

"Shit yes, man! Makes the rush that much better. You can't bungee without the blindfold." Levon laughed deep and sincere like that was something everybody ought to know. He helped Virgil up onto the railing, his skinny calves twitching under the filthy jeans. Levon grabbed a length of winching chain from the back of the truck and wrapped it around both Virgil's legs, then hooked it onto the harness.

"Levon," Byard said, still wanting to believe this was another of those practical jokes, the not-funny ones. Somebody needed to teach his brother the difference between funny and not funny. The soft whimpering sounds coming from the stranger reminded Byard of a rabid dog he once watched his mother shoot. And in that instant, he remembered the gun. Byard slipped it from the pocket of Levon's jacket. The gun was some fifty years old. Byard didn't even know if it was loaded. Levon turned, just the head, looked at Byard, and gave Virgil a shove off the railing.

There was no scream, only a faint *Yieee!* He hit headfirst, the blade of the stranger's body so thin he scarcely made a splash.

Byard continued to hold the gun on his brother.

"We'd better pull him up, Byard." Levon's eyes did not flicker, and he stood there, his hollow stare more horrible even than the silence below the bridge. He started to reach for the rope.

"Leave him be, or I swear to God I will kill you." Byard felt himself swaying there on the bridge, even though he was certain he was no longer drunk. He wanted to look into his brother's face and see a piece of remorse, or something resembling it anyway, behind the unflickering eyes. Levon's mouth seemed lower in his face, somehow, than it was just a day or two ago. Lips set like concrete slabs. Surely there must have been a time when he was not poison. Poisoned.

Levon walked toward him, his hand out. Byard gave him the gun. He clapped Byard on the shoulder. "You had me going there for a minute, little brother." He wrapped the rope around his fist and pulled until Virgil's limp form hung over the railing. Together they lifted him and stretched him out on the bridge. He was light, might weigh a hundred twenty, hundred thirty at the most. Byard loosened the chain and ropes and pulled the spanking new tree harness off the skinny wet butt. Virgil Grundy's face was a color not associated with human flesh. The lips hung flabby and blue.

Levon looked at Byard, aghast.

"This equipment goddamn better be dry come Monday morning," Byard muttered, his voice breaking.

Levon grabbed him by the shoulder. "The motherfucker is dead! Now what? Mister World Traveler, what are we supposed to do with a dead fucking body?"

"Maybe you should have thought of that before," Byard said. "Besides, who was it crowing about keeping the streets clear of trash?"

Levon leaned against the rail. A sound came from deep in him, bled out like a cougar scream, like the rebel yells they had let fly through the woods as boys. He stood gripping the railing for a while. His back still to Byard, his shoulders jerked with a mirthless chuckle.

"I got to hand it to you." Levon turned to face Byard and shook a cigarette out of his pack. His hands trembled too much to light it so he tucked it unlit behind his ear. "You really looked like you were about to shoot me." He bent and picked up the body and cradled it in his arms. He lifted it up like a sacrifice to a vengeful god then chucked it over the railing. He pulled Virgil Grundy's bicycle from the truck, gave the frame three or four powerful kicks, and slammed it into the bridge abutment. Streaks of shit-green scribbled across the concrete.

Levon inhaled deeply, let out a sigh, himself again.

"People don't know how to say it, Byard, but they're grateful. We got to take care of our town, don't we?" Then he drew himself up straight as though standing at attention, hand stiff at his forehead in a salute. He pursed his big lips together and hummed a few bars of Taps in the direction of Virgil's watery grave. Arlene always said Levon inherited their Uncle Johnny's singing voice.

Byard remembered the strange haunting song Levon sang at Augrey's service just before the pallbearers took her out to the burial ground. It was one of those nearly forgotten mountain arias that could be taken as a hymn of mourning or a paean to love that must be released: *Fly away little pretty bird / And pretty you'll always stay / Fly far beyond the dark mountain / To where you'll be free ever more.*

Levon stared into the muddy river now as if transfixed.

The two of them sat on the side of the bridge dangling their legs the way they did when they were squirts. Levon struck a match across the scabbed iron rail and let it fall toward the water, momentarily providing a swath of dim light. He was the one to break the silence.

"It was you, wasn't it?"

Byard didn't answer.

"Jimmy Smith's wife," Levon said. "You?"

Byard could feel his brother's eyes searching him. He imagined Levon breathing in a new respect for him, a new fear. Giang Smith had been easy; the look on her face was one of gratitude. Byard understood how she felt, that particular sorrow of people who know they can never really find home again. It was Augrey who fought. But their little sister wasn't suffering anymore. Byard had helped her go with something of her pure and precious heart intact, her beautiful white skin still unblemished by the afflictions of this godless world. And he had saved her from Levon too, hadn't he?

"Police believe the deceased struck the abutment with his bicycle while driving intoxicated sometime early Saturday," Levon intoned in the melodious announcer voice that used to crack Byard up when they were kids. He gave the stranger's backpack and bike over to the dark with his good left arm. The splash was distant, weak. It was raining hard now and the river was creeping out of its banks. The bicycle folded into the churning water like walnuts in chocolate cake batter. Byard would have given an arm or an eyeball, almost anything to be somewhere, anywhere else.

IT IS OUT OF HIM. He has fed the truth of himself to himself, and the truth of Levon to the sheriff. *Yes, brother*, he thinks, *it is up to us to rid our town of all that is tearing it down.*

Byard writes the last line of the story that ought to put his brother away: I am sorry I will not be here to confirm the identity of the man whose body will wash up on the riverbank. And Sheriff, I do apologize that I will not be able to testify in what I hope and pray will be a successful murder conviction against my brother.

He folds the letter into his pocket, returns Martha's notepad and pencil to the telephone drawer. From the bedroom come the sounds of his wife waking up, opening and shutting the bureau drawers. Byard pictures her looking in the mirror, brushing her hair.

He will sit with MaLou at the breakfast table this morning, the map spread out in front of them. He will give her time to forget she is pissed at him for being out late with Levon.

And when the moment is right he will stroke her forearm with one finger and he will say, "We're good, aren't we, Baby?"

Then they will plot the route they will take out of here.

# SEVENTEEN

It is fall, and yet Wanda still hoes. She had only planted a quarter of what she and her mother would have put out a few years ago, but it is still more than she can possibly eat, and more than a single woman can keep looking decent, too. Not that anyone would notice. It is rare for anybody but Carl and his niece and Katherine Juell to make the slow crawl up Crooked Creek Road now.

At first, after Loretta's funeral, Wanda had a steady stream of visitors. Simple curiosity—she wasn't fooling herself. People thought she was crazy, trying to keep a garden. *What with your new circumstances,* they would say, as though she had contracted some rare disease. But now she has not seen even June and Charlene Cahill for weeks.

"It has to be pretty bad when you are too strange for June and Charlene," Wanda says to Jimbo. She has tied the mule to a post at the edge of the garden and is letting him have at the old vegetable marrows in the compost bin. October's harvest moon is rising in the clear blue sky. First frost will be here before she can blink, and Wanda herself is perplexed as to why she bothers hoeing. She doesn't mind admitting she's a bit daft.

The new deep-freeze is stocked with vegetables and a side of beef she split with Katherine Juell. There is blackberry jam from Charlene, and whole-wheat flour and plenty of cornmeal in Tupperware tubs in the pantry. The hens will lay the occasional egg, and Carl will bring her anything she wants from the A&P, if she asks him. They have rekindled the old friendship, or whatever this new thing is. It's nice, having him around again. If Wanda plays her cards right, she will not have to come down off this hill for a year. Who knows, come spring she may even get some sheep. Dig Loretta's spinning wheel out from under all the junk in the meat house. She has no encumbrances. Wanda can do anything she wants to do.

A car's whine rises from below, the familiar sound of Katherine Juell's station wagon struggling up the steep gravel road. Wanda and Katherine have developed an odd friendship, falling into a casual pattern of afternoon get-togethers over a cup of coffee. Wanda takes credit for convincing Carl's sister-in-law that he is a big, peculiar oaf and nothing more. That spending half a life institutionalized would make an oddball out of anyone. That Katherine should keep Carl around, and who knows, maybe someday Wanda will take him off her hands.

Katherine gets out, dragging a couple of grocery sacks off the front seat and slamming the car door with her foot. The two women walk toward the farmhouse together. Inside, Wanda heaves another log into the Fisher Mama Bear stove—the only extravagance since her inheritance—and shuts its cast-iron door. Katherine sets her bags on the table while Wanda spoons instant coffee into two waiting mugs. She takes a steaming kettle from the stove.

"I swear I am going to buy you a percolator myself, Wanda." Katherine slips out of a light jacket and eases herself into a chair. She pulls a long flat box out of one sack and pushes it across the table.

"I found this. Under Maureen's bed."

Wanda lifts the lid of the box. "Maureen has been playing with a Ouija board? Who is she after talking to?"

"I have no idea where she got such a thing." Katherine looks out the window toward her own house across the valley as if worried her daughter might be spying on them. "Do you know, I caught her leaving the house Saturday morning wearing fishnet hose? Said she was meeting friends downtown. She's gotten in with this crowd at school, apparently they're kids that belong to the new families that moved here with the paper plant. Top-brass people, managers and so forth. I used to be concerned that Maureen had no friends, and now these girls—loud, disrespectful, spoiled . . . I've been so consumed with worry over Billy—but I tell you, that girl is giving me a run for my money. Oh, listen to me. It's just normal teenage stuff." She shakes her head and taps her fingers on the table as if summoning herself back into the room. She pushes the Ouija board nearer to Wanda. "It's silliness. Of course you can't talk to dead people . . . "

The two women shift under the weight of mutual grief.

"Katherine, you aren't thinking . . . ?"

"Why not?" Katherine's eyes are glistening, and Wanda, out of respect, casts her own eyes to the table. She reaches over and rubs Katherine's arm.

Wanda unfolds and studies the board for a minute. She holds the plastic pointer and glances at Katherine. She cannot gauge from the tense line of Katherine's mouth whether she is serious about this, whether her friend really believes they can summon dead soldiers or murdered girls. Billy is still at the veterans hospital in Louisville, and while Katherine does seem confident that he's getting better, she also seems to want to swallow the burden of all the town's grief into herself. Wanda feels bad that she hasn't been able to bring herself to go with Katherine and visit him. She has told Katherine that her own *condition*—even named it aloud for her friend—is improving too, and soon she will ride into Louisville and walk into the VA hospital. She will sit and talk with Billy Juell and wish him good health.

She folds the Ouija board back into the box.

Katherine hugs her arms tight to herself, but the fire blazes and crackles in the cast-iron stove in the corner, maybe even a little too hot for real comfort.

"I'm thinking about taking a trip!" Wanda says brightly. The way Katherine raises an eyebrow reminds Wanda eerily of her own mother. "London, I think. For starters."

"For *starters*—Wanda Slidell!"

"Can you feature me even saying such a thing?" How Wanda wants to believe this to be true. But she feels the shrill disbelief in her voice. She clears her throat, puts a hand over her chest, regains control. "Lots of libraries. I think my grandmother fancied the idea of me surrounded by all those dead poets. Maybe you could come with me. You and Maureen. Our little chronicler." A sense of floating, a momentary dizziness, weaves in and out of her undulating threads of thought, visions of this new translation of who she is now, the woman of the world her grandmother envisioned, and somehow Wanda rights herself, the floating sensation gone. She has the sense of alighting in her chair by the window like a homing pigeon who always knows the way back.

They sip their coffee in silence for a bit.

"I expect I won't be going anywhere for a good long while," Katherine says. "I'm waiting. You know. For Billy to get home. And I've got Maureen, she's really becoming a handful—" she comes as close to a laugh as Wanda has seen from her, making Wanda think that perhaps Katherine is glad to have a somewhat surly, perfectly normal teenager around the house. "And, well, there are too many animals to feed to think about going anywhere. Willis is talking about buying a horse!"

Katherine seems to lose herself for a while in the flame flickering through the stove's glass door. "They want to watch him a while longer. It really is the best place for him. At least he's safe there." Katherine tries to smile. "Willis and I, we'll go on."

"That husband of yours doing okay?"

"He isn't the kind to grieve out loud. You just know the sadness by the way he doesn't look at anything straight on."

"Men," Wanda says.

Outside the kitchen window, one of the barn cats startles a

flock of grackles that had settled in Wanda's straggling autumn garden. The birds shoot into the air as one winged body against a field of blue.

THE SUN IS GOING DOWN, setting fire to the sprawling cement plant in the center of town. Wanda walks out to Weeping Rock and sits, gathering her skirt around her legs. When she was small, she and Poose would sit on the outcropping overlooking Cementville and watch the evening clouds roll into the valley. Poose would make up stories about the gargantuan structure that stretched like a bony reptile over the valley floor, how it had once been a great dragon, but a good witch had turned it into a cement factory so the people could have jobs. Only he and Wanda knew, Poose said.

"Not even Mother?" Wanda had asked him.

"Not even your mother. You and me, we're the only ones brave enough to stand the knowledge that a spirit walks this land," Poose would always say. Then he would sing in his good clear tenor, a different song for every night of the summer. That showed Wanda how many, many songs he knew.

"Look at me, Poose," Wanda says out loud. Jimbo brays softly at the sound of the name he still remembers.

# AFTERWORD

O n the night of June 19, 1969, a thunderstorm fell hard on a hillside fire support base in Vietnam. The base was shared by a platoon of infantrymen from the 101st Airborne Division of Fort Campbell and National Guardsmen of Battery C, 2nd Battalion, 138th Artillery from Bardstown, Kentucky. The storm's racket provided the cover needed by the North Vietnamese Army to overrun Fire Base Tomahawk. Using rocket-propelled grenades and satchel charges, which they threw into the bunkers where American soldiers slept, the NVA managed to destroy four of the six Howitzers belonging to Battery C. When the fighting was over, the Battery had lost nine men. Nelson County, of which Bardstown is the county seat, had a population of around 30,000 in the 1960s. During the Vietnam War, the county suffered the highest per capita loss of any community in the United States.*

---

* Detailed information about the June 1969 battle at Fire Support Base Tomahawk can be found in John M. Towbridge's book *Kentucky Thunder* (2010); in Jim Wilson's *The Sons of Bardstown: 25 Years of Vietnam in an American Town* (Crown Publishing, 1994); and in the *After-Action Report—Attack on FB TOMAHAWK*, dated 7 July 1969, Headquarters, 2nd Battalion, 138th Artillery.

When news of the tragedy reached my hometown, the loss was palpable everywhere. The husband of the second-grade teacher at my elementary school was one of the Guardsmen who came home alive. My older sister's best friend wasn't as lucky. More than one new bride lost her young groom on that hillside near Phu Bai. The husband of another friend survived, but his brother did not. Not everyone in our rural community had lost a relative or close friend, but no one seemed immune to the sense of communal grief. Over the coming years, the war brought more tragedy. A celebrated POW would come home, more changed and damaged than anyone could know. He would later shoot dead a neighbor in a dispute over tractor parts. Some of the boys I had known would serve their time and come home belligerent and addicted or smoldering and withdrawn. My older brother, a paratrooper of the 101st, would be discharged from the Army and wander for a time on the streets of some California city. We'd had photographs from him: of a sky raining young men hanging from parachutes; of the side of his head bloodied by the debris of an exploded grenade; of him with an Asian wife we never met, a tiny, beautiful girl who died from a ruptured appendix, just outside the doors of an Army hospital. I put notes in my father's letters to him, begging him to come home.

People who write novels are often asked whether a particular work is autobiographical. With varying degrees of equivocation, we generally respond, No. But many of the events that have occurred during my lifetime—both to me and to people close to me, and even far off events—have stuck with me. They go into the making of who I am and sometimes provide the germ of an idea for a story. Beyond the obvious parallels between the historical 1969 war tragedy that occurred for the very real people of Nelson County and the fictional tragedies that affect the fictional families of the fictional town in this book, all direct relationship to real places, people, and events comes to an end. This maker of stories asks that readers please keep in mind the nature of fiction, an enterprise of imaginative exploration into what it is to be human.

# ACKNOWLEDGMENTS

First recognition for what lies at the heart of this novel goes to those who have lost loved ones to fighting everywhere. Men and women for centuries have marched away from home, either under force of draft or to defend what they believed was right. I honor them. I also honor the people they left behind, people like the families who live in the pages between these covers.

This book would not have been written without the generous support of the Artcroft Foundation, Aspen Writers Foundation, the Bedell Foundation, Key West Literary Seminars, the Meyerson Family Foundation, Ox-Bow Artist Residence, the Sewanee Writers' Conference, Squaw Valley Community of Writers, and the University of Colorado at Boulder. I am especially indebted to Maureen and Robert Barker whose noble hearts sustained me during long visits at Artcroft, their magical farm and artist residence in the Appalachian foothills.

Thanks to fellow writers who have read for me, listened to my blather, or simply were there to tell me to keep going. Among them: Lisa Birman, Mary Cantrell, Jane Hill, Patricia Grace King,

Aryn Kyle, Dylan Landis, Anna Leahy, Michael Poore, Max Regan, Christopher Rosales, Claudia Manz Savage, Christine Sneed, Evelyn Spence, Cheryl Strayed, and Rachel Weaver. Grateful acknowledgment goes to writers who have encouraged me in countless ways, and whose work has taught me to see with new eyes, among them: Richard Bausch, Robert Bausch, Mark Childress, Marcia Douglas, Brian Evenson, the late James D. Houston, Pam Houston, Laird Hunt, Stephen Graham Jones, Tim O'Brien, Christine Schutt, Elisabeth Sheffield, Lee Smith, and Mark Winokur. Joshua Kendall, thank you for telling me at just the right moment not to stop.

My agent Michelle Brower was willing to sink her teeth into this thing and push me and prod me to make it the best it could be. The brilliant guidance of my editor Dan Smetanka turned the hard labor of revision into an adventure. The fine staff at Counterpoint Press has showered this book with attentive care: Megan Fishmann, Kelly Winton, Ryan Quinn, thank you. Michael Kellner is responsible for the beautiful cover.

My children, Rachel Lambert, Lesley Lambert, and Graham Kirsh, have given me the kind of support about which most parents can only fantasize. You three, I adore you.

The dear man with whom I have the blessed fortune to share this life deserves much more than my skimpy words can muster. David Kirsh is my light, my partner, my knight, my love. May this book be worthy of the unfailing support and belief he has put into me and my work. There is no woman luckier in love.

## A NOTE ABOUT THE AUTHOR

Paulette Livers is a Kentucky transplant to Chicago via Atlanta and Boulder, where she completed the MFA at the University of Colorado. Her work has appeared in *The Dos Passos Review, Southwest Review, Spring Gun Press*, and elsewhere, and can be heard at the audio-journal *Bound Off*. Selections from *Cementville* were awarded the Meyerson Prize for Fiction, Honorable Mention for the Red Hen Press Short Story Award, and shortlisted for the Bridport Prize. *Cementville* is her first novel. Visit her website at www. PauletteLivers.com.

Printed in the United States
by Baker & Taylor Publisher Services